Advance Praise for

The Wardrobe Mistress

"A charming portrait of Marie Antoinette's inner circle and the intimate connections between politics and fashion."
—Jennifer Laam, author of *The Secret Daughter of the Tsar*

"Silk isn't the only thing whispering through the halls of the royal palaces in Meghan Masterson's captivating debut. . . . *The Wardrobe Mistress* is a romantic, tension-filled coming-of-age story set in a time of dangerous and uncertain revolution. You will root for Giselle; you will applaud her; and you will also fear for her."
—Sophie Perinot, author of *Médicis Daughter*

"In *The Wardrobe Mistress*, Masterson deftly captures the tumult of the French Revolution and the tragic unmaking of history's most infamous queen—Marie Antoinette—through the eyes of clever and likable dressmaker Giselle Aubry. . . . I grew impatient to return to the book each night. By turns sexy, absorbing, and suspenseful, this story sweeps you along to its riveting conclusion."
—Heather Webb, author of *Becoming Josephine* and coauthor of *Last Christmas in Paris*

The
Wardrobe Mistress

A NOVEL OF MARIE ANTOINETTE

Meghan Masterson

ST. MARTIN'S GRIFFIN ☒ NEW YORK

THE WARDROBE MISTRESS. Copyright © 2017 by Meghan Masterson. All rights reserved. Printed in the United States of America. For information, address St. Martin's Press, 175 Fifth Avenue, New York, N.Y. 10010.

www.stmartins.com

The Library of Congress Cataloging-in-Publication Data is available upon request.

ISBN 978-1-250-12666-5 (trade paperback)
ISBN 978-1-250-12667-2 (ebook)

Our books may be purchased in bulk for promotional, educational, or business use. Please contact your local bookseller or the Macmillan Corporate and Premium Sales Department at 1-800-221-7945, extension 5442, or by email at MacmillanSpecialMarkets@ macmillan.com.

First Edition: August 2017

10 9 8 7 6 5 4 3 2 1

FOR MY PARENTS.
AND I'LL BRING COFFEE.

Acknowledgments

Many thanks to Carrie Pestritto, agent extraordinaire, whose enthusiasm helped me remain patient through the submission process and whose love of historic fashion and food contributed to the inspiration for this novel. Thank you also to Lauren Jablonski, the best editor I could ask for, whose keen eye polished up this book like one of Marie Antoinette's diamonds. Much gratitude also to the rest of the team at St. Martin's Press—everyone is a dream to work with.

Lastly, thank you to Ken, for all your support and for filling in the gaps while I was lost in the gallop to the finish on this book. I'm still reminded of it sometimes, with appreciation, when one of us is washing dishes. You're my favorite.

The
Wardrobe Mistress

Chapter One

No one looks regal or elegant in their underclothes on a cold February morning, no matter how much lace or satin trims the garment, and the queen is no exception. She stands with her hands clasped over her stomach, bunching the loose fall of fine white fabric. Her skin gleams nearly as pale as her chemise, and a trace of blue veins shows at her throat, undisguised by the snowflakes of lace cascading across the bosom of her gown. She smooths the garment with delicate hands, and blue veins show at her wrists, too.

Though I'm the newest of her under-tirewomen, having only been here for five days, I know I ought not to speak to her without being addressed first. I can't help but feel sorry for her though, shivering in the chilly room in her nightgown, waiting for the heated bathwater to be wheeled into the chamber. The rest of us are fully dressed and warm, which heightens the faint awkwardness of this situation. I suppose I'll grow accustomed to it, but for now it feels strange to be in a position of greater comfort than the queen. I don't enjoy it. Perhaps I can soothe her a little by speaking.

We're strangers, and yet she stands before me in a state of undress, at a disadvantage. My tongue feels dry; her presence makes me nervous, in spite of the intimacy created by the situation, but I lick my lips and force myself to speak.

"It won't be much longer, Your Majesty. It's a cold morning— by the time you've completed your bath, the fire should have warmed the rooms."

I half-expect her to ignore me, or scold me, especially when Madame Campan, the first femme de chambre, twitches her mouth in a disapproving manner.

Instead the queen smiles slightly, softening the line of her lower lip, which protrudes a little. "It is indeed cold. There's frost on the window. It's rather pretty."

"One of my father's poems is about frosted windows," I say impulsively. Her gracious tone eases my nerves. "At least, the imagery is. I think the poem itself is really about time, but he will never confirm it. He dislikes talking about his poems in detail." I avoid Madame Campan's glance, since I can imagine what it looks like after my casual, impetuous chatter, and stare apologetically at the sloped tile floor. My cousin Eugénie teases me that I can converse with anyone I want. She probably exaggerates, but I like connecting with others. A thrill darts through me that I'm speaking to the queen, and I glance up again.

"Perhaps you will be kind enough to read the poem to me someday," says the queen.

Before I can reply, the bustle of the bath being wheeled into the room ends all opportunity for more conversation. The queen withdraws behind a curtain with Madame Campan, to change into the long English flannel gown she customarily wears in the bath. Her modesty is such that the gown buttons all the way from her neck to her ankles, and the collar and sleeves are trimmed with linen. It surprised me greatly on my first day at the palace. The satirical newspaper cartoons and marketplace gossip led me to believe she would flit about her rooms in shockingly wispy silks and transparent shifts, possibly even flaunting scandalous piercings or painted nipples. It's a relief to find she behaves with elegance and decorum. I wouldn't know where to look if she dressed and behaved like one of the maenads in Papa's books of Greek plays. Once she is seated in the bathtub, with a tray perched on the edges of the tub, no skin except that of the queen's hands and face can be seen.

"Would you like coffee or chocolate this morning?" asks Madame Campan, going to the table on which both selections have been placed. Though her tone is deferential, she has served the queen long enough that she doesn't always address her by a title when they are in private.

"Chocolate, please, Henriette." The queen gives Madame Campan a glance tinged with fondness.

It's rather dull, waiting while the queen has her bath, although the heavy scent of sweet almonds and jasmine wafting through the air with the steam makes the room a pleasant place to linger. In spite of the sloped back of the tub, her posture stays correct and firm, and she sips at the chocolate placed on the tray, her large gray-blue eyes misty and unfocused, as if she dreams of something else.

Afterward Marie Antoinette climbs back into bed, tucking the chemise about her and pulling the warmed blankets over her legs, and unfolds a swath of tapestry. Her eyes squint as she concentrates on making tiny stitches.

"I wager you never knew it could take a grown woman four

hours to get dressed," whispers one of the other tirewomen, once we are out of sight and earshot. "Lord, I wish I could go back to bed now, like she does. It sounds heavenly."

Though slightly taken aback by her tone, I can't help smiling in response to her infectious grin. "Especially in such a huge bed. It must be like sleeping on a cloud."

"You're Giselle?" she asks. "The new girl? Nice to meet you. I'm Geneviève."

Together, we lay the queen's dresses for the day out on the large tables within the wardrobe, making sure they are ready to wear. As soon as she discards one gown, changing to another, we immediately clean and press it. Even dresses that have been worn multiple times look nearly new, because we take such care brushing the skirts clean and mending loose threads. Most of them are new, though, stored in three wardrobe rooms lined with enormous cupboards.

"Have you ever managed to get a good look at the book of dress samples?" I ask Geneviève. Madame Campan brings the book to the queen every morning so she can choose the costumes she wishes to wear by poking pins into the sample swatches of fabric. I long to get my hands on the book, to pore over the patterned squares, examining the flowers and stripes and dots while brushing my fingertips over the smoothness of *chiné* silks and soft muslin, imagining the creations I could design someday.

"No," replies Geneviève. Her tone of longing matches mine. No wonder Madame Campan closely guards the book. We're all eager to see it, but it's too delicate to be pawed at by all the wardrobe women.

At noon Léonard, the queen's hairdresser, arrives, along with an entire entourage of people, including the Duchesse de Polignac, famed both for her beauty and her spending habits. Following Geneviève's lead and discreetly peeking through the door of the wardrobe, I eagerly try to see if her eyes really are violet, as the rumors say, but the distance between us tells me nothing. The Princesse de Lamballe has arrived too, and the queen seems quite happy in the presence of her friends. Her mouth forms a small, perpetual smile, and her expression lightens. She sits at her dressing table while Léonard works with her fading reddish-gold hair, and the other grand ladies perch on sofas arranged specifically for this function of the queen's day.

"Sometimes the princes of the blood and the captains of the Guard come at this hour too, to pay their respects," whispers Geneviève. "It's like a madhouse of etiquette in here then. Even more than today."

"I know. They were here yesterday." I'd been struck by the queen's ability to maintain her composure during what surely must be a taxing daily routine, and the seamlessly elegant way she bent her body, leaning slightly on the dressing table as if ready to rise in greeting to the princes. Secretly, I want to try to imitate the gesture, once I'm home again for my days off. The routine seems faintly ridiculous to me, though. Why should everyone want to watch as her hair is dressed? It seems the completed effect would be more remarkable if some mystery remained to it.

Geneviève grabs my arm. "Oh, hush. They're talking of politics now, I think."

Although I hadn't been speaking, I obediently refrain, straining my ears. The beautiful dresses are the main reason I leapt at the chance to work in the queen's household, for I'd love to design my own someday, making a name for myself as Rose Bertin has. The chance to pick up a smattering of interesting political information is an extra benefit, especially with the current troubled state of the economy.

"Do you suppose the recent election of representatives will matter a great deal?" That soft voice belongs to the Princesse de Lamballe. "They officially decreed for the books of complaint to be drawn up."

The duchesse scoffs, setting her cup down on a table with a soft clink. "Yes, but that's a tradition. I shouldn't wonder if no one reads the cahiers. There must be hundreds of them in the end, gathered from all over the country, and probably half of them are incomprehensible."

Geneviève and I exchange a glance, silently appalled by the duchesse's derisive tone. My brief time at court has already shown me that the nobles have a limited understanding of what life outside the palace walls is like, but her scorn for the legislative processes of the Estates-General, the assembly that represents the states of the realm in the government, is practically offensive. There are three Estates, although my father has been wont to say that there might as well be only two. The first and second, made of nobles and clergy, outweigh the third, comprised of the rest of the people, in influence but not numbers.

The duchesse has not finished speaking. Even through the cracked opening of the wardrobe door, I see the arrogant tilt of her head. Her pale hands, gleaming with rings, flick dismissively through the air.

"The people of France cannot understand the great responsibility of ruling that falls upon the shoulders of the king. He has been bred for it, trained for it. The Estates-General likes to imagine it understands everything about running a country, but the king is the only one who does. It is his duty—it's in his blood. Besides, state secrets and diplomacies can hardly be shared among the masses."

"They would not be secrets, then," remarks the queen dryly. "Louis tells me he may read the essay published last month by Abbé Sieyès. It has apparently become quite popular. He thinks it shall be interesting."

"I think it's rather nice he wants to share the interests of the people," says the duchesse.

Geneviève presses her fingers to her lips, as though she can hardly keep from confronting the duchesse about the condescension of this remark. I motion with my hand that she must keep quiet, and she nods, rolling her eyes at the same time.

"Of course he does. He's always been very proud of the people's affection for him. He loves his subjects dearly. And he does enjoy reading."

Geneviève nudges me, her voice scarcely audible. "I have a copy of that essay, *What Is the Third Estate?* I could lend it to you, but you must keep it a secret."

I don't need to ask why. It wouldn't make a good impression to be caught reading such an inflammatory text at court, provoking new ways of viewing society. From what I've heard, the essay suggests that the Third Estate, the common people, should have as much representation in government as the nobles. "I'll not breathe a word, I promise." The idea of reading it intrigues me, especially after overhearing this conversation between royal ladies. Their naïve callousness shocks me. I've never before questioned the king's right to rule—it is the normal way for society to function— but I didn't expect such condescension about serious issues affecting so many people. I return Geneviève's solemn look. "Thank you."

"I'll get it for you later. You can take it home during your leisure time."

My whispered conversation with Geneviève ends abruptly when the queen rises from her seat, her coiffure perfected, and turns to her companions before moving toward the wardrobe.

"Here she comes," says Geneviève quickly. "You know, she used to dress out there as well. It's only since she insists on having Rose Bertin as her dresser that she retires to the closet. The duchesse and the princesse would not suffer sharing the task with a common woman like Rose, so the queen changed the way things are done. She is very fond of Rose's creations."

"Don't you like Rose Bertin?" I ask, surprised. I haven't spoken with her much, and she seems rather smug, but it's difficult not to admire her brisk efficiency and the beauty of her gowns.

"Oh, I do. But she is common. You and I are no duchesses, but our fathers are gentlemen, at least. Her mother was a nurse for sick people, for heaven's sakes. I don't mind, though—she certainly rose higher than anyone could have expected. That's admirable ambition." Geneviève winks and then wipes her expression solemn as the queen reaches the doorway, Madame Campan in tow.

Marie Antoinette looks serious now, and the light smile she wore earlier has vanished, emphasizing the haughty angle of her nose. I curse myself for letting Geneviève distract me from the conversation, for the look in her eyes suggests it must have saddened her, and I wonder what had been said.

She catches my eye, startling me out of my thoughts. I smile tentatively.

"The sun has decided to shine," she says. "A welcome sight. I hope we shall have an early spring this year. It would do us all good." She looks wistfully at the patterned spray of flowers on the dress laid out.

"All will be well, Your Majesty." Still surprised that she has addressed me again, I can't think of anything cleverer to say, and she looks like she needs reassurance, somehow. Even royalty grows weary of winter, I suppose.

"Of course," she says confidently. "Of course it shall."

Chapter Two

As I walk home, a billow of smoke rises into the dusky violet sky, and the muted roar of wild voices tumbles through the air. My steps slow, and a middle-aged man with a tattered hat nearly bumps into me.

"There's a riot outside the Réveillon wallpaper factory—everyone who believes in change is there now." Eyes glazed with excitement, he dashes off in the direction of the thundercloud of smoke.

I edge toward the street. Around me, dozens of people hurry toward the smoke and the sound of shouting, wearing mingled expressions of excitement and nervousness. I'm not the only curious one. Revolution has sparked in Paris, and I want to see it. For months the subject of conversation in the marketplace, and everyone's parlor, has centered on the exorbitant price of bread, the shamefully low wages, the extravagance of the royal family. On the last, I have personal experience. People have been threatening riots over the cost of bread, but I never truly believed it would happen.

I've often walked past the Réveillon wallpaper factory, sprawled along the corner of the rue du Montreuil and the rue du Faubourg Saint-Antoine, admiring the lavish windows overlooking the street. The owner of the factory, Jean-Baptiste Réveillon, lives above it, and one can frequently see a fancy carriage pausing outside, while Madame Réveillon alights, swinging the voluminous skirts of her opulent gown. She's probably one of the few women outside of nobility who can afford to wear Rose Bertin's supremely fashionable creations. Her prices are fit for a queen, and with good reason, since she's Marie Antoinette's favored dress designer.

The view of the factory and the house are blocked by a swarm of people, clogging the street and shoving past one another. Everyone's clothes are dusted with soot and ash, and a dozen or so nearby watchers carry uncorked wine bottles. All around me voices are calling and boots are stomping in a cacophony of manic excitement. I can hardly pick out individual words, just muffled cries of wages and wine and change. "First Réveillon's wine, then his blood!" someone shouts near my ear, painfully. The jumbling crowd sweeps me into the maelstrom of people. I turn back, wanting to escape.

When a group of people make a mad dash for the thick of the fray, one of them collides roughly against me. A buckle from his coat snags the sleeve of my dress, ripping the seam.

"Watch it, clumsy elephant!"

The culprit, a man with a long brown coat and a matching beard, misses my scathing glare, already busy knocking into someone else several strides away.

My fingers curl around a fold of soft wool at the same time that a deep voice speaks, near enough to my ear to keep the words from being lost in the din.

"Watch it, yourself—that's my sleeve you're yanking on."

"Oh! I'm so sorry. I was trying to catch my balance." I look up into the glittering dark eyes and sharp features of a man approximately my own age.

His mouth quirks in a small smile. "As long as you weren't referring to me as the clumsy elephant, I don't mind."

A woman shoves past me, her elbow stabbing into the small of my back. "Réveillon deserves all of this!" she shrieks. "He wants to reduce wages—death to the rich!"

I stumble again, victim to her battering-ram steps. In retaliation, I stomp my foot down on hers, raising my arms to make spears of my elbows.

"Come on." The man grabs my wrist, dragging me forward a couple of steps and then slides behind me, moving his hand to my shoulder, pushing me forward. His breath hisses through his teeth once, sharply.

"What are you doing?" I try to plant my feet, but he's strong, and if I don't walk, he'll probably push me over. "Stop at once."

He doesn't reply until we have traveled all the way across the street, where the crowd thins. I hadn't realized how many people had swarmed around me. The perimeter of the raucous crowd had grown quickly.

"I'm getting you clear of the riot," he says crossly. "Unless you'd like to be beaten and crushed?"

"What? Of course not."

"Then stop insulting already-incited people and stamping on their toes. I took a blow meant for you, I'll have you know. The woman whose toes you attempted to crush whacked me across the back with a heavy book." Shaking his head, he raises a bottle of wine to his lips and swallows.

"I'm sorry." I promise myself it will be the last time I apologize to this stranger. Only a dozen words spoken, and half of them expressions of regret—how ridiculous. "Er, why do so many people have wine bottles?"

"The mob raided Réveillon's wine cellar. He's rather a connoisseur, as it turns out. Apparently, there were nearly two thousand bottles stored away, all very good quality." He tilts the bottle to me. "Would you like a sample?"

More shaken than I want to admit, I reach for the bottle. My fingers tremble, and I grip the smooth glass tightly to quell the motion. It's good wine, ranking among the best I've tasted, even given my uncle's fondness for collecting exceptional vintages. Rich and smooth and intense, it washes away the tension, warming my insides. Even after one sip, I feel braver.

"Apparently? Didn't you see the wine cellar for yourself?"

"No." He grins sheepishly and pushes a strand of dark hair away from his forehead. "Someone pushed the bottle into my hands, shouting 'share the wealth.'"

My laughter makes his smile widen, which softens his sharp features, making him look less fierce. "Thank you for helping me out of the crowd, and for the wine. I only wanted to watch from the edge, but somehow I got swept into the thick of the fray. I'm Giselle Aubry, by the way."

"Léon Gauvain," he says. "And you're welcome. Even the edge of a riot can be dangerous. In fact, we should probably retreat a little farther. Unless you do want to start a fight after all?" He takes the wine bottle back from me, drinking again.

"No, I've had enough for one day."

"Come on, then." He marches down the street, away from the smoke and shouts of the riot.

Scarcely hesitating, I follow. I'm afraid to linger near the crowd, but that isn't the real reason. The air practically hums with exhilaration, and I'm not ready to go home yet.

"Do you know what started the riot?" I ask. "I know Monsieur Réveillon made a suggestion about wages that wasn't well received, but that was nearly a week ago."

"Was it? I suppose it takes time for the word to spread." Léon passes the wine back to me.

"I know about the wine now, but what about the smoke? Is the factory on fire?"

"Just wallpaper, I think, although I didn't see it well. I wasn't eager to linger near a bonfire surrounded by a thousand raging men and women."

"A pity, as the wallpaper was already made," I observe. While it would be worse to see the factory burned, the wallpaper is still a significant loss. "It seems almost unfair to the workers to burn it now."

He narrows his eyes. "Unfair? I'll tell you what's unfair here— Réveillon owns a mansion filled with expensive wine and first-edition books, while his workers labor long hours, six days a week, for less than fifty *sous* per day. And then he has the gall to suggest lowering their wages."

I don't flinch back from his stare, although he leans closer and the corners of his mouth are tight with anger. "I do think it's un-fair. You talk of the laborers, and they worked hard to create that wallpaper. Now it's destroyed. And Monsieur Réveillon didn't sug-gest reducing wages, as a matter of fact. At least, not only that— it's complicated. He said that if the price of bread would go down, wages could also be slightly decreased, and it would still stimulate the economy. The economy needs that."

"Slightly decreased." He rolls his eyes at my too-diplomatic phrasing. "How do you know he said that?"

"My uncle told me."

"And he knows Réveillon?"

"They're acquainted."

He throws his head back derisively. "No wonder you were about to get trampled. You're one of them, aren't you? Privileged and wealthy?"

"No. My family isn't so badly off as some, but we're still Third Estate." I do know more about the nobility than most, though. I wonder what he would think if he knew of my connection to Versailles, that I live there when on duty as one of the queen's under-tirewomen.

His brow tilts suspiciously, but he doesn't question me further. "Pass the wine back."

Meeting his eyes, I take a deliberately slow sip before handing it back.

He shakes his head, but the sternness in his expression melts back into amusement. I like the way his mouth softens, a smile blossoming at the corners of his lips. It makes his straight brows and sharp jawline seem less severe. "Where are you from, Léon? Your accent is not quite Parisian."

"Toulouse." He lifts his chin with the air of someone who has seen much of the world.

I realize he's forgotten the bottle of wine in his hand and hasn't taken any since I returned it. I snatch it back, laughing. "What brought you to Paris?"

"I'm a watchmaker's apprentice, at a shop not too far from here." He reaches for the wine again, and this time his warm fingertips brush mine.

"You work for Monsieur Renard?"

"Yes." He stares in surprise.

"I know him, a little. My uncle used to be a watchmaker too. They worked together occasionally. My uncle designed a ring with a watch mounted on it, and the old king purchased it as a gift for his mistress, and I think Monsieur Renard was always a little envious. Uncle Pierre writes plays now, though."

"Your uncle must know everyone," Léon observes.

"Almost," I concede.

"Now that you've learned so much about me, I think it's my turn to ask you a question, Giselle."

Inexplicably, I like the way my name falls from his lips, the second syllable dropping into a purr. "All right."

"Where did you learn to lift your head in that haughty way?" His eyes gleam wickedly. "Your uncle again?"

"I do that?" I feel a little shocked, and thrilled, too. I can think of only one person I could be unconsciously imitating. In my three months as part of Marie Antoinette's household, I've secretly admired her poise. Even though a revolutionary like Léon might not approve, I'm pleased to possess even a fraction of her elegance.

"Yes. To the first man who bumped into you, and then the woman who clobbered me with a book, and again to me, at first."

"I can't tell you."

"Why?"

"I don't think you'll like the answer, Léon."

"You have to tell me. I shared my wine with you." His voice is teasing, but I can see by his expression that he really wants to know.

"Not here," I relent. "We have to move farther away from the crowd."

"How mysterious you are."

"I'm one of the under-tirewomen serving the queen," I say at last, once we have found a quiet patch of street.

He sighs. "I can see why you didn't want any of the rioters to overhear that. Wait—you learned that haughty expression from the queen? In person?" He sounds faintly stricken.

Annoyed, I shove at his chest and take the wine bottle again, sipping quickly to hide my distraction by the hard warmth of his body. "I suppose I must have. And don't look like that. It's a good job, Léon." It's a coveted position in the queen's wardrobe, only a step below her ladies-in-waiting.

"I'll bet. How much do you make?"

"What a rude question."

"In regular times, yes. But this is different—the majority of people can hardly afford food, and in Versailles no one wants for anything. Help me put this into perspective, please, Giselle."

"I have a salary of two thousand and one hundred livres per year," I say reluctantly. Léon had said the wallpaper workers made fifty *sous* per day—a little over two livres. The comparison makes me squirm guiltily. If my family lived closer to Versailles, I'd make even more, but part of my income goes toward the cost of living in the palace while I serve the queen.

Eyes wide, he ostentatiously takes the bottle back and takes a long swig. "Dear God. And plenty of days off, too, probably?"

"One week of work and then two weeks of leisure," I mumble. "Sometimes more, if I'm wanted as a substitute for one of the other wardrobe women."

"I don't know if I should be impressed or disappointed."

"It's not all easy," I say defensively. "The hours are very long—we rise before Her Majesty to prepare her clothing for the day, and can't retire until she does, which is often very late. I sew for hours each day. And there are so many rules and intricacies of court etiquette. It's a good thing I'm only in the background, working with other ladies, because I could never hope to master it all."

"Do you see the royal family often?" he asks. "Does the king roll his eyes over the plight of the Third Estate, dismissing them with his mouth full of delicacies?"

I laugh at his specifics, but it also makes me feel worldly to know so much about court. "No. I've only seen him a handful of times, and never spoken to him. He likes languages and locks. It's terribly boring."

"Locks? How strange. And the queen? Does she throw away her gowns after wearing them once?"

"No, they're immediately cleaned and put away in the wardrobe. She wears them again, usually. Even though she decreased the amount of occasions that full court dress must be worn, she still has to change several times a day for different functions."

Léon wrinkles his nose. "No wonder she needs several under-tirewomen. Does she pity her subjects who are starving?"

"She doesn't speak of politics to me," I say cautiously. "She's a kind woman, though." Seeing his brows arched in disbelief, I hasten to add, "It surprised me, too."

"This is very interesting," says Léon. His voice sounds warm, soothing my ears as the last of the riotous din fades away behind us. "I like hearing about the royal family. The more you tell me about the palace, the better understanding I gain about the need for change."

"What changes do you want to see?"

He smiles and tugs at his dark hair, which curls a little over his forehead. "There are a great many—I hope you don't regret asking. For a start, I want the Third Estate to have the appropriate amount of representation in the government, and I want the disparity between wealth and poverty to be narrowed. People toil all day, for weeks on end, and yet have scarcely anything to show for it and can't even afford bread."

As he speaks, his passion for the ideals shows in his face, sparking in his eyes and lifting his shoulders with pride. His hands flit through the air in constant, thoughtless gestures as he describes the improvements for society.

"Can you imagine if the people had adequate representation?" he asks. "Not like now, Giselle. Proper, proportional representation, and real input in the governing of the country. Why shouldn't we have our opinions heard? We live in France just as much as the king—even more, I think. Versailles must be like a paradise, but an isolated one, closed away from the realities." He looks to me for confirmation.

"You're right," I admit. "I don't have freedom to roam the palace, but the parts that I do see are opulent. Have you ever had hot chocolate infused with orange blossoms, Léon? The queen has it every day, a delicacy that starving people could scarcely imagine."

"You understand perfectly. How could someone who regularly dines on such luxuries understand the true depth of the problem? Of course the king doesn't understand. He couldn't possibly, and that is the heart of the problem."

Regret stabs through me when we reach the lane before my house. When we started walking, we ended up going in the right direction, and since I knew my parents would worry if I didn't return soon, I kept to that course. Léon hardly seems to notice where we walked. I wish the conversation didn't have to end already.

"I live just over there." I point vaguely toward the row of shimmering yellow lights gleaming in the windows facing the street.

"Oh." He sounds disappointed. "You let me talk too long about revolutionary ideas, and now I don't have time to find out more about you, let alone think of a way to kiss you."

My heart hammers in my chest, and I feel suddenly breathless at the thought of his mouth on mine. I strive to keep my tone light, matching all of our earlier banter. "Are you drunk, Léon?"

"Yes, a little," he says frankly. "Watchmaker's apprentices don't often get much to drink. Are you?"

I part my lips to say no, but as I shuffle a step closer to him, the world spins more than it ought to, and it almost makes me giggle. I suddenly want to touch his face, explore the angular slope of his cheekbones. "Yes, I think I am."

He chuckles, and the low, happy sound unleashes an echo of laughter from me. It's dark enough now that I can't see him clearly, but his teeth gleam as he smiles and his blue coat blends in with the shadows. One of his hands reaches forward, fingertips stirring the strand of chestnut hair that falls over my shoulder. My scalp immediately tingles, the sensation spreading all the way to my toes.

"You have pretty hair, Giselle."

"I don't believe you can see it in the dark."

"I noticed before." His hand follows the length of my hair, fingertips brushing along my neck to my ear slowly, almost uncertainly.

The wine makes me forward, or maybe it's Léon who takes away my reservations. Leaning into his hand until his palm cups my cheek, fingers curling delicately behind my ear, I slide forward and brush my lips over his easily, because we're close to the same height. He smells like woodsmoke and leather; the warmth of him makes my breath catch in my throat.

I retreat, pleasantly surprised by the brief sensation. This is the first time I've kissed anyone, and I like it.

Léon catches my wrist. "Wait, Giselle. I wasn't expecting that. Can we do it again?"

This makes me smile. "Next time, maybe."

"Tomorrow?" he asks hopefully, fingers playing with the edge of my sleeve, gently touching my wrist.

"No, I have to go back to Versailles in two days. I'll find you at the watchmaker's shop after." Tugging my hand free and taking a couple of steps toward my house, I pause to look back at him over my shoulder. "I'm glad I met you, Léon."

"So am I, Giselle."

My parents had heard of the riot, and rushed to me the moment I opened the door, relieved. Trying very hard to appear dignified and calm and not at all tipsy, I reassure them that I'm unharmed, and though I saw the riot from a distance, I took a long detour home to be safe.

"Still, you must be shaken," says Maman. "Your color is a bit high. Perhaps you ought to retire early tonight."

I take her advice, gratefully pulling the white coverlet over me and stretching my legs against the sheets. The adventure has left me weary and simultaneously full of excited energy. I want to reflect on everything, the scene of the riot, the way the meaning of Réveillon's words exploded out of control, and especially Léon, with his shining dark eyes and sharp voice, but the excess wine drugs me into a deep sleep almost at once.

Chapter Three

Compared with the splendor of Versailles, the house always feels strangely small and delightfully cozy at the same time. The sphere of gold lamplight spilling over the curtains and making the carved wooden furniture gleam gives the parlor an aura of warmth. It feels soothing after the tense excitement of the Réveillon riot.

"Eugénie and Pierre and Marie-Thérèse are coming for supper," says Maman, referring to my cousin and maternal uncle and aunt, who live just down the street. "They want to see you before you return to Versailles tomorrow."

"I've missed Eugénie." She's been away in the country for a few months, visiting family on her mother's side. Though only twelve, four years younger than I am, my cousin Eugénie is my dearest friend. We grew up together, and our families are very close. I can't wait to tell her all about Versailles. Since I started working in the queen's household, I haven't seen my aunt and uncle, either.

Eugénie barely steps through the doorway before a lightning-quick smile brightens her face, and she rushes to embrace me, her fair hair waving about her small cheeks the volume of her blue-striped skirt making her seem even more petite.

"Did you see the Hall of Mirrors?" she asks.

"Not yet. The days are so full, and there are separate corridors for the servants. They're faster, especially when crowds are viewing the parts of Versailles that are open to the public."

Her golden brows arch. "Secret passageways?"

"Not that I know of, yet."

"Well, have you tried on any of Marie Antoinette's dresses?"

"I would never dare! Although, the idea is tempting, I must admit." Alone in the wardrobe, I'd held a pale rose *gaulle* gown to my chest, admiring the layers of draping muslin and the wide white sash to be tied around the waist. The queen herself had begun the fashion of simpler dresses such as this, and although they were at first derisively compared to a chemise and condemned for not using French silk, I like the airy, light quality to them, the flattering softness. Holding the queen's gown, I knew I would never wear it— she is so thin, I don't believe it would even fit me—but I'll sew my own version someday, and improve on the design, too.

"I managed to get us a loaf of bread for tonight," says Maman. "I went to the bakery early, before they sold out, in spite of the moon-high prices. I almost changed my mind at the last moment— fifteen *sous* is very dear, even though we're not so badly off as others, but I thought today was a special occasion, since Giselle is home again."

"We would be better off if my Voltaire project had been more lucrative," grumbles Pierre, grousing over the financially unsuccessful attempt to collect and reprint the works of Voltaire. Though my father and I are both impressed by his efforts, and happy to read through the works, Pierre spent more money than he made on the venture.

"In a better economy, it might improve," says Maman, soothing him, even though it's no secret that Pierre is quite wealthy, thanks to the success of his *Figaro* plays and other business ventures.

"Thank you, Charlotte. You're eternally optimistic, and that's probably why you are my favorite sister." Pierre grins at her. "Well, we didn't bring bread, but we did bring wine."

"I prefer wine over bread." Papa smiles.

We all sit down, and I eagerly inhale the savory aroma of garlic, suddenly famished. "Maman, are you serving my favorite soup?"

"Of course I am. I always miss you when you're away."

After Pierre finishes his soup, he turns to me. "Do they talk much of the situation outside the walls of Versailles? The famine? The inflation?"

"A little. To be honest, I don't think they understand the extent of the discontent. The queen mentioned, very casually, that the king wants to read Abbé Sieyès's work, as if it were a passing interest for him. The Duchesse de Polignac was more dismissive of the situation. It nearly sounded as if she's determined to believe that the problems are only exaggerated rumors."

He grunts in response, sipping his wine. Pierre has the gift of masking his thoughts, a talent that must have been quite useful to him when he worked for the old king, Louis XV. Before he found success as a playwright, my uncle was a member of the Secret du Roi, a group of spies who reported exclusively to the king. Eugénie and I adore hearing tales of his experiences in espionage, and used to take turns playing courtier and spy, wishing we could have such adventures. Between tales of diplomacy, intrigue, and carefully guided conversations, Pierre likes to remind us that serving the king was a very solemn task.

"A king needs information to make the best decisions," he would say, cheeks turning rosy with enthusiasm. "And the king rules the people, so the information benefits them, too, in a way. It's a complicated task, gathering information, but an important one." Then he would smile suddenly. "And it taught me to read people, and that understanding has been most helpful for writing my plays."

Now he gives me a serious look. "I suppose the king believes that he did enough in December, when he agreed that the Third Estate would have twice the number of representatives as the Second Estate." He shakes his head. "Keep your eyes and ears open, Giselle. You're in an interesting position to see both sides, especially in these tense times. I confess, what happened to the Réveillon factory disturbed me. Monsieur Réveillon and I are not so different, though I may flatter myself with the comparison." He lifts a hand self-deprecatingly. "I don't quite have his success, but times are growing dangerous. Your insights may help our family stay abreast of upcoming changes. If you wouldn't mind keeping me apprised of some of the details of the court and the queen, I'd be grateful."

Meeting my uncle's steady gaze, I disguise the little flip of excitement that goes through me. This is not the Secret du Roi, nothing so prestigious, or so serious, since I would only share information with my own uncle, but it's an opportunity for adventure nonetheless, a chance to join in the family legacy of court intrigue.

"I see her every day that I'm serving at Versailles, so it shouldn't be difficult." My tone sounds nonchalant.

Pierre's shrewd eyes glint as his mouth twitches in a subtly approving smile.

"Only if you feel comfortable doing so, Giselle," interjects Papa. "You do have a choice."

"I don't mind. It feels natural to tell my family about my days

at the palace, and it's also rather exciting to have an inside perspective to the traditions of court, when the rest of Paris is so eager
for change." Léon helped me see the necessity for change.

Papa leans back in his chair, his worries assuaged. "I see no
harm in it. I know you'll be careful. It wouldn't be prudent to
share your information widely—some of the proponents of change
are positively revolutionary, their zeal is so great. You understand
any information is for family only, for myself or your uncle." He
pauses. "I can't deny I will look forward to hearing your tales of
l'Autrichienne."

"Félix," scolds my mother. "Such language at the table. It might
be clever wordplay," she concedes reluctantly, "but I don't believe
one ought to refer to any woman that way, queen or not."

Although I've heard this slur before, combining the queen's
Austrian heritage with the word for a female dog, and used to find
it clever, I don't like hearing it now. It brings to mind a bold, li-
centious woman with a sultry grin and greedy eyes. Maybe she
used to smile more, when she was younger, but in person, Marie
Antoinette does not fit this impression. Her solemnity and the
nervous way her fingers fidget at anything in their reach makes
me think of a person far too gentle for such a name.

"She's not perfect, but she can't help her blood, and she's too
kind to be called a bitch," I say.

Maman sighs. "I give up. I have a family of barbarians."

Before my aunt and uncle and cousin depart for the evening,
Pierre draws me aside in the parlor. Linking his fingers together,
he gives me a measured look nearly as stern as his voice. "If
I may, I'll give you some advice. You must maintain impartiality
when passing along information to me. It's one of the first things
we all learned as members of the Secret du Roi. Do not interpret;
only observe and report."

"I'll do my best."

"Your best shall be fine indeed. If you can, pay specific attention to whom the queen sees, if she receives anyone to her chambers. I don't know if you will have opportunity to see her correspondence, but if you see her writing lots of letters, it may be useful."

"I'll watch for it, but I surmise she does receive and send a great deal of correspondence. None of her family lives in France."

"Exactly." He pounces on my observation. "If things change, if the tension over the famine rises into riots, we may discover whether she is truly loyal to France or Austria. Her response will reveal it."

I purse my lips. "It would be impossible for me to read any letters, I think. But perhaps I can contrive to see who they are for, at least."

"Nothing is impossible," he says automatically. "But that will be good enough."

"Do you miss it, Uncle? Being a spy?" It occurs to me that he must feel nostalgic for the grandeur and excitement of his past in the Secret du Roi.

"I often preferred the term *diplomat*. They are not entirely unconnected, after all—how better to help gently persuade a person of something than to use what you know of them? But I do sometimes miss it. I occasionally miss being a watchmaker, too," he adds, referring to his earliest career. "I liked the precision of it. Each of my careers has required intelligence and careful attention to detail. The watchmaker must be meticulous with the mechanics, the spy watchful for nuance, and the playwright for the right words. The last two are more related than you think, my dear." He pats my shoulder. "You shall do well; you're a clever girl."

"Thank you, Uncle. I'm glad you helped me obtain a place at Versailles."

His hand brushes through the air as if to scatter the words. "What are connections for, if not to be used?"

※

It's not easy to forget the Réveillon riot, even back at the luxurious shelter of Versailles. The wallpaper adorning Marie Antoinette's private apartments is one of Monsieur Réveillon's designs, a pretty floral pattern called *papier bleu d'Angleterre*. The ornate gilded trim decorating the room frames panels of wallpaper, and my gaze is drawn to it more than usual as memories of the riot crowd my mind.

Somehow the queen discovers that I witnessed the riot, probably through a private conversation with Madame Campan, whom I told. Having served her for years, she is very close to the queen. Marie Antoinette beckons me to her side just before departing the chamber, dressed in an elegant rose gown of muslin, a soft hat pinned to her elaborately styled hair.

"Was it very frightening, Giselle?" Her pale brows draw together in concern.

"A little. I took care to keep my distance, and did not linger."

She nods seriously. "That was a wise choice. And Monsieur Réveillon and his family? Do you know if they were harmed?"

"I believe they have left France for England," I reply, drawing on information gleaned from my father and uncle. "None of them were injured, although there were casualties and people wounded in the crowd." This last part seems strange to me. After witnessing the chaos, I can well believe the escalation of violence that claimed lives, but it's hard to believe that this was happening while Léon and I walked and laughed together. We were fortunate to stay safe.

"I am very sorry for their families." The queen's mouth, with its too-full lower lip, droops in sorrow. "I sincerely wish that the tension and unhappiness in Paris shall be resolved soon. The Estates-General is commencing here next week, and I have high hopes that they will come to a resolution. The king is working on proposals for reform."

"I'm sure he will find a solution."

Though I meant to be polite and reassuring, and she nods in agreement, she bites the inside of her lip, looking suddenly doubtful. "All of this is rather stressful. I want nothing more than to seek a few days of quiet at le Petit Trianon."

Secretly, I hope she does go there, for I've heard much about the queen's favored retreat, a picturesque pastoral hamlet located within Versailles. Designed to appear rural and quaint, it's apparently still very expensively furnished, and only the queen's closest companions are invited to accompany her there, although she must take some of her servants as well. Rumor says the king has never spent a night there, though he occasionally pays a visit in order to spend an afternoon of leisure, reading in a rowboat on the pond. The queen stays there sometimes, and the cruelest of the gossips infer that she uses le Petit Trianon as a love nest, her name most often paired with Count Axel von Fersen, and even, shockingly, with the Duchesse de Polignac and the Princesse de Lamballe, her closest companions.

"A visit there would lift my spirits," says the queen, though not with any certainty.

"I'm sure it must be especially peaceful now, in the springtime."

She smiles. "Yes. If I go, you will be able to see it, Giselle. I have the freedom to dress more simply at le Petit Trianon, but I still take some of my wardrobe women with me."

I curtsy deeply. "It would be an honor, Your Majesty."

After the queen has departed, Madame Campan pauses by my side, her arms full of linen chemises and a worried expression on her oval face. "Her Majesty has been gloomy lately." She sighs. "I can't blame her. I hope she does retreat to le Petit Trianon for a few days. She could use a respite from the pressure. I don't like seeing her so thin. She was once rather plump, when the last baby was born, but you would never know it now, poor dear."

"Is it the politics that put pressure on her?" I ask curiously.

"Not only that. She is always watched. Her life is like a stage, and she the actress. Her reactions to everything are noted, and too often mocked." The concerned line crossing Madame Campan's forehead deepens. "It doesn't help that her eldest son, Louis Joseph, hasn't been well lately."

"I hope he recovers soon."

"He has always been fragile." Madame Campan shifts the heap of garments in her arms and clears her throat. "Thank you for trying to cheer her, Giselle."

I dip my head, acknowledging the praise. It feels strange to pity the queen, when she has so much wealth. After hearing Léon's passionate ideas for reform, and seeing the people clamor for bread, I don't quite want to. But when I began at Versailles, it didn't take long for me to see her for herself, not only as a symbol of the monarchy. The intimacy of the wardrobe allows few illusions.

Since the Réveillon riot, Marie Antoinette's nerves seem to fray as much as the hem of her favored purple wool shawl, which she twists while sitting in bed or being read to. Perhaps attempting to distract her troubled mind, she asks to be read to more than usual. Madame Campan is her preferred reader. It's easy to see why, for she has a pleasant reading voice and excellent enunciation.

I hover nearby, waiting for the queen to finish her bath before Léonard arrives to pouf up her hair. It's pleasant to sit in a corner where the spring sunshine streams like ribbons through the gauze-draped window, listening to Madame Campan read from Rous-seau's *Confessions*.

Marie Antoinette seems to be relaxing for once. Her mouth curls at the corners in a tiny smile, and she eats her brioche with a greater appetite than usual, sipping her chocolate after each bite.

" 'At length I recollected the thoughtless saying of a great—' " Madame Campan's smooth tones suddenly vanish into a fit of coughing. Blinking against watering eyes, she puts the leather bookmark along the page and closes the book. "My apologies, Madame. I seem to have a dry throat. I don't believe I can read again until I've had a sip of water."

"Yes, go ahead. That's enough reading for now. I'm ready to get out of the bath."

My gaze flicks to Madame Campan. Her voice has returned to its mellow tone, not scratchy and harsh sounding like some-one who had a coughing fit would usually sound. When she tucks the book underneath two more, hiding it under a stack on the side table, I wonder if she faked her coughing fit, though I don't know why she should bother.

It takes an hour, but at last I have an opportunity to slip Rous-seau's *Confessions* out from the bottom of the book pile. I search for the passage Madame Campan had been reading, tracing my finger under the words. *At length I recollected the thoughtless saying of a great princess, who, on being informed that the country people had no bread, replied, "Then let them eat cake."* Snapping the book firmly closed, I feel a surge of respect for Madame Campan's pro-tection of the queen. It's no secret that Marie Antoinette has re-cently been blamed for saying these precise words in response to the famine scraping France down to its ribs. It wounded her,

I know, for she had spoken of it, sighing over the malice of the rumor and wondering how to correct it.

"To address the matter directly would only lend credence to the rumor," she concluded sadly.

Privately, I didn't believe there was anything she could do, and I had said as much to my uncle while relaying the story, and his minute nod told me he agreed. The people referred to her as *Madame Déficit*, and found her an ideal scapegoat for the poor financial state of France. The queen did spend a lot on her wardrobe, along with the rest of the nobles at Versailles, but the strange comparison of blaming her, who ate sparingly and preferred surprisingly simple fare, for a grotesque misunderstanding of true hunger, was not lost on me.

Understanding now that the queen's rumored words have been lifted from a book written several years ago gives me sympathy for Marie Antoinette. In my spare time, I've been embroidering a row of purple violets on a linen handkerchief, and I finished it this morning. Impulsively, I give it to the queen just before she leaves the wardrobe, dressed in a mauve gown with white satin ribbon at the waist.

"It's only a small thing," I say humbly. She may not want my simple gift—she has so much already. "But I know how much you favor the color purple, Your Majesty."

She smiles, taking the cloth from me and holding it against the belling curve of her gown. "It complements very well, I think. Thank you, Giselle." She pauses by the door, turning back. "I would be interested to hear another of your father's poems, if he would be kind enough to allow you to read one to me."

I bow my head. "Of course, Your Majesty."

"You must be fond of reading, coming from such a literary family. Your father is a writer, and your uncle is Monsieur Pierre-

Augustin Caron de Beaumarchais, is he not? I greatly enjoyed his *Figaro* plays." Her tone drops confidentially. "The king did not wish them to be performed because of the satire of the aristocracy. I still found the plays to be quite witty, and persuaded him to allow them to be shown. It took a long time, but he finally relented."

"I'm sure His Majesty is always anxious to please you," I say cautiously. Actually, from what I have seen, the royal couple keeps very different hours, and seems to have few shared interests aside from their children. It makes me curious about the depth of feeling they have, or do not have, for each other. "My uncle will be pleased to hear you enjoyed his play. He likes to make people laugh."

"I thought so. His plays are proof of that, of course, but when we met once, after the private showing of his play, I thought he had a twinkle of humor in his eye, in spite of the rest of his face."

I laugh genuinely. "Yes, he can have a stern look. I was terrified of him until I turned six and he plunked me down on the sofa beside him and told me the story of *Cendrillon*. For weeks afterward I pretended to wear glass slippers."

"Mousseline adores that tale," she says, referring to her eldest child. The rest of us know her as Marie-Thérèse Charlotte, and must refer to her as Madame Royale. When speaking of her daughter, Marie Antoinette's eyes gleam, turning almost silver with delight. "She used to ask to hear it every night before bed. Though I eventually grew weary of telling it, I could never bear to disappoint her. Lately she has tired of stories and prefers asking questions about me, about stories she has heard from my younger days."

"Such as the winegrower wounded by a passing carriage?" Though it happened the year before I was born, my father had told me about the time a man toiling in a field was run over by one of the carriages of the royal hunting party. Marie Antoinette had apparently been more sympathetic than any of the nobles, and rushed to help him. Afterward she donated enough funds to provide for his family for the next year, while he recovered from his broken bones.

Pink roses bloom across her cheeks, and when she half-shrugs, the gesture is immaculately elegant. "Well, yes. Goodness, that was long ago. I was still dauphine. I had to help him; I felt such compassion. After all, I have the privilege of being able to afford to pay his yearly salary."

As the clock chimes noon, she gives me a tiny nod that manages to be regal, friendly, and dismissive all at the same time, and sweeps out of the wardrobe in a swirl of silk and rosewater, a train of attendants forming behind her.

I know her schedule well, after four months in her service. It is Sunday, and she always dines publicly with the king after mass, and later in the day, noble ladies are presented to her, before evening card playing begins. Except for a brief stop to change into her evening attire, it's unlikely she will return to her chambers until quite late in the evening. If I can find an unobserved moment, when all the others are occupied, I may be able to glance through the stack of sealed letters on the side table, ready to be sent, and see who they are addressed to. Last time I managed to do so, I had wondered whether my uncle ever opened any letters during his time in the Secret du Roi. Tracing my fingertip over the lavish spread of stamped wax, I knew I would never dare.

"Fawning over the queen?" Geneviève crosses her arms. "I bet you want to be one of her favorites."

I match her stare calmly. Even though she has been complimented a few times by the queen for her exceptionally fast and tidy sewing skills, Geneviève is jealous every time the queen shows favor to any of the other under-tirewomen, which is not infrequent. She treats us well. I think Geneviève, who is always reading revolutionary texts, resists liking the queen and resents it when others do. "I want to get ahead in this job."

"Right. You fancy being the next dressmaker. Well, giving gifts to the queen and simpering over her boring stories shall likely help."

"I don't mind talking with her. I don't find it dull." I pass her the *pret de la nuit* we are preparing, the covered basket containing the queen's nightclothes. A clean nightgown and nightcap lie carefully folded inside. Geneviève needs to add the morning stockings, and then the basket will be ready for Madame Campan to present at bedtime.

Geneviève slaps a stocking down on the table. "Giselle, you and I are the only two in the wardrobe. You can speak your mind to me."

"I am. Why do you serve her if you dislike her so much? Why are you here?"

Her expression locks down, and she doesn't answer for a moment. "There's always enough to eat, and I can boast about living here during my weeks on shift."

"I like those parts too."

She laughs, more cheerful again. "Of course you do; anyone would."

"I also like how the queen's rooms are so full of flowers that we are perfumed just from being present," I confess. "My favorite is when she has a lot of lavender and violets piled in every corner."

"Mine is the orange blossoms and roses, for both the scent and the bright colors." She smiles, and it's somehow less brittle than before.

"Come on, Geneviève. Let's see if we can scrounge a pastry from the kitchen to share."

As we divide the chocolate pastry between us, I tell her all about the Réveillon riot, describing the excitement and the wine, and meeting Léon. I brush off the frightening parts, encouraged by Geneviève's impressed reaction.

"I wish I had been there," she laments. "How lucky, to see change in the making."

"Are you a revolutionary?" I ask.

She shrugs, pastry in hand. "In these times, how can anyone not be?"

It's a good point, and I nod agreeably.

Geneviève gives me a thoughtful smile. "You know, you aren't as much of a snob as you seem at first, Giselle."

"I seem like a snob?" I echo, dismayed.

Geneviève giggles, not unkindly. "Well, I felt a bit defensive at first. I thought you were judging me. You seemed very serious, and you still speak to the queen so easily."

"That isn't any kind of arrogance; I simply never know when to hold my tongue."

"Well, now we can have some lovely conversations. I think we shall be friends."

Chapter Four

On the fifth day of May, the Estates-General meets at Versailles. I rise before dawn, for the queen's wardrobe is more complicated than ever. She will join the king at the ceremony to open the Estates-General, and the formality of the ritual means it will be no small task to dress her. She commissioned a gown from Rose Bertin to wear for the ceremony. Geneviève and I blink against the lamplight, grumbling sleepily as we hasten to the wardrobe to begin the preparations.

We work in silence for half an hour, neither of us being particularly chatty at this early hour, but the quiet is companionable. Geneviève and I have found a routine in our work, easily sharing the tasks, and it has brought us closer.

"This will be an interesting day," says Geneviève at last. "I'm glad we'll get to witness it. I pray that the Estates-General will be able to do something productive. We need change desperately."

"I hope so." My reply is distracted; while polishing the queen's shoes, I keep thinking how my uncle will expect a detailed report, running over his possible questions in my mind. So far he has seemed happy with whatever information I bring, no matter how

small, but the opening of the Estates-General is a significant event
and will surely interest him more deeply. I wish I could bring him
an important tale, for once. I won't be present at the ceremony, however, and will only be able to comment on things within the queen's
rooms. I wish I had the opportunity to witness more. I like being
the person who knows everything.

When Marie Antoinette is finally laced into her gown, Madame
Campan clucks over her like a fastidious mother hen, and Geneviève and I exchange a look of dismay. The queen's gown is stun-
ningly beautiful, like all of Rose Bertin's creations. Each fold of
material hangs perfectly, and the graceful cut of the collar makes
the queen's neck look as elegant as a swan's. But it's all wrong for
the occasion. It could hardly be less appropriate. The gown is purple satin over a white skirt, utterly royal, since purple is the color
of nobility and white is the color of the Bourbon house. Even worse,
the skirt swells to the floor, its hem dragging under the weight
of embroidery and hundreds of tiny diamonds and bright metal
sequins.

"No necklace today," the queen says to Madame Campan.

Geneviève shoots a surprised glance toward me, apparently assuming, as I had, that she would deck herself out with jewelry to
rival the glittering splendor of her gown.

"This will be enough." Her slender fingers drift over the shimmering diamond band fastened into her voluminous hair.

"And a fan?" asks Madame Campan.

"Where is the clutch of white ostrich feathers?" The queen casts
her gaze around the jewelry table.

"Here it is, Your Majesty." Geneviève hands it to her with def-
erence, voice polite and eyes lowered, but I detect a hint of disapproval in her tone, perhaps because I share the feeling. It is a
terrible choice, another item of luxury, and white again.

Marie Antoinette evidently picks up on the undercurrent of condemnation. She tilts her head in Geneviève's direction. "Do you think it an ill choice?"

I wish Geneviève would say yes, but her trademark bluntness doesn't extend to the queen. She stares at the floor. "No, Your Majesty."

"It's very luxurious." As soon as I blurt the words, I clamp my mouth shut and match Geneviève's humble downward gaze.

She turns to me, and her diamond-crusted skirt scrapes against the floor as she takes a step. "Yes, it is." Her voice grows louder, sharper. "This is an important event, and I shall dress to treat it thusly. I have been dressing for court functions for decades, and setting the fashions for nearly as long."

"Yes, Your Majesty." I make an apologetic bow.

After she has departed and we are able to speak freely, Geneviève turns to me in horror. "No one will be paying attention to the ceremony at all. They'll be calculating how much bread could be bought for each of the diamonds."

"Flaunting her wealth won't be received kindly, no matter how gracefully she curtsies and greets the Estates-General."

"It was brave of you to speak up. Foolish, but brave."

"It doesn't matter," I say. "She won't learn from it." It gives me a sad little pang to say that. Secretly, Geneviève and I often mock the court, even the queen. With her, I sometimes say harsher things than I would to anyone else. But it hurts me to truly admit that Marie Antoinette might not realize the danger of misunderstanding the dire need of the people of France, that she might not be clever enough to change her ways.

"Probably not," says Geneviève calmly. "Well, I suppose we had best get out the day's sewing."

Later Madame Campan's quick steps echo across the decorated

floor of the queen's apartments, where I am sitting by the window and sewing new ribbon onto a ruffled petticoat.

"Hurry, Giselle. I found us a place to watch the procession." She tugs at the corner of the petticoat. "Leave that for now. I thought you'd like to see our queen in her finery at the ceremony."

"Thank you, Madame Campan."

"Where is Geneviève?" she asks, already heading for the door.

I quicken my pace, my mint-green skirt flying behind me as I catch up to her. "She went to fetch clean items from the laundress." She should have been back a few minutes ago, but I suspect she paused on the way to flirt with the soldiers. Geneviève likes uniforms.

"We don't have time to wait. Perhaps she'll find a place to watch from." Madame Campan straightens the yellow sash at her waist, and her already hasty pace quickens, her heels rapping in a staccato rhythm on the tiled floor.

She leads me to a quiet alcove near a window taller than I am, where we can watch discreetly from around the edge of the blue velvet curtain as the king and queen walk across the courtyard outside. My gaze is immediately drawn to them, and not just because of the deferential space cleared for them as they slowly march through together. In her purple and white satin trimmed with a ransom of diamonds and paillettes, Marie Antoinette stands out like a swan among ravens. The king matches her, dressed in his fancy velvet jacket and with a few jewels of his own. Across the distance, her elegance lends him dignity.

The crowd of Third Estate onlookers shuffle, shoulders hunched in resentment. A few whisper to one another, faces sneering. They're all dressed in somber, plain colors; black, gray, brown, dark blue. Sensible clothing for those who cannot afford a diverse wardrobe and make do with the same coat for all occasions.

"She looks every inch a queen," murmurs Madame Campan fondly.

"Yes." By keeping my response to one syllable, it helps to hide my sour tone. I admire the queen's beautiful gown—who could not?—but seeing the contrast of her with the people makes me cringe.

"Oh—look—the sun is coming out even though it's still raining a little." Madame Campan gestures, forgetting her fingers clutch the edge of the curtain, making the whole fall of cloth wiggle. "Look at the rainbows."

As a sunbeam overpowers the thinning rain clouds, it lights up the droplets cascading over the courtyard and through the air like diamonds. And the diamonds themselves catch the light and shatter it into hundreds of colors, rainbow pinpricks after the other, hovering around the queen, dancing with each of her steps and floating away from the people as she progresses through the courtyard.

"It is like she is made of light," says Madame Campan poetically.

It's like she is stealing the light from everyone else, I think. Some of the people below seem to see it that way. They mutter and stamp, and while a few wear smiles of enjoyment, others have sullen expressions.

"No one could have planned such an effect," adds Madame Campan. "Not even Rose Bertin, though she will be so pleased to know how the dress looked today."

And so will the queen's detractors, I think. She has unwittingly given them more ammunition for their hatred of her.

✳

While she was out, Geneviève did glimpse the excitement of the procession, and we happily compare notes back in the queen's apartments.

"Did you see the Duc d'Orleans?" she asks.

"No, why?" The *duc* is the king's cousin, although they appear to have very different ideals.

"He wore a bourgeois outfit." Her eyes light up, entertained. "I wish I could have seen the king's face when he noticed his cousin dressed like a common merchant instead of wearing sumptuous court garb. Seeing the crowd's gleeful reaction was good, though."

"How very Third Estate of him," I say mockingly, and Geneviève giggles with hectic laughter.

"Some call him the people's prince," she says after a moment, growing sober. "What do you think of that?"

"It's interesting," I reply. "What do you think?"

She only smiles like she has a secret, and shrugs in an elaborate, casual motion. "God knows what will happen. But something has to change; that's for certain."

"What is the Third Estate?" I ask quietly, guessing Geneviève must be thinking of the text. We have both read it several times, and can practically quote passages to each other. It helps to pass the time while pressing stockings.

"Everything," she replies promptly. "What has it been up until now, in the political order?"

The answer comes quick to my lips. "Nothing. What is it asking for?"

"To become something." Geneviève tilts her head, a stubborn glint in her eye.

❊

Though I think of Léon frequently, blushing over the memory of our brief kiss and his passionate way of talking, my first week at home passes without my visiting the watchmaker's shop. Since the Réveillon riot and the continued malcontent throughout Paris, my parents don't let me wander alone. I consider fabricating a reason to visit the shop, perhaps with my father to escort me, but the longer I wait, the more it seems like a fool's errand. The spark between us might have been created by the adventurous setting or the indulgence of the wine.

One day I stroll into the parlor of my uncle's house and find Léon seated in the high-backed and yellow-cushioned chair by the window, deep in conversation with Uncle Pierre.

Léon rises as I enter the room, eyes gleaming in a way that's instantly familiar, direct and full of mischief. The sharpness of his cheekbones and straight nose reminds me of a hawk, but no bird of prey ever carried such warmth of expression.

My uncle stands too, though I scarcely pay attention to him. Léon's unexpected presence snatches all my attention. I falter in the doorway, swept with memories of my reckless behavior last time I saw him. I sipped wine from a bottle. I kissed him. And as my pulse flutters with excitement, I know I would do it again, given the chance. The rioting nighttime street provided the freedom for me to indulge in my desires, but as they all come flooding back even in the austere surroundings of my uncle's parlor, I learn the setting wasn't the trigger for them. Léon himself is the spark.

Maman bumps into my elbow. "Excuse me, Giselle." Her gentle voice carries a hint of reprimand.

Realizing I still hover in the doorway, blocking the way for my parents, my cheeks and ears scald with embarrassed heat, and I hasten forward, avoiding eye contact with everyone. I feel a sudden respectful kinship with Marie Antoinette. It's an incongruous time to think of her, but she is often in my thoughts now that she has become such a central figure of my life. I imagine she must have felt this same dazed exhilaration when she was young and full of gaiety, when she met von Fersen at a masked ball.

"Good afternoon," says Uncle Pierre. "I'm glad you've arrived, though not so much as Eugénie will be, once she returns from her music lesson. She was quite anxious for a visit with you." He grins at me. "May I introduce Léon Gauvain? He is apprenticing with Monsieur Renard—you remember the watchmaker?—and wanted to speak to me about the mechanical device I invented to maintain accuracy in pocket watches."

Papa greets Léon politely. "Watchmaking? A fine trade."

"I enjoy it," says Léon. "I like the precise art of it, but I'm interested in the innovative parts as well, such as the miniature watch set into a ring that Monsieur de Beaumarchais made for Madame de Pompadour. I'm fortunate he agreed to share his insights with me."

Papa chuckles. "No wonder you persuaded him to talk about his past life as a watchmaker. Pierre loves talking about that ring. It brought him into court circles at Versailles."

"It did change the course of my career." Shrugging complacently, Uncle Pierre pours brandy from the sideboard for himself and my father. "It's chilly today. Here's something to cut through the dampness."

"I trust you've been well, Mademoiselle Aubry?" Léon takes my fingertips lightly in his own and makes a small bow over my hand. The elaborate elegance of the gesture would not be out of place at Versailles, although the etiquette isn't quite proper. I see laughter glinting in his eyes and realize he is teasing me about the queenly head tilt I learned at court.

"Yes, thank you, Monsieur Gauvain." I lift my chin with nobility-inspired pride, and the corners of his lips quirk in response.

"Are you two already acquainted?" asks Maman curiously. Her light tone doesn't match the glint of intense interest in her eyes. I hope I'm the only one who notices. I think she might be a little amused, too. I suppose my reaction to seeing Léon was obvious.

"Only slightly," I reply. "Monsieur Gauvain was kind enough to escort me home on the night of the Réveillon riot. He'd been walking down the rue du Faubourg Saint-Antoine himself, and saw I was fearful of the crowd."

"How kind of you." Her smile warms. "Such a dreadful event. I'm glad you were not hurt, and kept Giselle safe as well." As she chats with him, I observe dryly that my parents warm to Léon quickly because of my uncle's introduction, and it adds to the pleasant thrill of his surprise visit. When my aunt comes into the room, my mother goes to her side, and Léon and I are left alone by the blue velvet–draped window.

"I didn't expect to see you here," I say quietly.

"You don't mind, do you? You never came to the shop, and I didn't know which house you lived in. It's fortunate you have a well-known watchmaker in the family, or I may not have been able to track you down. I asked Monsieur Renard about the ring timepiece, and used it as a premise to talk to your uncle. Before that, I managed to find out from the baker down the road that your uncle usually has family over for supper on Fridays, so I waited until today to call, in hopes that you would be here." His grin flashes as bright as moonlight breaking through a haze of midnight clouds, and I feel like it kindles light inside me, too. "And you are." He lowers his voice even further, to a rasp I can scarcely hear, although it shivers along my skin. "Good God, Giselle, it's like you want a man to be a detective."

"You're very confident, Léon. What if I'd been avoiding you?"

He shakes his head, unfazed. "Then you wouldn't have looked so delighted to see me here."

Happiness bubbles through me. I do want to know him better. My liking for him is much stronger than it ought to be, logically, given our short acquaintance. "All right, I will confess. It was a pleasant surprise. I did intend to visit the shop, but since the riot, I don't walk alone anymore."

"Perhaps you shall be allowed to go walking with me."

His hopeful look sends a swirl of excitement through me. "I'd like that."

"I'll ask your father. I almost wish they had offered me some of that brandy, for courage." He brightens. "I think it helps, though, that I was introduced through your uncle. And I did enjoy our conversation about watchmaking. Is he a supporter of equality for the Third Estate?"

The true answer is that I believe Uncle Pierre is waiting to see which side prevails, the revolutionary thinkers or the traditional royalists. My parents are slightly more liberal in their thoughts, but they're being cautious as well. In spite of my attraction to Léon, perhaps I do not know him well enough to divulge family opinions on politics, not in this rebellious time. "Let's not talk about politics here. I prefer walking and fresh air to broach that subject."

Léon nods, and when his eyes meet mine, I feel a jolt of heat, a connection, and a reminder that the spark between us earlier is real, not created by the wine or the riot. "I look forward to it." His voice drops to a murmur. "Especially because I want to kiss you again, and unfortunately this room is not the place for it."

"We'll see." Realizing my coy laughter has caught the attention of my mother and aunt, I ask him in a louder voice about his apprenticeship. He answers easily, switching to a more conversational tone, but I see a glint of challenge in his eyes, and a thrill quivers through me. He looks like he is determined to persuade me to give a more positive answer. Even without the wine and dramatic excitement of the riot to spark passion, I want to kiss him again, more thoroughly this time. I wonder how it would feel to slowly trace my lips over the angular shape of his mouth, the Cupid's bow arch of his upper lip.

Later, when Léon courteously asks my father if he may call on me, I notice Maman subtly nudging his arm, and I suspect Papa's cautious agreement is partly induced by her signal. Perhaps Léon and I didn't appear as casual while speaking as we thought, but it's just as well, if our friendliness helped grant us freedom to visit together again. As he departs the house, I can feel that the brilliance of my smile matches his.

Chapter Five

Through the last week of May, I have little to share with my uncle aside from Marie Antoinette's continuing air of despondency. She tends to be rather reserved at the best of times, but now she grows quieter, often gazing into the folds of her velvet skirt or out the window to the sprawling green lawn. She asks to be read to more than usual, and wakes in the mornings with dark circles under her eyes.

I know she worries over her seven-year-old son, Louis Joseph, more than the volatile political situation, and with good cause. No longer strong enough to walk and increasingly hindered by the deformity of his spine, he's forced to use a wheelchair upholstered in green velvet and pillowed with white wool cushions. On the fourth day of June, he succumbs to his illness. This occurs during my time off, and the queen is not at Versailles in any case, having gone to the Château of Meudon, which is the official residence of the dauphin of France, but hardly used. Near to Versailles and situated on a hill, Meudon is said to have one of the most stunning views in Europe. I like to think that the beauty of the setting provided some comfort to the dying boy and the grieving mother. Feeling sympathy for the queen, who loves her children greatly, I'm relieved to not witness her immediate sorrow. I wouldn't report her personal grief to my uncle, in spite of the calm, nonjudgmental manner in which he receives all my news.

Returning to Versailles, I'm immediately whirled into a tempest of high emotion and political drama. The Estates-General has been meeting at Versailles since early May, and it's no secret that they're no closer to reaching an agreement with King Louis in June than they were a month ago. Frustrated by the lack of progress, leaders of the Estates-General apply pressure to the king, even after the death of his eldest son.

"I feel such pity for Their Majesties," Madame Campan confides to me privately. "The poor queen—I've never seen her eyes so red and swollen. I wish she didn't have to leave her private chamber and face the court during this time. She ordered the portrait removed from the Salon de Mars, you know, the one that showed the late dauphin next to an empty crib. It seems cruel that she should lose two children when she already carries such burdens. You never met Madame Sophie, did you? It's nearly two years exactly since she passed away at eleven months."

"I pray that her other two children remain in good health," I murmur sincerely. Madame Royale, the eldest, is healthy and clever, and the other son, Louis-Charles, is by all accounts bright and eager to please.

Madame Campan crosses herself. "The king is having a horrid time of it too, though it's more difficult for him to show it. He refused to receive the Third Estate on the day of his son's death, and the next two days after. And well he should—he is in mourning! The next day, the representatives insisted on visiting him. Quite unsympathetic. I've never heard the king sound so bitter, in all my years at court. 'Are there no fathers among the Third Estate?' he

asked. They all shuffled their feet awkwardly but would not leave."
Her mouth twists into a frown.

I feel torn. I know heart-wrenching grief tears at the king and
queen. I've witnessed it myself. Last night he visited her chamber
while I was still in the wardrobe, folding her clothes. They sat on
the bed together and wept, no longer monarchs but simply heartbroken parents. I feared they'd hear me and feel watched again,
so I stayed up later than usual to finish tending to the dresses after
he'd gone and Marie Antoinette had fallen into an exhausted sleep.
But I also know from my conversations with Léon that the need
for change is so great that the Third Estate cannot afford to waste
time. In the letter I received from him yesterday, he'd written about
the desperate situation of France's farmers.

> I spoke with a man who came to Paris from the
> countryside, hoping for work, being entirely in debt due
> to the poor harvest last year and the impossible level
> of taxation farmers are faced with. Along with owing
> the government and the church, they also pay taxes
> to their landowners. It's contemptible to pay to spend
> backbreaking hours of labor to grow the crops, which
> are also then taxed. At least farmers can hope to grow
> their own food. Factory workers in the cities must rely
> on purchasing bread, and you know the cost has dou-
> bled over the last two years. I pray the king will come to
> understand how urgently change is needed.
>
> Thinking of you, as always, and counting the days
> until I can hear your voice again.
> Léon

A couple of weeks after the death of the dauphin, both sides reach snapping points of frustration, and the king orders the meeting hall to be closed. Outraged and determined, the Third Estate chooses a more patriotic name for itself, becoming the National Assembly and adjourns to one of the tennis courts at Versailles to continue their meetings. They swear not to disband until a constitution is made.

When I share this information with my uncle, he leans forward in his chair, resting his chin on his hand. It is an intent pose, and the glitter of interest in his eyes shows me that he listens very closely.

"And what do the king's advisers say?" he asks. He knows that Louis always asks for advice. It's one of his habits.

"Jacques Necker presses the king to make concessions to diffuse the situation."

Pierre nods approvingly. "Necker is very popular with the people. I've never known a finance minister to be so well liked. I hope the king will listen to him. Who opposes the concessions?"

"The Comte d'Artois and the Comte de Provence," I say, referring to Louis's brothers. "They urge him to apply his authority as king."

"That's not surprising." My uncle rubs his forehead. "If the king loses some of his power, so do they. And the queen?"

I hesitate. "She sides with the princes of the blood."

"Pah," my uncle scoffs. "She is ill liked enough, and this will only make it worse. Artois is hated by the people. The two of them allied only worsens each other's public image."

"The queen has never been overly political," I defend her. "And it's different now. She's lost her confidence."

His brow arches, and he leans forward again, eagerness written all over his face. He likes personal information such as this. If not for the political unrest, I'd almost believe his obsession with the royal family is merely love of gossip. This is my chance, though, to help him see that the public perception of the queen differs from her true self. I wish others could see through her shield of elegance and understand her kindness, her devotion to her children, her love of beauty.

"She grieves deeply for her son, and she's aware of the odious view the people have of her. She endures it, but it takes a toll." I search for words. I don't think I can tell my uncle that Marie Antoinette believes herself to be ill-fated. Such a glum superstition is too personal, and I only know from overhearing a whispered conversation between her and Madame Campan.

"How do you know?" asks Uncle Pierre, pressing me for details. He always does. It must be a lingering habit from his time during the Secret du Roi.

Omitting the conversation I heard, I think of another example. "When Léonard was dressing her hair the other day, she looked very weary, like a shadow of herself, and her skin was as thin and brittle as paper. She looked at her reflection in the mirror and saw Léonard fussing with hairpieces—her hair has grown quite thin—and she said, 'If I began my life again . . .'"

"Yes?" prompted my uncle.

I shrug. "That is all. She sighed and then asked Léonard to cheer her up with a story."

"Does she drink?"

I feel a flash of irritation. "Not at all. The gossips like to paint a picture of her as a drunken whore, indulging in orgies and wine simultaneously, but it's well known among the servants that she now abstains from liquor of all kinds. And she is more prudish than wanton. She wears a shift in the bath, for heaven's sake. She couldn't possibly be more modest."

"I know it's frustrating to hear obvious lies," says Uncle Pierre soothingly. "Clever people, like you and I, always see straight through them." The impatient lines of his face relax. "Gossip is a weapon, and it's used against her. You're doing very well, though, Giselle. If the Secret du Roi still existed, I'd recommend you to the Marquis de Ruffec—Charles-François de Broglie, you know, who was the leader of the network, reporting directly to the king. I'd tell him that you'd be a valuable member."

His praise makes me straighten with pride. "I'm glad you understand about the gossip."

"Of course I do. Every spy should. Speaking of gossip, I've been hearing some from Eugénie—she says that Léon Gauvain has called on you several times." He smiles. "Anything to tease you about there?"

I shake my head, though I feel my cheeks color a little. "I like him." Ever since I began spying for my uncle, I can talk to him frankly, even more so than to my own father. It is a strange effect of the arrangement. Still, I hesitate to talk about my private feelings too much. Léon makes me feel beautiful, even when I'm worrying that my brows are not as delicate and arched as the queen's, and I could talk with him for hours. I wish I could see him every day. These are my secrets, though, and I cherish them close to me.

"Watchmaking is a good trade, even if I do say it myself. Is he a revolutionary?"

"Yes."

"Good. I think you and I both know that it is rapidly becoming the safest thing to be. Outside of Versailles, of course. Keep your eyes and ears open at court, Giselle. It shall be very interesting to see whose advice the king decides to accept. I know there's nothing we can do about it either way, but I can't help feeling curious." He reaches for a stack of papers on his desk, sweeping them together, and one of the pages flutters to the floor. I glimpse writing in a bold, unfamiliar hand, only a few lines, and I don't read any of the words, except that it's dated from April. I don't mean to pry into his correspondence, but the letter is written with rich scarlet ink and lures the gaze. My uncle pinches the paper between his fingertips and shuffles it meticulously back into the pile, muttering about too much paperwork.

"May I ask you a question, Uncle Pierre?"

"Yes."

"Am I obtaining the right kind of information? We've never discussed the purpose of my information, so I tell you everything I think might be remarkable, but I've little notion if it's what you seek."

Dropping a paperweight onto the stack of letters with rather more force than necessary, he turns his attention back to me. "You're doing very well, Giselle. I myself do not know what information I seek." His mouth curls in a wan smile. "Anything to keep this old politician's mind sharp. I've a vague idea of setting my next play at court, maybe a historical setting."

"I'd enjoy that."

"When it's the right time." He centers the paperweight, twirling it slowly. "The plot isn't fully formed in my mind yet."

⚜

We don't have to wait long to learn whose advice Louis will follow. The king dismisses Necker and replaces him with Breteuil, a baron known for being notoriously conservative.

Scarcely four days later, furious at Necker's removal from office, a horde of revolutionaries advances on the Bastille, the eight-towered stone prison, attacking it as an ancient symbol of tyranny, and also, more practically, to obtain the gunpowder and weaponry stored inside, spurred on by the recently increased presence of the royal army.

On the day of the storming of the Bastille, I'm at Versailles, where the queen devotes her day to her children, and I to sewing. Surrounded by gilded paneling and tiled floors, we know nothing of the chaos rending Paris. We learn only the next morning, when the news is broken to King Louis, who is still lying in his crimson-blanketed bed.

"Is it a revolt?" he's said to have asked, frightened out of drowsiness.

"No, Sire. It is a revolution," came the reply. The conversation is repeated in the servants' corridors, and likely the noble ones too, throughout the day, a mantra of dread and wonder.

When the queen was informed, I was alone in the wardrobe, polishing one of her delicate heeled shoes, and the sound of voices reached me easily, as dark and sober as distant thunder.

"The Bastille is under attack," says the man. I can't tell who it is, but someone titled would have been sent to tell the queen. He must be someone important. "There's no doubt that it will fall."

Marie Antoinette's voice sounds thin. "Is this because of Necker's dismissal?"

A pause. "He was very popular with the people. They didn't like to see him go."

I clutch the shoe between my fingers, ears straining.

The queen sighs, but apparently appreciates his diplomatic honesty. Her voice cracks, though. "Thank you for telling me personally. I must see the king now."

The voices fade as they move toward the antechamber. I rub a fingernail mark out of the shoe, wondering if the queen's cheeks burn with guilt, since she advocated Necker's dismissal.

Later Madame Campan orders hot chocolate infused with

orange blossom to soothe the queen, who seems glumly unsurprised but still horrified by the news. I try to think of small ways to comfort her. Her gray eyes look wide and ghostly with fear. Seeing her hands tremble, I fetch one of her soft woolen shawls and place it near her. She reaches for it blindly, burying her fingers into the purple folds, turning away from the brightness of the open window. Moving quietly, I cross the room and partially draw the curtains to make her feel that the room is private and safe.

I long to see Léon, desperate to hear his account of the storming of the Bastille. He'll know the details. Within the walls of Versailles, the event is an affront to tradition, a terrible symbol of chaos and danger. In Paris, I wonder if it's something more, a herald of progress and much-needed change.

Chapter Six

Léon calls at the house soon after my return from Versailles. Impatient to see him, I glance up from my book every few minutes to scan the street through the window. In anticipation, I wear a deep blue gown that brings out the hints of gold in my hair, making the chestnut color less drab. It's an old dress, for cloth is dearly expensive these days, but I made it over after being inspired by some of the queen's fine clothes. I'm certain Léon will approve of the blue-white-and-red-striped ribbon in my hair. Tricolor is exceedingly fashionable these days as a symbol of the exciting revolution.

When I greet him at the door, the way Léon's mouth lifts at the corners and his dark eyes gleam as rich and dark as chocolate, tells me that he does indeed approve of my appearance. My cheeks warm with faint rosiness.

He greets my parents, and then we excuse ourselves to go for a walk outside. I try to minimize my excitement as we leave, to keep them from noticing, but it's the first time Léon and I have been allowed to walk alone together, and delight bubbles through me.

All of our previous visits were chaperoned until my parents got to
know him.

"I brought you something," he says, taking my hand and
pressing a small object into it. Part of it feels like a delicate chain,
the metal warm from his palm. I open my fingers and smile in
delight at the slender chain, though the small rock fastened to it
puzzles me.

"Is this a special sort of stone?"

"Indeed. It's from the Bastille."

I glance at him in astonishment, and inspect it more closely. A
little bigger than my thumbnail, the stone has been filed into an
oval shape. The file has left a white scratch across the back of the
sandy-gray colored stone. How odd, to think of wearing part of a
building around my neck. The stone is pretty, though, in a rustic
way, and I predict it will be at the height of fashion in weeks to
come. People have been carting away the stones of the Bastille as
souvenirs of the historic event. Geneviève will envy my necklace.
Holding it up to the light, I realize the chain is made of interlock-
ing sections of gold and silver, each gleaming in the sun. It's very
pretty; the chain is my favorite part.

"I made it myself," says Léon. The shy tilt of his head and the
tentative tone of his voice betray his worry over the reception of
the gift. "I had to use scraps leftover from repairing pocket watches
for the chain; that's why it doesn't quite match. I hope you don't
mind." He hesitates. "While I was making it, I liked to think the
gold and silver together are like the sun and the moon."

The idea brings a smile to my lips, and I trace my fingers over
the stone and the softly glittering chain. "It means a lot to me that
you fashioned it yourself, Léon." I lift my braid away from my
neck. "Will you help me fasten it?"

His fingers brush across the nape of my neck as he fusses with the clasp. The light touch makes my heart quicken, and I turn to look at him over my shoulder. "Thank you for the gift."

"You're welcome, Giselle." His fingertips slide along the length of the chain, skimming across my throat. It feels very pleasant. For a second I can't remember what I meant to say, and when I do recall, the words tumble too quickly out of my mouth.

"I should have known you would manage to get a piece of history." Léon is far too fervent of a revolutionary to miss this opportunity. Even though the fall of the Bastille is a blow to the king and queen, I can't help feeling a frisson of excitement about it. I can hardly help it, now that I'm back home, away from the palace. The streets are full of optimism for the revolution, and it's a little contagious. I feel like Léon and I hold a piece of the future. The Bastille was solid rock, something that should have been unshakable, and now here is a small piece of it, made into something new. This is what our country needs: the old, ineffective ways dismantled and remade into laws that better serve the whole population. I pray that the royal family will see it and aid the much-needed reforms before any further violence happens.

"I was eager to," he admits, dropping his hands. We resume walking, our sleeves close together. "Holding a piece of history is interesting. It's a good thing I only wanted small pieces, because it was amazing how quickly the stones began to be carted away. The Bastille represented the *ancien regime*." His lip curls around the words. "I daresay people are happy to see it pulled down. Now the stone will be used to build the future, and anyone can use it to remember the oppressiveness that wrought vital change."

"Did you see the riot?" I ask. Privately, I marvel at his passion for reform, that he can switch from romance to politics so quickly,

and with equal fervency for both, but after witnessing the fear at
Versailles that the storming of the Bastille had provoked, curiosity grips me and I want to hear more. Léon and I had entirely different experiences of the two events, and I'm desperate to hear his
account of them. It feels like a story out of one of my father's history books, and yet it truly happened. "Tell me everything, Léon."

"I arrived when it was nearly over." He sounds disappointed.
"I would have liked to have witnessed more—historians will speak
of that day for years, you know. The attack on the Bastille was truly
history in the making."

"Of course, but wasn't it dangerous? Were you frightened?"

He shrugs carelessly. "It was a dangerous place to be. . . . I suppose it was for the best that I missed most of the action. The
worst of the fighting was over when I got there, but the sound of
gunfire continued to pepper the air, and people were still shouting and rioting. Children were there, even, running forward every
time the round of fire ended, to pick up bullets. They seemed
utterly fearless." Léon hesitates, and I think the sight must have
been rather more disturbing than he wants to let on.

I put my hand gently on his sleeve. "I read an account of the
fall of the Bastille in the paper. I brought the clipping if you want
to read it."

We pause on the side of the road and read it together. Nothing
in the account is new to us, but it is fascinating anyway, for such
an act of revolution and violence is shocking. Only seven prisoners were housed in the Bastille at the time. Once the mob pene-
trated the outer courtyard of the fortress, a previously unheard-of
feat, the artillery fire began, resulting in death and many injuries.
The assault from the guards did not deter the mob that had located
a cannon and advanced from various directions. The governor of

the Bastille, a man called de Launay, was killed, his head impaled upon a pike.

"That was the worst part," confides Léon. At some point in our conversation, he has given up pretending to be worldly and untouched by the event, and speaks candidly. I like him more for it. "I dreamed about it later, remembering. Blood trickled down the pike, making horrid wet tendrils around the wood. His eyes stared, too, wide with the fear and pain he felt at the end, but so empty. It was a terrible sight, but it grew worse when someone pried them out and tossed them away. I left, then. I'd been staying near the back anyway, just like we did during the riot at the Réveillon wallpaper factory."

"I'm glad you didn't venture any closer."

"I went back later for the stone. The bodies had already been collected, and someone came for de Launay's head as well. His family, I expect."

"It's a pity so many people had to die." I touch the stone resting against my chest. The chain is long enough that I can hide it under my dress, which is probably a good thing, though I shall never dare wear it to Versailles.

"Yes," agrees Léon. "It would have been better if the Bastille guards had stepped aside. But I think the riot achieved what it was meant to. No one can deny it was a rallying point for the revolution. It gave people courage, and it united them. Perhaps the king will take the plight of his people more seriously now."

"He recalled Necker to his post as Director-General of the Finances," I say. "That is a start."

"Wisely. The king made a mistake dismissing him."

I mimic Léon's rather stuffy, knowing tone. "Yes, he was very popular."

His eyes light up, glimmering with amusement even before his mouth quirks. "Are you mocking me, Giselle?"

"A little."

"Well, that is very unkind of you." Laughing, he pokes gently at my waist, tickling me.

I shriek with laughter and sprint away from him, my blue skirt flying around my legs. Léon catches me easily, reaching for my hand with his. His face glows with merriment, and with his dark hair mussed from the wind, he looks carefree again. I feel that way myself. The push for societal change might be spiraling into something powerful and unpredictable, sometimes frightening, but today the sun shines and Léon and I have the whole afternoon to spend together.

He bends close to me, and just when I think he will kiss me, he pauses. His expression shifts, intensity overtaking the lightheartedness.

"Do you want to kiss me?" I whisper, remembering the day in my uncle's parlor when Léon told me of his desire to.

His smile causes my heart to lurch, and I want to press my own lips against it.

"Yes. More than anything. But I also want to know you want me to. I want us to kiss each other."

I do not answer with words, and instead close the small distance between us and kiss him first. He likes that response better anyway, I think, because now his arms have gone around me and his mouth slants over mine, heating me all through as I kiss him back.

"*Vive l'amour,*" someone shouts jovially behind us, clapping hard.

Léon and I withdraw from our embrace, breathless and grinning over the attention we unwittingly attracted.

"Shall we walk past the remains of the Bastille?" Léon suggests. "We seem to have been walking in that direction."

"Yes, I want to see it. It's about an hour walk to the rue Saint-Antoine, and then an hour back. It'll give us lots of time to talk."

"Excellent plan. I like spending time with you, Giselle."

"I like being with you, too. I suppose you know that now."

He surprises me by kissing my cheek, a quick soft caress that blossoms inside of me even more than our earlier more passionate embrace.

I smile at him, feeling shy and excited at the same time, my cheeks warm. He takes my hand, twining my fingers with his, and we continue to walk down the street, heading for the demolition site of the Bastille.

"Do you ever see Necker at court?" asks Léon curiously. "I imagine he must be relieved to be recalled to his post."

"I hardly see anyone important," I admit. "I did see him once, though, from a distance. He was heading to the Estates-General. I heard later that he gave a very boring speech that day, a long recitation of finances, instead of the political reform people wanted to hear."

"I suppose numbers are important too, if a little drier." Léon sounds only half-convinced; like most people, I think he is swept up in the urgency of the need for change, looking for grandiose ideas and not minute fiscal detail. I feel the same, most of the time, until I remember my uncle's chastisements to always watch for the little things.

"The queen is responsible for his recall, you know." I drop my voice to a confiding tone, leaning closer to Léon's shoulder. "I see that surprises you," I say, noticing his eyes widen and his angular brows twitch.

"It does. Everyone says she dislikes him greatly. Is that true, do you know?"

"Probably, but I don't know for certain. I think she must have known it needed to be done."

"It did. He is extremely popular now," agrees Léon. "When he was first dismissed, I was at Café du Foy—you know, the coffee-house by the Palais-Royal—and everyone was talking about what an outrage it was. Camille Desmoulins was there too. I haven't met him, but others told me who he was. He couldn't be missed—he leapt onto a table and made a fervent speech, urging us to take up arms and wear the tricolor cockades. He had a large one pinned to his lapel, and he took it off to wave it like a banner during his speech."

"Desmoulins the journalist?" I ask.

"Yes. He's an ardent revolutionary." Léon looks like he'll say more, but then his attention is caught by the scuffle happening across the street from us. A group of people, all decked out with tricolor rosettes, surround a nervous-looking woman in a gray dress, a black cockade pinned to the white fichu tied around her shoulders. Though all the rosettes are sewn in a similar shape, the somber dark color of hers contrasts with their bright patriotic ones.

"Take off that black rosette," demands one member of the revolutionary group, a woman carrying a basket heaped with knotted tricolor ribbons. "Remove that horrid Hapsburg emblem at once and wear a proper tricolor one." She waves the bright red-white-and-blue rosette in the woman's face, thrusting it into her hand when she doesn't take it.

"Black is for the queen, one of the royal colors of Austria," sneers a man with a drooping mustache and a tricolor band around his hat. "You ought never been seen with a black cockade again."

"It's for mourning," says the woman timidly. Her fingers clutch at her white shawl. "For the dauphin who died."

"If things don't change, we'll all be in mourning for many more people. Do you want to see them starve?" The revolutionary woman plucks the black rosette from the royalist lady's fichu and tosses it to the man, who promptly throws it to the ground and grinds dust into it with his heel. The rest of the group cackles.

The woman in the gray gown pins the tricolor ribbon to her dress with shaking fingers and hurries away, head down and her cheeks flaming as bright as a sunburn.

Shocked by the aggressiveness of the group handing out tricolor cockades, I turn to Léon. "That poor woman. She looks so frightened."

His mouth tightens, forming a grim line. "They could have just handed her a ribbon and let her continue on. It's a better way to spread the revolutionary cause."

Voices rise again, and I tighten my fingers around Léon's. "It isn't over yet—look, that tall man is yelling at them about it."

"He wears a black rosette too," notes Léon. "He must be feeling pretty defensive about it now."

"I would have just slipped away quietly, avoiding them completely."

The man may be wishing he had done so now, for the people with the tricolor cockades seem immune to all of his strongly worded rebukes, circling around him like vultures and jeering at his black cockade. Eventually one of the revolutionary women shoves at him, snatching at the black ribbons, and he steps back, pushing his hand against her shoulder to establish personal space again. The man with the mustache and tricolored hat shouts an obscenity, and his pale lumpy fist crashes into the other man's jaw, triggering chaos in the street. People swarm closer to the fight, circling while their voices rise in harsh excitement and anger.

Léon's hand grips mine hard. "Let's get out of here before this spins out of control. Soldiers will be along in a moment."

We run down the street, stopping only when the noise of the sudden brawl fades and the only sounds above our quickened breaths are the chirps of birds and the occasional calls of a man selling stones from the Bastille.

"Perhaps I overreacted," says Léon, pausing in the thin shade of a young tree.

I shrug. "I don't mind running." It was rather fun, the two of us careening down the street, flying but anchored together by our held hands. "The way the crowd grew so quickly was unexpected. . . . I'm glad we aren't there anymore."

"I worry about riots lately. In my last letter from my parents, they mentioned hardships the farmers outside of Toulouse are facing. It was a very poor harvest last year, and this one isn't shaping up much better. Some families are apparently forced to eat wheat that has been wet and spoiled—it's a terrible situation. And now this week we keep hearing rumors through the city of peasant riots in the south countryside; it's happening at home, too." His thin brows draw together, creasing his forehead with concern.

"They aren't landholders, right?" I squeeze his hand sympathetically. Everyone knows the peasants are revolting against the seigneurs, taking back tithes and grain. They're too desperate not to. "I'm sure they'll be fine. Artisan families like yours are probably the safest—not rich enough to be targeted, but not quite at the mercy of poverty, either."

He summons a small smile. "Are you saying it is better to be middle class?"

"I think so." Worry still lurks in the shadows under his eyes, so I reach up and gently touch his cheek, brushing a dark curl of hair behind his ear. "I'm sure your family is safe. We've had riots here, too, and we're fine. They're probably sitting at home in Toulouse right now, worrying just as much about you."

He straightens, his worries evidently assuaged in part by my words. "You're right, Giselle. I'll write them a letter tonight. I did last week, but it's not too soon to send another."

"They'll be happy to hear from you again."

Léon's mouth quirks sheepishly. "I know I'm probably reacting strongly. But ever since I came here, I've been so thrilled with Paris, I never wanted to be back in Toulouse. This is the first time I've wished for less distance between the two cities." He offers his arm to me for us to continue strolling, and his voice lowers to a confessional tone. "I did write to them last week, but it had been over a month before that. Maybe longer. I wanted to feel independent, living here in Paris, and I thought that it would help me achieve that if I distanced myself."

"Léon," I chide him. "Your mother will thank me for telling you to write home more often. You came to a new city for your apprenticeship, and you've witnessed many revolutionary events already. I'd say that's independence enough."

"I think my sister is more frustrated by the space of time between my letters." He looks reflective. "My mother understands that boys grow up."

"And men don't disappoint their mothers and sisters," I tell him in a teasing tone, but I mean my words.

His fingers stroke along my wrist, his warm gaze seeking mine in a way that makes my pulse dance like a butterfly.

"You haven't spoken much about your sister to me yet," I say. "Is she younger?"

"Yes, by three years. I used to tease her mercilessly, I'm afraid, bringing frogs and grass snakes to the house to scare her. Claudine used to shriek with outrage, until one day when she was about nine, and she took the tiny grass snake from me and commented that it had a pretty green pattern on its back. We got along better after that, and used to roam through the orchard near our house together."

His story makes me smile, and I think his sister sounds interesting. "I am learning a great many new things about you today, Léon. Tell me something else. Please?"

The tips of his ears turn red. "I hardly know what to say. I had a dog back home that I was very fond of. I had to leave her with my parents. I didn't know if Monsieur Renard would appreciate a dog in his house."

"I haven't had any pets," I say wistfully. "Our cook had a black cat once, and I used to slip into the pantry to feed it cream."

"I found Octavia hiding underneath a collapsed fence."

"You named your dog Octavia?" I ask, entertained.

"I'd been reading about the lives of the Caesars, and the name stayed in my mind. She was the sister of Augustus. Claudine thought it an amusing choice too."

"I like it." I link my arm through his. "You've read many books, it seems. If you tell me your favorites, I'll read them too. Papa has a well-stocked library; he may have some of them."

"Perhaps he will let me borrow a few books?"

"I'm sure he would." We talk of books for a while, and our childhoods after that. By the time we pay attention to our surroundings again, I realize we have looped back closer to my house, and that every person around us wears a tricolor cockade.

"I'm going to make up some proper tricolor rosettes for us to wear," I say. "It seems safer."

"Yes, it does. I'd like to show my support for the revolution, as well. I'd like it if change could be achieved without chaos, but it's unrealistic not to expect a few riots. The Third Estate isn't asking for anything small."

Chapter Seven

My parents are relieved Léon and I avoided the scuffle on the street over the rosettes.

"Pierre told me that one man was nearly hung for resisting the removal of his black cockade," says Maman. "Only the timely arrival of two passing soldiers saved him. It's madness." Her teacup clinks against the table when she sets it down too quickly.

Papa leans forward over the dining room table, rumpling his hair. He has ink stains on his fingertips, and one smudged under his eye as well. He looks tired. I know he has been writing frantically over the past several weeks, essays as well as his usual poetry, and staying up far too late.

"It can't last for much longer," he says. "The king seems to be taking the requests of the Third Estate seriously. Aside from recalling Necker, he also traveled to Paris from Versailles to meet with the mayor of Paris for the National Assembly. He seems to be engaging."

"They say he even placed a blue-and-red ribbon on his hat," says Maman. "A crowd of people shouted 'Long live the nation' and the king seemed very pleased."

"He looks on himself as a father figure to the people. Accord-

ing to court gossip, he likes to refer to them as 'his good people.' "
It's the kind of thing I would tell my uncle, and I automatically
look for him before remembering he's not present.

Maman pushes her cup away and reaches for her knitting. "I am
glad you're being careful, Giselle. I know I don't need to warn you
to continue to be so, but a mother always worries."

I collect the dishes to take them to the kitchen for washing. "Don't
worry. I promise to stay away from riots and brawls of all kinds."

Papa rises from his chair. "I know you're still watching things
at court for Pierre. Be cautious there, too."

"What could happen?" I ask.

"I don't know," he admits. "I just don't believe it's good for anyone to be too close to the royal family these days."

"To them, I'm only a servant. It's nothing," I say, to soothe his
nerves.

The next day, Léon stops by, bringing a book. "This is one of my
favorites, as you can see." His thumb glides along the bent edges,
crossing over the cracked spine, tracing the embossed title: *Robin-
son Crusoe.* "My father read it to us when we were children, and
I've reread it many times since. It's an adventure story." He smiles
shyly. "I hope you like it. The translation of this copy is de-
cent. . . . I can't stay long. Monsieur Renard needs me back at
the shop. But I wanted to bring it to you, after our conversation
yesterday. I liked talking about books."

"I enjoyed it too. Thank you." After he reluctantly departs, I
find a note tucked into the corner. Léon's writing is smooth and
sure, with no wasted blots of ink.

*Giselle—I confess, at first I thought to try to impress
you by bringing something by Voltaire, or maybe even*

older poetry, like Petrarch. But then I realized I wanted
you to know what stories make me the happiest, and this
is one of them. I hope you shall escape in your mind to a
sea-swept beach when reading this, just as I do.

I slip the note into the pocket of my gown, smiling. His endearing honesty is far more impressive to me than any list of highly
regarded books.

⚜

When I tell her of witnessing the street fight over the rosettes,
Geneviève is appalled by the resistance of the people with black
rosettes, instead of sympathetic.

"What fools." She fluffs the underskirt of a dress with rather
more vigor than necessary. "Don't look at me like that, Giselle; I'm
not heartless. I'm practical. It's madness to resist a crowd of revolutionaries. They have more energy than a pack of hunting hounds,
and just as much viciousness, although maybe it's justified. I would
have taken the rosette with a smile, no matter what I thought."

"It's easy to say that when you do fervently support the tricolor."

Geneviève grins at me, pushing a frizz of red hair behind her
ear. "And what about you? I saw you sewing a rosette after supper
yesterday."

"I decided to make one for myself, to wear on my days off."
We both know that wearing a tricolor ribbon at Versailles right
now would likely result in our immediate dismissal. I don't wear
my Bastille necklace here either, although I've seen ladies of the
court wearing similar items, though much fancier. One locket appeared to be set with a Bastille stone, and tiny diamonds spelled
out the word *Liberté*. Another woman wore a complex and slightly

ridiculous headdress with white satin towers to represent the Bastille. Against this, my simple locket can hardly be noticed, but I remain cautious. "I'm sewing one for my friend Léon as well."

"Your special friend Léon?" Geneviève giggles when the faint burn of rosiness spreads across my cheeks and an unbidden smile bends my lips. "The dark-haired revolutionary you told me about, the one you met at the Réveillon riot?"

"The very same," I admit happily. "We have been seeing each other for a while now."

"Good for you. I liked the story of how you met; it's very romantic. We should meet up one day, back in Paris. I could introduce you to my fiancé, Étienne. He's a revolutionary too—he'll get along with your Léon."

"I'd like that." When we first met, Geneviève's prickly way of speaking and direct manner had been off-putting, but the more we work together, the more I enjoy her company. We are indeed friends now. Her blunt honesty is refreshing, and we find ways to make the repetitive tasks of caring for the queen's wardrobe entertaining. A couple of times we have sneaked out of bed in the middle of the night to roam the dim and mostly empty halls of Versailles, exploring the long corridors, avoiding the corners that stank suspiciously of urine, and searching for secret passages. We haven't found any, but we have learned new shortcuts around the palace.

The first time we slipped out to explore, we ran down a long marble-tiled hallway so quickly that our feet skidded on the floor, and we suppressed giggles of hilarity, speaking in whispers that were probably too loud. I hushed Geneviève in earnest when I noticed a slight figure through the window, crossing the garden like a gray-cloaked ghost. The woman entered through the side door down the hall from us. Even though she walked in the opposite direction, we recognized her at the same time. Neither of us could mistake Marie Antoinette's long neck, proudly lifted head, and elegant steps. As the queen rounded the corner, we caught a glimpse of her loosely belted gown, sliding slightly off her shoulder to show the delicate arch of her collarbone. It was lucky she never deigned to turn her head and look toward us, for we certainly must have been within sight, although the darkness in our section of the corridor, away from the moonlit window, helped to shield us.

Eyes meeting in astonishment and silent accord, we crept back to our room before launching into speculation as to where she could have been.

"An assignation with a lover," Geneviève declared. "What else could it be? I wonder if Count von Fersen is at court now."

"It might not be. What if she is having secret meetings with royalists?"

"She didn't look dressed for that."

"She couldn't dress herself properly, not without waking her ladies. Insomnia, perhaps?"

"I still think it's a lover. Von Fersen, probably. I wouldn't blame her one bit. I can't imagine being married to Louis would be remotely satisfying."

I wrinkled my nose. "He probably makes awful puns about locks and keys."

Geneviève let out a burst of shocked laughter. "Giselle! Why must you put such things in my head?"

"Sorry. You know, it's rather nice that she gets out on her own sometimes at night. It makes her seem more relatable. Everyone wants love—it's natural."

"Yes. I judge her for a lot of things, but this is one thing I can't."

In that moment I knew that I would never speak of this to my uncle. The queen deserved this secret. Though I had little proof, I shared Geneviève's suspicion about her having a lover. Maybe my happiness with Léon influenced me, but I felt that everyone deserves some romance. My uncle preferred political information, and anyway, I doubt he would approve of my sneaking around at night.

⚜

Geneviève and I go exploring one more time after that, hoping to see the queen again. Instead we encounter the Comte d'Artois, drunk and mumbling to himself as he staggers down the hall in a red velvet jacket and white satin culottes. We hide behind the corner of an enormous and elaborately carved mahogany clock, ducking into the shadows and pressing our hands to our mouths to stay quiet until he has passed.

Unlike our sighting of the queen, which rather impressed us, this seemed a hilarious secret at the time. However, now that Artois has fled France, escaping the people's hatred of him and his unwavering royalist beliefs, it seems almost sad, a trifle pathetic.

After Geneviève disappears to visit one of her friends from the kitchens, leaving me alone in the room, I stroll toward the queen's desk. It's been a while since I had anything interesting to report to my uncle. Perhaps I'll see who she receives letters from in the pile of correspondence. I carry one pearl-gray glove in my hand so that I may have the excuse of searching for the other if anyone comes by, but since Madame Campan has gone to meet with the dressmaker Rose Bertin, now that the queen's mourning period for the young prince is ending, I think I'm safe. The rooms are quiet, patched with sunlight, and two of the queen's white cats sleep on a chaise longue, their luxurious long fur piled together so it's difficult to tell where one cat begins and the other ends.

Marie Antoinette spent at least an hour writing letters this morning, as has increasingly become her habit. I've never managed to see any of her letters before; she seals them at once and sends them away. This morning, however, she sat at the desk a little too long, and had to rush to have her hair done in time to join the king for another court function, and perhaps she didn't have time.

I nudge the papers on the desk, uncovering the half-finished one underneath. The queen's handwriting is as elegant as expected, written with rich, dark ink. I have to squint to make out some of the letters. I'm afraid to lean over the desk in case someone comes in and catches me snooping through the papers.

> *I am trembling—forgive me this weakness—at the idea that it is I who am bringing about his return. My destiny is to bring misfortune, and if vile scheming makes things go wrong for him once more, alternatively if he diminishes the authority of the king, I shall be detested still further.*

Heels click on the floor, growing louder and nearer. I slide back one step and look at the cats, like I'd been doing that all along. One of them peers at me, its green slit of an eye sleepy and disdainful.

"Hello, Giselle," says Madame Campan, coming into the room. "Is everything all right?"

"Yes. Just collecting a stray glove." As I lift it in demonstration, the fragrance of violet and hyacinth drifts through the air. The queen has dozens of pairs of gloves, all in light colors, and exquisitely scented by Jean-Louis Fargeon, her perfumer. "How was the meeting? Is the queen having some new dresses made?"

"A few, though more of them shall be made over by Madame Éloffe." Madame Campan's voice drops lower, even though we're alone. "Poor thing, I think the queen would like to stay in mourning longer. A mother's sorrow may last forever, but the official mourning period does not, and she has a public image to maintain. Do you want to see the list of new items?"

"Yes, please." I love seeing the latest fashions and learning how they are made, poring over the swatches of fabric and lace, reading the descriptions, and tracing my fingertips over sketches. It is a rare treat to see the list, usually deemed by Madame Campan to be above the tasks of tirewomen like myself.

"Come sit by the window," says Madame Campan kindly. "You did such a tidy job of mending the worn hem on the queen's skirt yesterday, I thought you might like to see the new train designed by Madame Éloffe."

I thank her, already skimming over the list with interest, silently praising certain items and imagining how I would have redesigned others. As I near the last new dress, I notice the colors aren't exactly revolutionary. There's hardly any white, blue, or red to be seen, mostly an array of greens and purples and grays in solid colors, sometimes decorated with stripes. All of Paris might be going wild for tricolor, but not the queen.

❋

Near bedtime, when Geneviève and I are laying out the queen's voluminous nightdress and slippers, Marie Antoinette rushes into the room, her face whiter than usual. At first I think she is angry, with the grim set of her mouth, but then I see her eyes show too much white at the corners, her gaze darting and indirect. She is afraid.

"Is there anything we can help with, Your Majesty?" As I speak, Geneviève and I both sink into a deep curtsy.

"No." She licks her lips. "Well, perhaps. Did you see anyone in my rooms today who should not have been here?"

Solemnly, I shake my head. "No one." Geneviève echoes the same response.

"Are you certain? Not near my desk?"

A frisson of alarm and guilt prickles over my skin, and I'm glad of the nightgown to hide my suddenly nervous fingers. "No, Your Majesty. I saw no one. I'm sorry."

Marie Antoinette gnaws on her lower lip, eyes to the ground. At last she seems to resolve something in her mind. Straightening, she looks directly at me, her confidence mostly restored. "Fetch me a warm shawl, Giselle. It feels damp in here tonight."

I bring a soft knitted one, the yarn woven from long Angora rabbit hair.

"Thank you," says the queen, taking it quickly from me and wrapping it about her shoulders, though she has not yet changed into her nightdress. "Send Madame Campan in. You and Geneviève can go for the night."

Madame Campan already hurries into the outer chamber, a worried line etched between her brows. The lamplight turns her hair pale.

"The queen has asked for you," I say.

"What happened?" asks Geneviève sharply.

Madame Campan glares at her impertinence, but she does answer. "The queen found an anonymous note on her desk. It's not kind." She sighs, taking one step toward the queen's bedchamber, then whirls on us fiercely. "Do not say a word. Your jobs depend on it."

Geneviève and I both promise. As soon as Madame Campan is out of sight, we hurry to the massive expanse of the desk, hoping the offending note remains. One of the cats strolls across the desk, sniffing at the papers curiously, batting at a bent corner. Geneviève pets it absentmindedly, her eyes roving through the pages of script.

I find it first, maybe because I am already familiar with the desk's contents. "Here it is." The note is short, written in messy capital letters, as if someone tried to disguise their hand.

It is long past time you paid your debts, Madame
Déficit. The consequences are mounting. How many more
do you need?

A bold signature reads *Dame de la Révolution*. Underneath,
two sketches fill the rest of the page. One depicts the Bastille, half-
demolished, with a cannon and crumpled human figures lying
in front of it, clearly meant to represent corpses. The other is of an
eyeless head mounted on a pike. At first I think it must be an il-
lustration of de Launay, the late governor of the Bastille, but seeing how it is set aside from the other drawing, its mouth stuffed
with hay, I realize it may be Foulon, the man who was appointed
Controller-General of Finances after Necker's dismissal. Allegedly
corrupt, and hated by varying groups for both his severity and his
wealth, he was captured by a mob and murdered in mid-July.
Afterward, the most fashionable color of the season became *sang de
Foulon*. The striking crimson color is pretty, although its patriotic
popularity feels a little macabre to me.

Looking up from the drawings, Geneviève stares at me, her eyes
wide and puzzled and surprised. I know, because I can tell my expression mirrors hers. Who would have written such a note?

I pick up an empty, unmarked envelope, its wax seal broken,
wondering if it could have been delivered within. The envelope
could have been delivered from anywhere, slipped into a stack of
the queen's correspondence.

My uncle will be intrigued by my latest information. He likes
a mystery, and lacking my sympathy for the queen, will be interested
only in the puzzle of it. I hope he may help, for I can't forget the fear
flickering in her eyes, and I hope she receives no further notes.

Chapter Eight

As soon as he hears that I managed to read some of Marie Antoinette's correspondence, my uncle leans forward in his chair, elbows on his knees. His eyes gleam with interest, and his already reddish complexion brightens further.

"Do you remember the wording, exactly?"

"I think so. Close enough, at least." I recite it back to him three times before he is satisfied.

"And do you know who it was written to?"

"No, I didn't have time to see the salutation. I've thought about it though, and based on the wording, I suspect it's about Necker."

My uncle frowns dismissively. "What makes you say that?"

"She was instrumental in his return to office."

This surprises him, and he straightens again, leaning back in the chair, eyeing me with a new respect that makes me feel clever and proud. "How do you know?"

"It's common knowledge among the servants at Versailles. The king said everyone would probably regret bringing him back, but the queen knew it would appease the people."

"Temporarily," adds my uncle. "I shouldn't be surprised, but I am. Louis has ever been indecisive and prone to sulkiness, so they say. And so do his actions."

"A girl from the kitchen told me she heard that the Comte de Provence remarked that trying to get Louis to make up his mind is like trying to hold a set of oiled billiard balls together."

My uncle barks with laughter. "I met Provence once. He made a sarcastic comment then, too. I like him for his wit."

"Uncle Pierre, this is not the most important thing." Hearing the earnestness in my voice, he cuts his amusement off and watches intently. I tell him about the anonymous note threatening the queen. I've been anxious to discuss it with him, feeling that he is the only one who will truly understand. Geneviève, caught up in revolutionary furor, is not as sympathetic as I am, and my parents would react with equal amounts of empathy, but no theories as to the culprit. Léon wouldn't like to hear of anyone facing secret harassment, even the queen, but he knows too little of court to provide helpful ideas. My uncle is the only one who can do that.

He blinks rapidly in surprise, and harsh lines crease either side of his mouth as he frowns. "Someone is writing anonymous notes to the queen? In her own chambers?" He isn't actually asking me. He stares into space, his brows pulling together and making his eyes narrow and cold. He transfers his gaze to me. "And you saw no one near her desk?"

"No. As far as I know, I'm the only one who went near it all day, except for her. But I'm not certain it was written at the desk. It might have been delivered."

He clears his throat, a rough sound. "You will have to keep a better watch, then."

My spine stiffens. I resent the blame that crept into his tone. "I didn't know threatening and anonymous notes would appear. I could hardly watch for something that no one expected—not even you."

For a heartbeat, he glares as though he'll reprimand me for speaking so tartly to my elder, but then he subsides, leaning back in the chair again and sighing heavily. "I know. I'm sorry, Giselle, my dear. It took me by surprise. I knew you couldn't be the only spy at court, maybe even in her household, but having proof of it is rather a disappointment."

"A spy or an enemy?"

"Aren't they the same?" He brushes my question away.

"No." My cheeks flush. "I don't believe so. I don't *want* to believe so." That would make me the queen's enemy, and the idea makes guilt stab along my scalp. I shift uncomfortably in my chair. I remember the way her fingers trembled as she took the shawl from me, her skin pale and taut, highlighting the dark hollows under her eyes and making her seem frail. She needs no more enemies.

"I meant in this case," amends my uncle quickly. "Giselle, of course I did. You are merely watchful, and useful to her, nothing more. But whoever wrote the note may be close to her, and quite malicious." He has leaned forward again, watching me with contrition written in his eyes.

I manage a small smile. "I daresay I'm more equipped to talk of gossip and fashion, not mysteries like this one."

"That's all I ask of you," he says gently. "I'm sorry for making you feel as though I wanted more. After all, this is just a game between us, isn't it? I miss the days of the Secret du Roi, and you were always so curious about them. . . . Here we are, arguing over information that benefits us not at all, providing fodder only for a nostalgic family interest."

Feeling calmer again, I shrug. "Well, perhaps we can attempt to solve this mystery, for amusement's sake. We may never know if we are right."

"She has so many enemies, the culprit could be anyone. But we can exercise our minds in an attempt to solve this. Tell me about fashion and gossip. There may be a clue there we haven't recognized. Tell me everything, and then let me think."

I tell him about the queen's new wardrobe, now that her mourning period for her son must end, and how she has ordered very little from Madame Bertin, instead hiring Madame Éloffe to rework many of her old gowns for a smaller cost. He grows bored when I describe some of the items, and fidgets with his sleeve, his attention wandering.

"I don't think you understand," I say. "I should have summarized better. I'm not telling you that the queen hasn't requested to have any red ribbon sewn to her gowns or that she's adding Alençon lace to a blue-and-black-striped satin redingote because I'm overly excited about the details of her fine clothing. I'm telling you because she is studiously avoiding revolutionary colors."

His attention perks. "She is?"

I can't help laughing. He knew so little of fashion, for a worldly man. "Yes. She is mostly wearing the opposite of revolutionary colors, and bringing out her jewels again more often. Most other women in Paris are dressing themselves in *sang de Foulon* red, and wearing blue-and-white ribbons, but the queen is avoiding all three colors and certainly not mixing them."

"One could hardly expect her to support the revolutionaries," muses my uncle, "but she ought to portray a slightly more neutral position. She's being threatened daily, for God's sake." He pauses. "Wait—*sang de Foulon* red? Is that why Eugénie keeps pestering me for yards and yards of red ribbon?"

"It's very fashionable," I say persuasively. I purchased some red ribbon of my own with my wages, and I already shared some with my cousin, but I don't want to get her in trouble. "And trimming gowns with red ribbon is a very economical way to make them over and bring them into style again."

"Red ribbon named after the blood of a murdered man," grumbles my uncle.

"I didn't name it, and neither did Eugénie. Red is very popular these days. It's becoming safer to wear revolutionary colors like red and blue than not."

"I believe you, and if the queen eschews it, all the better to wear it. The way things are going, I think it might be better to wear the opposite of the queen's fashion, rather than letting her set the style like she used to." He grimaces. People must have praised the queen's elegance once, but lately everyone only remembers her extravagance. "I'll let Eugénie have some ribbon, then."

Pleased, I excuse myself from his study to go and meet with her. We made plans to sew red ribbon to the hems of our skirts this afternoon, so his agreement could hardly be timelier.

❦

Late in August, the queen continues her post-mourning habit of dressing to remind everyone of her royal bloodline, and greets the mayor of Paris, Monsieur Bailly, and the popular general Marquis de Lafayette, who have come to Versailles as representatives of the people of Paris, in an everyday gown cascading with diamonds. I know that most of the larger stones have been plucked from the purple-and-white gown she wore to the opening of the Estates-General and sewn into this one, but this knowledge is not common, and her opulent gown draws all eyes. The skirt sways and shimmers with each step, and as the queen bends her head, the eardrops swallow and then project the light like chips of ice, en-

hancing her grace and sparking scowls on many faces in the audi-
ence. People don't want to be reminded of the queen's beauty and
delicacy, her vast wealth, and the blue blood that runs in her veins,
nearly visible under her translucent skin, which has never seen the
harshness of a summer of labor. They want to see someone with
wise eyes and calloused hands, someone who understands their
plight and cares to help.

"She doesn't need the help of the papers to make herself look
like a fool," whispers Geneviève to me.

Although Geneviève uses the term habitually, and calls someone a fool at least twice a day, I agree with her. Even more so in
early September, when a group of eleven women, mostly artists or
the wives and daughters of artists, come to the Assembly at Versailles to express their concern over the state of the French economy. Their clean, unpowdered hair, simple white bonnets, and
floating ivory dresses making a stark contrast to the queen's os-
tentatious finery. I didn't see them during the Assembly, since I
couldn't shirk my duties and enter the hall, but I did manage to
glimpse them strolling proudly through the courtyard on their departure from Versailles. I would have loved to witness their gener-
osity at the Assembly. They declared they cared more about the
nation's financial health than they did for their personal finery, and
placed heavy cases stuffed with jewelry on the table at the front,
before the Assembly's stunned eyes.

"I would have given an entire month's wages to have been
there." Geneviève clasps her hands fervently, and for once no
trace of mocking amusement lurks around her mouth or in her
eyes. I've rarely seen her so serious. "I'm sewing a modest white
muslin fichu for myself now. Those generous ladies all wore them.
I think it looks ever so elegant. Simple clothing makes everyone
look so much cleverer and graceful, don't you think?"

"Like classical heroines." I'm rather taken with the floaty white dresses, and have already begun sewing one for myself. Even with the tightening budget my family is living on, I can justify it, for the latest fashion is to wear a simple white dress with a muslin scarf, tied into a debonair careless knot, with touches of blue and red to support the revolution and override the plain white, which is historically a Bourbon color. One can wear the same dress several days a week, with different scarves and belts and rosettes, and no one would never know it was the same garment being recycled.

On the morning of October fifth, a chestnut horse gallops to Versailles, its sides heaving and speckled with white foam. Pulling the horse to a sliding stop, its hooves clattering on the patterned stone of the courtyard, its rider leaps from the saddle. His cheeks glow red from the whip of the chilly autumn wind, and his coat and trousers are spattered with mud from the hard ride along the damp roads.

I watch from the window on the second floor, my arms full of the white linen cloths Madame Campan sent me to fetch. The courier barks a command to the nearest of the royal guards, who immediately hurries away, beckoning to one of his comrades. Whatever information the courier has brought, it must be of vital importance. I haven't seen a royal guard move that quickly since I've been at Versailles. Wishing I possessed the ability to read lips, I hurry back toward the queen's chambers, regretting the detour I'd taken on my errand, wanting to enjoy strolling down the long hall with its marble floors, stately windows, and walls decorated with carved wood and gold leaf.

The news explodes through the castle, spreading like smoke into every corner, where people huddle to whisper together, their words hissing through the air. A random footman stops me at the bottom of the stairs, quite close to the queen's chambers.

"The women of Paris are marching to Versailles." His hushed tone belies the tightness of his fingers on my shoulder. "Lafayette sent the courier as a warning. The people are out for blood, they say. Seething over the lack of bread. They've had enough, and are coming here to demand something be done. He says revolutionary men follow behind the women. It's a mob."

I pry his fingers from my arm, noticing his wide eyes, the whites flashing as he darts nervous glances through the high-ceilinged hall, as if he expects an angry pitchfork-bearing mob to burst through the doorways at any second. "Something will be done," I say, trying to sound firm. "We will be safe."

His uncertain glance tells me he's not convinced. He looks younger than me.

"Just put on some tricolor when they get here, if you're worried for yourself." I sound impatient, I know, but I must find Geneviève.

The footman blinks in surprise and confusion. "I don't have any. Do you?"

Uncertain whether his reaction will be supportive or not, I gesture for him to continue down the hall. "Go on—spread the news! Everyone must know."

Spurred by a renewed sense of purpose, he rushes down the hall, his boot buckles jingling with each heavy step.

"Where were you?" Geneviève links her arm with mine, dragging me into the shadowy corner near the wardrobe room. "Did you hear?" Her whisper is scarcely audible.

"Yes."

The king and queen move toward us, their gazes focused on the window. I hadn't realized they were in the chambers, but it explains why Geneviève is whispering.

Though they aren't watching us, we grab the nearest cloth item, which turns out to be a blanket draped over the back of a chair, and fold it together, careful to keep our eyes down. I don't need to remind Geneviève to be quiet. We both silently work, but I know she is straining to hear them just as much as I am.

Marie Antoinette twists her ring-laden fingers, biting her protruding lower lip fretfully. "We must thank the Marquis de Lafayette for his loyalty. I'm grateful that he sent a courier to warn us." Under her relief, her voice has a slight edge, probably because Lafayette had been an early supporter of granting the Third Estate greater representation.

The king bends his head close to hers, clucking soothingly, rather like an overlarge hen. "There, there." The voluminous velvet sleeve of his jacket billows as he raises his hand and pats her shoulder, the motion gentle and rapid. He scarcely touches her, but I see her shoulders shake as she exhales, calming. "We have friends yet." He clears his throat. "Besides, I don't believe the mob will reach Versailles. It's a six-hour walk. Boisterous as they are, the people must have better ways to spend the day."

Geneviève rolls her eyes, clearly indicating her opinion of the king's naïveté.

My own optimism that something will finally be done to alleviate the tension over bread fades a little too. While I secretly hope that the angry mob does not march all the way to Versailles, the fact that the king seems to regard their actions as caused by feistiness and high spirits makes me grind my teeth. Léon will have a great deal to say about this. Thinking of Léon sends a stab of loneliness through me, spiked with fear. I don't truly believe that harm will come to me if the mob arrives at Versailles, but another riot isn't a welcoming event. If it has to happen, I wish I could see it with Léon. At least I can comfort myself with the knowledge that he and my family are safe in Paris.

As the day wears on, Madame Campan tries to get the tire-women to perform our tasks as usual, but everyone is distracted, including the first femme de chambre herself. While sewing, far more slowly than usual, I notice Madame Campan folds the same freshly repaired chemise seven times before finally thrusting it back into the mending basket. Sometimes, because we are quieter than usual, the shouts of the royal guards drift through the shuttered windows as the men mobilize at the palace gates to prepare for the arrival of the mob.

"I wonder how many guards are posted." Geneviève leans close so I can hear her whisper. "The revolutionaries marching here will have members of the national guard with them."

I nod solemnly. It seems likely. The national guard, a citizen's militia was formed shortly before the fall of the Bastille with the goal of defending Paris from outside threats, as well as the dangers within caused by the revolutionary tensions. It is also filled with representatives of the Third Estate, people who are growing increasingly frustrated with the incompetence of the king and the pressing issues affecting daily life. The national guard has already proven to be itself revolutionary at times, siding with the people instead of following the orders of the king. It's an unpredictable entity, and all the more because it is commanded by the Marquis de Lafayette, ostensibly a royalist, yet also famous for aiding the revolution in America.

"The national guard might outnumber the royal guard," I murmur back. It's impossible to predict how many men may have joined the national guard at the last moment, caught up in the passion for change and the excitement of facing the king and queen at Versailles to demand a solution to the bread shortage and prices that cost as much as blackmail. Even Léon has talked of joining, although he seems to have decided to wait until he finishes the current year of his apprenticeship.

"Étienne joined the national guard." Geneviève's brown eyes gleam with pride for her fiancé.

This is another good indication that the national guard is turning away from tradition and the king's command, at least some of the time. Like Geneviève, Étienne is a fervent revolutionary. He would not join unless it matched his ideals. Étienne must be one of the revolutionaries who admires Lafayette for his role in the American Revolution, and for his earlier efforts to have the Third Estate represented fairly at the Estates-General.

Madame Campan clears her throat gently, and Geneviève and I subside into silence, expecting a reprimand for whispering. To my surprise, she straightens her skirt and leans back in her chair. "If only there were enough bread and food for everyone. We would not have these troubles then."

"That would be a relief indeed," I say cautiously. Madame Campan never discusses such things with us.

Geneviève frowns. "It is not only about food, although that situation is dire enough. The people are also angry because the king hasn't fully accepted the Declaration."

"How could he?" asks Madame Campan. "That document, the Declaration of the Rights of Man and of the Citizen, takes away his inherent rights, his divine granted power."

"Perhaps it should. Things have been the same for hundreds of years. Life should not be static."

Her soft eyes widening, Madame Campan watches Geneviève with a look of surprised sorrow, but she does not offer a reprimand.

"All the same, one should be able to understand why it is no simple matter for the king to accept these changes."

"I suppose so." Geneviève stabs her needle through the cloth. Knowing her as I do, I suspect she is biting back a retort that the king is allowing hundreds of people to suffer to keep his own luxurious habits from being uprooted.

I understand Madame Campan's point of view and loyalty to the royal family, but Geneviève's words that life should not be static circle through my mind, echoing powerfully. It gives me much to think about as the day wears on. Waiting for a horde of angry rioting women to arrive turns out to be a frazzling business. I almost begin to sympathize with them before they even show up at the gates.

Chapter Nine

In the afternoon, the mob arrives. All through Versailles, people announce it in hissed prayers and frightened exclamations, scurrying through the long corridors and dashing through doorways, but the clamoring racket of the horde of angry people at the gate is quite a sufficient proclamation of the fact. I wipe my palms on my skirt, wishing I was not at Versailles today. As a shrieking voice crying for the queen's head cuts through the din, loud enough to be heard through the door of the balcony, I think I would be safer at home, and quell a wave of homesickness.

Geneviève stares out the window. "I wonder what it's like out there."

"I'd keep my distance," I say honestly, thinking of the way Léon and I skirted the Réveillon riot and the fall of the Bastille.

"I'd watch it all," she says fervently. "I'd soak it all up."

"Nonsense," says Madame Campan with uncharacteristic harshness. "Get back to work. We may be under extraordinary circumstances, but Her Majesty needs us now, more than ever."

We do not get much accomplished, aside from sharing every bit of news about the riot happening outside in the courtyards, but

Madame Campan doesn't seem to mind as long as we keep our chatter quiet, and refrain from making revolutionary remarks that could be overheard. I listen carefully to every snippet of gossip, trying to memorize details, certain that my uncle will want to know it all. My family and Léon will too, for that matter. This is a rare event for a lifetime.

As the day wears on, more slowly than it ought, given the tense circumstances, my head starts to ache, and edginess pumps through my veins with each heartbeat, jangling my nerves until I start expecting rioters to burst through the door at any moment. I wish I didn't feel afraid, but the mob shows no signs of dispersing, even as darkness falls, cloaking them in midnight and frosting the autumn air outside. I never thought they would linger so long.

I can't go to bed, and am not certain if I'd be allowed. Near twelve o'clock, Madame Campan sits down beside me, where I'm pretending to sew and failing to concentrate. Her eyes squint over dark pouchy circles, and her usually immaculately dressed hair frizzes out a little above her ears. I've never seen her look so exhausted. Even her movements indicate her weariness, her steps slower and her fingers less deft than usual as she halfheartedly plumps the cushion on the chair and leans back, closing her eyes.

"Is everything all right?" I ask, my voice tentative. Geneviève has disappeared for the moment, probably questioning footmen about the events outside, and I think Madame Campan will speak truthfully to me when we're alone.

Her eyes remain closed while her mouth pinches into a sour line. "There are approximately six thousand angry men and women swarming the courtyards of Versailles, perhaps even more. Everything is most certainly not all right."

"I didn't mean—I am sorry, Madame. I know the situation is

dire." I lick my lips, taking a breath to steady my voice. "I'm frightened. Everyone is, I think."

Madame Campan opens her eyes this time, lifting her head slightly to see me better. Most of the customary gentleness returns to her tone and expression. "I know, Giselle, my dear. It has been a most nerve-racking day, and I'm afraid none of us will be able to relax for a while yet. I can't understand how such madness has taken hold of so many people. . . ." She clicks her tongue, pondering. "You heard, I suppose, that His Majesty the king graciously agreed to meet with a delegation of women representing the crowd in regards to their need for bread."

"Yes, but not many details. I do know that the king ordered for all the loaves in the palace to be distributed to the people." As the people working in the kitchen and bakery scrambled to obey, chaos had reigned in the back hallways of Versailles.

"Indeed, and promised that more would be granted to them. He does not want to see them hungry, no matter what they say." She shakes her head sadly. "The delegation seemed pleased, by all accounts, and I am told that some of the mob dispersed after this. As you know from the infernal racket outdoors, not all of them did. As he was given to understand, the people are angry the king hasn't been wholly accepting of the Declaration of the Rights of Man, he amended this, and announced that he will support it without reservations."

I blink in surprise. This is undoubtedly a victory for the Third Estate and for progress, but I didn't expect the king to take this action. "Why are they still here, then?"

Sorrow and worry make shadows around her eyes and mouth. "Many of them are demanding that the monarchy move to Paris instead of remaining outside the city at Versailles. Most of them continue to denounce the queen, fearing that she will use her influence with the king to change his mind about the concessions he made."

"She wouldn't do that." I don't know her well, in spite of being near to her for months, but am still certain of this. Besides, she doesn't have as much power over the king as some of her detractors seem to think. He's as obstinate as a mule, and so indecisive that no one can predictably influence him.

"Of course she wouldn't. But to hear them—I've never heard such viciousness." Madame Campan's hands fidget at her skirt. "We mustn't leave her alone tonight. She is so fearful, it wouldn't be fair. My sister is one of her waiting women tonight, and I will be here. I may need you, too, Giselle."

"I'll stay awake." My words cue a yawn, but even the thought of sleeping with the mob outside stifles it. There's so much going on that I couldn't possibly rest, and I don't want to miss anything. Six thousand people have never swarmed the courtyards of Versailles before, and God willing, they shall never need to again.

The queen doesn't go to bed until two in the morning. Her skin looks gray with fatigue, and though she protests she's too fretful to sleep, she drifts into unconsciousness soon enough. It's not my place to go near her bed, but from the doorway I see she lies as still as a corpse, although her breathing is fast and shallow, like someone ill and feverish. I doubt she has pleasant dreams tonight.

Geneviève and I sit together on a chaise longue in the antechamber, pushed near to the queen's bedroom door. We lean against each other drowsily, listening to the faint sound of voices outside. The mob seems to be quieting down, and I wonder if we might be able to sleep soon.

"I don't know why we have to be awake," mutters Geneviève. "The Gardes du Corps are here. What can we do anyway?"

"If it gets much quieter, we'll likely fall asleep right here." I've been awake for nearly twenty-four hours, and even the hard, crowded chaise is starting to feel comforting and soft.

"My laces are digging into me," Geneviève grumbles, poking at her side and tugging at her dress.

"Mine too." While I understand her tired grumpiness, I don't have the energy to join in.

"Pass me that ugly little yellow cushion, will you?" Geneviève tucks it behind her head, half-pressed against my shoulder, and leans back, her eyes already drifting closed.

I tell myself I'll let her sleep for an hour or so, and then maybe I can wake her and take a turn. Better, maybe the mob will have dispersed and we can both sleep. I yawn with so much force, my jaw aches, and my eyelids droop.

The loud crack of metal on wood batters through the relative quiet of the queen's rooms. My heart jolts and I lurch forward, confused and half-awake. I must have fallen asleep, but I don't know how long ago. The antechamber is still dim, only a few candles giving light.

Geneviève snorts, sitting up and blinking with sleep-narrowed eyes and a muzzy expression. "What's going on?"

"Get back!" shouts another voice, sharp with a mixture of terror and anger.

"I don't know." Fear erases the stiffness from my limbs, and I stride toward the wide, heavy door that opens to the corridor. On my way, I pick up a silver candlestick, discarding the unlit candle. I brandish it in my hand, listening before I open the door in case there's anyone on the other side. I still hear sounds of a scuffle— terse voices and heavy footsteps—but I think it's coming from farther down the long corridor, perhaps around the corner. The sounds seem to be moving in the other direction.

The door opens just as I put my hand on the knob, and I rear back in fright, hefting the candlestick high. My knuckles tighten around it and my whole arm quakes, ready to bring it down on the intruder's head, if necessary.

"Stop!" A man wearing the uniform of the Gardes de Corps swings his hand toward the candlestick. He misses as I jump back out of his reach, bumping into Geneviève, who has followed me. The candlestick smacks into her elbow as we both stumble, and she lets out a low and vicious curse.

"Why are you here?" she spits out at the guard.

His cheekbone is red and swollen, the flesh puffing and darkening around his eye. "I'm here to warn you. The queen must get to safety." Blood soaks his sleeve, shockingly dark and wet from his arm all the way to his elbow. A few drops have already fallen to the floor. I do not know much about wounds, but based on the spattered marking of the blood on his jacket, I don't think it's his.

My heart lurches into my throat. "What's happening?"

"Get her to the king's rooms," he says forcefully. "More royal guards are on their way."

"Shouldn't more of them be here now?" My voice is higher than usual, edging on panic.

"They were probably removed from their additional posts at bedtime, thinking the riot was over." Geneviève sounds scathing, but there's a nervous undercurrent to her tone as well.

The bodyguard doesn't argue. "Some of the rioters found a way into the palace, led by some fugitive members of the Gardes du Corps. Myself and other loyal guards are fending them off, but you must hurry." He turns to go, calling over his shoulder. The angle makes the bruise on his face more prominent. "Get her out as quickly as possible. They're calling for her blood."

Madame Campan, probably hearing the noise of us talking to the guard, has slipped out of the queen's bedchamber in time to hear this last sentence, and seems to immediately understand its significance.

"We must get Madame into L'Oeil de Boeuf." Madame Campan beckons us wildly. "Hurry, hurry." I've never been inside the salon, the second antechamber to the king's rooms, but I know it is not far from the queen's chambers and is named for the oval bull's-eye window on one wall. They say guards are posted within it at all times. As we swarm into the queen's bedroom, Madame Campan goes to wake her. "Girls, fetch her something to wear."

Geneviève and I dash to the wardrobe together, skirts flying. In our haste, my slippered feet skid on the tiled floor.

She catches my elbow as I flail. "I'll get the dress. You fetch the rest."

Fumbling through the cupboard, I snatch up the first warm shawl I can find, knitted in charcoal. She'll need to cover her hair, loosely braided for the night, but the nearest hat is red, too bright and cheerful for the circumstances. I take precious extra seconds to find a somber black one.

Geneviève waits in the doorway, a pale yellow redingote draped over her arm. "Is this everything?"

I clutch a velvety yellow fold, heart sinking. "We can't take these—you got a yellow dress, and I picked a black shawl and hat." Our hasty choices make a terrible combination for the circumstances. Black and yellow are the colors of the Austrian monarchy, and the people have always feared that Marie Antoinette remains loyal to her home country over France.

Geneviève winces. "Yellow was the first thing at hand."

"I'll look for a white shawl," I say.

"Hurry," cries Madame Campan. "The guards can't keep them at bay for long!"

"We must go." Geneviève swings the yellow dress higher over

her arm. Seeing me hesitate, her voice sharpens. "Better she wears these colors than she gets caught in here by the mob."

I know she's right, but I can't quell my dismay as we dash back to the queen's room and huddle nervously together while Madame Campan helps the queen slip the yellow redingote over her nightdress. Trembling violently, the queen wraps the black shawl tightly around her shoulders. Madame Campan urges us toward the inner wall of the queen's chamber.

"I thought we were going to L'Oeil de Boeuf." I look uncertainly toward the door that leads to the antechambers and the main corridor, where angry rioters and the rogue members of the Gardes du Corps could be lurking.

"There is a passageway." Madame Campan twitches her fingers, beckoning me to move faster. "It is secret."

"The chamber used to be part of the queen's apartments, a long time ago," adds Marie Antoinette, staring at the wall ahead of us. I understand she speaks not of herself, but of the women who preceded her. "When it was turned into part of the king's rooms, they left the connecting door but disguised it."

Deftly, she feels along the wall with its gilded panels and many mirrors until she finds the hidden latch. She opens it so quickly that I'm not certain I could find the door again on my own. I let Geneviève go first so I can count the mirrors that are on the left, between the corner of the chamber and the doorway. It could be useful knowledge.

The queen halts in the threshold of the doorway, her breath catching with an audible rattle. She stiffens as her hands press against her mouth.

Madame Campan reaches her side in an instant, putting her hand on the queen's arm and making reassuring noises. "Forget it, Madame; it's only malicious."

Marie Antoinette doesn't seem able to speak. Her mouth works, but no words come out. She nods, her eyes too wide and bright, and ducks through the doorway to the L'Oeil de Boeuf.

Hesitating for a second, I see what shocked her so. Another anonymous, vicious note has been left for her, this one painted on the inside of the door with crimson ink.

Red as roses,
red as Foulon's blood, red for revolution,
symbolism the queen's blood poses.
Her skin of white
for ribbons fine, at last she shall see
how the downtrodden can bite.

With no time to comment, I follow Geneviève through the doorway, and Madame Campan slams it shut behind us. The passageway is very narrow, nothing more than a tiny alcove before another door opens into the outer salon of the king's quarters.

The queen sinks into a stiff brocaded chair in the corner, her face in her hands. She lets out her breath in a long, quivering sigh. Madame Campan pats her back in a maternal fashion, her eyes daring anyone to come near.

I do, but not close enough to touch Marie Antoinette. She looks up as I pause in front of her, staring at me almost accusingly. I swallow back my fear. "It was not a good poem, Your Majesty. Very forgettable."

Her lips quirk, but the gleam of her eyes tells me she is closer to hysteria than true amusement. "You're right, Giselle."

"Terrible," says Madame Campan warmly.

The doorway to the king's chamber opens, and a member of the Gardes du Corps ushers us inside as quickly as possible, his musket balanced on his arm and his sword at his belt. "The children are on their way here," he tells the queen, to her obvious relief.

King Louis puts his hands on his wife's shoulders, meeting her eyes. "The worst has happened."

Mutely, the queen shakes her head. Her pale complexion and wide eyes make me think she fears the worst that could happen is yet to come, that perhaps it is violence against her.

"I hope this is the worst, that it's nearly over," she murmurs through cracked lips. "But I cannot get their shouts out of my head. Even now I hear the drum of footsteps."

The dread in her voice evokes the sound of them for me, too, and I hear the rapid staccato beat of boots on the marbled floors. The volume of the sound escalates, and when the jarring hammer of someone pounding on the door shatters the tense quiet of the salon, I twitch violently, startled by the noise. My heartbeat echoes in my ears.

"Take a deep breath, Giselle," says Madame Campan gently. "It is only one of the Gardes du Corps. It's all right."

I recognize the same guard who came to the queen's chambers to warn us. In the short time since we saw him, his black eye has darkened noticeably. His shoulders loosen with noticeable relief when he sees the king and queen standing together.

"Thank God you're both here." He bows, low and crooked, his legs shaking from exertion. "I've just left your chambers, Your Majesty," he says to the queen. "I am sorry to tell you that some of the rioters forced their way inside." His eyes flicker. "I had to flee, once I saw you were not there."

"What have they done?" asks the king sharply. "Tell me," he adds, when the guard seems reluctant to answer.

The guard looks carefully past the queen. "They slashed at the bed with knives." His voice is colorless. "When they realized it was only the heaped coverlets and pillows, they angrily smashed the mirrors that lined the walls. There are feathers and broken glass everywhere."

Marie Antoinette sags slightly, as if weariness is finally over-taking her. It looks odd to see her stooped with worry, when she is usually the epitome of correct posture. Her eyes close, masking her thoughts.

Quieter footsteps herald the arrival of Madame de Tourzel, the governess, and the royal children. Praying audibly, the queen springs back to life and leaps forward, folding her children in her arms. Being reunited with them seems to restore her strength. After a moment, she rises and thanks the guard for his loyalty in a sem-blance of her usual majestic manner.

I let myself relax slightly too. I hate to think of what might have happened if we had not left the queen's bedchamber as quickly as we did, but for now we are safe, and more of the Gardes du Corps are lining up outside the door. The first one, who brought the news, has disappeared again to take reinforcements to eject the rioters from the queen's chambers. Reaching into the deep pocket of my skirt, I wrap my fingers around the soft ribbons of my tri-color rosette, reminding myself I can always pin it to my collar, that it could keep me safe and help me blend harmlessly into the crowd if I need to.

Eventually, the monarchs accept they cannot remain inside Ver-sailles, avoiding the increasingly rowdy crowd outside. Even the high and gilded walls of the palace cannot entirely block out the panicky cacophony, rising through the air to the chimneys, push-ing into passageways, chasing people as they hurry through mul-titudes of doorways. Thousands of feet rumble against the patterned ground of the Marble Courtyard, stamping and shuffling as the shout of voices pierce any remembrance of quiet. My head aches with tension, and I can't stop curling and uncurling my toes inside my shoes.

"I fancy I can hear them breathing," murmurs Marie Antoinette in a shaky voice. "Like hungry dragons."

I understand her rather fanciful words. The vitriol of the crowd is such, and directed most toward her, that she must feel helpless and targeted. Her face is pale enough that she consents to let Madame Campan apply a small amount of rouge to her lips and cheeks.

"You mustn't look afraid," says Madame Campan very gently. "You must appear vital and strong."

Marie Antoinette nods once, the motion stiff as though the delicate bones of her neck have frozen. Tension draws the skin taut over her bones, making her look older and fragile. Shadows crouch under her eyes and her mouth twitches endlessly, drooping one moment, and pursed into a grim line the next. Even under the rouge, her lower lip is raw from fretting at it with her teeth.

The king hesitates, waiting for her, his shoulders slumped and his complexion grayish. He seems to be breathing in short pants. The queen pats his hand once and follows him toward the balcony door. She insists on bringing her two children with her, and their wide, nervous eyes flick alternately between the crowd outside, impossible to ignore, and the relative safety of the inner chambers.

"I won't be parted from them," says Marie Antoinette. "They must see the children."

I think she believes the presence of innocence will curb the mob's violence, and perhaps remind them that she has done her duty and provided heirs. It's a sound idea, but I don't envy Madame Royale and the little prince Louis-Charles for having to face the crowd. Still, perhaps they would rather stay with their mother than risk being parted for even a moment.

Standing back from the window, I see them on the balcony,

but am well enough away that the crowd can't see me inside. The queen's head disappears from sight as she dips into a low, humble curtsy. The raucous shouts for bread and blood fade momentarily, and the silence is painful, scraping my nerves. My heartbeat thuds in my ears. Geneviève's nails claw at my wrist. She watches as intently as I do, and I remember her comment that some people in the crowd carry muskets. When the queen rises, a cheer goes up, but it is by no means echoed by all of the thousands in the crowd. She pulls her children close and folds her arms in front of her, resting on their shoulders, her expression and posture calm and correct. She disguises her fear well, managing to evoke an air of dignity.

"Remove the children!" shouts a harsh voice, perhaps near the front, for the words rise clearly over the hubbub. Soon the phrase is repeated by others. My heart leaps into my throat when I see that a row of men on the front left of the crowd swing their muskets carelessly, pointing them toward the queen, teeth showing as they sneer.

"Take them away!" The chant rises through the damp air and slaps the queen in the face. Eyes wide with shock and fear, she presses her son and daughter close to her, squeezing them so hard that her arms tremble with the effort. The children's fingers wrap themselves in her heavy yellow skirt, the shade like misguided sunshine, reminding everyone that Marie Antoinette came from Austria. Her lips move as she whispers something to the children, and then they bolt back through the balcony doors and directly into their governess's arms.

The queen lifts her head high, chin straight and defiant. Sparks flare in her eyes as she presses her lips together, and I think she is angry now. It eases some of her fear. Acknowledging the crowd again with a dignified dip of her head, she sweeps into another magnificent curtsy, holding this one so long that my own legs feel a ghost of a cramp in sympathy.

The Marquis de Lafayette, mostly beloved by the people, seizes the opportunity to move to the queen's side. When she rises at last, he bows deeply and kisses her hand. The cheers that began upon her show of respect to the people slide exponentially upward in volume at his encouraging action. The shrieks of approval are almost worse to my twitchy nerves than the jeers, but it helps to reassure the queen. The musket-wavers throughout the crowd now appear to be hoisting them skyward and yelling.

"Vive la Reine!" The cry floats to the sky like a ghost from the past. It has been years since anyone cheered for the queen in such a way. She forces a tiny smile to her face, and curtsies once again. I think I see the wet gleam of a tear on her cheek. Lafayette murmurs something to her, his expression empathetic, and that tells me I'm probably right. I'd weep too. This scene could have ended so differently.

"They threaten to shoot her one moment and praise her life the next," whispers Geneviève to me, her brow wrinkled in frightened awe. None of us can predict what the rioters will do.

"For now," I say. I wish I could go far away from Versailles. It doesn't feel safe here yet, not at all.

The king and queen may have won a temporary victory on the balcony over the Cour de Marbre when the crowd cheered for them, but it's fleeting. Less than an hour passes before the crowd resumes clamoring for the monarchs to travel to Paris instead of isolating themselves at Versailles.

"They say Paris is their heart," says King Louis tiredly, pressing his fingers against his temples. "They say I must be located there. There is merit in it; just as a father must be near his family to guide them, I must lead my people again."

"Your children are here," says Marie Antoinette. There is an edge to her voice, and her eyes narrow impatiently.

Louis turns to her in surprise. His lips part to argue with her, but she waves him away, her fingers curled into irritable claws.

"We must go. It is the only choice." She pinches her lips together, pressing them into a tight, bloodless line. It is the sort of expression one makes when trying to hold back words, and I think she has a great many more things she wishes to say on the subject, but not in this place, with dozens of servants and guards nearby.

I straighten, trying to look alert. My feet ache from standing, and exhaustion makes my limbs as heavy and stiff as iron. If the journey to Paris is inevitable, I wish to God we would get on with it. Versailles has lost its opulent grandeur for me, and begins to feel like a too-crowded and overly decorated prison. Under normal circumstances, perhaps I'd enjoy seeing the gilt-trimmed walls and the enormous oval window of the L'Oeil de Boeuf, but now I just want to escape the chamber. The window, framed with gold stucco frieze, does resemble the bull's-eye the room is named for, and I feel like a target inside the walls. For a moment I imagine snatching up one of the pale green vases sitting on either end of the mantel, and hurling it up to the oval window. The pretend smash of glass and china suits my mood.

Now that he has finally made up his mind, the king makes arrangements to travel to Paris. There's little arrangement involved, in truth. The mob plans to escort him the entire way, and there's no time or space to bring much. Madame Campan and I go to the queen's wardrobe under escort of a mix of Gardes du Corps and members of the national guard, who glare at one another, making irritable remarks under their breath, and fetch a few essential items for the queen.

The king and queen are herded into a carriage, along with the children and some of their most high-ranking attendants. Madame Campan stays as close to the carriage as she can, pacing anxiously back and forth until she disappears around the corner of it. Lafayette flanks the carriage, mounted on his horse and accompanied by several soldiers, but it doesn't stop a group of rioters from singing a cheerful tune with vicious lyrics. In the swell of the crowd, I lose sight of Geneviève, too, and panic flutters in my throat. A trio of middle-aged women pushes past me, elbowing others without care as they caw and jeer at the fearful faces of the king and queen. I stumble into another knot of people, their voices raucous with triumph. The crowd seems drunk, even more so than at the Réveillon riot. Maybe some of the people are, or perhaps they are exhausted and running on the vestigial energy of their victory. Remembering Léon's advice during the Réveillon riot, I don't shove or shout back. Instead I slip through the narrow gap between two women with red shawls, worming my way through the crowd until I reach the outskirts. My fingers feel stiff and cold as I pin my tricolor cockade to my fichu, resolutely looking away from the carriage carrying the king and queen, even though I'm too far for them to isolate my face from the crowd.

"Stand aside, *petite*." A man's hand sprawls over my shoulder, casually shoving me aside. I skitter away from him like a frightened young horse before he has to apply much pressure, but once I've moved out of his way, he doesn't look at me again. He's too busy beckoning to his companions, all wearing revolutionary colors, a few of them in uniforms of the national guard. Two of them carry long pikes with heads impaled upon them.

Time ticks by distantly as the sight registers in my mind, and then my heart lurches in my chest, twisting the air in my lungs into something heavy and choking. Blood spirals down the pikes, droplets leaking from the ragged severed necks. A vein dangles from one of them, bouncing and flipping with every step of the man who carries the head. The face is chalky white, so devoid of rosiness that the phrase *pale as death* sinks through my head, heavy with a new and dark understanding. The man's neatly trimmed blond beard looks dark against the ghastly flesh. The other head has a squishy splotch on the side of his face, remnants of bruising, purplish against his marble-pale skin, and I recognize his face with another pang of horror. It is the same guard who warned Geneviève and me about the rioters searching for the queen, who told us of the attack on the queen's bedchambers. The one who was brave, and unfailingly loyal to her.

Swallowing back bile, my throat burning, I let my trembling legs totter to a halt. The crowd surges past me, some carrying shovels and pitchforks, others with kitchen knives tucked into their belts and aprons. A few people ride scrawny horses and gallop to the front to avoid being swarmed. In spite of the distance and vast number of people now between myself and the guards with their grisly trophies, I can still see the heads bobbing above the crowd, the pikes hoisted high.

Keeping my eyes fixed directly ahead, watching the rise and fall of the feet of the person walking in front of me, I force myself to take a deep breath, and settle in to endure the long trek back to Paris.

Chapter Ten

OCTOBER 1789

Outside the Tuileries Palace in Paris, I manage to send a message to my parents to let them know I'm safe. It costs me my tricolor rosette, which I'd made from queenly scraps of cloth, but a girl of about twelve, loitering in the street to watch the king and queen's carriage wheel up to the palace doors, agrees to go to my house and deliver a verbal message. I pray she keeps her word.

⚜

The abrupt move to Tuileries shatters our routine, and the daily tasks of the queen's household fall into utter confusion on the first day. Geneviève and I unpack what little clothing has been brought, while Madame Campan reroutes orders by Rose Bertin and Madame Éloffe to be delivered to Tuileries instead, and sends for items from Versailles.

Although the Tuileries was once a luxurious royal residence, and still appears commanding, with an arched tower flanked by long and vast walls lined with many windows, Versailles has overshadowed it as the primary palace for years. As a result, the Tuileries shows signs of deterioration. Cobwebs and dust and cracked tiles detract from the elegance of its once splendid rooms. The gardens, visible through the window of the queens' new rooms on the second floor, are well maintained. When Madame Campan gives me leave to go outside for an hour for fresh air, I halfheartedly wander through the unfamiliar corridors, searching for the way to the gardens. All I really want is to go home. Thinking of my parents surges homesickness and loneliness in me.

Reaching a staircase with a large rectangular window at the top, I trudge up the wide, shallow steps. Perhaps from the window, I'll be able to see which courtyard leads to the gardens. Crossing the last step, I trail my fingers across the sleekness of a decorative pillar, peering toward the window.

"Giselle?"

My step hitches when I hear my name. I recognize the cadence of the voice, the soft way it carries the second syllable. It sounds like Léon. My spirits lift, hovering uncertainly. I'm afraid to turn around in case it proves my ears deceive me. I do so slowly.

"Giselle, it is you!" A happy smile lights up his face, softening the sharp angles, and he sprints up the stairs to my side.

"I never expected to see you here, but oh God, I'm glad you are." I reach for him.

Léon takes both of my hands, and my fingers twine themselves around his. His skin feels warm and comforting against mine. He squeezes my hands tight, once, then slides his fingers up my arms, around my shoulders, pushing me close to the wall behind the pillar, out of the way of the walkway at the top of the stairs. My heart lurches as he bends his face close to mine, my back pressing against the wall. A shiver of pure excitement flutters through me, and then his lips claim mine in a fierce, possessive kiss. I wrap my arms tight around him, feeling the visceral urge to keep him close to me, that everything will be so much better now that I'm not alone here at the Tuileries.

Léon draws back, touching my cheek lightly. "Are you all right, *mon coeur*?" His breath seems accelerated, like mine. I feel his chest moving under my hands with each breath.

"Yes. I wasn't hurt, but it was rather an ordeal. I stayed awake for hours and hours—everyone did; no one could sleep through the riots outside Versailles. By the time we left, I was almost too tired to be afraid."

Perhaps Léon knows that I'm being a bit blasé about my fear. He drifts a tender row of kisses from my temple to the corner of my mouth. "We were so worried about you, once we heard about the storming of Versailles. I visited your parents several times to see if they had updates. I happened to be there when your messenger arrived."

"She did keep her word, then? I'm so glad. I sent a letter yesterday, but I don't know if it'll be delivered yet. It's still chaotic around here."

"I noticed. I've been hanging around the corridors all morning, hoping you'd pass by. When anyone asked, I told them I was here for the National Assembly. It always worked to placate them, and only two people asked anyway, out of dozens of official-looking people walking past me. Your parents are in the gardens. We split up to have a better chance of finding you."

I smile at him, and my eyes prick at the corners. Only moments before I'd been wallowing in my loneliness, and now my loved ones are all here. "I was heading for the gardens before I found you."

"It'll be a better tour of them now," says Léon gently, seeing my emotion. He bends close to my ear. "I'm glad I found you first. I couldn't have kissed you like that with your parents nearby."

I arch a brow, my mouth quirking in a smile. "But random courtiers are no deterrent?"

"Not at all," he assures me, brushing his lips against mine. This kiss starts slower, softer, without the wild hard edge of the first one, but it builds, lingering, and ends with both of us flushed from its heat. My pulse feels like a staccato drumbeat, pounding against my throat. It's a sensation that should be uncomfortable, but is instead breathlessly thrilling.

"I'm torn," Léon murmurs against my neck. "I want to keep holding you, but I also want to hear all about the riot at Versailles." He draws back slightly. "If you want to talk about it, of course."

"It would feel good to speak of it, I think. It's not easy to do here. . . . Everyone has a personal stake in the event."

"Tell me everything as you're ready, then," says Léon.

"In the garden, so my parents can hear too."

The gardens are the best kept part of the Tuileries, and from walking in them, one would hardly know that the palace hasn't been the primary royal residence for years. I let go of Léon's hand to rush toward my parents once they come into sight. I'm always happy to see them again after being at Versailles for a week, but this time the relief is strong and their smiles comfort me.

"I hope you weren't too worried," I tell them.

Maman shakes her head. "Impossible not to be. But I'm glad you are here, and safe." She hugs me, and she smells like lavender, just like always.

I tell them about the storming of Versailles, leaving nothing out, though I don't like the way my father's jaw tightens when I talk about being shoved into the crowd and seeing the heads on pikes. My mother's face looks pinched.

"Those poor men," she says. "The mob forced some hairdressers at Sèvres to frizzle and powder their hair to make them

look like aristocrats." She shakes her head solemnly. "So disre-
spectful."

"I met one of the guards, briefly," I tell her. "He was very brave.
He deserved better."

"I hope the king will provide some sort of assistance to the
man's family," says Papa.

Léon seems surprised by the destruction of the queen's bedchamber. "Thank God you weren't there. I'm surprised they got
that far into the palace, but I did hear that someone saw the Duc
d'Orleans disguised in an unassuming gray coat, leading them
toward the queen's rooms."

I blink in surprise. It's the first I've heard of that rumor, and it
seems impossible. I don't think it's true, but that day and night
was so chaotic, I wonder if I'll ever know the full extent of events.

"I think it's just as well the court is located at Tuileries now,"
says Papa. "You'll be closer to home. Paris is growing increasingly
volatile—I like knowing you'll be able to slip away and come to
us if you need to." His brow creases, wrinkling his heavy eyebrows
with concern. "Perhaps you ought to leave your post."

For a moment the idea tempts me. "No," I say, thinking it over.
I enjoy my work overall, and the queen is fascinating. Even if I
weren't spying for my uncle, I'd be curious about her. I like being
at court, too, at the center of everything. I'm not ready to give up
the prestige of it. "Not yet. Things are bound to be better now that
the king is in Paris, not isolated at Versailles. If something else happens, I'll leave then. I promise." The last phrase comes out in a
questioning tone as I look to my parents for approval.

Papa sighs. "All right, Giselle. But please be careful."

"I can meet you here when your days off start," offers Léon.
"I'll escort you home. It might not be safe to walk alone."

My parents nod in agreement, and I like the idea too.

On my last day at Tuileries before my days off commence, the queen calls me to her side after her bath. She sits upright in the bed, pillows and heavy blankets heaped all around her. In spite of this, her knuckles look faintly purple, as if she caught a chill immediately after exiting the tub of hot water.

"I would like your assistance in choosing my outfit today, Giselle," she says.

I gape at her in shock. "Me, Your Majesty?" It's not a clever response, but it springs to my lips before I can think of a better one.

"Yes. I will wear something tricolor. Madame Campan tells me you have an understanding of the fashion for these colors and an eye for detail."

"Madame Campan is very kind to say so."

"She also never gives unwarranted praise." Marie Antoinette nods toward the book of dress samples lying on the table not far from the bed. "Fetch it here." I bring it back, and she hands me a pincushion. "Choose something elegant and undeniably tricolor."

I've dreamed of holding the book of dress samples and poring over it in detail. Now that I finally have the chance, the pressure of the task overwhelms most of the pleasure. I forget to admire the variety of patterns and materials, and flip through briskly, searching for suitable colors. Marie Antoinette watches me closely, and though it makes me nervous, I'm determined to please her. Fortunately, I know which dresses of the book are here and which were left at Versailles, since I helped unpack.

In the end, I select a blue-and-white-striped gown, and a plain white bonnet and fichu. "Geneviève and I will sew red ribbon on the edges of the bonnet and fichu," I say. "It will pull the colors together nicely." I hesitate and force my expression to stay neutral. "Will you wear jewels, Your Majesty?"

She shakes her head immediately, eyes flashing. "No. They are here, but keep them locked away. I will dress more simply while we are at Tuileries." Her voice rings with decision, but when her gaze flicks to the window overlooking the gardens, I think she believes they will return to Versailles soon.

"These are good choices, Giselle," the queen tells me, although she doesn't smile. I suppose she hates to wear the revolutionary colors, even though she knows it is the wise choice. I can't really blame her.

⚜

In the weeks to follow, she insists I accompany Madame Campan when the orders to Rose Bertin and Madame Éloffe are put in. I do not presume to expect I would have final say over the decisions, and keep quiet most of the time, but Madame Campan sometimes asks for my opinion on colors. In spite of her offhand tone, I know she never asks unless she finds herself hesitating over the revolutionary choices. The queen orders only a few formal gowns from Rose Bertin, needed since the formal ceremonies of Versailles have since been adopted at Tuileries, but spends most of her reduced budget on silken tricolor cockades and ribbons, and orders for Madame Éloffe to make over old blue, white, and rose-colored gowns to be more revolution appropriate. She begins dressing her hair more simply, and wears modest bonnets and fichus in the fashionable tricolors for her daily walks in the sculpted Tuileries gardens.

Part of me thrills every time the queen or Madame Campan asks my advice, but it also gives me a pang of sorrow whenever I see the faint, mostly concealed resentment felt by the queen for the limited and personally offensive choices, or the worry that tightens the lines around Madame Campan's eyes.

My uncle will be pleased, at least, knowing that I have entered the queen's inner circle at last. The idea doesn't excite me as much as it once would have. For all of his expertise with espionage, it has crossed my mind that perhaps he should have predicted the march on Versailles or, if not something so specific, at least foreseen a large-scale riot. Since he did not, I sometimes wonder what the point of spying is at all.

Chapter Eleven

In the new year, three months after the move to the Tuileries, my uncle focuses intently on political intrigue and international affairs, specifically where the queen is concerned.

"The unrest in Paris—all of France—is capturing attention throughout Europe," he says, not for the first time. "Of course, the queen's Austrian relatives will have a particular interest. She must correspond with them frequently. Doubtlessly, she tells them everything, and expects them to extricate her from this wretched mess." Like nearly everyone else, he seems to believe that Marie Antoinette cherishes greater loyalty for her native country and siblings than she does for her French husband and children.

I am not so sure. "She writes a lot of correspondence lately," I say cautiously. "More than previously." Some of it is secret, but I don't say this. I only suspect because of the furtive way she hunches over the paper, sometimes splattering tiny droplets of ink onto the table in her haste to scrawl the sentences. Once the letter is completed and folded closed, she regains her customary straight-backed composure and stamps the wax with efficient vigor. If I hadn't been working as a tirewoman for months, becoming familiar with nearly every aspect of her daily routine, I probably wouldn't have perceived the minute differences in her actions.

"Correspondence to foreign powers?" My uncle's eyes narrow.

I've never managed to read any of the letters. Truthfully, I've hardly tried. While I have gained a greater measure of trust from the queen, she also notices me more than before. "I know she corresponds with Leopold of Austria, but that's hardly a surprise. He's her brother."

Uncle Pierre's mouth twists. "I don't believe they were ever close. I never heard of it. She used to be very close to her late mother, who advised her on multitudes of things, but never her brother."

"Lots of the letters are for people in Paris." Not knowing how to confirm nor contradict his assertion about the queen's family, I shift the subject. "They get sorted into a different pile for delivery."

His head comes up like a hound on the scent, eyes glinting with interest. "Do they?"

"The same servant fetches them from her desk all at once when she commands it, but before that happens, I've noticed she keeps them differently. The local ones are stacked diagonal to the inkwell, with the foreign ones overlapping but straight to the back of the desk."

"Good work, Giselle, my dear girl. Not many would notice a nervous habit like that. You're very clever." His smile rounds his cheeks briefly before he leans back in his chair again, thinking. "So most are for Paris? Well, it makes sense that she would write to as many royalists as she can. She needs their support."

"And their comfort."

His brows arch, and I'm surprised he neglected to think of this angle, given his vast experience for examining and interpreting every action, monitoring every detail for the Secret du Roi.

"She was nearly killed last time she was at Versailles, people scorn her all through the city, and more and more often she hears that her role, which she was raised for from birth, is wrong and disastrous for society. She fears for the future of France, and her own life, and it's natural that she seeks reassurance and advice from friends."

My uncle nods sadly. Pressing his fingertips together, he leans forward, shaking his head slightly. "She always was charming, when she wanted to be. Is she bringing you under her spell now too? I suppose it isn't unexpected now that you've received a promotion of sorts."

This isn't at all the response I anticipated upon seeing his pitying reaction. At first I'd thought he understood the angle of sympathy I attempted to present, but now understanding that patronizing tone is directed entirely at me stings. Resentment makes my spine stiff, and I stare down my nose at him. My brows probably reach my hairline. "Not at all, and I don't appreciate the accusation, Uncle. I've always been careful to remain unbiased and to view everything from objective angles, as you directed me to. When I have a personal opinion on an incident I report to you, I'm careful not to let it color my words, just as if this really were the Secret du Roi—even though it is not. You missed this angle, because you dislike her so much that you imagine her not to be human, and because you obsess so much over ulterior motives that sometimes you overlook the simplest ones."

His eyelids twitch, and his frown lines deepen with displeasure while his cheeks redden. I brace myself for a reprimand but match his stare. I'm not afraid of him. My uncle might fancy himself the head of our family, but I've survived the storming of Versailles and I will not be treated like a child. Besides, while perhaps a bit harshly stated, my point has a ring of truth. He taught me to observe, and I see him now too.

"I am sorry to offend you, Giselle. I didn't mean you're failing in your task. Such empathy is a credit to anyone, and if I forgot it, it's only because such depth was unfortunately a lacking feature of the Secret du Roi."

I rise, smoothing my skirt so it falls in a haughty line down to my feet. "The queen isn't the sort to dissemble and pretend. She's accustomed to being independent, frank, and headstrong. Born into royalty, she never had to curb those aspects of her personality."

"I know," he says, fingers flicking impatiently. "I knew her when she was a young dauphine, just come to court. Sit down, Giselle. I said I'm sorry."

"In the most noncommittal way possible. You apologized for offending me, not for saying something offensive. There is a difference. Besides, I have to be home for lunch. My father will be here any moment. He's walking me home. I don't walk anywhere in Paris alone these days."

Uncle Pierre sees me to the door. "Is this the end of our spy work, then, Giselle? Are you ready to give up the family legacy?"

I sweep past him without answering, but before I close the door, I twist my head over my shoulder. Standing in the doorway, he looks slighter than usual, his hair glistening with gray.

"I don't know," I say. "Perhaps."

"Please don't give it up so quickly. I know you enjoy the intellectual side of it, gathering observations and putting them together into conclusions. It's a puzzle only the clever can do. You'd miss it."

"I do enjoy it. But I think you would miss it more."

The silence expands for a long moment. "Indeed I would," he says heavily.

"I'm glad you can admit it. Perhaps I'll continue, then."

Seeing my father approaching along the street, I proceed down the steps. I don't look back, but I can practically feel my uncle's satisfaction as he lingers before closing the door. It pleases me, because if he cares about his spying on the queen during all this political upheaval, he needs me, and I hope I've shown him that I won't be taken for granted.

My uncle doesn't contact me for weeks, and although I see him a couple of times at family dinners, we don't speak of spy work. We hardly converse at all. He seems weary and tense, excusing himself early on several occasions, withdrawing to his study or hastening his family home in their carriage. I'm curious about what he could be working on that takes up so much of his time, hoping he has finally begun writing another play, as we discussed so long ago. Papa scoffs at the idea when I mention it in passing.

"I think Pierre prefers politics over plays, and there are plenty of those to go around at the moment."

At last, in late February, I arrange our next meeting myself, bringing a carefully prepared list of the most notable items to discuss. The winter has been quiet, so these are small enough, but I don't mind. The events of October were sufficiently dramatic to last a long time. As well, Léon and I spend as much of our spare time together as we can, and this keeps me busy. Sometimes we walk around Paris or in the Jardins des Tuileries. On rainy days, we slip into the library, which is usually empty and neglected, and the books receive no attention from us, either. He often calls for me at home, too, and my parents seem to approve of him. Maman spoils him, sending him home with extra food like biscuits and apples. Though he is a grown man, I think she pities him for having to live so far away from his own family. After one of his visits on a drizzly March evening, Papa calls me into his study and gently enquires about the depth of my regard for Léon.

"I see the softness in his eyes when he looks at you, which is almost constantly." Papa smiles, teasing and bittersweet at the same time. "You're all grown up now, Giselle, and maybe you will be married soon. If Léon asks for my permission to wed you, shall I give it?"

My cheeks tingle with the self-conscious blush that I cannot suppress, but excitement sings through me. "Yes. I love him, Papa."

"I know he loves you too. Has he told you yet?"

"No, not yet. Not in words."

"It's a life-changing thrill, hearing it from someone who you have requited feelings for." Papa stares into the fireplace, eyes glazing with memory. "I still remember when Charlotte said those magical words back to me."

"Did you court Maman with poetry?" I ask lightly. Even now, his index fingertip bears a blue ink splotch.

He smiles wryly. "Poetry and roses every day for two months." He rises from his chair, his grin widening. "It's a good thing we settled things between us then, because I was running out of poems. She confided afterward she knew she would marry me after one month, but she didn't want the poems to cease."

I giggle. "Perhaps it's just as well that Léon doesn't write poetry, for his sake."

"Ah well, he's practical. Not like your romantic fool of a father." His dark brows draw together in cheerful self-deprecation. "Léon will take good care of you, I think, not that you need someone to coddle you."

I embrace my father. He smells like parchment and smoke from the fireplace. He knows me so well, even when he seems to be immersed in his books for weeks at a time, and I love him dearly.

Just as I turn to leave the study, he puts his hand on my arm to pause me. "One more thing, Giselle—if you are tired of spying for Pierre, you only have to tell me or your mother. I think she would be secretly relieved if you were to stop. She worries, now that the court atmosphere is so volatile."

"I'm very careful. It isn't dangerous—at least, no more dangerous than simply being at court is, and it's been much better since the king and queen moved to the Tuileries and have been making an effort to support the revolution."

"I can't stop you, and I wouldn't anyway. I trust your judgment, Giselle. But I wouldn't be a proper father if I didn't remind you to continue to be careful."

"I will," I promise solemnly.

"Not just at court," he adds. "Pierre can be a bit of a bully at times. He thinks of himself first, always. Don't let him get to you."

"We did argue," I admit. "It was my fault as much as his. I think we have come to a better understanding now. He knows I won't be pushed around."

Papa gives me a small, strange smile. It's proud and also cold, somehow. "Good. Make sure he never forgets it, and trust yourself first."

"I shall." His seriousness seems almost excessive, but I suppose he worries now that the revolution makes each day unpredictable. I do too, even while I enjoy the excitement of it.

As the snow melts and the trickling icy paths give way to mud and then sun-warmed grass, time flies in a blur for me. My head and heart are both full, and I am content.

In mid-June, all aristocratic, hereditary titles are abolished. The king is to be called merely citizen, his title changing to *Citoyen* Louis Capet. The queen, I suppose, must be *Citoyenne* Capet. However, it's an unspoken but ironclad law that this new development does not permeate either of their households, or indeed, life at Tuileries at all.

"The audacity of it," says Madame Campan, fists clenched with shock. "If they are not king and queen, then why do they live in a palace and administer the government, I ask?"

There are no words to soothe her, so I make a sympathetic noise. It's been a long while since Louis administered any government laws, and they live in the Tuileries by force, after being evicted from Versailles. On the day the title change happens, the queen walks about the garden for several hours, making the rounds over and over, until her cheeks have grown quite pink from the fresh air and sunshine. She looks healthier than she has in a long while, if one doesn't notice the anguish in her eyes.

In the following weeks, it becomes exceedingly fashionable in revolutionary circles to adopt the use of *citoyen* in everyday conversation. Instead of being addressed as Mademoiselle Aubry, all of my acquaintances outside of Tuileries greet me as *Citoyenne* Aubry, and I must do the same. It feels strange. On one hand, the title invokes equality, but it feels impersonal, too. Geneviève likes it, and she and her fiancé, Étienne, address each other in this way all the time, laughing and grinning at each other.

"Come out with us, your next day off." Geneviève smiles coaxingly. "I know Étienne and Léon would be fast friends, just as we are. They'd enjoy talking of politics together."

"Léon likes Café du Foy. Perhaps we could go there?" I'm intrigued by the idea of visiting the coffeehouse, located in the garden of the Palais Royal. Though there are many cafés in the area, few have such a reputation for attracting idealists, revolutionaries, and political dissidents. The company is the draw for Léon, who could happily talk reform for hours. It's a relatively new thing for women to be allowed into coffeehouses at all. Only a few years ago they were viewed as places for men—only—to network and share ideas. I've never been to a café.

"I've been there once." Geneviève tosses her head, but her grin is more mischievous than lofty. "You'll enjoy it, I think."

"Was it very exciting?"

"Oh yes, although I don't know how much I like coffee, really. So bitter. The café got a little loud and rowdy last time, when two men started arguing. They had to be escorted out."

"Let's meet there," I say. "I know Léon will want to."

Geneviève's eyes sparkle. "What time? I think late afternoon would be best."

It requires no persuasion to convince Léon of the plan. "I'd thought of asking you to accompany me to Café du Foy one of these days," he says. "I confess, after hearing all of your stories of Geneviève, especially when the two of you explored Versailles by night, I've been curious to meet her."

Étienne is older than I expected, nearing thirty. Silver shines at his temples, perhaps a little prematurely, but his smile is broad, youthful, and infectious. Geneviève lights up like a candle whenever he smiles at her, his gray eyes turning smoky with warmth. He towers over her, and when she nestles close to his chest, his broad shoulders and stocky build nearly shield her lanky figure from view if one is standing behind them.

Léon hands me a cup of coffee, sipping at his own. Although Papa adores the beverage, I've rarely tasted it. The bitterness fills my mouth, and I pinch back a cringe, keeping my expression neutral. After a moment, though, only a dusky richness is left, and I find myself taking another sip, more willingly. I wish I could've had more sugar, though.

"That's Desmoulins over there." Léon's fingertips nudge against my wrist, and his lips brush my ear as he leans closer, whispering. "The one with the dark hair, gesturing profusely as he talks."

I study the man unobtrusively, until it occurs to me that the busy café, full of animated, excited people, doesn't require much subtlety. With his wavy dark hair and fine features, Desmoulins looks almost effeminate. The spark of fervor burns in his eyes, though, making him appear strong and fierce as well.

He sees me looking at him, and I hastily take another sip of coffee, regretting my gawking. I overestimated the busyness of the café, it appears. After a few minutes, when his conversation has ended, he crosses the room toward us, greeting a few others along the way. He seems to know almost everyone.

"H-have we met?" he asks politely, his gaze sidling to Léon as well.

"No, I have not yet had the honor, *Citoyen* Desmoulins. I'm Giselle Aubry, and this is Léon Gauvain. Léon tells me that we have you to thank for the wonderful popularity of the tricolor cockades."

"I heard your speech last July, when Necker was dismissed. It was very convincing." Léon glances down at the tricolor rosette pinned to his coat, grinning ruefully.

Desmoulins inclines his head. He doesn't smile, but his expression seems to warm somehow. "You give m-me too much credit, but I thank you for the compliment. The cockades are a symbol of a very powerful movement—I daresay it scarcely needed my encouragement." As he speaks, his faint stammer fades, and his voice gains the confidence to match his assured posture.

He continues to speak of the ideals of the revolution, and I feel a spike of shyness, afraid to say the wrong thing or mention that I work for the queen. I don't know how well that would be accepted here, and I notice that Geneviève keeps her mouth shut on that subject too. Léon carries the conversation though, drawing Desmoulins into a discussion of the ways in which equality might be improved.

"Equality is so *logical*," says Léon, waving his hands. His eyes flash. "I cannot see how the king can deny the changes much longer, especially when the Assembly is so determined to make them."

The corners of Desmoulins's mouth twitch. "Any man can make mistakes, but only an idiot persists in his error. Cicero said that, and I think he was quite right. I fear our king may be an idiot."

It's a shocking statement, treasonous in normal times, but no one blinks at it here. I sip my coffee again, to hide my reaction. I wonder if the king will see past his mistakes. Truthfully, I don't believe they are all his; he inherited some from generations of predecessors, but that doesn't mean he can't be held accountable for setting things right now.

"I haven't read as much as I would like, but I've recently obtained a copy of one of Cicero's works on rhetoric." Léon tries to sound casual, but I know him well enough to hear the excitement in his voice. No wonder he likes it at Café du Foy so much; it's the center point for a storm of revolutionary and political ideals, much frequented by intellectuals. Léon wishes to be seen as a scholar as well as a craftsman, I think, given his love of books. I resolve to raid my father's library for books that may interest Léon, for both of us to read. I'd like to be able to talk with him about them too.

"I studied the classics quite extensively," admits Desmoulins. "I always admired Cicero, and Tacitus, as well."

I can see Geneviève, who has been engrossed in a separate

conversation with Étienne and another couple approximately ten years older than we are, lose interest in their chat, and listen in to Léon and Desmoulins. A slight wrinkle appears between her eyes as she deems this just as boring, and she catches my eye, grinning. "Do you like your coffee?" she murmurs, so as not to interrupt too loudly.

"It's interesting here," I say.

"About to get more so." She lifts her chin in the direction of a newcomer making his way purposefully toward our group. "That's Maximilien de Robespierre. Also very revolutionary."

I recognize the name from reading the newspapers and political pamphlets. He's a member of the Jacobin club, a revolutionary political group comprised mostly of professional men, at least in Paris, although there are other branches throughout France. The Comte de Mirabeau is the current leader of the group, which I have always found vaguely surprising, because I've seen correspondence from the queen addressed to him lying on her desk.

Robespierre's countenance is also easily recognized from the political sketches. He has a sloping forehead, and his alleged strong-mindedness is matched by the strength of his features.

"Are you talking of Cicero again?" he scolds Desmoulins. "What could he possibly have to say that would be relevant nowadays?"

Desmoulins smiles. "How about this? 'Peace is liberty in tranquility.'"

Robespierre grins back wolfishly. "Not bad, and I like the sentiment behind it. We need peace, if that's what it may be defined as. It will come; I have faith."

Desmoulins turns to Léon. "Robespierre believes the people of France are fundamentally good, and therefore capable of advancing the well-being of the nation above their own individual desires."

"I never said it'd be easy, though," Robespierre adds. He makes introductions with Léon, who remembers my presence and presents me as well. Robespierre studies me in a way that makes me blush, not because it is improper or lewd, but because he has the focus of a man learning a face, memorizing a name, someone accustomed to remembering everyone he meets. They continue their political and philosophical conversation, and I leave them for a while to visit with Geneviève and Étienne, until Robespierre's powerful voice catches my attention again, extolling the brilliance of Rousseau.

"You admire the writings of Rousseau?" I ask, accidentally interrupting.

Fortunately, no one seems to mind. Robespierre stares down at me in approval. "Indeed. Have you read his work?"

I nod. Papa has all of his works, and besides, I've heard Madame Campan read from his books to the queen many times. I'm surprised to hear such a fervent revolutionary quoting him though. I think back to the passage where the princess ignorantly declared that her starving people could eat cake, and remember that contemporary people have accused Marie Antoinette of saying it. Someone who studied Rousseau would surely see through the sham, realize it's a fiction dating from the queen's childhood.

Curious as I am, it's too dangerous to ask the question here. Instead I bring up an unrelated passage from Rousseau and ask Robespierre for his opinion. He seems glad to give it, and later on, when the conversation has trickled in another direction, Léon squeezes my hand.

"I like that you are well-read," he says, his voice a low vibration close to my ear. "I like being able to talk to you about anything, even books. Some people find it a dry topic. . . . I think my father does sometimes. He used to say that I was the smartest of the family, but he was always happy to leave anything bookish to me."

"I see why you enjoy it here. There is plenty of intellectual conversation to go around." I nudge his arm teasingly.

He smiles back briefly before slanting a serious gaze toward me. "I get a little uncertain sometimes. The revolution grows so complicated. . . . Sometimes I fear I misunderstand it. It eased me to have you here with me today. A man cannot help but feel confident with a lovely woman at his side."

I kiss his cheek. "I enjoyed our outing too. The conversations were quite stimulating." It was interesting to see Léon surrounded by other revolutionaries. I knew of his passion for reform, of course, but I feel now that I understand the depth of it. I make a silent promise to myself that I shall do my best not to let my place at court and my secret sympathies for Marie Antoinette cause arguments between us. We don't have to agree on everything—Lord knows Geneviève and I don't, and our friendship is strong—but we can respect each other's boundaries. I regard Léon with too much esteem for anything less.

✦

A fortnight after our visit to Café du Foy, on the fourteenth day of July, there's a fête for the one-year anniversary of the fall of the Bastille. Léon and I make plans to attend the celebration together. Most of Paris will be there, convening at the Champs de Mars.

Léon meets me in the gardens, near my favorite small fountain, hiding in a corner. "It's a shame the sky is so cloudy. The whole world should be dazzled with sunlight today."

Amused by his enthusiasm for the *fête de la fédération*, I smile and squeeze his hand in mine. "Little chance of that, I'm afraid."

"A few raindrops won't stop us." He hesitates. "Will they still be able to do the fireworks in this wet weather, do you think? I was looking forward holding you close to me while we watched them." His eyes gleam with warmth, heating my blood and quickening my heartbeat.

I tilt my face toward his. "I don't think we need fireworks for that."

Léon bends his head to mine, moving slowly, and his gaze traces across the shape of my face, from my cheekbones to my mouth, an almost palpable caress. Our eyes meet intensely, as though he wants me to read the depth of his feeling, to peer into his soul. My anticipation for our kiss sweeps through me, fluttering low and sweet through my belly as my lips part.

Sunlight pierces the roil of gray clouds, slanting down over us, throwing sparks of light off the shifting water of the fountain. I half-close my eyes against the brightness, but I don't want to stop looking at Léon. Dipped in sunshine and pressed close to him, I feel utterly happy.

"Giselle, you're so beautiful." Léon's voice drops to a purr, and his breath whispers across my lips, tempting me even more to kiss him. "It breaks me. I planned to wait, but this moment is perfect and I don't want to waste it." He strokes his fingers along the side of my neck, cradling his hand under my jaw. "I love you. Will you marry me?"

I close the gap between us, pressing my lips to his, sliding my hands behind his head to play with the silky strands of hair curling along the nape of his neck. He tightens his arms around my waist, embracing me with a fierce joy that echoes mine.

"Yes, Léon. I will marry you."

His eyes glitter, as soft and warm as velvet. "I'm so glad you said yes, Giselle." His voice sounds throaty and rich. "I was fairly sure you cared for me as much as I do for you, but apparently a man always has a frightening lurch of doubt when asking such a significant question." He grins. "I had a special day all planned, but—"

"This was perfect," I assure him. "It isn't often we get to be alone in this busy garden, and the sunshine singled us out on a dreary day." I can't stop smiling.

Léon touches the corner of my mouth gently, grinning back at me. "A marvelous omen for us. We'll be so happy, Giselle. I promise I'll be a good husband to you."

"I know you will be. And I'll try to be a good wife."

"What, you won't promise?" He chuckles, knowing that I'm teasing him.

"I can't promise to never be haughty or impatient or not to talk about the queen's gowns for an hour at a time. But I do swear to always love you and to be open with you, to build a life with you."

"It will be a good life," Léon says, growing earnest. "I won't be an apprentice too much longer, and then I hope I'll make a comfortable living. Watchmakers often do, and I have some ideas for patriotic watch designs. They should be popular. I know you dream of becoming a famous dress designer like Rose Bertin. Maybe we'll put together matching combinations of cloaks and pocket watches." He grins.

"I like that idea. Especially since I've given up wanting to model myself after Rose Bertin. I'd rather be known for clothes that are both sensible and fashionable."

The corner of the garden is still deserted apart from us, but I lower my voice anyway. "Léon, I promised I'd be open with you, and since you're going to be my husband, there are some things you ought to know." Wariness creeps over him, shadowing his eyes and tightening his shoulders. I suppose I didn't begin very well, so I make up for it by jumping straight to the point, albeit through a whisper to his ear. "I've been spying on the queen for over a year."

He stiffens in surprise and stares at me curiously. "What do you mean?"

I tell him about my uncle, and the family legacy of the Secret du Roi, even, for added explanation, a few of the specific things I have reported to my uncle. "I don't know what he does with the information. . . . As far as I know, he does nothing, storing it away for himself. Perhaps he is only nostalgic for the days of the Secret du Roi."

"Or perhaps he corresponds with other people. Other writers, politicians . . ." His mouth quirks in thought, and then he gives me a serious look. "Are you good at espionage?" asks Léon.

"I believe so. You didn't suspect."

"I'm not part of the queen's household, either. Ought I to count?"

"Always, with me." I trail my fingers along the back of his hand.

He flips his hand over, twining my fingers with his. "But not as someone whose suspicion matters."

"Madame Campan likes me, and she would be the most likely to suspect. I'm sure no one else does. Anyway, it doesn't matter much; it's just for my family, which you will now be part of."

"Remember when we first met, and I talked to you of revolutionary ideals for hours? You had a reasonable counter for nearly all of my points—"

"I enjoyed the debate," I interject.

"But the whole time, you were secretly being a revolutionary. How mysterious you are, Giselle." His smile lights his face, rounding out the hollows under his cheekbones and making his eyes gleam with affection.

I try to shrug away the sudden bashfulness that washes over me. "I wasn't trying to be mysterious."

"I know; I'm only teasing. You always surprise me in good ways. When we met, I was so pleased when you first spoke to me. You were so pretty, but you seemed a little haughty, with your queenly head tilts." He grins. "As we spent more time together, and I discovered your kindness and cleverness, I fell in love. I'm so glad we'll get to spend our lives together."

His gentle teasing and tender words make me smile. "I'm happy too." The simple words seem insufficient to express the swell of joy in my heart, but he kisses me gently, and I think he understands.

By the time we arrive at the Champs de Mars for the *fête de la fédération*, a sizable crowd has already gathered. I watch in awe as people surge toward the amphitheater in a tide of tricolor, foamy white dresses swirling with deep red sashes and blue coats and hats, a sea of revolutionary fervor. Given that I wear similar garb, dressed in a simple, long-sleeved white dress that I've embroidered with bouquets of red, white, and blue flowers, with a wide red sash and a muslin fichu, I blend into the crowd. Léon looks every bit the handsome young revolutionary, with his jaunty tricolor cockade, blue jacket, and the popular style of breeches and buttons that look vaguely like military uniforms. It suits him well.

"There's the Altar of Liberty." Léon gestures to a flight of steps across the amphitheater. "I heard they built it with stones taken from the Bastille."

I strain my eyes to see across the distance. The grandly named Altar of Liberty houses traditional symbols of royalty, such as the scepter and the Hand of Justice, but a Liberty Cap adorns the peak, its bright tricolor unmistakable.

We find a place to sit, and huddle close together for warmth against the damp weather. The king and queen are both here, and

I see the slight form of the young dauphin at the queen's side. She has dressed him in the tricolor uniform of the national guard, and the cheer of the crowd at the patriotic sight howls through the air. I knew of the wardrobe choices in advance—Geneviève and I helped to put the finishing touches on the dauphin's costume— but it relieves me to see that Marie Antoinette hasn't changed her mind and reverted back to something more royal.

The queen herself wears an outfit that Madame Campan and I created. Her simple white dress is not unlike those of the other women in the crowd, especially since the distance hides the better quality of the cloth, and a tricolor sash provides brightness to off-set the white. Her headpiece is my favorite part of the outfit, gracefully designed with dyed tricolor feathers and matching ribbons that flutter with every movement.

Monsieur Talleyrand, the president of the Assembly, is to celebrate mass with the monarchs and the members of the Assembly all in attendance, and they take their places near the Altar of Liberty. Just before mass begins, a shower of rain falls from the sky, streaming like silver ribbons down the tiers of seats. I hasten to open my parasol, leaning close to Léon in a mostly futile attempt to keep both of us dry. Across the distance, Marie Antoinette opens her shawl, the diaphanous white fabric spreading like wings, and swathes it around her young son.

"Vive la Reine!" The cry echoes across the Champs de Mars, taken up by hundreds of voices rising and falling in a tuneless chant but airy with enthusiasm. The same cheer for the king echoes through the air. Those titles aren't supposed to be used anymore, and yet they ring familiarly across the field like old times, when the monarchs were not so loathed. Seeing them pledge to uphold the constitution for the good of France, with the young dauphin present, seems to herald a bright future. I shout praise for the queen

too, wondering if she smiles to hear the enthusiastic phrase once again after its long absence. The storming of Versailles was a harsh lesson, but she doesn't forget it. Her wardrobe choices are proof enough. The queen has come a long way since her days of wearing ropes of diamonds to the opening of the Estates-General.

"You look lost in thought," Léon whispers. "Not listening to mass?"

"I can hardly hear it." All around us, people fidget, uncomfortable on the hard seats and unable to make out most of the words.

"Neither can I. We're near the end of the row—fancy sneaking out of here?"

"Yes." Gratefully, I take his hand. I wanted to see the queen, and now that I have, the rest of the fête feels rather impersonal and crowded.

Apologizing to the people we have to squeeze past, Léon and I hurry out of the amphitheater. We shall miss Talleyrand, the Assembly members, and the king and queen swearing an oath of fealty to the nation and the constitution, but since I doubt we will be able to hear it anyway, we won't be missing much.

We spend a glorious day together. We smile at the sight of the statue of Henri IV, now decorated with a voluminous tricolor scarf, and we wander for hours before eventually finding our way back to the Tuileries Palace. Weary from walking, we stretch out side by side on a stone bench under a vast tree, its branches forming a canopy to protect us from most of the rain. The bench is hard, but when Léon kisses me until I'm breathless, his mouth and hands growing more urgent, I forget about the setting and allow myself to imagine the future delights of our marriage bed.

The faint crackle of the fireworks being lit on the Pont Neuf brings us back to our senses. I feel about as dazed as Léon looks, his eyes dark and blurred, lips softly parted.

"I guess we missed the fireworks," he says.

"We might be able to see them from here." Holding hands, we run to an open part of the garden, scanning the sky. A fan of sparks trails across the sky like stars, except for the strange orange color. A burst of white ones follow, harder to see because the dark sky is still veiled with clouds, which swallow them up.

"Come here," says Léon, pulling me into his arms, leaning me against his chest. "It isn't the best view, but we can see the fireworks after all, and I promised to hold you during them."

❧

My parents are pleased, and altogether unsurprised by the new development in my relationship with Léon.

"You know I think he is very kind," says Maman. "I've grown fond of him already. And it feels right to have another watchmaker in the family."

Papa chuckles. "Another watchmaker? Pierre hasn't worked as a watchmaker in years. As far as I'm concerned, Léon will be the sole craftsman in the family, and I like him for himself, not for his trade. He has a good head on his shoulders. That's more important; although of course the most significant thing is that he makes you happy, Giselle."

I give him a sideways glance, wondering at the sharpness of his response to an indirect reference to my uncle, but it's not the time to address it. Though he has said nothing to me since our chat about Uncle Pierre's occasional bullying tendencies, Papa has seemed bitter toward him lately. They have not visited as frequently as they used to. In fact, I haven't seen my cousin Eugénie for nearly a month. The revolution tugs us apart, it seems.

My parents persuade Léon and me to wait until the following spring to be married, at which time he will have completed his apprenticeship. His apprenticeship hours are as strict as mine when I'm at the palace, and both of us know we'd have to spend much time apart if we married hastily. In the spring, I think I may leave my post and find work in a dress shop. Two years in the queen's household should be enough to help my reputation as a dressmaker.

Chapter Twelve

"Tell me about Saint-Cloud." My uncle rises from his chair at the imposing mahogany desk by the window as I enter the study.

"Good morning to you, too. Lovely weather, isn't it? The roses have done well this year."

He has the grace to look chastened, and ducks his head. "Pardon my brusqueness, please, Giselle. It's only that I'm anxious to hear your account of the assassination attempt."

"Understandably." I offer him a small smile.

"Tea?" He jerks his head in the direction of the tea tray on the side table. "I could call for biscuits."

"Please don't bother. Tea will be fine." I pour myself a cup, offering one for him as well, which he declines. I confess I feel a small pleasure in taking my time pouring the tea carefully and stirring in a spoonful of honey. His eagerness to hear the story beats palpably in the room, like the ticking of a clock. Having information that is so keenly desired gives me a surge of power, although I feel a little guilty at the same time for keeping him waiting.

He leans back in his chair, one hand resting on his thigh, the other cupping his chin. The pose is only a veneer of calmness, of relaxation. His fingers curl into a fist at his lip, and the tip of his little finger taps on his cheekbone.

I perch on the wicker chair in the corner and sip my tea twice before speaking. To make up for the delay, I launch into the story at once, without waiting for further prompting from my uncle.

"As you know, the queen went to Saint-Cloud, and there was an assassination attempt upon her there." It still seems shocking to me. I'd believed that her public support for the revolution of late, and the approval shown for her at the *fête de la fédération* showed that she was successfully changing the public's opinion of her, and the country retreat of Saint-Cloud seemed a pastoral (albeit luxurious), peaceful place, a temporary haven against the turmoil of city politics. I'd felt fortunate to be invited to attend to her there, even though it meant leaving Paris again. Overlooking the Seine, the chateau is located about five miles west of the city, and is one of Marie Antoinette's favorite residences. She enlarged it in the previous decade, working with a personally selected architect to redesign the stone stairs leading to the royal apartments, and to rebuild the front garden. None of this will interest my uncle, but Madame Campan told me all about it while we were there, and indeed, I could see touches of the queen's elegant taste in all of the designs. It seemed a safe, quiet place, making the attempt on her life all the more appalling.

"A national guardsman apprehended a man in the gardens and discovered that he'd come to Saint-Cloud with the intention of murdering the queen. I haven't been able to clarify the details of how the man was found to be suspicious, but I expect the guard questioned him as a matter of routine. Saint-Cloud is not like Tuileries, or even Versailles, where sightseers and Assembly members come and go at all hours of the day. A man roaming the garden and looking for a way inside, unaccounted for by all parties, would raise suspicion."

"He ought to have known the way inside in advance," says my uncle scathingly. "Inept planning."

"Remember, I'm only guessing." I sip my tea slowly. His harsh response gives me a twinge of discomfort. It is almost as if he wanted the man to use greater finesse. As if he wanted harm to come to Marie Antoinette.

"What sort of weapon did he carry?"

"Unconfirmed rumors indicate that it was a knife."

"Bloody," murmurs my uncle thoughtfully, gazing into the floral pattern of the rug at his feet.

An image comes to my head of rose-tinted silk, the delicate shade the queen favored at Saint-Cloud, where she felt free from the judging eyes of the city, streaming with scarlet blood, rivulets of it running through the folds of the silk, bright rivers that stained the rosy color red that darkened into black. I shiver, thrusting the unwilling image aside, and clear my throat to continue my account.

"Although the man never made it into the same room as the queen, she was understandably shaken." She had consented, uncharacteristically, to take a sleeping draught, and retired to bed early, pale and quivering, while Madame Campan and two of her most trusted ladies sat near the bedside. Guards were posted outside the bedroom door. "The king, also afraid and angry, hired secret investigators to root out all the facts of the assassination attempt, to see if the man was acting on his own or had been hired."

"How do you know this, if they were *secret* investigators?" demands my uncle, staring with an impressed arch of his brows.

"One of them questioned me, as well as some of the other

servants close to the queen." Forestalling his nervous outburst as he stiffens in the chair, I raise my hand and speak over him. "I was not a suspect; let me be clear on that. However, he thought perhaps someone would have come to some of the servants and questioned us about the queen's habits."

"Had they?"

"Not me—I would never volunteer information to a stranger in any case. Word is that one of the chambermaids may have divulged some information of the queen's routine. One of them was sent away the next day, at least."

"If they found the assassin and at least one of the informants, that plot is long since doomed then," says Uncle Pierre.

"Yes, that one is." I hesitate. "But the investigator unearthed another plot. This one to be carried out with poison."

The breath heaves out of his lungs in an exclamation of surprise. "Another attempt? By God, she'd best be careful. Someone is determined to see her demise."

"This one was rather more terrifying to the household, although I don't think the majority of the staff at Saint-Cloud was informed. All of the women who work in the queen's chambers were told, so we could be on our guard." I meet his eyes squarely. "Poison, they say, is a delicate art, but can so easily go wrong. Someone tastes a delicious-looking pastry not meant for them, or steals a nip out of a wine bottle. . . ."

"You're being careful, aren't you?"

"Of course." I glare sourly. I feel he wouldn't have asked unless I pointed out the risks, that he was too caught up in glee over the scandal to think it through. "I didn't tell my parents of the poisoning plot. It would only cause them worry, and I'm careful to eat nothing meant for the queen's plate or cup. Please do not mention it to them." The most likely means of poison might be through the bowl of sugar the queen likes to keep in her chambers, to stir into water before she drinks it. Madame Campan has seen to it that precautions are taken there, though, and none of us would dare touch the queen's sugar.

"The fewer people who know about this, the better," he says decisively. "Does she have a taster?"

"I don't know. Not that I've seen, but she often doesn't eat in her chambers."

He grunts thoughtfully. "Well, I won't say we ought to have seen this coming—attempted murder is no simple matter—but pamphlets have been circulating about the queen lately, stirring up ill feeling toward her."

I frown, pitying her. "I haven't seen any. What do they say?"

"I'm sure they are kept away from court," he says wryly. "Your young man, Léon, may have seen them. Most of them paint her as a depraved adulteress."

"I'm sure that's not true," I say. "If she is having an affair, it's certainly more discreet than depraved."

Uncle Pierre leans forward, cracking his knuckles. "There is a purpose to the writings, true or not. Consider, Giselle, what would happen to the queen if she were found to be philandering?"

"She would be sent away, probably to spend her days locked in a rural convent."

"Correct. Perhaps even executed—it happened to more than one English queen; it could possibly be arranged in our country." He leans back again, watching me with approval. "And then what?" he prompts.

"The king would be free to marry again," I say slowly. "Ideally to a woman whom the revolutionaries approve of, someone entirely

French instead of coming from a foreign monarchy." The idea sounds alien—kings have always wed for diplomacy. "But he needn't wed again; he has an heir."

"One boy," says my uncle. "Two of his children have already gone to early graves. Another son would help him. Besides, the public hates a single king. They want a queen to admire." His teeth show through his thin smile. "Just not our queen."

"I can't see the king marrying again." The idea is almost amusing, given how shy and odd and unromantic he seems. "This is all speculation."

"Lots of people are doing it these days," agrees my uncle. "What else has happened? Nothing so dramatic as assassinations gone awry, I'm sure, but do you have any other news?"

"The queen has met with the Comte de Mirabeau," I offer. Seeing Uncle Pierre's expression sharpen with interest, I smile. "I thought that might intrigue you. Her earlier dislike of him seems to be well-known, though I'm not sure how."

"She never liked any politicians," grumbles my uncle. "But you know she doesn't like Mirabeau?"

"Well, Madame Campan confessed to me that he once asked the queen if he could be a minister, last year I think, and she turned him down very indignantly. Madame Campan was piqued too, in the retelling. She often is about any perceived slight to the queen."

"What did they meet about?"

"I was not invited to the meeting," I remind him. "I have no idea. I would hesitantly assume, however, that the king asked his advice for this current political climate."

"It fits," muses my uncle. "Louis always asks for advice, and Mirabeau is known to be a more conservative member of the Jacobin club. It's odd that he's a member, really. The Jacobins tend to have such extreme political ideas in regards to the revolution and egalitarianism. He was one of the chief men who drafted the Declaration of the Rights of Man and of the Citizen, of course, but he denounced all of the Assembly's fine speeches after the fall of the Bastille, saying that inaction would only give the revolution more room to follow a violent course."

"He may be correct, given what later happened at Versailles."

"True." He frowns, thinking. "As you must already know, he advised the king to distance himself from Paris, from the revolution, until it blows over. He recommended Rouen." His lip curls. "Do you know, Mirabeau even suggested that the capital of France ought to be moved away from Paris? To kill the revolution, one ought to kill its place of birth," he adds, presumably summarizing the rationale he'd heard.

I straighten, outraged myself now. "That's ridiculous. Paris has always been the capital." Ruefully, it occurs to me that I'm precisely one of the Parisian snobs Léon sometimes teases me about. I do love my city, though.

"I feel the same way, much as I am loathe to admit the idea slips out of the grasp of my imagination. Writers," he says airily, "never want to admit to a lack of imagination."

On my way out, I bump into Eugénie in the hall, wearing a muslin gown with blue and white stripes, and a bright red fichu.

"Giselle," she exclaims, throwing her gloves aside. Evidently she has just returned home. "I haven't seen you in ages; can you stay?"

"I'd like that. I've missed you."

"I'm anxious to hear all about your wedding plans." Eugénie shrugs out of her shawl.

"They're not very far along yet, I'm afraid. You must help me with them."

She leads me to the parlor and flops onto the sofa. "Tell me all about Léon. I've met him, of course, but it's different now that he is to be your husband." Her voice drops, even though I know very well that she scanned the hallway to make sure there is no one in earshot of the parlor before we entered. "Do you kiss all the time? Are you going to sleep—or rather, *not* sleep—with him before the wedding?"

"Eugénie!" I protest, mildly scandalized by her questions. My cheeks sear with embarrassment.

"I know very well that my parents were together for twelve years before they married," she retorts. "I doubt they were chaste for over a decade."

"Let's not think of that," I advise, wrinkling my nose.

"I agree," she says calmly. "Let's talk about you and Léon instead."

"All right," I relent, laughing. "I don't know."

"That's the best answer." She nods seriously. "If you do, it ought to be spontaneous and romantic."

"How do you know so much? You're only thirteen."

"Almost fourteen. Besides, Juliet was thirteen. I think."

"And she was a marvelous example of a successful marriage."

Eugénie grins. "Well, I just finished reading *Romeo and Juliet*. I have been reading a great many romances lately, mostly in secret. I have to stay indoors more often than before, now that there have been so many riots, and I have to amuse myself somehow."

Laughing, I feel my spirits lift. In spite of her complaints, Eugénie seems almost untouched by the drama of the revolution, and it's freeing to push those cares away for an afternoon.

❀

As the months pass, we take in dozens of the queen's gowns, narrowing the already slight waists and sleeves. Marie Antoinette's reddish-gold hair begins to fade to a more ashy shade, threading with silver strands, and a single streak of white forms above her left ear and seems to grow a bit wider every day. Worse, her pale face etches with permanent creases of worry, deepening around the corners of her mouth and puckering her proud forehead.

One afternoon, the queen calls me to her side. "Giselle, would you tell me if any strange domestics came near my chambers?"

"Yes, of course, Your Majesty."

She studies my face intently, perhaps looking for signals of a lie. I make an expression of concern, easy to do because the feeling comes easily to the surface when I see her up close, ravaged by stress.

"Forgive the question if it is impudent, but has there been another anonymous note?" I ask quietly.

Her eyes harden. "From *dame de la révolution*, you mean?" Her voice scrapes across the alias. "No, not since the last night at Versailles. I believe that the perpetrator must not have been relocated to Tuileries."

"I would tell you," I say, returning to her original question. She looks as though she needs the reassurance. A knot forms in my stomach as I speak, and I stare at her earnestly, trying to reassure myself of it as well. I'm not the most loyal servant, but I don't want to see her harmed.

"Thank you, Giselle." Her gaze darts around the room, though no one is close to us, and she licks her lips nervously. "I am watched constantly—even more than usual, and I am accustomed to it. A queen is never alone, nor is a dauphine, and I have been both. Perhaps that tells you how intense the scrutiny is now. The national guard is always watching. . . . One of them protected me at Saint-Cloud, but any man can join their ranks, and many of them are fervent revolutionaries. I don't know who to trust. Even some of my household staff . . ." She trails off, and I wonder if, like me, she thinks of the failed poison plot uncovered at Saint-Cloud, which might have been successful if it had the participation of someone with intimate access to her household.

"I won't let any strangers near you," I promise. "If it pleases you, I'll come to you at once if anything suspicious happens. I won't interrupt, but I could arrange a signal meant only for you."

She doesn't answer at once, but her shoulders loosen slightly. In contrast, her gaze sharpens, and I think she will stare all the way into my soul. I try not to flinch. She's had years of practice in staring down the most haughty aristocrats, and I'm no match for her.

"Carry a red-and-white handkerchief with you," she commands at last, her voice gentle. Her eyes have softened now. "Drop it on the floor if we are not alone and cannot speak. Don't look back— pretend you haven't noticed its absence. If the circumstances won't allow this, you can always speak to Madame Campan."

The plan strikes me as needlessly complicated, that going to Madame Campan might always be the best course of action, but I nod solemnly. She seems calmer now, and I don't want to make her panic again. Perhaps the complexity of the plan is an indication of the great depth of her unease. "I will, Your Majesty."

"Good." Her small mouth twitches in a tiny smile. "Now hand me the gray silk shawl, please. I am meeting someone in the receiving room in a few moments."

A short time later, I find an excuse to go past the outer rooms of the queen's chamber, where she sometimes entertains high-ranking guests and her few close friends. Axel von Fersen sits across from her, leaning forward with his hands resting on his knees, speaking in a low voice. I can't make out the words, but I'd have to be blind not to see the tender regard lighting his eyes, the way his body orients toward hers, hunching protectively. Recalling the rumors that they used to be lovers, and witnessing the warm affection between them, I wonder if it was true then, and true again now. It doesn't matter to me, but I'm glad to see her with someone who cares for her. There are few enough of them, God knows.

Chapter Thirteen

"I am sorry there isn't a proper cake." Maman puts the plate down in the center of the table. The best blue china gleams against the crocheted white lace of the tablecloth. "The flour prices are erratic. I never expected prices would still be so outrageous two years later. All these riots don't seem to change anything."

"I don't mind. I like baked apples."

"I know. But you're eighteen now, and it's a special age. You deserve a beautiful cake with cream and preserved cherries. Besides, these apples are from last fall. I asked our cook to bake them; they're a bit soft now."

"You said that seventeen was a special age too, and sixteen, and fifteen before that. . . ." I grin at her. "The apples look delicious."

"Yes, they do," says Léon, with enough fervency that Papa laughs.

"Let's serve it now, and not deprive the poor boy any longer."

"There's rum sauce to go with them, at least," says Maman. "To make it a little more fancy."

"Everything is perfect, Maman. I haven't eaten roast beef in a long time. I couldn't have asked for a better birthday supper, or better company." I smile fondly at everyone around the table. We are a small, intimate group, only my parents and Léon.

Papa turns to Léon. "Will it affect your work, now that the guilds have been abolished?"

He shrugs. "I was a member, and it wasn't easy to join, but a lot of people see the guilds as a remnant of feudalism. If the economy is to move forward, change has to happen. I confess, I won't miss the guild very much. They talked of going on strike, and I don't want to. It would lengthen my apprenticeship. Even afterward, I'd rather be working and providing for my household." His hand brushes mine.

I smile at him. It's hard to believe two years have passed since our first meeting. My happiness makes it feel as though he's been part of my life forever, but our moments together still glow with excitement, too.

After supper, Léon and I excuse ourselves to go for a short walk. The full moon splashes filmy light over the street, bathing the city in gradients of silver and gray, and we pause in the fathomless shadows of quiet corners and the dark privacy under the heavy branches of trees to snatch kisses.

"I can hardly wait to be your wife," I whisper, as his mouth leaves mine and roves down my neck, pressing soft, lingering kisses to my skin.

His fingers tighten on my waist, pressing me closer to the tree trunk at my back, and he makes a low rumble of pleasure in his throat. "I can hardly say how happy it makes me to hear that." His lips move close to my ear, his breath tickling in an erotic way that makes me shiver. "I think about you all the time, Giselle."

"I do too." Resting my palm along his cheek, I bring his face closer to mine for another bone-melting kiss.

After a while, we reluctantly drift apart, but keep our hands twined together.

"We'll have to walk a bit now," I say, feeling the warmth of my flushed cheeks and slightly swollen lips.

"We wouldn't look innocent at all," agrees Léon. "My heart's still racing."

I flatten my palm against his chest to feel its flutter, and instead become distracted by the enticing feel of his hard muscles, the angular shape of his collarbones, the breadth of his shoulders.

He sucks in a breath, holding still, and then evidently gives up on self-control, because his hand grasps the back of my neck and his mouth crashes down on mine again.

"Soon we'll walk," I say breathlessly a moment later. "In just a bit."

"If you say so." The corners of his mouth quirk briefly, until I kiss his smile away.

🙵

As a month passes and May closes, I notice a marked change in Marie Antoinette.

The first sign is that she begins ordering new gowns from Rose Bertin again, instead of relying on made-over ones. The new items aren't strategically colored, and she appears to favor green and white, as well as purple and black. She also rejects many of the tricolor items in her daily dress choices, instead gravitating to green, which brings out the near-lost glint of red in her curls, and lavender, which emphasizes the milkiness of her skin and the shadows under her eyes.

Gowns aside, her demeanor shifts as well, albeit in a less noticeable way than her drastic change in color choices. Perhaps someone who has not watched her as closely as I have would remain oblivious, but I observe the way she paces along the long row of windows, gazing outside wistfully, staring as though she imagines seeing past the rooftops of Paris and into freedom beyond. Sometimes she sits at her desk for hours at a time, writing more slowly than usual, her lips moving as she thinks of the words to write, although she never speaks loud enough for me to hear anything. Indeed, her mouth twitches in concentration only; I don't think she's saying words at all. Once, she asks for a list of all the contents of her closet at the Tuileries, and spends two hours poring over it alone. And she sees Count Axel von Fersen every day, murmuring to him with their heads bent close together, locked in their own private conversation.

"I thought this might look well with your cornflower-blue gown, Your Majesty," I say to her one morning, proffering a blue sash edged in scarlet and embroidered with small white fleur-de-lis. I've sewn it myself, but I don't say so to the queen. It isn't my place.

She gives it a cursory glance. "No. I will wear purple today, and that will not suit."

"Of course, Your Majesty. Shall I put this aside for tomorrow, then?"

"No."

I hear the finality in her voice, but since I worry about her, the words spring almost unbidden to my lips. "It's only that it's very fashionable at the moment. . . ."

Her gray eyes flare angrily, sparking with silver. "*I* make the fashion."

I bow my head, averting my gaze to the floor. "Yes, Your Majesty."

She makes me wait for a moment before releasing me, either by stalking away or giving me leave to look up, but when she does speak at last, her voice softens a little. "You are concerned for me, Giselle, and your loyalty is commendable. But our days of planning tricolor outfits together have ended, I believe. The people ceased believing it. They see me as an actress, playing the part of revolutionary and never truly caring for a moment. I would rather dress as myself, be seen as myself, than be seen to be costumed like a charlatan."

I don't know what to say, especially as the thought has often crossed my mind that she does not understand the need for change that drives the revolution, and wishes the whole thing would simply vanish. "I—I am sorry."

"Do not be. None of this is your doing." Giving me a strange smile, half-kind but still with a hard edge that thins her lips, she turns and walks away, managing to convey all the sweeping haughtiness of royalty, even while dressed simply in her nightgown and a purple wool shawl.

Madame Campan pauses at my side, her arms folded, hands clasping her elbows as if protecting herself from the cold. "It's good of you to try, Giselle. The revolution is not easy for her."

"She has been ordering many new dresses from Rose Bertin," I say, trying to keep my voice neutral.

"She must amuse herself somehow," says Madame Campan roughly. "Everything else is slowly being taken away from her."

"I hope she doesn't spend too much. They will revile her for that."

I expect a reprimand for my impertinence, but Madame Campan sighs, her shoulders sagging. "I know. I have warned her that acquiring too much clothing now could be dangerous, but she doesn't listen to me." Her mouth twitches in a wan smile. "She has always been headstrong, and while I'm her friend, I am below her."

"She may listen to you yet." I pat her hand comfortingly. I don't think I've ever touched Madame Campan before. The bones of her hand feel delicate and frail, like a bird's, though she's not elderly. "She knows you love her." I explain my arrangement to warn Marie Antoinette of danger by means of dropping a red-and-white handkerchief.

Her eyes grow thoughtful, her thin, sculpted eyebrows dropping as her face grows more serious. "I think perhaps I haven't given you enough credit," she says very quietly. "Thank you, Giselle."

"It's the least I could do," I say honestly. It isn't enough, I know. It won't atone for spying, although I like to think I've never reported anything that changed the course of her life, and it won't comfort her through the threats she receives daily. But it's something.

Late the next day, when I'm nearly ready for bed, Madame Campan pulls me aside. "Giselle, one of Her Majesty's earrings is missing. Have you seen it?" She sounds a little sharp.

Across the room, I see Geneviève's eyes widen in surprise, and then she glares, miming pouring a bottle of perfume over Madame Campan's head. While I appreciate her loyalty, nervousness ripples over me, and I'm not comforted.

"I haven't seen a lone earring." My lips feel very dry. "Which one is it? I'll search."

"Are you certain you haven't seen it?" Madame Campan grasps my arm, not tightly, but I daren't resist her. She leads me into the antechamber of the queen's bedroom. "Nothing with pearls?"

"No, nothing. I promise."

"It could have been an accident," she says. "Caught in your skirt, perhaps." She closes the door behind us.

"I swear, Madame Campan, I would never touch Her Majesty's jewelry." I feel cold, certain that my face is pale with fear.

Being accused of theft is the last thing I expected to happen to me here.

She pulls me across the room, farther away from the door. "I know, Giselle. I'm sorry, but I had to get you away from the others without making them believe you were receiving special treatment. That would make them pay a great deal of attention, all of it born of jealousy."

"Special treatment?" I stare blankly.

"Of a sort." She bends her face closer to me, peering into my eyes. "Giselle, I need to know that I can trust you."

"You can."

"And the queen may trust you?"

"Yes." I meet her stare unwaveringly. "I promised to protect her as well as I could, didn't I? I meant it, every word."

Relief washes some of the lines from her face. "I believe you. I never thought to be in this situation with you, putting all my trust in you. You were always a good tirewoman, right from the start, but sometimes a little irreverent, and so close with Geneviève."

"She means well," I say, understanding that Madame Campan will not forgive nor forget Geneviève's revolutionary proclivities.

"I'm going to tell you a secret, because I require your assistance. It's potentially dangerous, and if you betray me, it puts more than one life at risk."

Speechless, I scan her face for signs of jesting. She regards me calmly, but with a serious edge to her glance that tells me she watches me for signs of slyness. I think through the implications of her words before I say anything, wondering if I even want to know.

"If I help you, I may potentially help save lives?" It seems to be the logical reverse of her warning.

"Four lives, possibly eight," she confirms. "Maybe even more."

I think about it a moment longer but there's only one answer I can give. Sighing slowly and gently, trying to relax even though tension floods me, I nod. "I keep secrets very well. I'll help you."

"Sit down," commands Madame Campan, eyes glittering with approval and purpose. She points to the low cushioned bench along the wall. Once we're both seated, she tells me the king and queen have been plotting, with the aid of Count Axel von Fersen and herself, to flee Paris, taking their children with them.

"They will be killed if they remain here," she says.

"Surely not." Even I hear the confusion in my voice, the doubt. I saw the wreckage of Marie Antoinette's bedchamber at Versailles, after all, the glitter of mirror shards and silks ripped and torn, feathers scattered everywhere, drowning everything like the blood the rioters wanted, only white and soft instead of scarlet and sticky.

"It's not safe for them, especially our queen." Madame Campan sounds resolute. "They must get to Austria, where the queen's brother may offer them protection."

"But Austria is so far. . . . How can they leave France?" *They are supposed to rule it,* I want to say. They can't abandon it.

"The king wanted to remain in France," admits Madame Campan grudgingly. "But he agreed it's not safe just now. The hope is that they'll return when things are settled, and with the support of Austria to protect them. They are losing allies here every day. Even the army can't be trusted."

I can't argue with this truth, and the plans are clearly far enough along that there's little point anyway. "What do you need me for?"

"I'd hoped we wouldn't have to tell anyone else, but one of the tirewomen must know," says Madame Campan. "I need you to help pack, in secret." She hesitates, meeting my eyes. "I also need you to distract Geneviève. I fear she suspects something is going on."

"Of course she does. I did too. It's because the queen is ordering so many new gowns, and in risky colors."

Madame Campan's mouth curls sorrowfully. "I know. I did warn her to be careful. She can acquire everything she needs when she's safe. I think impatience has overtaken her." She clears her throat. "I also need you to help procure common-looking clothing for them to wear to escape. They can't wear anything they own."

"They would certainly be recognized at once." I want to giggle suddenly, struck with hilarity at the thought of fleeing in one of the queen's wide skirts, and I realize it must be nerves. I dig my fingernails into my palms, using the pain to calm myself again. "Tell me everything I need to know. Leave no detail out."

"There are tunnels in the kitchen," says Madame Campan. "They'll escape the palace that way, and a coach will be waiting." She clasps her fingers together, steadily talking in a low voice until I understand what I must do.

I walk slowly to my room after Madame Campan dismisses me. My heart feels heavy under the pressure of this new secret—the greatest of them all, and the one that must be protected the most closely. There are hundreds of people who would condemn me for helping the king and queen flee Paris, and as dangerous as that is, I fear the reaction of the people closest to me instead if they find out. My uncle would not be pleased. Léon would feel betrayed. In doing this task, I am working in direct opposition to his loyalty to the revolution.

None of these fears affect my decision, though. I feel in my bones that it's the right thing to do. Marie Antoinette and her family aren't strangers to me, and I must help them. Even though my mind whirls under the weight of my decision, my soul feels free.

It's late by the time I go to bed, but Geneviève sits up when I come into the room, pushing her nightcap out of her eyes. "Well? Are you in trouble?"

"For a while." I scowl, rubbing my back. "I had to scour every inch of the floor. My back feels like a mule kicked it. I found the wretched earring, though; Madame Campan can't complain or blame me for theft anymore." I glower. "Cow, accusing me like that when the earring was on the floor the whole time."

"The *Citoyenne* probably made her," says Geneviève, referring to the queen. "She would've ordered a new one anyway and hung the cost, but she had to blame someone, didn't she?"

"Just be glad she didn't accuse you," I say darkly, pulling my nightdress over my head and climbing into bed.

"She's been dressing like a tyrant again, hasn't she?" remarks Geneviève conversationally. "I thought the days of purple velvets were over."

"If they ever truly were, we might not have jobs." I'm glad she can't see my face in the dark. She's my friend, and I wish I didn't have to lie to her, but she doesn't share my sympathy for the queen. "She's so spoiled; she can't stand not wearing whatever expensive thing she likes."

"True." Geneviève rolls over, the sheets rustling audibly. "Well, five o'clock will be here far too soon, as usual. Good night, Giselle."

The next day, Madame Campan gives me leave to go home for the night to have supper with my family, an easy thing to do now that we are living at Tuileries. My uncle is there with his family. I avoid him as much as I can, joking and talking with Eugénie, but after the plates are cleared and he holds a glass of claret, he summons me to the study.

As he closes the door behind us, I marvel at his ability to commandeer the room of a house that is not his own. My father is quite private about his study, and I wonder if he resents the intrusion. I think the time for spying has come to an end, since I'm not enjoying it anymore. I turn to my uncle with a trace of bitterness, tired of being ordered around.

"The queen hasn't been wearing revolutionary colors," he says without preamble. "What does it mean?"

"How do you know?" I ask instead. Does he have another spy? It never occurred to me before, but his question strikes me as oddly specific.

He waves impatiently. "She's been seen in the Tuileries gardens a number of times this week, one day wearing green and white, another purple, another black. As I'm sure you've noticed too. You miss nothing, after all, Giselle." He smiles, apparently attempting to be conciliatory.

"She grows bored with tricolor, I suppose." I shrug, careful to remain nonchalant. "Fashion has always been her chief amusement, and she's accustomed to setting her own trends. She dislikes having to follow the strictures of others."

He stares at me for a moment and then nods, evidently satisfied. "I'm sure you're right. She always has seemed quite vain. Anything else to report?"

"No. Wait—one thing. The queen received another threatening note, the first one since Versailles."

"Indeed?" His eyes widen in curious surprise. "And? What did it say?"

I shake my head regretfully. "It was burned before I could see it. I'm told it was the same."

"By whom?" The question fires back as quick as a musket shot.

"Madame Campan."

His face relaxes into approval. "She trusts you, then. Well done."

"If anything else happens, I'll come and visit you," I say, wanting our interview to end.

"Of course. Eugénie wanted us to invite you all for supper next week. I will see you again then."

I make an excuse to search for a book from my father's shelves, and stay behind while my uncle exits the room, dragging the tension away with him as if he is the magnet for it. I lean back against the corner of the bookshelf and close my eyes, praying I have lied well enough. I ought to have had enough practice by now, God knows. My pulse flutters nervously, and I think of the plot I've become tangled in, hoping it doesn't turn into a terrible mess. I doubt I'll sleep well tonight.

Chapter Fourteen

While not directly involved in the planning, the pending flight of the monarchs hovers at the forefront of my mind as the weeks pass, plaguing my sleep and my conscience. It's not an easy secret to keep, not one to be quietly locked away and forgotten. Sometimes I ponder their weakness for even considering leaving their country. Other times, the memory of the queen's frightened face comes to me like a ghost begging for long-lost sympathy, and knowing she truly fears for her life, I can't blame her.

Madame Campan frets about it worse than I, although I don't believe she ever doubts the legitimacy of their decision. "The date is still uncertain," she tells me one evening, a week into June. "Count von Fersen had been ready with the arrangements for this Saturday, but the king has delayed again." Disapproval makes her tone leaden.

"The plan cannot be treated carelessly," I warn. "It increases the possibility of mischance."

Madame Campan flicks a panicked look toward me, fluttering her hands. "I know. I don't like it either. Madame," she says, referring to the queen, "is going to speak to him about it tonight.

Between us—like everything now—he has grown so indecisive and fearful. It's a good thing she is strong for both of them."

Her mouth still puckers with concern, and I feel sorry for her. "At least you have the disguises all ready for use." Madame Campan and I put them together ourselves, raiding our own wardrobes, the queen's closet, sewing a few things, and even taking a few misplaced items from the clean laundry baskets. The royal party will go disguised as members of the household of Madame de Tourzel, the governess for the children. She will play the part of a Russian baroness. The king will be her butler, a ludicrous idea that makes me want to giggle, while his sister and the queen shall pretend to be her maids. The royal children will pose as Madame de Tourzel's daughters, which I think may be the most difficult ruse to pull off. As far as I have seen, the royal children are fond of Madame de Tourzel, but given their parents will also be present, they will have to take great care to treat the monarchs as servants.

"Does Madame de Tourzel speak Russian?" I ask. "I know her disguise as a foreigner is imperative to help them leave the country, but it seems like a risky façade."

"No need," says Madame Campan. "Russian nobility prefers to speak French. It's cultured."

It seems strange to me that a country so far away would revere our language as much as that, but I'm still patriotic enough to feel a vague sense of pride. Léon will be interested to learn this. Along with the revolutionary progress to change the government and the growing equality, he will see this as another symbol of France's enlightenment.

"Still, it's a dangerous plan. No doubt about that." Madame Campan sighs, resting her delicate pink cheeks in her hands. "I pray constantly that they'll make it to Montmédy safely."

"Montmédy? I thought they were bound for Austria." I stare

blankly. Is this another change to the plan, which grows ever more flimsy?

"Yes, it's a citadel northwest of Paris. The Marquis de Bouillé there is loyal to the king, and he has an army of mercenaries at his disposal. The French soldiers cannot be trusted at present time, I'm sorry to say. However, the marquis suppressed a mutiny last year, and according to Madame, the king approved of his efficiency and strong-mindedness. The marquis will be able to control the mercenaries, and the king needs a strong force at his command."

"But the national guard is made up of a large number of soldiers."

"Mostly untrained and ill equipped," retorts Madame Campan. "Though I hope it should never come to fighting. We've seen enough already. Once the king is protected, I'm sure the more faithful subjects outside of Paris will want to see order restored without the need for civil war."

Remembering Léon's concern for his family in Toulouse, also dealing with riots, I wonder if the revolution is really as centered in Paris as Madame Campan seems to believe. Unfortunately, she's the wrong person to ask. Marie Antoinette is not present, even if I dared to question her, and deep down, I'm not convinced she would know the truth anyway.

My uncle might, and this is the one thing I cannot discuss with him. I gnaw on the inside of my lip, wishing the escape would happen already, freeing me of its tangles.

"One more thing," says Madame Campan. Her tone shifts, growing gentler. "I've been thinking about your role in this. I think that on the night of the escape, you ought not to be here."

I shake my head vigorously enough that a sleek strand of hair falls across my eyes. I push it away with impatience. "You might need me to help you deflect other servants away from the queen's bedchamber if we're to pretend she is asleep inside."

"I'll manage on my own. My sister will help me." Madame Campan's sister is another of the queen's ladies-in-waiting: trustworthy, a pinnacle of discretion. "It could be dangerous, Giselle. If the plan goes awry . . ." She presses her knuckles to her mouth, cutting the sentence off, as if vocalizing her fears will somehow make them come true. She closes her eyes briefly, regaining her composure. "You are young, my dear, and it's better if you aren't implicated. Just in case it goes badly."

Later, when Geneviève and I braid our hair before bedtime, it occurs to me that if I pretend to have seen a Russian baroness in the halls, it could reinforce Madame de Tourzel's eventual persona as such. Tuileries is busy and chaotic enough that there's little chance of Geneviève—or anyone else—finding it suspicious. And God knows those disguises need all the credibility that can be mustered. When I think of Marie Antoinette pretending to be a maid, I shudder. There's nothing deferential about her manner, ever.

"I saw a lady with the ugliest dress today," I say, knowing Geneviève will be amused. "Black with olive-green trim, and such a stiff collar." I make a face, mirroring Geneviève's reaction. She hates olive green. "The lady walked down the hall like she owned the palace though. When I asked Madame Campan, she told me the woman is a Russian baroness visiting Paris."

"Out of sympathy for the revolution?" asks Geneviève, perking up.

"Maybe. After all, she isn't Austrian."

Geneviève grins. "Probably not a supporter of *l'Autrichienne*, then."

"One would hope not. Here, let me fix your hair. You've missed

a curl." I take her ginger braid in my hands and untwist it, beginning again. She's always too impatient to do it properly. "How's
Étienne?"

She tilts her head back, relaxing under my hands. Her voice
sounds dreamy when she speaks. "Wonderful. I'm counting the
days until we meet in his rooms again. It was only last week that I
saw him but it's never enough." She turns her head, eyeing me slyly
over her shoulder. "What about you? Have you been with Léon
yet, or are you waiting until your wedding?"

"It's not far away now." Her words have given me an idea,
though. If I'm to be away on the night of the escape, perhaps I
could arrange a tryst with Léon. I can't go home easily; my parents know my schedule at Tuileries and would wonder why I had
the night off. Of course, I could tell them that Madame Campan
had given me the night off, which is what I shall have to tell Léon.
The truth is that I ache for the chance to be alone with him, and
now that the opportunity presents itself, my heart flutters with excitement.

"I want to," I tell Geneviève honestly. "Maybe soon, if I can
find a place to meet him. He lives in a room over the watchmaker's shop, where the family also lives, so that isn't an option."

"I'll help you find somewhere," offers Geneviève. "I like arranging trysts. Now that Étienne has his own rooms, we don't have to
sneak around. I *almost* miss it." She smiles lazily. "But being un-
restrained is much better."

⚜

Although I know, given the context, Geneviève had been referring
to her love affair with Étienne, over the next few days, she seems
to adopt this frank attitude for everything else. She has always been
bold and outspoken, but she tosses revolutionary remarks without

regard, peppering them into conversations in the queen's chambers at Tuileries.

"Étienne was recently elected as an officer in the national guard," she tells me, speaking at normal volume, in spite of the fact that Madame Campan sits only a few feet away from us, sewing. "I'm so proud of him. He's been wearing his uniform more often, and he looks very fine in it. Don't you like the uniforms of the national guard, Giselle?"

Madame Campan looks up at me, her gaze prodding almost tangibly, and my tongue feels stuck to the roof of my mouth. "They have an air of dignity."

Geneviève rolls her eyes at my mumbled response, stabbing the needle through the muslin fichu she is nearly finished hemming. "Well, I adore the combination of the tricolor. The dark blue coats are rather elegant, and having the red collars and white lapels doesn't overwhelm the severity of the uniform. Léon would look nice in that uniform, wouldn't he?"

"I suppose so." I accidentally prick my finger with my own needle and clench my fingers together underneath the satin petticoat to hide it and stop the tiny bubble of blood rising from my skin.

We sew in silence for a moment. I can tell Geneviève is annoyed at me, for her mouth pinches into a button of disappointment and her eyes flash more than usual. Madame Campan inflicts both of us with a severe look, lingering longer on Geneviève, and then resumes sewing, her face turning unreadable.

"People would approve so much if the king wore something similar to the national guard uniform to the next public appearance," says Geneviève, evidently undeterred by the tension choking the room. "Those glittering jackets and plumed hats he favors are a thing of the past, and they look it too."

I widen my eyes at her, astonished that she would speak so

frankly in front of Madame Campan, whose loyalty to the queen, and by extension, the king, is unrivaled.

In response, Madame Campan exhales loudly, staring down her nose in disapproval. "Geneviève, perhaps you ought to focus on your sewing instead of proclaiming on matters of which you know nothing. I need you to have completed sewing all three fichus before bedtime."

"Oh, this is the last one." Geneviève speaks airily, fluffing the muslin over her lap.

Madame Campan rises and strides across the room, peering condescendingly down at Geneviève's handiwork, but she can find nothing to complain about. As usual, Geneviève has made neat, economical stitches, and in record time.

"You should have time to darn some stockings as well, then," she says coolly.

"Of course." Geneviève's voice drips with exaggerated sweetness.

Later, when we're alone in our shared room, I grab her arm, halting her careless, quick steps. "What are you doing? Madame Campan could have you dismissed for such disloyal talk."

"Come now, Giselle, you're just as much a revolutionary as I am."

Not quite as much, as it turns out, but I can't reveal it to Geneviève. I find it rather pains me not to. The secrets I carry grow heavy, but they are fragile and need protecting, too. "Not here I'm not," I say firmly instead. "I don't want to get in trouble at work."

Her eyes narrow in annoyance. "Is it really the work, or do you just want the queen to approve of you?"

"It seems to me the two are irrevocably intertwined."

"They aren't. I've worked here longer than you, and she has never approved fully of me. Then again, I never tripped over myself trying to fawn up to her, telling her about poems and frosty windows."

Geneviève's temper isn't unfamiliar, but it has never been directed so harshly at me. Stung, I feel too hurt to be angry, and my voice sounds small. "I just wanted to talk to her. I wanted to feel like I fit in at Versailles. I was new and feeling a bit lost."

"Talk to her? Or see if she would talk to you? There's a big difference between the two, Giselle. Don't fool yourself."

I cross my arms and lean against the wardrobe. Maybe she's right, but it doesn't justify her vindictiveness. It also doesn't make me feel better to admit that possibility. "And so? I want to keep my job here, and if that means ingratiating myself toward the queen or Madame Campan, so be it."

She flounces across the room, sits down heavily on the bed, and throws her hands up. "I've given up caring. The revolution is happening all around us, and they refuse to talk about it, even though it's their fault. It's ridiculous. I'm tired of the games and the deceit. It was amusing for a while, but I'm finished now."

"Amusing? There have been a great many dangerous moments as well."

"Oh yes, but they were exciting, too. I felt drunk on it, you know, when the rioters stormed Versailles. If not for the exhilaration, I never would have dared to write that silly poem on the inside of the door, on the way to the king's rooms. I was nearly caught then—there was so little time. I'd only just discovered that door a few hours earlier."

Aghast, I stare at her. My eyes widen so much that they feel cold. "That was you?"

She shrugs, but from the way she looks aside, I think she feels a wash of shame. "I thought you guessed."

"And the poison plots? Were you behind them, too?" My voice

grates harshly. I can hardly believe what I'm hearing. Geneviève has always been headstrong and brave and a bit outrageous, but she pushed it further than I ever dreamed she could.

"No! Good God, Giselle, you know me better than that. When things like that were happening, I didn't need the cruel little notes. I'd hoped they would spur change at the palace, that they'd help the queen see the revolution was a real, *important* thing, something that she was causing, but I don't think she ever thought of it. Perhaps years of overly elaborate hairstyles have numbed her brain." She smirks briefly. "But if poison attempts would not persuade her to face the revolution, I realized my notes were utterly useless, and I gave them up. For all the fright they caused Marie Antoinette, they weren't spurring her to any action, so there was no point in continuing."

I sit down beside her, still shocked. "I can't believe that was you." Geneviève has a sharpness about her and can say rather spiteful things sometimes, but this still surprises me.

"I was angry," says Geneviève slowly. "People were starving, desperately trying to scrape two *sous* together. People were drowning under years of oppression. They still are; we are only now breaking free. Some might say the royal family deserved a little trouble." She sounds defensive.

I sigh, racked by torn loyalties I can't articulate. "It's a hard world, everywhere." She looks frightened, eyes bright and shoulders hunched, and when I realize it's out of worry that I'll repudiate her, our argument dissolves away. She's still my closest friend, and I can't judge her too harshly in light of my own spy work. I squeeze her hand. "I won't tell anyone."

"Thank you. You're a good friend. I don't care if they find out, anyway. I've had just about enough of working here. I can't be here, in the middle of the wrong side of the revolution. I just don't believe in it."

"You know yourself so well." I feel a pang of envy for her self-assurance. Truthfully, I've rarely paused to seriously consider my own beliefs as to the revolution. I've been caught up in the perceived glamour of spying, enthralled by Léon's passion for change, reflective of the new laws and shifting politics, and even with all that involvement, I let myself be swept into the personal turmoil of the queen. I have supported the revolution, but I continue to protect her, too. Every day Paris turns into a more divided city, and I don't properly belong on either side.

"What isn't to know?" she asks, with apparently genuine curiosity. "I'm the only person I'll ever have to live with for my whole life—I ought to know exactly how I feel about everything. It makes sense."

"It isn't that simple, not for everyone."

"Oh. Well, I'm sure you know everything about yourself, too. You just have to stop to think about it." She offers me a tentative smile. "You often seem to have your head in the clouds, Giselle."

"Are you going to give notice, then?"

"Yes. I probably have to, after today. Madame Campan wasn't pleased. Even as I was speaking, I knew it would be better to bite my tongue, but I was dreadfully weary of holding things back."

"I wish you didn't write the notes," I say, before I think it through. At once, I wish I hadn't spoken.

The remnants of Geneviève's smile vanish, and her eyes turn smoky. "I did, and I can't take it back."

We fall quiet as we climb into our beds and blow out the candles. I lie still, hoping that if I remain silent and motionless, I'll suddenly find it is morning.

The blankets rustle as Geneviève sits up. I see her silhouette, the faintest shadowy impression against the dark. "I'm not proud of the notes. I thought I would be."

"I know. I'm sorry."

"I felt—the circumstances. . . . I only wanted to help." She sits up a moment longer, and I can feel her peering at me, before she flops back down, yawning audibly. "Things always look better in the morning, I think."

A wave of sleepiness crashes over me. "Yes, they always do. Good night, Geneviève." The pillows seem softer, and I drift away, feeling a little more optimistic.

In the morning Madame Campan sends Geneviève and me on separate errands. When I return from mine, there is no sign of my friend, and Madame Campan greets me with a satisfied tilt to her head and a faintly smug curl to her mouth.

"Where is Geneviève?" I ask, suspecting I know the answer already.

"I dismissed her. Such a fervent revolutionary has no place here. It was also hazardous to continue with the plan as long as she remained in service. The queen is convinced she was a spy."

"I don't think she was." I was the spy, only I have stopped now. Geneviève had her own vendetta against the queen, however, which I cannot defend, and remembering it trills my voice with hesitancy.

"I'm sorry; I know you were friends. But her incendiary ideas didn't belong here." Madame Campan's voice softens. "You may need to consider your friends more carefully, Giselle." Somehow the gentle tone makes the words more insulting.

I bob my head stiffly. "Yes, Madame."

She seems not to notice the resentment making me look down, glaring at the floor. Though hushed, her voice gains a note of excitement. "I didn't find an opportunity to tell you yesterday, but

I have news. The plan shall proceed tomorrow night. The king wanted to leave tonight, but the queen persuaded him to wait a day, until Geneviève was gone. She would not move while under that girl's watchful gaze."

"I did everything I could to make sure Geneviève didn't suspect. I even mentioned seeing a Russian baroness, to set up Madame de Tourzel's disguise."

Madame Campan presses her fingers together. "Oh no, my dear—I didn't intend to imply you failed. The shortcoming was mine. I should have dismissed Geneviève long ago."

Since the rooms seem dull to me without her, I turn the subject back to the plan. "We'll be busy with the last-minute preparations, then," I say to Madame Campan, grateful for the prospect of being busy, distracted by the impending escape.

"Yes," she agrees, and commences to outline a list of tasks we must complete to ready the disguises.

The day passes in a whirl of preparations, piled on my regular tasks as a tirewoman. In fact, with Geneviève's absence, I have more work than usual. I manage to sneak away to the garden for a few minutes around lunchtime, when Léon and I often meet.

He waits near the fountain, holding three flowers in his hand: a white rose, a red carnation, and a blue delphinium. Upon seeing me, his face beams with more warmth than the sun, eyes lighting up and a bright smile growing. I sink into his arms, pressing my mouth to his neck. His arms wind around me, hands sliding up my back, and it feels comfortable and exciting. I never want to move. Things are simple in Léon's arms. There are no schemes or artifices here, only love and loyalty.

"I picked a bouquet for you," he says at last, releasing me from our embrace. His fingers curl around mine, and he presses the stems into my hand with his free one. "I snapped off the rose thorns with my pocketknife. You deserve more flowers, *ma belle*, but I saw a rather grouchy-looking gardener, and I confess to being afraid to pick more." He laughs low in his throat. "If I was evicted from the gardens today, I wouldn't get to see you."

"I'm glad you're here." I lean closer to him, brushing my lips against his earlobe. I like the way his fingers tighten around mine. His other hand curves around my hip. "I have a plan to see even more of you."

He licks his lips and stares at me. The sunlight makes his dark brown eyes gleam with flecks of molten gold, melting every sinew in my body. I lean against him, feeling suddenly feverish.

"Due to an unexpected schedule change, Madame Campan gave me the night off. My parents don't know of it. Tonight I have the freedom to go anywhere." I tilt my face up, brushing my lips against his. I'm not even trying to be teasing or seductive anymore. The heat in his eyes makes me feel deliciously wanton. "I could spend the night with you."

Our lips are already tantalizingly close, and Léon fastens his mouth to mine with a low groan, kissing me with such passion and enthusiasm that I wish I'd thought of this sooner. The heady feeling outrivals being drunk on wine.

"If you didn't already know, I hope my reaction told you how much I'd like that," he murmurs, stroking my hair. "I can't invite you to my room, though. Monsieur Renard would know if I had someone over."

"I thought of that. I know of an inn we can use. I have a bit of money; I just received my wages. We can meet there."

"Are you sure, Giselle? We'll be married soon, after all."

"Don't you want to?"

He smiles in the crooked, endearing way I love so much, the left corner of his mouth rising slightly higher, lifting his eyebrow with it. His eyes glitter with a mixture of desire and humor. "More than anything. I'm not a madman. But I want to be certain you want to. . . . I've waited for you, for someone I love, my whole life. I could wait a few more weeks if you weren't sure."

"I'm absolutely certain. I don't want to wait a few more weeks."

He gathers me into his arms, resting his cheek against my hair. "Tonight, then." The tremor quaking through his body echoes mine. "What time shall we meet?"

Chapter Fifteen

After my interlude with Léon in the Tuileries gardens, the rest of the afternoon seems strangely paced. Sometimes it drags, and I squirm with anxious anticipation for the hour of our meeting. But the secretive preparations for the queen's flight do not stop. The tasks, rushed to meet the strict deadline, tussle with the vital importance of maintaining the secret. They keep me so busy that sometimes I find an hour has passed in a flicker of moments.

The queen retires to her rooms early, pleading a headache. Her eyes gleam bright silver with purpose, and her footsteps flutter with grace and lightness. Rosy pink stains her cheeks. She looks far brighter and more animated than I've seen her in a long while. Frankly, it's a good thing she's in the privacy of her own rooms, because anyone seeing her would never believe the story of a headache. Supper is brought to her room, chicken broth with soft white bread, a suitable meal for someone feeling ill. She sends it away after eating only a few bites.

"I can't eat," she says restlessly to Madame Campan. "My nerves jangle too much."

"You need your strength," says Madame Campan, her tone mild.

"It's just as well," I say. "Lack of appetite fits with headache symptoms."

"The idea occurred to me as well." Marie Antoinette smiles at me unexpectedly. "You have served me very well, Giselle. I wanted to tell you that before I go. When we return, when Paris has grown safer and the revolution is under control, I hope you'll return to my household. There will always be a place for you here."

Her warm, charming smile catches me off guard, and eases some of the weight of the preparations from my shoulders. I feel myself relax a little, the way one does when sitting in the sunshine after a busy morning. I curtsy slightly. "Thank you, Your Majesty. I would like that."

"I have something for you. Come here." The words ring crisp and clear, an unmistakable command. When I stand directly in front of her, she reaches into a small silk bag knotted with a blue cord. The item she pulls out is small enough to be nearly disguised by her smooth fingertips, but the glitter of rubies catches the lamp-light, tossing sparks of fire over the pale skin of her hand. "I would like you to have it."

Marie Antoinette puts the brooch into my hand before I can reply. It feels cool and hard, the gold trim heavy. It's the shape of a rose, with dozens of tiny rubies making up the petals. The whole thing is probably the size of my thumb. For her, it is a small thing, hardly more than a trifle. For me, it is a rich gift, and an honorable one too. I balance it on my fingertips, resting it gently, and look to her in surprise.

"Are you certain? Your Majesty, I have no need for anything."

She laughs at my expression and that I have thoughtlessly

questioned her. The sound reminds me of delicate wind chimes. I've never heard her laugh like that. She's always been reserved, detached, and the gaiety bubbling from her lips like champagne makes her seem like a different person, a younger one. The pending flight from Paris has imbued her with hope, and it has changed her. I wonder if this is her true self.

"Yes. You're taking a risk, helping me. I want to reward you. The work of this night may extend into the future. It seems right that I give you something that may help you then." Her mouth still softens in a faint smile, but a serious glint forms in her eyes.

Having a sudden, disconcerting notion that the brooch is also meant to buy my continued silence, I feel my cheeks grow warm. I meet her eyes steadily. "I will guard this secret, Your Majesty."

She nods as regally as if she wore a crown and held a scepter, instead of sitting in a chair near the bed with her hair half-unpinned, a trunk near her feet. When she doesn't argue or seek elaboration on my words, I know I interpreted correctly.

"Take care of yourself, Giselle," she says. "May God protect you."

"And you, Your Majesty." I hesitate, feeling inadequate for this rather formal farewell. "I hope—Have a safe journey. I will pray for you and the children. I wish you luck."

Her hand moves, and for a startling second, I think she is going to grasp my own. She is a queen, though, accustomed to remaining a step higher than most other people, born of noble blood. She nods in a way that reminds me of a blessing instead, and gives me a serene smile. "Thank you, Giselle."

Madame Campan's farewell is warmer and less confusing, and also less final. "Perhaps we will see each other in Paris on occasion." I think she wants to have someone to reminisce about the queen with, counting the days until they are reunited. "I may follow her to Montmédy later. If it's safe, if she'll be there long enough. She'll send for me if I'm needed."

"She will miss you," I tell Madame Campan. The nervousness lurking around her hands and eyes tells me she needs to hear the words, but I know they're true. "She relies on you."

"Be careful tonight, Giselle," she says to me in parting. "Don't forget to arrange the rooms as you go."

"I won't. Good-bye, Madame Campan." Impulsively, I squeeze her hand, and she pulls me into a hug. I never thought we were so close, but becoming conspirators has created a bond between us. She smells of rosewater and pats my back in a motherly fashion.

On my way through the outer chambers, I put out the candles and arrange the cushions on the chaise longues, just as I normally would before bed. I put away all the clothes and a spare pair of slippers the queen left lying out. She has so many clothes that no one will notice any are missing, at least not quickly, in spite of the fact that she packed a great deal of them. Too many, I think, but I suppose she isn't used to traveling light.

Lastly, I say good night to the other tirewomen, who have been dismissed from waiting on the queen for the night, and sit sewing in the outer antechamber. "The queen has gone to sleep early, with her headache," I say, yawning. "Madame Campan said you can retire for the night. I cleaned up in the inner rooms, so that's all done."

They wander off, pleased to put their sewing aside early. I follow, and slip into the bedroom that I used to share with Geneviève. I think it's unlikely anyone will enter here or look for me until morning. I debate plumping the pillows under the blanket to make it look like I am asleep, and then I decide it will be less suspicious if it is left made and tidy. It will fit better if anyone asks later, since the queen will be gone from Paris, but I will not. I will simply tell the partial truth that Madame Campan sent me away for the night.

This is probably the last time I will see this little bedroom in Tuileries. It seems lonely without Geneviève, and too tidy. She always left her hair ribbons strewn around. I'm glad I don't have to spend the night in this empty room alone, and think happily of Léon.

Before I leave to meet him for our tryst, I take precautions to prevent pregnancy. I want to be able to make love to him without fearing for the future, although since our wedding is only a couple of weeks away, I suppose it wouldn't matter drastically if we started a baby early. Still, I want to be married to him for a few months first. I want to enjoy Léon to myself for a while, and while I dream of being a mother someday, I'm only eighteen and there is no need to hurry. My own mother was twenty when she gave birth to me.

I'd asked Geneviève what to do, for I knew she and Étienne regularly met at his home. She confided about the physical delights of their relationship often to me, in private.

"Lemon juice," she had advised briskly. "You can push half a small lemon up there, but if you can, I'd soak a scrap of soft wool in lemon juice instead. It's easier to remove again, and you can make the lemon go farther that way. Vinegar works too, in a pinch, but lemon juice smells much nicer."

Thinking of Geneviève and her endless practicality in all things makes me feel a pang of loss. I didn't know her as well as I had thought, perhaps. But when I think of all the times we laughed together, sharing confidences, I know that we did have a true friendship.

Léon meets me outside the inn. Geneviève helped me find this place, too, for I'd no experience arranging lover's liaisons. I've never stayed at an inn before, but I know many of them have several beds in one room, and that will not do for us, not tonight. We need a private room. A frisson of excitement rockets through my body at the thought of being alone with him in this way.

Murmuring a sweet, rather shy greeting, Léon takes my hand and presses his lips to my knuckles before holding it close to his chest, our fingers clinging together. "Can you feel how fast my heart is beating?" he whispers, laughing a little. "You look lovely, Giselle." He touches my hair where it curls over my ears, smoothing it back.

"Thank you." He looks handsome himself, and I tell him so. His eyes gleam as dark as midnight, but soft somehow too, like candlelight, and his sculpted mouth looks gentle, its sometimes severe lines erased by the small smile he wears. His wiry arm pulls me closer, and he presses a light kiss to my temple.

Once in our room, we explore the plain furnishings. The blanket on the bed is a pale wheat color and looks clean, to my relief. I fluff the pillows and tug the corner of the coverlet straighter. Once I realize I'm fussing to hide my apprehension, I drop the pillows again and turn to Léon with a sheepish smile on my face.

"I suppose I'm a bit nervous, though it doesn't make sense to be. I'm happy to be here with you, my love. It feels like a gift to have our wedding night early." I kick off my shoes and move closer to him, pulling my braid over my shoulder and unraveling the plaits. My hair spills over my shoulders in a silken heap of chestnut waves smelling of rosewater. I took care to scent it lightly, hoping it would please him.

His eyes flare with warm sparks, and he watches my movements very intently. "I always assumed we would wait until our wedding night." The light tone does not quite hide the huskiness in his voice. "I proposed early too. It appears we're an impatient couple."

"Love doesn't wait." I smile back at him. "I love you, Léon."

"I love you too, Giselle, very much."

"Untie the sash of my dress?" I'm perfectly able to do it myself, but I pull my loose hair over my shoulder and present him with my back. His hands skim along the sides of my waist, and he takes a while, treating the soft blue sash of my *gaulle* gown far more gently than I would have. As the layered muslin loosens, the neckline drops off my shoulders. His lips brush the back of my neck, and the warmth of his breath shoots arrows of desire all through me. When his fingers curl around the collar of my dress, sliding it farther away from my skin, I help by tugging it past my hips, letting it fall to the floor. Aware that my chemise is not quite opaque, I turn slowly around to face him. Self-consciousness threatens to douse my eagerness, but then I see the heat in his eyes and I feel beautiful.

Léon swallows, his fingers hesitating over the thin material of my chemise. "I—I've never done this before."

"Neither have I," I whisper. "But I want to now, with you."

His breath hisses faintly as he exhales shakily, and his hands tighten on me, twisting the loose fabric of my chemise, drawing me closer to him. He slides one palm up my back, between my shoulder blades, bending his face close to mine. His eyes gleam in the candlelight, his gaze as rich and hot as a cup of chocolate, and he bends his head close to mine. "I want it to be pleasurable for both of us; I don't want to hurt you." He twists the cloth at my waist in his fingers. "You have to tell me if I need to go slower, to be more gentle."

Feeling a surge of tenderness for him, touched by his concern, I stroke his hair and smile at him. I think it reassures both of us. "I will. I'm not afraid, Léon. I'm looking forward to it." Licking my lips and taking a breath to steel myself against a new burst of self-consciousness, I pull my chemise over my head, baring myself before him.

The candlelight flickers over my skin, making patterns of gold and shadow, and as Léon's scorching gaze traces the movement, eyes roving over every inch of me, I fancy that I can feel the heat of the flame and his eyes like a tangible, feathery caress.

He kicks the cloudy heap of my white clothing aside and strips off his shirt and breeches, undressing quickly. "It's only fair," he says roughly.

I feel as though he read my thoughts, for while I trembled with excited anticipation under his stare, I also felt slightly at a disadvantage, since he was still clothed. Nude, his body shows tan lines at his wrists and throat, and his arms are lean, faintly sinewy. His chest is flat and hard with a sparse scattering of dusky hair, although a heavier line of it trails from his navel to his groin, which I observe with a mixture of interest, arousal, and slight fear. Everyone says that the first time is often painful for a woman, and seeing his sizable hardness makes me nervous even as it excites me.

"Your skin is perfect, Giselle." His voice sounds jagged and throaty. "Soft as satin and pale as moonlight." His fingertips trace the curve of my waist, sliding tentatively over the slope of my breast, circling the nipple. The sensation makes me arch closer to him, surprised by the pleasant intensity.

Hands moving to my hips, he guides me toward the bed and gently lays me down. Fanning my hair across the pillow, I settle in the middle of the mattress, opening my legs and feeling a little awkward.

"Move over, *mon ange*." He nuzzles at my neck. "Oh, it feels so good to touch you." Stretching his body beside mine, our skin brushes together, and the warmth of his body and the intimacy of the touch scatters flickers of lightning through me. He threads his fingers through my hair, stroking my neck, and moves his lips against mine in a gentle, slow kiss. I know he is excited, for his breath feels fast and shallow, and his erection presses against my bare thigh, but he holds back the kiss, keeping it light and soft until I sink my fingers into his silky dark hair, pulling him closer and searching for his tongue with mine.

Fierce now, increasingly urgent, his mouth moves over mine until dizziness spirals behind my eyes and I am making soft sighs of enjoyment that match the rhythm of his hand stroking my breast. When he at last ends the kiss, I hazily expect him to poise his body over mine, but instead he nudges at my jaw, turning my head slightly to the side so he can press his lips to my neck. He takes a long, sweet time exploring there, lingering whenever he finds a spot that makes me writhe and gasp, flicking his tongue against the sensitive skin behind my ear, grazing my earlobe with his teeth. Just when I think I can't stand the pleasurable, but ticklish, sensations anymore, he leans over me and switches to the other side of my neck. All the while, his fingertips drift over my skin, learning the map of my body, circling in gentle, unhurried caresses. He presses soft kisses along my collarbones, moving closer to my breasts as his hands skim past my hips and along my thighs, all the way to my knee, and back up again, so slowly that my body tenses with anticipation. His mouth closes over my nipple at the same time that his fingers stroke between my thighs, and I moan with delight, squirming against him.

"Do you like that?" he whispers. His already dark eyes look almost black now, the pupils dilated with desire. "I'll keep doing it, then . . . faster? Or slower?" He demonstrates both motions, flicking his tongue against my nipple, and I can't decide yet which I like better so I just tell him not to stop.

Léon kisses me for a long time, until my breath emerges in short pants, drying my throat, and I clutch at his shoulders and tug on his hair. I never want his teasing, wonderful touches to stop, and yet I also yearn for more, start to crave the weight of his body over mine.

At last he kisses his way back up my neck. "I can't wait anymore." His voice rasps in my ear, making me shiver with desire. "Oh, Giselle, I want you so much." He kisses me deeply, then coaxes my thighs farther apart with his hand. It takes a moment for us to get situated, neither of us having done this before, but then he joins his body to mine in a thrust that wrenches the breath from my lungs. It hurts. Pain sears through me, and I bite my lip hard. Léon also gasps as he enters me, only from the flutter of his eyelashes and soft mouth, I know he feels only pleasure, and I don't want him to know he has hurt me. I keep quiet, but he sees my bitten lip and strokes my hair with one hand, murmuring breathless endearments.

It does not last long, both to my relief and faint, surprising, regret. Near the end, the stinging had begun to fade, slowly being overwhelmed by enjoyable friction. I liked watching Léon's face suffused with desire. Seeing his pleasure, and his helplessness, gave me a powerful feeling, a sense of womanhood. I wish I could feel more of it, which seems a good sign for our next time.

"Was it all right?" Léon tucks my hair behind my ear, sounding shy. "Are you well?"

"Yes. I am fine." I run my hand down his back, slightly damp with sweat. "And you?"

He chuffs with laughter. "I've never been better, I promise." Lying down, he pulls me against his chest, curling his body around mine. I lean my head back against his chest, tucked under his chin, feeling sheltered and adored.

"I dreamed of making love to you," he says softly. "Especially these last months. But I also dreamed of this." He squeezes me gently, nuzzling my hair. "Of holding you close to me while we fall asleep, safe and warm and alone together in our own bed. I wanted to be the last person you saw before sleeping, and the first upon waking."

"And now you shall be." I twist my head around to smile at him. "I want that too." To show him how much, I nestle more comfortably against him, enjoying the thrilling novelty of his closeness. The groan of satisfaction he makes sounds like a purr, his throat poised near my ear.

We whisper to each other, talking of our plans for the future, when Léon will be a proper watchmaker, and I'll be creating dresses of my own design. We've been planning to visit Toulouse a few months after the wedding so I can meet his family, and he tells me more about them and his favorite parts of his native city while a transparent haze of moonlight stains the room. As we drift to sleep, our faces close together, I wish we could somehow share our dreams, a fanciful but sweet notion.

At dawn I wake first, skin suffocating from heat. My head is pillowed on his shoulder, my arm flung across his chest, fingertips tingling with limited blood flow. He wakes when I slide away from him, and stretches, throwing the coverlet off of us. The cooler air glides over my skin, raising goose bumps and revitalizing my senses.

"I like the look of you, lying on the tangled sheets," says Léon in a sleepy growl. "I wish it was brighter in here so I could admire you better."

"I suppose you'll have to use other senses, and not rely only on sight," I say, smiling lazily. "Come here and touch me."

We make love again, and this time it is both more and less urgent. Léon moves slowly, his quick breath and darkly gleaming eyes betraying the depth of his excitement, but he seems determined to focus on my pleasure, learning from my reactions what touches I like best. It's all new to me, too, but fire rushes through my veins, fanning my heartbeat, hurrying my breaths. The exquisite tension builds higher and tighter, coiling all through me, until I pant and cry out his name, begging him for more. I close my eyes against the burst of starlight searing through me, as bright and beautiful as the fireworks we once watched, and then Léon buries his face in my neck, shuddering with his own pleasure.

Although a bit sore and stiff, I also feel replete, almost boneless with relaxation. Pressing drowsy kisses to his shoulder, his skin warm and salty, I pull his hand across my waist again, thinking how remarkably decadent it is to lie abed like this.

Later, but still too soon for me—I don't want to give him up yet—Léon stretches his arms above his head, yawning. "I suppose we have to get up soon. Lord knows I don't want to." He grins at me. "Good thing we shall be married soon. One night with you isn't enough. I want a lifetime of them."

"I do too."

"Do you have to be back at Tuileries soon, or do you have the day off?"

"I have the day off." I hesitate. I know I have to tell him my employment is over, at least for now, but reluctance slows my speech. I trace the length of his fingers with mine, stalling. "I have the next day off too, and the one after that. . . . all of them, in fact, for the foreseeable future."

He sits up on his elbow, thin brows arching in surprise. "You do?"

"Yes. I'm finished at Tuileries, at least for now. I can start working on my own dress creations instead. It's sooner than planned, but just the same as we always talked about."

He lies flat on his back, squeezing my hand in his. "I'm happy to hear it. You know I think you'll be good at it, and if you are ready, who am I to argue? I confess, though, I didn't expect you to leave your post until we were married. You're full of surprises."

The gentle amusement in his eyes makes something crack around my heart. For an endless moment, I wonder if I can keep the secret of the queen's flight and never tell him of my role in it. I know it's impossible, though. Soon the news of her disappearance will spread throughout the country, and everyone will know what day she left, including Léon. He isn't a fool, and I love him too much to treat him so.

Still, it's not easy to speak. I fidget with a wrinkle of the bedsheet, looking away from his eyes. "My post is no longer available. I mean—you see," I stammer helplessly. Perhaps I ought to have told him earlier, but Madame Campan had instilled the absolute necessity for secrecy of the plan deep into my bones. I couldn't tell Léon before, but now that I can, it doesn't make it simpler.

"Are you trying to say that you were dismissed?" He rolls onto his side, facing me, sounding faintly outraged. "That's nonsense; you were one of the best workers. I know it. Unless—the spying?" He chews on his lower lip, worried for me, in case I have been suspected. "Tell me, Giselle."

"No, it isn't that." I take a deep breath, and to my horror, it sounds shaky. "I gave up spying a while ago. I should have said something—you're the first I've told. For what I am about to say next, you are also the first person to hear it. Maybe one of the first people in all of Paris to know."

"Secrets from the palace?" He sits up, grinning, folding his arms across his bare chest. "It must be shocking—you seem nervous. You can tell me anything."

I hope to God it is true. "The queen trusted me, and so did Madame Campan. They trusted me to help them with a—a scheme."

His smile fades into a serious expression. He listens intently, brow furrowed.

I knot the blanket into my fists and take a long, slow breath, which doesn't succeed in calming me. The confession spills out of me more rapidly than I intended. "The king and queen fled Tuileries for a royalist fortress in Montmédy, and I helped them."

Silence reigns, and after a few heartbeats echoing in my ears, I timidly peek up at Léon.

"Fled?" His voice grates over the word, turning it into something harsh. "They ran away from their responsibilities? Like children? Like cowards?"

"Not exactly. They don't feel safe here, surrounded by enemies. The queen has had multiple attempts on her life. I believe they desire to return France to peace, but from the safety of a place surrounded by loyal protectors. It's not a brave choice, perhaps, but she was so afraid. . . . Marie Antoinette thought she would die if she stayed here."

"Running away is as craven as it is foolish," says Léon flatly. His eyes have gone that way too, as dark and inscrutable as onyx. "It's desertion—soldiers can be executed for this sort of thing, but I suppose they think they're untouchable. This just proves they have never understood the cause of the revolution, the desperate need for change. They never will understand it, I see now. They cannot possibly grasp it, blinded as they are by their luxurious surroundings, ruined by their selfishness."

"Maybe." I squirm with misery. "I can't presume to know what they think. All I know is that I was asked to help, and I did. I couldn't refuse."

"I'm not sure it's as simple as that," says Léon slowly. Even though he sits in bed in what should be a relaxed pose, the blankets

pulled around his hips, he seems taut, ready to move at any moment. His face reminds me of a hawk again, fierce and angry. "You
had a choice, Giselle."

"Not much of one," I say. "The queen was my employer and
my sovereign. I could have been dismissed, punished, even arrested
for refusing. Don't assign nonexistent power to me in this, Léon."
My pride grasps at this excuse, feeble because I wanted to help her,
wasn't forced to. I'd known it would be difficult to tell Léon, that
my actions contradicted his beliefs, but I hoped that he would understand my sympathies. His harsh reaction leaves me feeling
small.

"The power is changing." His voice is very soft but not at all
gentle. "Even the king and queen know that, or they wouldn't have
fled like scared puppies. There are plenty of high-ranking people
who support the revolution, who could have used the information
of a planned flight to prevent it, to further the new constitution
and new ideas." He pauses. "Your uncle certainly has the connections. It wouldn't have been hard for you to find someone to tell.
You had just the right person sitting across from you at the Sunday
supper table."

"I swore I would keep it a secret. I keep my word, once given."
I shoot a stubborn glare at him. "It wasn't easy, Léon."

"I just don't understand why you would support the monarchs
in this." Confusion blurs his features, and he twists the blankets
too, wrenching them away from me without noticing. "You know
how bad things are, and you've been spying on the queen for
months. This sudden loyalty doesn't make sense to me. I can't suddenly change my whole opinion, even though it seems like you did.
I need time to think about it." He swings out of bed and reaches
for his discarded breeches, lying in a heap on the floor.

I pull my shift over my head, viciously tugging the sleeves

straight. One of the seams loosens with a tearing sound, but I'm too angry to care. I sit down on the edge of the rumpled bed and begin rolling my stockings up past my ankles. "Take all the time you need." My voice sounds wire-tight. "But I didn't change my whole opinion overnight. Give me some credit, please."

He whirls around, fingers automatically finishing fastening his pants. His eyes flare with fresh outrage. Bare-chested, his hair standing messily on end, and a scowl marking his face, he looks like some kind of barbarian warrior. If my feelings weren't smarting, I might have found it appealing.

"When did you change your opinion, then? You certainly didn't indicate it to me, and I thought we knew each other very well." He hesitates. "You promised to be honest with me, an oath you made on your own."

"I wanted to tell you," I say helplessly. "But I couldn't—it wasn't safe until they had actually slipped away in the night. I *had* to keep the secret until then, Léon. Don't you see?"

He flinches as though I slapped him. The dark fire fades from his eyes as the tension drains out of his shoulders. Sorrow flickers across his face, and then he guards his expression, straightening once more, ready to walk away. "You didn't trust me? Giselle, I'd do anything for you. I would have helped you, even, if I could, though God knows I can't condone the king deserting his own countrymen. But I can't control him, not any more than you can, and my loyalty is for you first. I would have helped you," he repeated.

My voice scrapes my throat. "It wasn't my secret to share. I wanted to trust you—I did trust you, always—but I had no power to share it until last night, until they were safely away—"

"Last night?" He strides forward and takes my wrists in his hands, pulling me roughly to my feet. His eyes stare into mine, shadowy and probing. "They fled last night—Giselle, that's why you had the night away from the palace? That's why you were free to arrange this?" He casts a pained look at the bed.

"Madame Campan said I shouldn't be there, for my protection. I saw an opportunity to spend the night with you, and I took it. I wanted you—I thought you wanted me, too." I stare at the floor, unable to meet his gaze any longer. "You seemed happy enough last night for us to be together."

We stand close enough that his breath hisses across the sensitive skin of my neck, and that somehow makes the words more tangible, makes them hurt more. "Last night I thought I was your lover, not your convenient alibi. Last night felt right—as if I unlocked a new part of my life with you, and our time together was going to be glorious. But it was a sham."

I dig my nails into his arms, clinging too tightly. "It wasn't! I felt like you were my husband already. I love you, Léon."

"Do you?" he asks. "You lied to me because you thought you couldn't trust me. Even though, if I were to betray your secret and blow open the whole escape plot, you'd be implicated and most likely punished. I wouldn't do that to you, and if you thought it was a risk, you must not know me at all."

"I never thought you would betray me." Tears streak down my face in hot bursts, salting my lips. "I didn't think of it much at all, I confess. I got caught up in the secrecy, and I shouldn't have."

Our fingers are still wrapped around each other's wrists. I've left nail marks in his arms, and he squeezes my bones together. He seems to realize, because his lashes flicker, veiling his eyes, and he slowly loosens his fingers. He pushes me away until I sit on the bed again.

"I don't think we should get married."

I stare at him in shock. My tears halt, but the burning in my eyes seems to double, scorching down my throat and into my lungs, squeezing tight. Inside, I am begging him to forgive me, to please understand, not to leave me. The words lock inside me, emerging only as a strangled gasp.

"I don't know if I can move past this." Léon looks older all of a sudden, with shadows smudged along his skin under his eyes and cheekbones. "I always knew I felt more strongly about the revolution than you, and I accepted that. But you helped the opposite cause and used me while you did it. This tainted our love—I know you didn't mean it to, but it did. I can hardly describe how I feel, but I know it would be a mistake for us to wed now. We wouldn't be happy." His voice twists with sorrow and bitterness. "I'm sorry, Giselle."

He pulls his shirt over his head, crams his feet into his boots, and snatches up his coat, all the while avoiding looking directly at me. Even in my haze of shattered dreams, I see that his skin has grown very pale, and he bites his lip while his eyes glitter, with fury or tears, I can't tell.

Léon pauses before opening the door, and for a hollow heartbeat, I think he will turn around and say that we will see each other, that this isn't over. Instead he visibly steels himself, spine stiffening, and slips out the door quickly and quietly.

It takes me a long time to get dressed. My body seems to have turned to stone, a statue of shocked sorrow and horrible self-guilt, because I made mistakes and they cost me my love. Once I thaw my fingers and manage to move again, I can't flee the room quickly enough, escaping the reminders of our night together, the tousled sheets, the two indents in the pillow, the faint scent of him lingering in the room.

I walk around for hours, afraid to go home and face reality, the consequences of my actions. At some point, people begin shouting about the noticeable absence of the monarchs, outraged and baffled. It acts as my cue. Hating the sunshine, for it feels like the day should be full of thunderstorms, I go home and tell my parents of my role in the plot and of my broken engagement.

The following days pass very slowly. I almost feel I can count the passing of each wretched moment by the pain in my head, throbbing with each pulse of my wounded heart.

Chapter Sixteen

A pool of sunshine spills into the parlor. I drag one of the chairs to its center, taking comfort in the warmth as I embroider a hand-kerchief. Desperate to keep my mind and hands busy, to lose minutes in concentration on a menial task, I design an elaborate pattern of violets. I considered roses, but red reminds me of tri-color, and revolutionary notions drag at me now, shadowing me in soul-sick weariness. I don't want to think about anything. Not about the queen, not about Léon, not about myself. I want to think of nothing but how precise I can make the tiny purple stitches.

Maman finds me after a while, giving me a gentle smile and a cup of tea. She seems to sense that I don't wish to speak, so she ruffles my hair, an affectionate gesture that has fallen out of habit since I was much younger, and leaves me alone with the quiet sunshine. I appreciate her understanding.

The next interruption is far less welcome: a knock on the door. The needle jabs my finger as I twitch with surprise, and I freeze, listening with anticipation and trepidation, hoping the visitor is Léon, fearing that it is not.

My uncle's smooth voice rings through the hall. Disappointment stabs through me so deeply that I feel ashamed for letting my hopes rise for Léon's presence. I remember the bitterness etched over his face when we parted, the way he wouldn't quite look at me, and I have to clench my lips together to keep fresh tears from starting.

"Good afternoon, Félix. I hope you're well. We haven't visited in some weeks," says Uncle Pierre.

"We are all well, thank you." Papa expresses his greetings for Eugénie and her mother, and they make small talk for a moment. I continue sewing, not looking up. By counting stitches and taking even, measured breaths, I bring my emotions under control again.

"Are you settled into your new house?" asks Papa.

"Oh yes, it's very comfortable."

"And the location?" I hear distaste in my father's tone. "Across from the remains of the Bastille, isn't it? It seems like a rather maudlin landmark to live near."

"There is hardly anything left of it now." Pierre sounds dismissive. "Once the workers are finished clearing away the last of it, I daresay the view will be splendid." He clears his throat. "I wanted a word with Giselle. Is she home?"

"She is. I'm not sure she's up to visiting, however. She's not well today."

"I am sorry to hear that. Perhaps, if I call back later?"

Sighing, I put my sewing aside and rise to my feet. My head feels heavy, temples throbbing, but I'd rather face the inevitable conversation with my uncle now instead of delaying. I want to get it over with, not let the dreadful anticipation build.

I clear my rusty throat. "Hello, Uncle. I'm well enough to speak for a few moments."

He smiles, but his eyes glint with steel. "Thank you, my dear. Should we go to the study?"

"The parlor will be fine." Without looking back to see if he follows, I return to my sun-splashed seat and pick up my sewing again. It makes me look unconcerned, bending my head over nonurgent embroidery while he paces around the room, clearly waiting for me to speak first.

After a while he admits defeat and sits down opposite me. "I've heard some extremely interesting news." His voice carries an edge of a quality akin to slyness.

My detached façade flickers. I'm certain he knows about the queen's departure, that he possibly suspects my role in it. Determined not to react, I find my fingers tightening around the cloth anyway. "Yes?" Striving to sound tranquil, I look up, letting my brows arch in a display of mild curiosity.

He reaches into the pocket of his waistcoat and pulls out a folded piece of paper, which considerably increases my bafflement. Opening it slowly, he proffers the paper, and I see that it is an assignat, a form of paper money that came into circulation a couple of years ago, issued by the National Assembly.

"It's odd, don't you think, that a bill as new as this would still include the king's portrait?" He peers at the profile of King Louis, then back at me. "This money was created after the start of the revolution, after hatred of the king was well rooted, and yet, here is his face." His shoulder lifts in a shrug. "I suppose tradition clings in ways we do not expect. It's just as well, for having the king's likeness can be very useful, as it turns out. A postmaster in Varennes, one Monsieur Jean-Baptiste Drouet, recognized the king's profile when he looked upon the face of a supposed butler passing through Varennes. This butler was part of the retinue of a Russian countess, I'm told, and she had children and other servants with her as well."

He still holds the assignat toward me. The paper drapes crookedly over his palm. I take it from him, studying the profile of the king. The soft bullfrog swell of his chin and his sloping nose really are quite distinctive. What a pity, since it triggered his recognition.

"You needn't carry on with the long-winded story," I tell my uncle tartly. "I'm quite intelligent enough to make the connection that the man truly was the king, and the queen and their children were there too. I'm aware they left Tuileries, after all."

His teeth show in a cool smile. "Of course. I beg your pardon, Giselle. It's such a good story. I get caught up in the telling. They say that, when the king's disguise was caught out, the queen herself straightened up like the empress of the world and peered down her Hapsburg nose at the onlookers and said, 'Since you recognize your sovereign, respect him.' And the mayor, who had been called to the scene as soon as suspicion was aroused, made a chagrined bow. It did not stop him from doing his duty, however, and the flight of the monarchs was halted."

"It sounds in character for her," I say numbly.

"You would know," replies my uncle. "You know her rather better than most people have had the opportunity to. Or the desire to."

Remaining silent, I pick up my needle again, but it's useless. I can't focus. I set it back down, this time on the side table instead of my lap.

Uncle Pierre's voice drops. He narrows his eyes, abandoning the show of light chitchat. While the earlier pretense was still glazed with malice, his anger rings unmistakably now, not contained by the low volume. "I know you helped them escape, Giselle."

I haven't the faintest idea how he knows, but a sick feeling coils in my stomach, tugging my limbs taut. Moving with the tension pulling me apart, I rise to my feet. I'm tall enough that we are almost the same height, and as his eyes bore into mine, I stare back. My brows draw closer together, scowling with me, and I've never been so glad of the fierce dark shape of them. Perhaps I don't have a delicate face, but I can stare down my bullying uncle enough to make him blink and rock back one step.

"Their lives were in danger," I say coldly. "You know this. I told you about several incidents of death threats and assassination attempts."

"And so you chose to protect them instead of your family? To keep this secret from me?" He waves his hand, palm flexing in frustration.

My lip curls. "We are safe enough. No one is sending us daily threats. No one is calling for your blood."

His voice slips to a low volume, but it doesn't sound soft. "Have you forgotten the Réveillon riot? That man and his family were targeted and nearly lost their lives. It could happen to any of us. Feudal privileges have already been abolished. Marat's bloody pamphlet, *L'Ami du Peuple*"—he rolls his eyes at the title—"rages against aristocrats. The threat is all around; a mob could storm the house any day, taking what they want and caring little for the consequences."

"You exaggerate, Uncle. We aren't titled. And if some starving people are envious of your lavish house across from the old Bastille, it's not because of me."

His hands twist. "And yet you would take such extreme action to help them escape to Austria? You thought the moral scales balanced, to let them abandon their country and suffering people in order to protect their wretched lives?"

"Not Austria. Montmédy."

Perplexity wrinkles his brow. Understanding dawns on him, lightening his expression. He knows where Montmédy is, of course, and knows the citadel is fortified and held by royalists. He throws back his head, and merry laughter bursts from his throat.

"Your hilarity seems misplaced." I watch him, baffled, feeling as though I have missed something important. I don't like it—the longer our conversation goes on, the more it seems like a cunning verbal chess game.

"I thought they'd flee to Austria, to beg for aid of the queen's brother. The obvious routes would take them through Varennes, to the east, or Compiègne, in the northeast. I had people watching in both cities. I meant to find them first." He shakes his head, eyes gleaming with ironic mirth. "I was wrong, utterly ill informed, and yet they passed through Varennes anyway."

"What do you mean, ill informed? By whom?" My voices rises, shockingly panicky and shrill. I wish I could bite my tongue, take the sound back.

"Another of the queen's women. She was dismissed a day or two before the event, but she suspected a flight, and had passed some information on to me. Her name was Geneviève. I assumed you must have been acquainted with her, but I found out from Eugénie that she is your good friend. I am sorry for that—mistrust and betrayal among our family is enough, without tarnishing friendships, too. But I had to hire her. I needed this information, and you weren't providing it. You succumbed to the queen's charms, and I could no longer trust you."

My cheeks burn. I feel like I've been slapped. I wish Geneviève had told me. Perhaps she would have, on the night she confessed to the notes, if not for my strongly disapproving response. Tightness clutches at my throat.

"How did Geneviève know? I was careful to keep the plan from her." The words leave my mouth stiffly.

"She didn't know the exact date, but her sudden dismissal was taken as a clue. A correct one, as it turns out. She knew the queen disliked her and suspected her. Her days at Tuileries were numbered. I believe she had been watching Count von Fersen's household as well. He was instrumental in the planning, was he not? Geneviève befriended one of his footmen."

The more I hear, the more ludicrous it seems that any of us, Madame Campan, myself, the queen, ever believed the monarchs would truly make it to safety at Montmédy. There are no secrets in the palace, and besides, the plan was ill formed, too spontaneous and dependent on luck that they would not be recognized, that they would make good time, even though each of the royal party brought too many belongings, weighing down the too-large coach. My fingers start to tremble as anger snakes through me, coiling around my heart, spinning the blood to my ringing ears.

"You've taken far too much pleasure in telling me of this betrayal." The words burn my throat, hoarse and dry. "I deceived you—I won't deny that. It wasn't kind of me, when we had a partnership. If I truly believed your life was at risk, as the queen's was, perhaps I would have chosen differently. But we are still family, and I won't listen to you taunt me any longer with my failure. I don't need you crowing over me that you managed to outsmart me. I'd like you to leave now."

Uncle Pierre's face changes during my speech. As my voice gains strength and clarity, his eyes grow narrow, his mouth opening with outrage. Pink blotches appear high on his cheekbones. His manners are still too good to interrupt, but only barely.

"Taunt you? You silly girl, it's not that simple. I'm not mocking you for the failed escape—do you even realize the gravity of what you have done? The consequences of your choice? Thanks to your deception and a damnable postman in Varennes, I came out empty-handed on this. I made promises to protect us all, and now I'll have to explain—" He pinches the bridge of his nose and takes a deep breath. "I had reservations about the revolution at first, but no more. The king, and especially the queen, cannot be allowed to continue with their mindless frivolity." His usually soft voice rings with anger, jaws opening wide with each word.

Papa walks into the room, his calm strides providing a stark foil to my uncle's erratic hand gestures. "Pierre, you must leave our house now."

"I spoke too harshly," admits my uncle. "The revolution makes short tempers, even for me. I'm sorry if it sounded like I was attacking Giselle." He glances at me, but I don't see apology in his eyes, and his phrasing sidestepped it as well. His voice turns silky. "But I think we need to discuss this further, as a family. What Giselle did is very dangerous, for her, and for all of us. If it's found out that she aided their attempted escape, we will all be associated with her crime."

When Papa puts his hand on my shoulder, I feel the tension vibrating through his fingers, taut like harp strings, and I realize he is not calm at all, in spite of his smooth countenance.

"Charlotte and I are happy to be associated with our daughter, no matter what may happen. She did what she thought right, and I'm proud of her for it. If we choose to discuss it as a family, you will not be a participant. This is for immediate family only." He pauses, grimness drawing lines around the corners of his mouth. "It shall be some time before we see each other again, Pierre."

It must have been years since anyone resisted my uncle's commanding attitude, refused to defer to his belief in his greater knowledge. Hearing my father's dismissal, he actually stammers in shock, something I've never heard him do in my entire life. Papa easily herds him to the door, his movements steady but implacable. Uncle Pierre jams his hat over his gray hair and pauses on the threshold, throwing a sharp, broken glance toward me.

"What shall I tell Eugénie? She will want to see you."

I want to tell him that she can visit anytime, without him, but the sting of his betrayal still burns through my veins, and I choke on the words. He used me and Geneviève both, playing us unwittingly against each other, knowing it might destroy our friendship and doing it anyway. Scorn clears my throat, lets the words loose. "Tell Eugénie the truth." I turn my back on him, and Papa closes the door with a solid, final click.

"I've wanted to tell him to leave for a long time," says Papa, sighing. A weight seems to have been lifted from his shoulders, but he also looks tired. He follows me back into the parlor and gives me a gentle smile. "Facts are not wisdom, Giselle, and you have already learned it. I'm so proud of you."

Hope flickers in my chest, but it doesn't take away the aching loss of losing Léon. My heart feels like shards of broken glass. "I'm not proud of myself. I learned the lesson too late." My voice sounds as small as I feel.

"There's no such thing," says Papa firmly. "Better late than never—it may be often said, but it holds true. And I don't believe you were too late, anyway. You were true to your beliefs when it came down to a difficult choice. Not many have the courage to face themselves in that way."

I want to talk about Léon, to ask my father if he thinks Léon will ever forgive me, but a lump clogs my throat. After a moment I find other words instead. "How long have you wanted to evict Uncle Pierre from our house? I had no idea you felt that way."

He shrugs. "You're an adult now, Giselle, so I'll speak frankly to you. I've never liked Pierre, but we got along well enough for your mother's sake. However, even she has grown impatient with him lately. The political unrest is just the kind of thing he glories in, the precise situation to let him pretend he isn't an obsolete, unemployed old spy, but he takes it too far. We are people, not puppets, and he's not always right."

"Maman is impatient with him too?" I'm surprised—they always seemed to be fairly close siblings.

"Yes. He's always treated her with a certain degree of condescension, but she used to attribute it to the protective, slightly skewed, attitude of an older brother to his younger sister. She could handle it and didn't mind doing so. But she resented his use of you for his games of spy work."

"She did? Why didn't she say anything?"

Papa smiles gently. "I will let her answer that."

Maman crosses the threshold of the room. "I don't mean to lurk, but I didn't want to interrupt. I heard everything, of course. Pierre can be so loud. Giselle, you did well. Please don't fret over it." She folds me in her arms, a delicate, lavender-scented embrace that makes me feel like a child again, in a comforting way.

"I'll try." I pause. "Maman, did you want me to quit spying for Pierre?"

"I hoped you would," she says, her voice soft and sweet. "I understood it was exciting at first—even I felt it. But as time passed, and the unrest grew, along with Pierre's smugness, I thought it was unhealthy."

"Why didn't you say something?"

"I wanted to," chimes in Papa. "I wanted to forbid it." His mouth twitches in a chagrined smile. "Charlotte reminded me that being too strict and blunt would only further set you on that

course. She said I should wait and let you make your own choice."
He bends his head indulgently toward me, at the same time squeezing Maman's hand. "She was always confident you would make the right one. I should have known not to let even a flicker of doubt cross my mind."

"Thank you." It relieves me to know that they stand firmly by my side. In my months of being an under-tirewoman and a spy, I imagined so much pressure on myself, battering down on all sides from my family, the queen, Madame Campan, even Léon, but in the end it was myself I had to be true to. I try to smile, but sorrow anchors my face away from too much happiness, in spite of all their support. "Uncle Pierre was right, though, that I brought danger close to us. I'm sorry for that."

"You're unlikely to be implicated," says Papa reassuringly. "They'll go after people like Count von Fersen first, and blame the king and queen most of all."

"If it ever does come back to you, my darling, you won't be held too accountable," says Maman quietly. "You were only a tirewoman, after all, unable to stand up to the queen." The glint in her eyes shows the obliqueness of her statement. She doesn't undermine my ability to make a choice, my own strong-mindedness, but it's a possible defense. I hope I shall never have to use it.

"I hope no one is punished," I say with foolish optimism.

"We can pray for that," agrees Papa.

"I wish—" The words stop in my throat, crushed by vulnerability. I look at the floor and speak very carefully. "I wish Léon understood as well as you do."

Maman strokes my hair back from my forehead like she used to do when I had a nightmare and could not sleep. "He may come to understand, in time."

"And if he does not, he's not worthy of you," Papa says authoritatively.

I try to believe him, but it doesn't erase the pain in my heart.

✷

As the weeks pass and gossip spreads faster than a grass fire on a dry August day, I piece together most of the facts about the ill-fated flight to Varennes, only thirty miles from Montmédy.

Von Fersen himself drove the coach as far as Bondy. Unfortunately, the royal family was delayed only forty miles outside of Paris, for the necessity of coach repairs. This stroke of bad fortune meant they missed the relays at Varennes. Even if Louis hadn't been recognized by the postmaster, it was already a serious setback in their plans. Apparently, Léonard, the queen's hairdresser, had passed through Varennes a few hours earlier without incident, as had a few of the queen's ladies.

Marie Antoinette had tried to persuade the wife of the mayor of Varennes to aid them in their flight, explaining that she could help restore tranquility to France by doing so. Knowing the queen as I do, I find it easy to imagine the charm she would have demonstrated, the gentle desperation, the quiet logic. She often has a rare talent for winning people to her side, in person at least, for her skill seems not to extend to crowds. However, the lady declined sorrowfully, saying that even though she loved her king, she loved her husband more, and he'd be held at fault if she let the royal family continue their frantic journey. The queen didn't give up easily, and the party remained at Varennes for some hours. Some gossipers insinuate that she displayed her poor judgment and lack of connection to reality by fighting so long for a lost cause when the mayor clearly would not help, but I believe Marie Antoinette had another end in mind with her delays. She hoped to give the

Marquis de Bouillé time to travel to Varennes with his soldiers and extricate them from the terrible situation. How she must have mourned when he never came to rescue them.

⚜

Two things happen to me in early July, bringing unwelcome reminders of the drastic ways my life has changed.

One morning, a letter is delivered to our house, addressed to me. Written in Madame Campan's sturdy, elegant script, it invites me back into service as one of the queen's tirewomen at Tuileries. I cringe to imagine how the palace must now feel like a prison to Marie Antoinette, in spite of its size and luxury. There is even a scrawled sentence at the end, written in rich blue ink, in the queen's own hand. I recognize it from seeing papers on her desk. She briefly thanks me for previous service and expresses her desire to have loyal friends near her.

Maman and Papa both watch me carefully while I set the letter aside and sit near the window, thinking the offer over, although they try not to be obvious about it. Maman fusses over a roll of yarn, and Papa sharpens a pencil so thoroughly that the lead snaps.

"I'm not going back," I tell them, to their obvious but unspoken relief. Even knowing the queen must be worried and constantly be spied upon by her enemies, that she could perhaps find comfort in having friends near, I can't return. It might not be entirely logical, but I feel that if I go back, I will have lost Léon for nothing.

A week after the delivery of the letter, Maman persuades me to go for a walk to enjoy some fresh air. I find myself wandering listlessly down the rue du Faubourg Saint-Antoine. In spite of my stern self-instructions not to think of Léon, I can't help remembering all the times we walked along this street together, talking and laughing, reaching for each other's hands. We met on this street even, sharing the stolen bottle of wine, our connection immediate and profound.

I step around a vegetable cart, and my heart lurches into my throat. Léon is across the street, walking with another man about the same age. I'd recognize Léon anywhere, whether I could see his face or not. I know the smooth springiness of his steps, the length of his arms, the shape of his shoulders. His hair, always just a bit curly, seems shorter, but it still clings to the back of his neck in the same way.

He wears the sleek navy coat and red-trimmed white shirt of the national guard.

Rooted to the spot, I stare at him in disbelief. Léon never had any military aspirations, and it surprises me that he joined. Hazily, I find myself agreeing with Geneviève's prediction. He does look well in the uniform. It makes him seem taller and very alert. Too late, I realize the alertness is not merely an illusion granted by the clothing; his gaze fastens upon me. I feel it sharply, and the air clenches in my lungs. He pauses midstride, still watching me. His lips part as if to speak, but his companion says something. Léon turns to him, fast and frowning with impatience. Before he can look back, I spin on my heel and slink home. I'm not brave enough to face him.

Chapter Seventeen

"There's a letter for you." Papa hands me an envelope sealed with an untidy blob of wax. The envelope is a bit tattered, one corner bent, as if someone carried it in their pocket for a while before sending it. I recognize the elaborate curls of Geneviève's writing at once, but it surprises me just the same. It's been a month since her dismissal, since Varennes, and I feared our paths had diverged forever.

I do miss her, in spite of everything. We parted very suddenly, and so soon after the shocking revelation of her role in the anonymous notes. I don't want to leave things unresolved, and it occurs to me that Geneviève probably doesn't know I'd also been spying on the queen. My uncle would never have told her. He'd have preferred to keep us both in ignorance, quietly comparing the information we obediently fetched back to him. He used us both.

The wax crumbles under my fingers, and I slide the paper out of its grimy envelope. The tone of the letter recalls Geneviève's animated voice to my mind, and carries the same wistful quality that I feel. She asks if we might meet at the Champs de Mars in a couple of days.

*I miss you, my friend. I thought I would find you
in the Tuileries gardens one day, but after the pathetic
flight attempt of the monarchs, I hear you are no longer
in the queen's service either. One of the footmen told me
when I saw him near Café du Foy.*

I wonder if it's the same footman who helped her monitor
Count von Fersen's plans as well, but it doesn't matter. It's over
now.

Briefly, I explain the contents of the note to my parents, who
are making little effort to disguise their curiosity.

A worried line creases Maman's forehead. "Are you certain? She
won't like that you took the queen's side."

"I won't tell her. I'll pretend I knew nothing about it." My
experience with Léon has filled me with caution. "I plan to never
tell anyone of my role in the flight to Varennes, ever. And I do want
to see her. We were very close while working at the palace, and
I miss my friend."

"I understand," says Maman.

"Be careful," says Papa. "There have been riots lately."

I manage a wry smile. "Nothing I haven't seen before." How
odd, that riots should have become almost an ordinary event.

On the morning of July seventeenth, I dress myself in tricolor,
preparing to meet Geneviève at the Champs de Mars. I've mostly
been wearing old housedresses in muted grays and browns while
holed up at home, and the boldness of the scarlet sash and the bril-
liant blue trim on my white dress feels startlingly bright.

Geneviève outdoes me in terms of revolutionary garb, however.
In spite of the exuberant crowd milling around the Champs de
Mars, I spot her almost at once at our agreed-upon meeting place,
in the southeast corner, a little away from most of the people. A

jaunty tricolor ribbon festoons her hair, and she has sewn red-white-and-blue-striped trim along the sleeves, hem, and waist of her dress.

"Giselle, how lovely to see you." Her exclamation sounds joyful, and her eyes glitter with all their old roguishness. She squeezes my hand, brief but fierce, tugging me closer to her and away from the meandering steps of a group of middle-aged women moving past us, arguing loudly over a petition. She has started using a new scent, I notice, something green and peppery, very different from the lily perfume she favored before.

"Hello, Geneviève."

She lets go of my hand, her exuberance fading into awkwardness. We stare at each other in silence.

"I confess, I'm glad you're not still in the employ of the *Citoyenne*," she says eventually, "Did she ask you back after Varennes? I bet she did, even after she turned tail and ran, leaving you without a job." Her nose wrinkles with scorn.

Relief settles over me like a warm cloak. Geneviève doesn't know that I helped to orchestrate the escape. Or if she does, she's going to pretend ignorance, and that's good enough for me right now. I need my friend.

Her smile wavers until I grin back at her, and then all of a sudden everything feels normal between us again.

"As if I would return after that. I'm rather sorry I had the night off when they fled. I'd have liked to witness all the panic and flabbergasted stammering in the morning, when the lady-in-waiting went to wake the queen and found that great big bed empty. Afterward, once they had returned to Tuileries, Madame Campan did write me a letter, asking me back."

"And clearly, you declined. I'm glad," says Geneviève. "It feels right that neither of us serve *her* anymore, when she tried to run away from it all. How cowardly—you know, I never liked her much, but I did think she had a sort of stiff-backed royal pride. I must have been mistaken. It seems at odds with the attempted escape."

"I thought so too." I am afraid to say too much on the subject. Greater verbosity increases the chance for me to slip up in the lie. I nod seriously to counteract my lack of elaboration, which seems to be enough for Geneviève. She slants a glance toward me. "I nearly forgot—you had an assignation with Léon that night, did you not? Did you go to the inn I suggested?" Her face is bright with girlish curiosity.

"Yes," I say unwillingly. It feels like talking through ice. "I don't want to talk about him, though."

She pats my shoulder, clucking with sympathy. "What happened? You two seemed deeply in love. I never expected you to call off your wedding. Léon simply told Étienne that the two of you wanted different things, and refused to speak more of it. Lord, the man can scowl. Even Étienne hardly dared inquire further."

Léon certainly can glower with notable fierceness. The memory of his thundercloud expression and black eyes during our last meeting frequently slips into my mind, especially at night when I restlessly fail to sleep. "He's right. We're very different people, as it turns out." The words are heavy to push from my throat, and fall into the air with a clipped, final tone.

"And you won't say anything more either?"

"No."

"Well, maybe someday you'll wish to talk of it. When the heartache has eased. Or when the two of you are reconciled?" Her small, hopeful smile withers when I shake my head. "I should warn you, then: Léon and Étienne may be here today, somewhere. They're both on duty as members of the national guard, and there seems to be a number of them here at the Champs de Mars this afternoon." She hesitates, voice growing even gentler. "Did you know he joined the national guard? I think it must have been after you ended your engagement."

"I know. I saw him once, on the rue du Faubourg Saint-Antoine. He was wearing his uniform." I clear my throat, as if doing so will magically infuse my voice with a carefree tone, erasing the miserable edge I can't quite keep out. "Remember when you guessed he would look well in one? You were right."

"Did you speak?" Her eyes grow wide. Her wish for our reconciliation is touching, or at least it would be if I didn't know our relationship was battered beyond repair.

"No," I say to the ground. "I avoided him."

"Oh." She is quiet for a moment. "Well, let's not talk about it now. I understand you don't want to." Her tone brightens as she seizes onto a new topic. "You must have heard the announcement this morning, that Louis will remain king of France under a constitutional monarchy?"

"Yes. I was surprised." The king is greatly despised for his perceived attempt to abandon his people, and the queen is hated even more. Many people, including myself, had speculated that he would be removed from office entirely. His power had been greatly reduced by the constitution and the political upheaval, and his title was technically abolished, but he still holds a significant role as the head of state. People can't seem to stop thinking of him as the king, in spite of the new laws, myself included. It's interesting to think that he might yet lose the position. Rumors had been flying that his brother, the Comte de Provence, would be the new ruler instead, or that the dauphin would succeed his father with the help of revolutionary advisers, given his tender age.

Geneviève knows each of these rumors but tosses them aside.

"Why do we need a king at all? What if the Assembly governed the nation?"

"A radical idea," I say doubtfully, but it is an intriguing one, too.

"The Americans are doing it," Geneviève points out. "Although it hasn't really been very long yet since their revolution. I suppose it's early to say if the system is effective. I have high hopes for a republic, though."

"Like the Romans."

"Yes. The fashions are taking a hint from the Romans; why not government, too?"

"Maybe we'll even get bathhouses," I joke, but Geneviève is not easy to scandalize and perks up at the thought.

"I should like to bathe in a pool with a fountain. It sounds very decadent. Anyway, back to serious matters. Not everyone is pleased with the announcement. They think Louis has had his last chance to lead the country. *Citoyen* Desmoulins and *Citoyen* Danton are going around with a petition to call for the removal of the king."

I remember meeting Desmoulins at the Café du Foy. He quoted Cicero and seemed very idealistic. Danton, I have never met, but his name is a prominent one in Jacobin circles, and his roughhewn features are frequently sketched in the papers.

"Where?" I ask curiously.

"Here—at the Champs de Mars. That's why it's so crowded. Isn't it lucky we came here today? We may see history in the making."

"We've done that already, at Versailles."

She laughs, breathless and exhilarated. "I know. These are exciting times, Giselle. Come on. Let's walk around and see if we can find them. Do you think women will be allowed to sign the petition?"

As she sets off toward the bustle of people, moving quickly, I follow with rather less enthusiasm. I still believe that change must correct our country's many social and economic problems—no matter how much Léon believes I've changed sides, it's not true. However, I've already been caught in the turmoil of two riots, and have no desire to be whirled into the midst of another. As Geneviève and I stalk through the moving crowd, twisting between clusters of people, I hear talk of the petition all around me, and people shouting about the monarchs, varying from declarations of loyalty to those of harsh castigation. The mood of the crowd seems volatile, and I begin to think that Geneviève and I ought to leave the area. She nods distractedly, eyes scanning the sea of people. "All right. After we see about the petition, we can go wherever you like."

It doesn't take long to cross paths with Desmoulins and Danton. As the two of them are gesturing wildly from the top of some steps and shouting out impassioned speeches to reel in more petitioners, we'd have to be blind and deaf not to notice them. The crowd surges around them, roiling like bubbles in a hot kettle, and making nearly as much noise as the two revolutionaries with cries of mingled praise and arguments. Geneviève and I keep our distance.

She bites her lip, looking a little crestfallen. "It doesn't look like we'll get close enough to sign. Maybe if we wait awhile?"

"I don't think so." Grabbing her arm, I point toward another face familiar to us, the Marquis de Lafayette, flanked by the national guard under his command. "They're marching toward the petitioners, and they look grim."

"I suppose they'll break up the crowd. I saw Étienne briefly just after lunch, and he said they already dispersed the petitioners this morning. It didn't stop them for long, of course. I think there must be twice as many now. He was rather disappointed—he approves of the petition, but he still has to obey commands from Lafayette, who leads the Guard."

"We should leave." Tightening my fingers on Geneviève's arm, I drag her away a few paces. Even though the crowd seems to be growing increasingly hostile at the sight of the national guard, she moves reluctantly.

"I want to watch," she says.

"We can from farther away," I bargain, moving faster. We have little time to waste. The situation escalates tangibly around us, taking my heart rate with it. My pulse hammers and my nerves jolt. Out of the corner of my eye, I see a nearby petitioner, mouth curled into a snarl, bend to pick up a loose stone. "It's going to be a riot in moment."

"Not this time," says Geneviève, but her brows quirk with doubt. "Where's Étienne?" Her gaze flicks past the press of people, peering between their heads and above their shoulders. "I hope he'll be all right."

Lafayette's voice rises above the hubbub, recognizable because it's rich with command. He volleys orders like one accustomed to absolute obedience. The members of the national guard with him surge forward, muskets raised toward the sky like empty flagstaffs. They march toward the petitioners, intending to scatter them away. I think I see Léon, and my heart lurches at the sight of his dark glittering eyes, winged brows, and long proud nose, but then the sweep of the crowd snatches him from my view, and Geneviève yanks on my hand, pulling me out of the way of a rampaging man, red-faced and angry with the presence of the national guard. I feel bereft, though I saw him so quickly that it may not have been Léon at all, only a desperate conjuring of my lonely imagination.

Lafayette's voice rises in another order for the crowd to disperse.

A few people near Geneviève and me obey him, and we move along with them, putting distance between us and the more fervent petitioners. Most of them root themselves to the spot, though, facing the national guard with rebellion. Lafayette commands them to leave again, and a stone flies through the air, bouncing roughly off the shoulder of one of the soldiers. More rocks follow, hurled with vicious strength by the riled-up protesters.

"Warning shots!" yells Lafayette. Before the echo of his stark command fades, the muskets crackle skyward, the sharp rumble leaving trails of smoke in its wake.

"They'll depart now," says Geneviève, but she herself seems frozen on the spot, staring fearfully, fascinated by the mad spectacle and fearful for Étienne. I understand her expression, because I feel the same way. I scan endlessly for Léon, but the soldiers all look the same from here.

The crowd doesn't disperse, and instead crushes forward, infuriated. More stones soar through the air, many of them finding meaty targets. One of the soldiers visibly grabs his head and stumbles, and Geneviève and I squeeze each other's hands, both praying it was not Étienne or Léon who was struck.

In the noise and the panic, I can't hear Lafayette's next words, but his voice rises and falls. The muskets spit fire and thunder again, and it takes me a disbelieving second to comprehend that the smoke spirals low, not circling into the sky like before, and the shrill pitch of screams harshly contrasts with the deep sound of the gunfire. Several petitioners stagger and fall. I watch as one man's white shirt slowly turns to match his red coat before his companions grab his shoulders and drag him from my view.

"We have to go." I turn to Geneviève, but she doesn't need my warning, and our feet already take us farther away from the scene.

My hand grips hers so tight that I feel like my fingers will be stiff forever, and my heart hammers so hard, I fancy I can see my pulse in the corners of my eyes.

"Oh God," whimpers Geneviève, half-running with me alongside her. Gunfire snaps again. "All those people. Étienne—"

"We'll find them later," I vow, quickening our pace until we're running, our skirts twisting around our legs, tendrils of our hair flying like flags of retreat.

When we stop at last, our lungs heave and Geneviève's face gleams with perspiration, almost red enough to match her hair. My skin feels wet too, and my hair clings to my forehead.

"I can't run anymore. I need to rest," Geneviève says, and gasps. We stagger over to a wooden bench near a green hedge and collapse into the rough seat. I want to talk about what just happened, but I don't know where to start or what to say. Geneviève must have the same struggle, because she leans her head back, though her eyes remain open and her face has a pinched look, and says nothing.

"My parents will be worried," I say at last. "I ought to get home."

"Mine too," she says. Neither of us move.

"When you see Étienne, will you ask him about Léon?"

"If I see him." She licks her lips. "If he's alive."

I sit up straight, rounding on her. "Of course he is. He's strong and brave, and he'll be fine." She looks comforted by my optimistic words, thankfully.

"I'll ask," she promises.

In spite of knowing we ought to go straight home, we stay on the bench for a long time, dazed. We find words, eventually, to cautiously speak of the terrible event we witnessed, and narrowly escaped.

"A massacre," says Geneviève.

"A catastrophe," I add.

"Étienne supported the petitioners, in his heart. To be forced to fire upon them . . ." She fades into silence again.

I don't know Léon's mind on this, not now, but I suspect he felt the same way. "They thought they were helping the revolution by joining the national guard. Léon always admired Lafayette for his role in the American Revolution."

"So did Étienne. How things have changed." She sighs heavily.

Finally, when the setting sun makes angled beams of light and velvet shadows, we leave our strange haven of the bench and start for home, walking quickly.

"Can we stop at the Soleil d'Or on the way?" asks Geneviève. "It's a public house on rue Saint-Antoine, not far from the old Bastille. I understand if you don't want to. It's just that Étienne frequents it, and if he was released from duty for the day, I think he may have gone straight there."

"I'll come with you." Even though the idea of talking to Léon frightens me, lest he accuse me of being a royalist, of being a liar, I must know he's safe.

We lurk outside the door of the Soleil d'Or, uncertain if we should go in. I've never been to a place that sells liquor, and I feel awkward. I'm not sure it's proper. The few women inside seem to be accompanied by men.

"I've never gone without Étienne," says Geneviève, squinting through the open doorway as a man in a black hat passes through.

I lift my chin, feigning confidence. "Let's just go in. Walk confidently, like you go there every day, and likely no one will question us."

"Maybe," she says dubiously.

"Geneviève?"

She whirls around at the sound of her name and dashes straight into Étienne's arms as he approaches the public house. His companion slows at his side and turns his head toward me. I recognize him instantly, with a flare of joy I can't suppress.

Léon's face is paler than I have ever seen it, and somehow looks thinner, the skin drawn tight with tension. His dark hair sticks up at the back, as though he's clutched at it with restless fingers. As I watch, he drags them through his hair, the movement distracted and anguished. He watches Geneviève embracing Étienne, murmuring to him so rapidly as to be incomprehensible, and then his eyes dart to me, and to the ground.

I approach him slowly, like one would a skittish horse. "Are you all right, Léon?" My voice sounds more tremulous than I would like.

He looks up at me, and his lustrous brown eyes are filled with shadows, which spill all across his features, curling around under his eyes in purple streaks, making his cheekbones stark against his pale skin. Without thinking, I close the gap between us and gently put my arms around him. For a split second, as his shoulders tense under my hands, I think he'll push me away and I brace myself for the humiliation. His breath empties in a shuddering sigh, and he hugs me back, wrapping his arms around me so hard that I'm wrenched closer to him.

"I killed a man, Giselle." His voice sounds hoarse, and his lips are crushed to my neck, as if he could muffle the words and make them somehow not true.

My hand strokes circles on his back, sliding up to his hair. "Sh," I whisper. "It's not your fault. You had to obey the command."

He draws back enough to see my face, his gaze piercing mine. "I wish it were so simple. The order was given, and I obeyed. I pulled the trigger. I watched the blood spill from a man's heart, and I wished I'd never fired. Even if I aimed badly instead, it would've been better. . . ."

I cup his cheeks in my hands, looking into his beloved face, wishing he would not feel such torment, loving him because he does. My Léon is an idealist, a craftsman, not a soldier. He is still the same man I loved. *And betrayed,* whispers something cruel in me, but I tug the painful thought free like a splinter.

"I don't even have very good aim." He sounds confused. "If it were target practice, I would have called it a lucky shot. Lucky!"

"You were a soldier acting under command. It wasn't your fault," I say again, although I know it won't make him feel differently. I don't know if there is anything I can say to ease his spirits, but I keep trying.

"I can't—I don't know—oh, Giselle." His voice cracks under the struggle to find the words to explain his current torment, and then he gives up. His eyes close as his arms squeeze my waist, and then his mouth crashes down on mine. It is not a soft kiss, nor gentle. It's desperate and fierce, and even as my mouth opens under his and I moan at the feel of his tongue stroking mine, I know he's seeking forgetfulness, something to momentarily banish the sight of the blood from his mind.

He nips my lower lip a little too hard, and it makes me squeak in protest. He lifts his head, though I don't want him to. My hands still curl around the back of his neck.

"Sorry," he whispers. Red flushes his cheeks now, and his eyes gleam too bright. "I shouldn't have used you like that."

"You didn't use me. You can't take advantage of the willing. I want to help you, Léon."

He does not speak, and something in his expression softens, triggering a leap of hope inside me.

Behind us, Étienne's voice carries loudly. "We can blame *l'Autrichienne* for this, too, if you ask me. She's probably got Lafayette in her pocket, just like von Fersen and dozens of others. . . ."

"You can't help me," says Léon. His voice has gone as hard as granite again. "I'm sorry." He releases me and stalks away so quickly that he might as well have shoved me away.

My heart cracks anew and my cheeks burn painfully hot. Blinking hard, refusing to let anyone see a single tear fall from my eyes, I go to Geneviève.

"I saw you kissing—engaged again?" asks Geneviève brightly, before she sees my face. "Never mind."

"I'm going home. I'll see you soon—be careful, all right?" I turn on my heel and walk as fast as I can before she can respond. I need to be alone.

❦

Over the following days, the newspapers have varying accounts of the number of casualties in the massacre at the Champs de Mars. Some wrote that a dozen had been killed, others that the dead numbered fifty.

"Some of them may be recording injuries as casualties," says Papa.

"To make it sound more disastrous?" I ask.

"Perhaps. It could also simply be poor reporting."

One thing all the papers have in common, except any royalist publications, is that they roundly blame Lafayette for the disaster. As the leader of the national guard, he already faced some blame for the king and queen's escape attempt, and now that he ordered the Guards to fire on a crowd of petitioners, he looked like the most devout of royalists, and was condemned by all revolutionaries.

Chapter Eighteen

As winter approaches, I avoid politics as much as possible, but it's not easy when new changes occur almost daily. In September another new constitution is proclaimed, and after swearing to uphold it, King Louis is restored to power. Popular opinion seems to be that he'll keep that promise, but I know the most fervent revolutionaries believe he'll continue to be as ineffectual as ever. For the queen's sake, I'm glad of her husband's restoration. It gives her a reprieve against the worst of the gossip. The government changes again too, and the two-year session of the National Constituent Assembly gives way to the new Legislative Assembly. As a constitutional monarchy, it's supposed to have greater representation of the people, but only the richest taxpayers are able to elect deputies and representatives to the district councils. I imagine the outrage Léon must feel about the latter, but I try not to think about him too often. I don't have much success.

In October the Marquis de Lafayette resigns as Commander of the national guard. His reputation never recovered since the flight to Varennes and the massacre on the Champs de Mars, and his voluntary removal from the post is generally looked upon with

favor. Geneviève and Étienne laud his absence and look forward
to the future. As has become routine for me, I try to remain aloof,
but sometimes I feel a private kinship with Lafayette. Although I
don't know his true motivations, I imagine he's like me, trying to
do the right thing and please everybody, and failing miserably. Perhaps he will be happier with less involvement, although it hasn't
happened for me. My life is more peaceful now, but not happier.

One day in late January, when I'm walking home empty-handed
from the bakery, I spy Maximilien de Robespierre striding down
the street toward me. His broad forehead and catlike eyes make
him easy to recognize. I intend to pass without speaking—after
all, we met only once at Café du Foy and it was a long time ago.
However, his step hitches as he passes me, and he turns around.

"Mademoiselle, I know you. You're affianced to Léon Gauvain.
Do me a favor, will you? Tell him I have moved."

"Oh, I suppose he hasn't told you—" I try to say, but Robespierre seems in a hurry and speaks over me, edging his feet down
the sidewalk.

"After the dreadful events at the Champs de Mars, I feared for
my safety, and I wanted to be nearer to the Assembly and the
Jacobin club. Tell him to ask Maurice Duplay; he can give him
directions. I'd be much obliged to you." He marches off, then
pauses to look back once more. "Tell him, please, to bring my
copy of Rousseau, as well. I lent it to him."

The strange interview leaves me with many questions, the chief
of which is if Robespierre knows that Léon was one of the national
guards at the Champs de Mars. I'm curious, too, about the loaned
book. Have Léon and Robespierre become such great friends? I
suppose I'll have to ask Geneviève.

A woman with a bouquet of tricolor rosettes pinned to her hat
stops me. "Was that Robespierre? The Incorruptible?"

"Er, yes." It's strange to refer to him by the nickname the papers sometimes use, gleaned from his well-known beliefs in revolutionary virtue based on the writings of Rousseau.

"And you know him? How remarkable. Do you think you could introduce me? I'm so curious about his opinion on the threat of war with Austria, and other countries against our revolution. Is it true that he believes France is ill prepared?"

"France *is* ill prepared," I say, thinking of the chaos of the government and Louis's chronic indecisiveness. Then I remember my personal vow to stay out of politics, and bite the rest of the words off short. "I'm sure Monsieur Robespierre has great knowledge on the subject. I don't know him well—I'm merely to pass on a message for him, but if you hurry, perhaps he will speak to you."

Before she can reply, I lengthen my strides and duck around the corner. If I ask her, Geneviève will give the message to Léon through Étienne, though I know it's the coward's choice and I ought to go see Léon myself. I've worried about him constantly since our last meeting after the massacre at the Champs de Mars, and although Geneviève assures me he is well, I want to see for myself. I still care about him.

I don't know how his schedule has changed since joining the national guard, but I know he still works at the watchmaker's shop, so I stop there before going home.

Léon's eyes widen in surprise to see me strolling through the doorway. The shadows under his eyes are accentuated by the dark, nondescript clothing he wears while working behind the counter.

"*Citoyenne* Aubry, what can I do for you today?" he asks.

A frisson of annoyance skips over me. "Hello, Léon." I deliberately refuse to match his formal style of greeting. "Are you well?" I clearly remember the trauma he felt after the massacre at the Champs de Mars, and have been worrying for him.

"Quite, thank you. Are you looking for a watch?"

"No. I came to see you."

A flare of intrigue gleams in his eyes, but he watches me silently, waiting for elaboration. The intensity of it makes me uncomfortable, longing desperately for our previous close relationship, and I speak too quickly as consequence.

"I have a message for you, from Robespierre." Rambling, I pass along all of the information, including the loaned book. "I was surprised to hear you borrowed a copy of Rousseau from him. I thought you had your own."

"He'd written his own notes in the margins. I wanted to read his interpretations."

"Oh." The word hangs. "I wasn't aware you knew him so well."

"We've met at Café du Foy a few more times." His shoulder twitches in a casual shrug, which irritates me. It feels like he is dismissing me.

"You must not be too well acquainted. He addressed me as your fiancée." Seeing the flicker of vulnerability crack across his stern expression gives me a perverse sort of satisfaction, though I'm not proud of it. At least I'm not the only one hurting here.

"We don't speak much of our personal lives," he says stiffly. "I haven't seen him in a long while. No wonder he's anxious for the return of his book."

"You must be very busy," I say. "With the national guard duties and your apprenticeship combined."

"I completed my apprenticeship, actually." For the first time he sounds natural, and proud, too. "Monsieur Renard agreed to let me stay on here for a while to increase my savings. We're doing a brisk trade in watches with tricolor designs on the face."

"That was your idea, wasn't it?" I say, delighted. "I'm so glad to hear they are a success."

"Thank you. I'm allowed an extra percentage of all profits on those watches, since I designed them. With my duties in the national guard three days a week, I hardly have time to spend any of the money, so it's a help to my savings." He hesitates. "I want to set up my own shop."

"I know." Sadness settles over me. His plan hasn't changed. If we were still a couple, we'd live together now, pooling our savings to open the shop. I could be sewing dresses of my own design while he fabricated new watches or repaired old ones. How things have gone wrong.

"And you? Are you designing fashions, like you always wanted?"

"No," I admit reluctantly.

"You should. Not for royalty anymore. That's over. But practical clothing, while still fashionable—that will always be needed."

"I miss you, Léon." As soon as the words escape my lips, I wish I could take them back and choke on them. I hadn't meant to bare my emotions before him.

He looks down, and his throat ripples as he swallows. When he meets my eyes again, his expression is guarded once more. "I miss the way we were. I wish it wasn't lost."

"Will you ever forgive me?" The words whisper across my lips, which feel as dry as parchment.

He stares into me. "I don't know."

"Can we at least be friends?"

"I don't think so."

I grit my teeth to hide the sudden tremble in my lips. "Congratulations again on your success." Turning on my heel, I reach for the doorknob. The bell clangs as I toss the door closed, and I fancy for a second that I hear my name. I don't look back, though. It seems unlikely that Léon truly called out to me, and I can't embarrass myself further by looking back to see proof of it.

❧

In April, Geneviève comes to see me at home, a rarity, for we usually just walk around, talking.

"Things are looking up," she says, spreading a pale blue skirt over her lap and picking up her embroidery needle.

"I wouldn't say that. There have been food riots for the last three months, and they say Austria will declare war on France any day."

"True, but these problems were caused by poor leadership, and the king has formed a new government. Most of the ministers are Jacobins, so that ought to push things in the right direction."

"I hope so." It seems heartening news. "If the revolutionary and royalist factions can begin to work together, perhaps it will make improvements. Assuming they can agree on anything, that is."

"As long as the royalists don't have too much sway over the decisions," she temporizes. "Did you hear about the new manner of executions? That contraption called a guillotine?"

"Yes, a highwayman was executed that way, I heard."

"What a strange idea," muses Geneviève. "An invention to slice off a person's head as efficiently as possible. They say it's painless, over in the blink of an eye."

"How could anyone know that without experiencing it?"

"Doctors know these things," says Geneviève confidently. "It's supposed to be the most humane method of carrying out the death penalty."

"Apparently they catch the head in a little basket." I wrinkle my nose. "A rather gruesome idea."

"Better than letting it roll around the ground like a chicken's." Geneviève snorts. "Oh drat, I ruined that stitch. I'll have to pull it out, or the butterfly I'm embroidering will be crooked." She lifts the cloth close to her face. "Have you gone to see Léon again yet?"

"You know I haven't," I say resentfully. "Hiding behind your sewing so you cannot see my annoyance doesn't mean it isn't there, you know."

She drops the material into her lap. "You should. I remember it didn't go well last time, at least according to you, but I still think it sounds like he misses you. Besides, I happen to know from Étienne that he never pays any attention to other girls. He's utterly thrown himself into his work. Étienne says he's grown quite dull. I think he means lovesick. Men never know the right words."

"There is a rather significant difference between the two." My voice sounds tart.

"You won't know until you find out, will you?" Geneviève is never fazed by my sharpest responses.

※

In May the leaves are out on the trees, bathing the streets in gold-green light, an appearance far more soothing than the political situation. Whether by the advice of his Jacobin ministers or not, the king declared war on Austria. They say he stood before the Legislative Assembly with an expression of rather vacant sadness, and made the declaration in the same flat tone he might have used for announcing the time of a meal to be served.

So far the state of war hasn't changed much of daily life, but I fret over the idea that the national guard will be sent to meet the Austrian armies, and Léon will have to go with them.

There's little I can do, though, so I focus on keeping my hands busy, sewing, and even making a few of my own designs. When I am not sewing, I read or help Maman with the household chores. I'm arranging flowers in a vase to brighten the parlor when I hear a knock at the door. Expecting canvassers for the poor, I go to open

it. Maman and Papa have gone out, and no one has been invited
to visit.

To my astonishment, Madame Campan shuffles awkwardly
on the step, her usually serene countenance marred by an uncomfortable frown. Her hands twitch inside the fur muff she carries.
"Hello, Giselle. May I come in?"

"What brings you here, Madame?" I don't think I quite hide
my surprise, but I open the door wider and move aside to let her
cross the threshold.

"I merely wanted to call on you. We were sorry you declined
to return to the queen's household."

By "we," I surmise she means to include the queen herself, for
I had no other close friends there besides Geneviève.

"I was grateful for the invitation but not inclined to take up
my old post."

"May I sit down?" she asks. "It was a long walk here. My legs
aren't accustomed to such a long journey."

She doesn't seem out of breath, but I lead her to the parlor and
direct her to the best chair, near the window.

"Thank you, Giselle." She folds her hands in her lap. "Are you
certain you won't reconsider? You're still welcome in Her Majesty's
household."

"Thank you, but I'm unlikely to change my mind."

"The queen's household is not what it used to be, I'm afraid,"
says Madame Campan, as if I had asked for details. "So many
people absent, and she dares not appoint new people, lest the old
household become obsolete. The court rituals are falling by the
wayside. It's a sad thing. Not everyone understands, of course; they
never do perceive the intricacies of Her Majesty's life. Many of the
remaining court ladies sulk because they haven't been appointed

into the empty roles in the queen's household, but how could they be? Others may return."

"Is that likely?" I ask, rather gratified to hear I am not the only one who did not return after Varennes.

"Perhaps. The Princesse de Lamballe returned. She fled after Varennes, being fearful for her safety, but she obeyed the queen's summons to return to Paris. They always were dear friends. She brought a dog for the queen, a little red-and-white spaniel. The queen calls it Mignon." Madame Campan pauses and watches for my reaction.

Still rather startled by her presence, and by her verbosity, I find it difficult to think of a reply. "She is very fond of her pets," I say neutrally, remembering the cats and dogs that lived at Versailles.

"Yes, more so now than ever. She takes comfort in them, I believe." She leans forward confidentially. "The queen is so lonely and so fearful. The princesse almost didn't return, because after Madame invited her back, she changed her mind and wrote a letter, begging her to stay away from the 'mouth of the tiger' here in Paris, where there are so many worries for her and the children. I was quite glad when the princesse eventually agreed to come back to Paris anyway. It's been good for the queen to have a friend with her again."

"She's fortunate to have you."

"How kind of you to say, my dear. I've missed you, Giselle. I could always count on you. Are you certain you won't come back?"

"I prefer a quiet life these days."

"Ah, but you're so young. Not like the queen . . . Her hair has turned white these last months, transformed by sorrow and worry."

Since I recall her hair had been fading and taking on gray

threads for months, I find this cause hard to believe, but I cluck sympathetically.

Madame Campan seizes on this speck of empathy. "I hoped you would understand. The queen liked you, and that means something. She didn't get to know most of her tirewomen very well, not when there were so many people at court already. But she noticed you."

Restlessly, I stand and pace in front of Madame Campan's chair. It's my own house, so she can't chastise me for rudeness. "Why are you telling me all of this?"

"Because we want you to come back to the Tuileries," she says baldly. "I can offer you a greater salary than previously, and a bonus for each month that you stay on."

"Have things grown so desperate at court, then?" A sardonic tone creeps into my voice.

Madame Campan meets my eyes, her expression serious and serene. "Yes. Please reconsider. You have plans to marry, don't you? You could undoubtedly use the extra money for your trousseau."

I don't bother correcting her about my marriage. It's true the income could be useful. My parents have always been reasonably well off, but the rising food prices are taking a toll, and Papa spends longer going over the account books than he used to, hunched over with frown lines on his face. He always tells me not to worry, and I have offered to work as a seamstress, but so far he has always turned down the suggestion.

"You have my interest," I say, careful to keep my tone flat, to disguise my thoughts. "But I still don't understand why you want me. I'm a good tirewoman, but not extraordinary. I know that."

"You are loyal, and that is a great virtue in these turbulent times."

"I have revolutionary friends and family members," I say. I almost want to tell her that I spied on them all for months and no one suspected, but I bite my tongue. "I understand their cause."

Her mouth twitches. "That may be so, but you also risked yourself to help the queen. Your actions have well proved your loyalty. Even if you have doubts about the monarchy, it's still more than can be found among most qualified ladies nowadays. Also, you're observant, and the queen is surrounded by enemies. You are needed, Giselle. Please come back."

I tell myself the money is the lure, not that I'm growing bored with reading philosophy and sitting at home. That I'm curious to see the changes wrought at court after the disaster of Varennes, not that there's a slim chance that Léon may think I have resumed my spy work and be more inclined to forgive me. I know it's a lie. Even crumbling, court is still alluring. "How much of a monthly bonus?" I ask.

※

A week later I return to Tuileries, resuming my old position as one of the queen's wardrobe women, although with a few more privileges and better wages. My parents weren't enthusiastic at first, but the new salary impressed them. Before going, I tell Geneviève I need the money, which is true, but also that I want to help the revolution from the inside. She believes me with ease—after all, she did it—but tells me that the queen has ceased to matter, and it would hardly be worth it. I suspect she's right.

Chapter Nineteen

In the streets and corners, people whisper that the queen has grown so hated that she'd be ripped apart if sent alone into the Legislative Assembly, and she looks as if she knows it. As Madame Campan described, Marie Antoinette's hair is quite white now, as wispy and pale as summer clouds. The color isn't shocking, for she used to powder her hair liberally, but the thin, dry quality of it is. She dresses it more simply than she used to, and it ages her.

So, too, does her new posture. Not as ramrod straight as previously, her shoulders hunch forward protectively, and she has picked up a habit of glancing around her, eyes flicking nervously. Her smile is still charming, though, on the rare occasions she finds it. She greets me very elegantly, and with apparently genuine warmth.

"We're glad to have you back, Giselle. Are your quarters comfortable?"

This time, I've been given my own room. It's in a small corner, with a stained ceiling where a leak trickled through the plaster, but I tugged the small bed to the other side of the room in case it happens again, and have found it comfortable enough. I suspect one of the main reasons I'm able to have my own room is because

there are far fewer servants now, although Madame Campan tries
to elevate the privacy to a special status granted to me for consent-
ing to return.

"Yes, thank you, Your Majesty. I feel myself quite at home." In
truth, the room is depressing, and the solitude reminds me of the
jokes that Geneviève and I used to share before going to bed. The
small lie seems to please her though. The corners of her eyes crin-
kle as the faintest of smiles crosses her face.

"Excellent." She pauses, shuffling her feet, clad in violet shoes.
Purple always was one of her favorite colors. "I thought you might
help me sew a dress for Mousseline," she says, referring to her
daughter. "She's thirteen now, and growing fast. I want one of my
old dresses to be made over for her."

I bow my head deeply; a curtsy seems too formal now. "Of
course, Your Majesty. I organized the wardrobe this morning, and
there are some dresses with very lovely cloth. Which color do you
prefer for her?"

She gnaws on her lip. "I haven't decided. Perhaps something
green? It would suit her."

"I'll select a few items and bring them to you to make the final
decision," I promise. There was a time when she would have known
exactly which ones she wanted, and selected them by putting pins
in the vast book of clothing swatches. She's too distracted now to
think of these things.

"Yes, do that." She goes to the window and stares out into the
courtyard, for so long that I think she doesn't see the cobblestones
or the people strolling around. Catching Madame Campan's worried gaze, I press my lips together sympathetically and take my
leave.

Being back at court feels odd. I continue to observe small details and pay close attention to Marie Antoinette, spying out of

habit, even though I have no one to report to, and little interest in doing so. Tuileries is bursting with spies these days anyway, most of them utterly lacking in subtlety. Since the ill-fated flight to Varennes, every footman and scullery maid watches the king and queen like hounds slavering over rabbits, fancying they might be the first to discover another escape plot, and thus be a savior to the nation. I wonder who they all report to. Some of them surely must be here at Robespierre's behest. As his reputation as the Incorruptible has grown, so too has his power.

One day a guard overhears Marie Antoinette talking about a project for June, and leaps to the conclusion that she means another escape attempt, perhaps for the one-year anniversary of Varennes. The atmosphere of mistrust and panic is so great that he actually succeeds in having the royal family confined to their rooms for twenty-four hours. I end up being confined as well, trapped in the inner chambers of the queen's apartments, and the ludicrous incompetence of the incident loses any potential amusement after I've missed a few hours of sleep and have been forced to watch Marie Antoinette's transition from ineffective anger to desperate resignation and finally to stark helplessness.

"As if the queen would be so foolish as to refer to another attempt to flee to safety as a 'little plan for June.'" Madame Campan scoffs, her breath hissing through her teeth in annoyance. "The people have gone mad, I think."

"Is there another plan to get the royal family to safety?" I ask in a neutral tone.

"Do you think it could possibly be successful, watched as they are?"

"No."

"Well, then." She briskly smooths her skirt and starts to turn away, reaching for a basket of yarn. The look she gives me over her shoulder shows greater sadness than her brusque movements. "It wouldn't be safe for them to venture out at all. Tuileries is where they must remain for the time being."

Given the constant presence of various soldiers, Swiss Guard, and members of the national guard, the Tuileries should feel safe, but it doesn't. Even discounting the constricting, prisonlike atmosphere, a sullen tension pervades the walls of the palace, an undercurrent that hints at a cusp of violence. I cease monitoring the queen's movements as closely as I've been accustomed to, and begin watching other servants instead. Watching a guard pacing slowly down a shadowy corridor, gaze sidling from one person to the next, fills me with more suspicion and worry than seeing the queen flit wearily around her chamber like a ragged-winged moth, her silken slippers silent and harmless on the floor tiles.

It's not an easy way to live, though, and I find my wariness growing daily. I keep to myself and trust no one. During the second week of June, Louis recklessly dismisses the Jacobin ministers he appointed previously and replaces them with more moderate ones who aren't as sympathetic to the revolution. Anyone with sense would foresee the decision would incite resentment among the growing ranks of revolutionaries, but Louis seems certain it will blow over. As usual, Marie Antoinette is afflicted with most of the blame; the papers begin calling her Madame Veto, in reference to the king's remaining veto power and her supposed influence over him. Louis is more likely to listen to the last person who advised him, but the queen makes a better scapegoat for the newssheets.

⚜

In mid-June, when I am walking home from the Tuileries, a familiar black carriage stops beside me, and my uncle leans out the window. "Let me give you a ride, Giselle. It's too rainy to walk."

"How did you know I would be walking at this hour?" I haven't spoken to him at all in nearly a year, and I don't think Papa has either.

"Your mother mentioned to Marie-Thérèse that she looks forward to Wednesday evenings, when you are often able to go home for supper. Today is Wednesday, so I thought you might be heading home."

"Thank you. I shall accept your offer of transportation," I say, but disdainfully. Part of me wants to decline, but the rain has already soaked my cloak, and my hair is starting to feel wet beneath my hat. I can't help being curious to learn why he wants to speak to me as well.

"I owe you an explanation," he says without preamble, once I am settled on the velvet upholstered seat across from him.

I stare at him in wide-eyed surprise. He sounds almost apologetic.

"I always encouraged you to believe I merely wanted to relive the days of the Secret du Roi, that our spy work was only between us. While I did enjoy aspects of being a spy again, I must confess that my motives were not so simple."

"Yes, I know. I distinctly received that impression when you had spies working against me, waiting in Varennes."

He has the grace to look abashed at my chilly tone, but he clears his throat and speaks with his usual infuriating authority. "I would like to explain, if you would kindly listen."

I wait in silence.

He clears his throat. "You know my reputation hasn't always been untarnished. I was close to Louis XV, as much as a man of my rank can be, and while I'm proud of my *Figaro* plays, their reception at court also ties me to the royal family. After the revolution broke out, I knew I needed to be prepared to be targeted.

I hoped it wouldn't happen, and so far it hasn't. I don't know if it's luck or my own actions. I admit, I didn't need much provocation to return to the patterns of the Secret du Roi. I did that on my own, to understand the situation. But as it escalated . . ." His hands drift through the air. "Information is valuable currency, Giselle. I regret that I worked against you in the matter of Varennes, but I had other commitments I had to meet."

I don't want to know who he delivers information to, what promises he's made. In the early days, I imagined our spy work to be serious, even though my information was mostly inconsequential. After Varennes, I had no illusions that spying could be casual anymore. I stare out the window, focusing on a streak of mud slashing across the tiny carriage window. "Why are you telling me this now?"

"It's been a year, and our families have hardly spoken. I owed you the truth."

"Thank you."

The carriage slows around a corner, the last one before my house. Uncle Pierre seems to realize he is almost out of time to speak to me, for he lifts a hand in a halting motion, his eyes pleading. "I could still use your help, Giselle. Now that you're back at Tuileries . . ."

He looks utterly serious. He truly believes I may go back to spying for him, after all that has happened. I suppose my return to Tuileries made him believe I haven't changed, but I know without hesitation that I don't want to begin spying again. "I've given that up, Uncle. You shall have to find someone else."

"I do have a servant in the king's household," he says, fingers knotting in frustration. "He hardly knows anything—he mostly comes in to light the fire and sweep the floor; he never speaks to Louis himself."

"He will have to be enough," I say without remorse. As the stuffy carriage lurches to a halt, I reach for the door with relief. "Thank you for the ride, and best of luck finding someone else to help you." I swing out of the carriage without giving him a chance to argue, and I do not look back.

❧

As June twentieth approaches, everyone seems to be thinking of the one-year anniversary of the flight to Varennes. A group of national guards, none of them familiar to me, stop muttering to one another as I pass through the courtyard, but not before I catch a few telltale phrases to let me know they are reminiscing resentfully about Varennes. The newspapers also use the anniversary to renew the story in the press, heightening anti-royalty fervor.

For me, the date brings the pain of knowing it has been a full year since I lost Léon.

On the day of the anniversary, the air is hot and humid for June, and I'm grateful when Madame Campan sends me to fetch bunches of dried lavender to freshen the queen's wardrobe, for it gives me an excuse to loiter in the cool, stone-lined corridor near the cellars.

I make my way slowly back to the queen's chambers, arms full of scratchy lavender, dizzy with the scent of it. Just past the launderer's, a burst of noise floats down the hall—strange for this part of the castle. Though the main corridor is not too far away, it's usually quiet this time of day. A large group of people stomps down the hall, singing a revolutionary song I've heard Geneviève hum. The thunder of their feet and raucous voices precede the sight of them, so I duck around a corner, taking a narrower passage that leads to a doorway to the courtyard, used only by servants. The drum of boot thumps adds a rhythm to the jaunty singing, but the revolutionary lyrics and great number of separate voices make my skin prickle with fear. After lasting through the storming of Versailles, I know the sound of a mob, and my pulse hammers at the thought of an invasion happening again. People died last time. I wait, hiding in the doorway, until the noise fades, and then I creep forward, thinking of the fastest, most discreet way to escape. It occurs to me that I could dash out to the gardens and be home before anyone would really wonder where I had gone. My feet hesitate, but I don't know how many people know of the presence of the mob as yet, and the queen and Madame Campan must be warned so they may retreat safely. Dropping the lavender and moving quickly, I take a shortcut through a servant's stairwell to run to the queen's apartments. It helps, but I have to exit a doorway and follow the main corridor for a short while in order to get to the right part of the castle, and the mob manages to arrive there before I do. I lurk in the doorway, watching as they pass, paying no attention to me in the narrow corridor. They follow the main hallway, chanting about finding the king's apartments.

As they pass, a wave of sweaty stench floods the air. The people must have been marching in the heat for some time. Some of them fan their hats, which undoubtedly feels cooling for them but does not help the odor. Most carry weapons, pikes and hatchets, that have been lavishly decorated with tricolor ribbons. The bright colors look garish against the steel spikes and blades, not at all cheerful. A man marching at the back of the group, his mouth moving in time with the song, swings a gibbet with a rag doll hanging from it. A little flag, also attached to the gibbet, reads *Marie Antoinette á la lanterne*. The symbol is quite clear—she is viewed as an enemy to be killed, her body then hung from a lamppost. I pray that she will not see it.

As the crowd tumbles past, I see another person carrying a

strange item. Raised high, above her head, proudly displayed, is a set of oxen horns. The woman tilts them from side to side as she walks, as if in a macabre sort of dance. I wonder if the horns are meant to indicate cuckoldry, dragging up old rumors of Marie Antoinette's unfaithfulness to her husband, but I'm not certain, and my thoughts are interrupted by the sight of a man carrying something squishy and red. Smears of blood have oozed between his fingers, which cup the piece of flesh. It must be an organ of some kind. Swallowing back disgust, I can only hope that it is animal, procured at a butcher shop, and not a signal that terrible violence has already happened. The idea instills new urgency in me, and as soon as the mob has passed, I lift my skirts above my ankles and run as fast as I can down a different corridor, going straight to the queen's chambers.

Someone has already warned her. As I dash into the room, lungs heaving, Madame Campan hurries to my side, squeezing my shoulder. Her skin is pale, and her lips tremble. "Are you all right, Giselle? Did you see the mob?"

"Yes. They're going to the king's apartments. They don't seem to know the way."

"They'll find it," says Madame Campan grimly. "He has guards with him, at least."

Marie Antoinette curls her thin fingers into fists and regards us with a fierce expression. "I must go to the king's side."

Madame Campan lets go of my shoulder and gestures pleadingly toward the queen. "It would not be safe."

"We must put on a united front and show we are not afraid," she insists. "I am the queen—it is my duty to face them, even if it's dangerous."

"You are a mother, too," reminds Madame Campan, her voice

soft but steely. "Take the children and go to safety until this is over."

I expect Marie Antoinette to argue, but she sags slightly, mouth moving as she nibbles on the inside of her lip uncertainly. Finally she nods once, a tiny movement.

"I sent for them. They should be here momentarily," says Madame Campan.

"I don't know if we should wait for them to arrive," I say. "The mob will come here, just like they did at Versailles. They will want to find the queen's chambers. We ought to go somewhere else."

The queen nods at this, eyes glinting with fresh decision, washing the uncertainty away. I think she's glad to have a course of action, to move instead of waiting helplessly. "We will go to the dauphin's chamber. Mousseline's rooms are close by, and we can escape through my son's rooms."

My breath shakes as we sneak down the hallway to their rooms. All of us twitch at the slightest noise, fearing the mob. They don't venture in our direction, however. Even if they did, I'm not sure they would recognize the queen, who has tugged a shawl around her shoulders and moves like an old woman. It's not a voluntary disguise, but one wrought by the ravages of the past year.

Both children are in the dauphin's rooms when we enter. Madame Campan says a prayer of relief, echoed by me, and the queen encircles them in her arms, tears streaming down her ashy cheeks.

"We must go to safety," she tells them. "Your father will meet with the revolutionaries, as is his duty, and then we will see him. We will get through this together."

Standing nearest to the door, I'm the first to hear when rowdy voices approach, wondering loudly about which room lays before them.

"Must be for one of the royal family," says a gruff-sounding man. "Look at the door, very fancy."

"They're outside," I hiss in panic. "Where will we go?"

"Bar the door." Madame Campan points wildly at the mechanism, and I run to obey, fingers trembling. By the time I've turned around, she has opened a door in the wall that I didn't know existed. I should have known that Tuileries has secret passages as well, after I saw some of them at Versailles.

As the main bedroom door rattles and thumps under a beating of axes and wooden pikes, we squeeze into the secret passage. The racket of the mob trying to break into the dauphin's room lends us speed, and my pulse rings in my ears. The passage is dark and stuffy, and by the time we're all crammed inside, the children and their attendants included, it's too crowded to move rapidly lest we trip one another. Taking small, patient steps is not easy. My nerves scrape with the urge to run, and from the fast, shallow breaths of the others around me, I think they must feel the same. Thankfully, the passage is not long, and we exit into an unfamiliar room. The double row of grim Swiss Guards standing across the doorway floods me with relief. Their ordered stance means that the mob hasn't arrived here yet, and they look ready to deal with it when it does inevitably work its way here. Madame Campan once told me all about how Swiss Guards are considered the best mercenaries available, loyal and disciplined, and that's why royal courts all over Europe have been hiring them for centuries.

"I can hardly believe the mob would try to violently enter the dauphin's rooms," I whisper to Madame Campan. "He's a child." Even as I speak, he presses close to his mother's voluminous skirt, eyes round with fear.

"They would do anything," says Madame Campan darkly. "Even harm a little boy." Her gaze flicks to the queen, who stares at the door like she wishes her vision could pierce the heavy oak and see beyond. Her posture looks stiff and statue-still. Madame Campan goes to her side. "Are you very afraid?" She sounds motherly.

Marie Antoinette twitches her head in a small, jerky movement. "No. But I suffer from being away from the king when his life is in danger."

"He would want you safe," says Madame Campan.

The queen doesn't react to this. "At least I have the consolation of staying with the children, which is also one of my duties. It's not a sign that I am weak, hiding."

"Of course it isn't."

It takes some time, and feels even longer, but eventually more guards come to the room, and King Louis follows. With a strangled cry of relief and joy, Marie Antoinette rushes into his arms, the children close behind her. Louis-Charles, the dauphin, flings his arms around both of his parents, holding on tight in spite of not having arms long enough to reach around them. Madame Royale murmurs a prayer of thankfulness, speaking to her parents in a voice too soft for me to hear.

Louis's voice carries better. "They broke into my apartments, but they didn't offer violence, in spite of carrying weapons. One of my subjects proffered a *bonnet rouge*, and I thought it best to humor him and put it on my head." The king pauses and blinks in mild confusion. I wonder if he even understands the significance of the *bonnet rouge*, a popular symbol of the revolution meant to recall the red caps that Roman slaves wore once they gained their freedom. "He addressed me as *Monsieur* and not as *Majesté*," Louis continues. "It sounded so strange. The cap was uncomfortable, perched tightly on my head, but it pleased them to see me wear it, and they grew calmer. I drank a toast to their health, and that made them cheer, waving their hats and ribbons. They were suddenly much more jovial." He bends toward the dauphin. "The people need a leader, always, and may be guided with a gentle hand."

I resist the impulse to roll my eyes at this. Louis is famous for not understanding and guiding the people. However, to give him credit, it sounds as though he's been successful today.

"There must be no repercussions to this," says Marie Antoinette. Her quiet voice slides through the room like the whisper of a steel blade. "The people must never be given the impression that we harbor resentment for what happened here today. It is our only protection."

Louis pats her hand. "Of course not. After the toast, they left quite happily, singing and waving their red hats. I carried mine for a while." He looks around for it, but one of the guards must have taken it away. "They are satisfied for now, but they insisted I return the Jacobin ministers to the government." He scowls. "I have no wish to. My God-given power may be sadly stripped, but I still have the veto, and I should be able to choose my own ministers."

⚜

The next month, Robespierre calls for the removal of the king.

"He's useless, hardly anything more than an outdated symbol by now, but it still sounds shocking, doesn't it?" muses Geneviève. "Such a thing has never happened."

"The English deposed one of their kings," I say. I suppose Louis will likely be deposed soon. The revolution has steadily chipped away at his power, even his title, although I often hear people using it still. Removing him entirely seems like the final step. "They executed him."

"I don't like to compare France to England." She waves her hand. "Removing Louis seems the logical step, though, doesn't it? He's not doing any good for our country, and we've evolved past being governed by one man simply because of who his parents were. It's an archaic system. Besides, he's hopelessly incompetent. He removed his Jacobin ministers in spite of their necessity, and even though he wore a *bonnet rouge* at Tuileries, he hasn't done anything else. He's nothing more than a waste-of-space figurehead."

"Who will lead instead?" I ask dubiously. Louis doesn't have the mettle or quick wit of a natural leader, but the idea of Robespierre ruling France is disconcerting too.

"There will be an election," says Geneviève firmly. "There has to be." She pauses. "Léon supports it. He told Étienne so." The words fly from her mouth as if desperate to escape, but she has the grace to look slightly abashed for mentioning him.

There are many who support the removal of the king, weary of his empty promises and continuous ineffectuality, and on the third day of August, petitions from all but one section of Paris are sent to the Legislative Assembly. The section of Saint-Antoine swears it will give the Assembly one week to carry out the will of the people and end the monarchy, or will do it alone.

The ultimatum frightens me; the Assembly itself has gone through several disruptive transformations, and nothing official seems to happen quickly. When August tenth approaches, nothing has been done. Another angry mob marches toward Tuileries, exactly as threatened.

It's my week off, so I'm home when Papa hears the news while visiting friends. Sober lines drag down the corners of his mouth, and he stares out the window before turning back to me. "Thank God you're safe at home."

Maman leans on his arm. "We were so worried last time, and to see Tuileries invaded again only a few weeks later . . . It's frightening. Perhaps you ought to leave your employment again."

"I think you're right." I pace the parlor, worrying for Madame Campan and Marie Antoinette, wishing the violence were over. Sometimes it seems as though it will never stop.

Chapter Twenty

Late the next day a message sent by Madame Campan comes to the house for me. She writes that the royal family sought refuge at the Assembly, while the loyal troops remained in a position of defense at Tuileries. There was fighting, and although she doesn't go into detail about the violence in her relatively brief missive, I know from the tales burning through the streets that there were many deaths, and Tuileries was ransacked. It was violent and disastrous.

> *The king and queen are housed in the Couvent des Feuillants, and sorely lacking in comforts. The escape from the invading mob at Tuileries happened so quickly that there was no time to organize clothing. They have all had to borrow items, even the queen and the dauphin. Please, gather some suitable items for them and bring them to the convent as quickly as you can.*

Madame Campan didn't specify whether I should try to fetch some of their own belongings or just procure whatever I can. Tuileries must be safe enough now that the riot is over and the royal

family is no longer in residence. I decide to see what remains of
the queen's wardrobe.

Before I even set foot inside the walls, I realize my assumption
had been naïve and overly optimistic. Tuileries is a disaster. Broken things lie scattered everywhere: shards of glass, jumbled heaps
of furniture, crumbled dishes and decorations, torn and dirty
pieces of cloth. Anything I can think of could probably be found
in the wreckage, except intact items of value.

As I move closer, the horrid scent of blood rises to my nostrils,
acrid and sweet and metallic. Half-dried pools of it congeal in scatters on the floors. One of them near my feet has been smeared
into a dry brownish streak, as if a gravely wounded person crawled
away on their belly. Bodies have been lined up in one of the
courtyards, waiting for family to claim them. I turn away from
the smell of death, pressing my lavender-scented handkerchief as
tight as I can against my nose. The hot August air makes the
pervasive aroma worse, and I quicken my steps, gasping into the
handkerchief and wishing to God I had not come. Rounding
a corner, I nearly stumble on a human arm, part of a red sleeve
still clinging to it. Too shocked to do anything but hurry away,
I cringe as a wave of nausea belatedly catches up with me a moment later. My legs tremble, but I dare not stop among the grisly
surroundings.

Perhaps because she hadn't been present, the queen's apartments
aren't as bad in terms of carnage. Strewn wreckage covers much
of the floor, and the patterns on the wall are marred with scratches,
but it smells more of perfume leaking from shattered bottles than
of blood.

Her wardrobe has already been vandalized, and many items pil-
fered. Two women rifle through a pile of fichus as I enter, muttering about jewelry and silk. They glare at me, fingers curling into

claws. I stare at them, my lip curling over my teeth. I've been through two palace invasions, and I walked through the wreckage. A couple of thieving crones will not stop me. I go straight past them, to the cupboard at the back where the chemises and petticoats are kept. The best of the queen's dresses are probably already gone, but hopefully some of her undergarments are here. No one likes to wear borrowed underwear, and if I can bring some of her own garments, it will no doubt be a comfort.

The women stare balefully for a moment, but when I continue to ignore them, they go back to searching for valuable items. As long as I don't try to take anything they've already claimed, I think they'll ignore me.

By the time I hurry away from Tuileries, gratefully turning my face into the fresh breeze, my bags are full, stuffed with clothing and a couple of sentimental items I found. Although I possessed no familiarity with the dauphin's chambers, I found his belongings to be the most intact. I suppose no one expected a child, even a royal one, to have many valuables in his room. I have clothing for him, as well as a toy dog that had been kicked under the corner of the stripped bed and forgotten. I found a loose page of poetry in Madame Royale's chamber, and folded it into the bag. It may not be important to her, but the room had already been well searched for jewelry, and it was the best I could find. I managed to cobble together two outfits for her out of the remaining items as well.

The queen's room was the worst, with many items deliberately ruined and tossed about the room. I only manage to find one item of value for her: knitting needles and a tapestry she'd been working on. I find two dresses for her, one in blue and one in dark pink, and a few undergarments. My familiarity with the wardrobe helps me to sift through the damage. Many items have been stolen, and some of the remaining ones have been torn and streaked with ink and dirt. Before I leave her rooms, I search for the little spaniel, Mignon, or any of the queen's cats, but there is no sign of them except for a patch of white hair clinging to a velvet cushion kicked into the corner.

I take everything to the Couvent des Feuillants, but no one will allow me to see the queen. No one seems to know anything about Madame Campan, either. One of the guards offers to pass along the bag, but I don't trust the eagerness on his face, and suspect he will keep what he wants and dispose of the rest. Just as I'm leaving, determined to come back tomorrow, Madame Campan finds me.

"Oh, thank goodness, Giselle." Her hair, frizzled out of its usual smoothness, makes her look wild and desperate. "You brought something? Thank goodness. Did you go into Tuileries?" She peers at me with wide eyes, her curiosity avid as though the place has become a lair of thieves and murderers, an accurate analogy, in truth.

"Yes." Sparsely, I tell her about the pillaged rooms and grim remainders of the fighting that happened. The sorrow of it makes us both fall into silence, so I clear my throat and give her an inventory of the items I have brought.

"Thank you, Giselle. This will help. The queen is fearful that they will move the family to the Tower, you know, the old building attached to the Temple? When the Comte d'Artois used the Temple as a residence, she always urged him to knock down the tower. What a pity he never listened."

"Is she in good spirits?" I ask, although I don't see how she could be.

"She has hardly any appetite, and grew rather annoyed with the king for managing to enjoy his dinner." The ghost of an indulgent smile crosses Madame Campan's face. "There are always contentious points in a marriage, even one as grand as theirs, and Madame never understood when the appetites of others remained unaffected by stressful circumstances. She is so sensitive to them. However, she seems strong, but prepared for the worst. I pray that it does not come."

"As do I." I bow my head fervently, because I know that our wishes will probably not make it true. There is so much hatred for our queen. "Madame Campan, do they have any money? They may need it in case the guards must be bribed."

She blinks in surprise at my question. I don't blame her. It is odd to think of the people who found it normal to wear cascades of diamonds to be suddenly without funds. "I'll take care of it. That's shrewd of you, my dear."

The corner of my mouth curves ruefully. Over the last three years, I've learned how the world works.

With the royal family imprisoned, events unfold swiftly within the government. The Assembly elects six ministers to oversee the national election of representatives to the Convention, which will be the next new government. Royalist newspapers are prohibited, and it would be dangerous to be caught reading one anyway, for the Assembly also authorizes the arrest of suspected enemies of the revolution.

Coldness grips my heart when I hear this threat. Though I believe changes are needed, I dislike the violence of the revolution, and my actions regarding Varennes would be seen as royalist loyalty. I must be cautious and publicly support the revolution to protect myself.

On August thirteenth, the royal family is moved to the small tower, the part of the Temple that the queen had always feared and disliked. Six days later Marie Antoinette's remaining companions and ladies-in-waiting are removed for interrogation. The Princesse de Lamballe, the governess the Marquise de Tourzel, and others I knew are sent to La Force Prison.

"Let them rot there," says a man on the street, folding up his newspaper. "Especially the Princesse de Lamballe." He elbows his companion in the ribs, leering. "You know what they say about her and *L'Autrichienne*, don't you? Damned unnatural relationship."

I straighten the tricolor rosette pinned to my shoulder and reach for a copy of the newspaper, fixing an expression of interest on my face, as though I could not be more pleased to hear of justice being meted out. Inside, I quake with sorrow. How frightened they all must be, feeling so helpless.

Madame Campan comes to my house the day after the other royal ladies are sent to prison. I hurry her through the door, checking to see if anyone on the street has noticed her presence, feeling guilty as I do so. She's not that recognizable, but my wariness has reached new heights.

"You look rather lost," I observe. "Would you like some tea?"

"No, thank you. I do feel lost. I suppose that's why I came. I've served Her Majesty for so long. Now that she's imprisoned, I hardly know what to do." Madame Campan's eyes shine with a gloss of held-back tears, but she still sits as straight as a board, chin held high.

I press my handkerchief into her hand. "There's nothing to be done but pray for her and keep yourself safe," I say as gently as I can.

She nods once, mouth working. "I asked to go to the Temple, where they're being imprisoned, but I wasn't allowed in. They have twenty guards at the gates. It seems a superfluous amount. . . . It shows how much they fear the king and queen, even now. At least I may speak freely about Her Majesty to you. Everyone wants to talk about her, but not with kindness. They all hope to hear salacious gossip, and I certainly won't provide it to them."

"I understand how isolating it is to love Her Majesty."

"Yes." Madame Campan squeezes her handkerchief. "I wish you could have known her even better."

Madame Campan knows more about the queen's current situation than I do. She informs me that the royal family was allowed to order new linens and undergarments, although the process for getting packages to the queen is rigorous, and her perfumer, Monsieur Fargeon, graciously sent the queen some of his scented *vinaigrettes* of *eaux revigorantes* to help her cope. The spaniel, Mignon, was also found and reunited with the queen. This, in particular, gives me a hollow sense of comfort. I think of the queen's pale hands stroking the spaniel's ears, and feel glad that she's not alone.

When another unexpected caller shows up on the doorstep later in the week, I open the door with some weariness, half-anticipating the somber presence of Madame Campan again. To my surprise, my cousin Eugénie stands on the threshold and pushes her way in before I can speak, her fingers twisting around my wrist.

"Giselle! Oh, thank God you are home. Father has been arrested and sent to prison."

"Uncle Pierre?" I echo blankly. The idea of him, with his suave arrogance, being contained against his will seems ludicrous. Based on our confrontation after Varennes, I know he is no royalist. "Why?"

"Suspicion of anti-revolutionary sentiments." Eugénie's fingernails dig into my skin. "You have to help, Giselle. Please, can you? He isn't anti-revolutionary. You know that—he told me all about your disagreement, and how you were on opposite sides in the matter of Varennes. I've missed you dreadfully since then, but he told me I ought to let you approach us first, because he had said unkind things and you weren't unfounded in resenting him over them."

It seems astonishing to me that he said that. I thought he was more likely hissing over my poor decision. I prize Eugénie's hand from my wrist and squeeze it between my own fingers. "I missed you too. I should have come to visit you, but the situation has been so complicated. . . ." I trail off and meet her worried eyes. "I don't know how I can help. I'm sorry."

My helpless response smashes through her composure, and tears gather in her eyes as she squeezes my fingers. "Please, Giselle, you have to try! I don't know who else to go to." Her breath heaves.

I fold her into a hug, patting her back and murmuring soothing endearments until she gulps and draws back, cheeks glistening with tears.

"Sit down," I say briskly, guiding her into the parlor. Papa's decanter of brandy sits on the sideboard, and I pour a small amount for her nerves. She stares at the cup blankly when I push it into her fingers, and then swallows the amber liquid in one gulp, not even making a face at the taste, like she did a year ago when we secretly tried it.

"I didn't say I wouldn't help. I just don't know how. I need to think."

Eugénie clears her throat, stiffens her back ramrod straight, and takes a deep breath. It seems to give her strength, but I see her fingers are white around the crystal glass. "We need to vouch for his revolutionary support, but I don't have the right contacts to make sure someone important hears us, and I don't know if they'll listen to me, anyway. Our connection is too close, as father and daughter. They'll say that any child would protect a parent, no matter the truth. But I think they would listen to you."

"I'll try, but I'm not anyone important. You have a great deal of faith in me."

Eugénie sets the glass down with a sharp sound, not looking

at the table. She leans forward, eyes gleaming fierce and bright. "Father did too. He remarked that you have a sharp mind. He also said you have a gift for connecting with people, and that it was your greatest asset and your worst drawback as a spy."

I can hear my uncle in her words, and realize she recites a quotation from him almost verbatim.

She keeps talking too fast, her voice rasping from her earlier tears. "He said you could get people to tell you things, but you also opened yourself up to them in the process and felt too much sympathy for them. He said you were likely to befriend anyone, if you wanted, but you probably wouldn't be able to remain distant afterward." She leans farther forward, arms resting on her knees, fingers outstretched beseechingly. She sounds like herself again when she speaks. "You see? You know the right people. I know you hate asking for favors, but you must. Please, Giselle."

I feel stunned, after listening to my uncle's cool appraisal of my personality, and then the contrast of Eugénie's urgent pleading. She doesn't need to beg me for help; I won't abandon her. My fingers fiddle with the stone pendant of my Bastille necklace as I consider possible options. "I do have some revolutionary contacts." I decide not to give Eugénie the details yet, in case my first plan fails and I need to come up with another. "I will talk to them and see what I can do."

Eugénie leaps from her chair and throws her arms around me. "Thank you." When she draws back, her eyes swell with tears again, but she manages to summon a tremulous smile. "At least one good thing came of this. We are friends again."

I pull her back into another hug. She's grown in the months we've spent apart, and is almost as tall as I am now. "Hopefully more than one good thing will happen, and we'll obtain his freedom, too."

After I see her into her carriage, I collapse back into the arm-chair, swept with a sense of dread.

I can think of only one person significant enough among the revolutionaries to help me. And to reach Robespierre, I need to enlist the aid of Léon.

Chapter Twenty-one

When I go to the watchmaker's shop in the evening, I'm told Léon is in his room above the store. I hesitate before knocking. It's one thing to speak to him at the shop counter, quite another to disturb his privacy.

Opening the door, he stares, clearly surprised to see me. I take the opportunity to study him, noticing the smudged shadows under his eyes and the new extra prominence of his cheekbones. He isn't too thin, exactly, but food prices have been erratic and many people are missing a few pounds for it, including myself. Léon looks like he'd benefit from a hearty meal and a long, restful night. An urge to stroke his hair while he lies with his head in my lap sweeps over me, and it fills me with sadness for the lost intimacy.

"I haven't borrowed any books lately," he says, referring to my last unexpected visit to see him. "You must be here for another reason."

I give a tiny nod. "Yes. I need to speak with you."

"Come in, then." He steps away from the door, sweeping his arm to invite me inside.

"I expected more argument," I admit, surveying the small room. The star-patterned quilt draped over the bed is a little rumpled, and judging by the lamplight nearby and the ragged copy of *Le Morte d'Arthur* on the dresser beside the bed, Léon had been reading before I came in.

His eyes look dark and unreadable. Finally his mouth quirks in a rueful half smile. "So did I." The smile fades as he notices my Bastille necklace, untucked from the collar of my white gown. He reaches out and touches the chain so lightly that I feel the heat of his fingertip more than the brush of his skin. A wave of emotion rocks through me: the burn of heartbreak, a shock of hope, a frisson of desire. I lick my lips, feeling my breath grow suddenly shallow and rapid as my heartbeat accelerates.

He looks up from the necklace, staring into my face with intensity. "You still wear this?"

"I do."

Léon flicks a glance back to the necklace and then to the floor. When his gaze returns to me, his aloofness has returned, and I can't tell what he's thinking. "It adds to your costume. You look quite the revolutionary lady."

I wear a long-sleeved white dress decorated with tricolor embroidery, the popular style I'd worn long before our engagement ended, but the sharpness of his tone implies I'm faking it, a royalist in disguise as a revolutionary, and it hurts.

"The necklace is one of my most treasured possessions." The stark truth of my answer strikes him, I think, for he turns away, hiding his expression, before sitting on the bed.

"Be seated in the chair, if you wish. Tell me what you came for." He folds his arms across his chest, and the posture highlights the lean muscles of his forearms, exposed by his casually rolled sleeves.

I want to hear more about him, but I sense he won't welcome

personal questions, and besides, Eugénie is relying on me. "My uncle has been arrested on suspicion of anti-revolutionary activity. The charges are false. He's not a royalist."

"Are you certain? Perhaps it runs in the family." His lip curls slightly.

I rise from my perched seat on the edge of the hard chair, only realizing I've done it when I find myself prowling forward toward him, scowling. "I'm certain. Like you, he was disgusted by my role in Varennes. Even without knowing this, you should never doubt his interests in the revolution. He initiated my spy work, and it turned out he had Geneviève working for him too." Dimly, I see that this information shocks him, but I'm too angry at the jab to pause. "Léon, I want to apologize for lying to you. I should never have done it, and I've regretted it every moment since. But I won't apologize for doing what I thought was right. You and my uncle have both treated me as though the matter was something to be simply compartmentalized and understood, like the colors black and white. But I was the one seeing the royal family day after day, witnessing the most intimate moments of their lives. I watched the queen weep with dread; I saw her children frozen with terror. Maybe I should have held myself back and tried not to care about them, but in the end I made the only choice I could. Maybe it wasn't the right one, but it was *mine*."

He rises too, standing so close to me that I feel the heat of his body and I have to tilt my head to stare furiously into his eyes.

"Is this what you came for? To shout at me for being angry at you?" The shadow in his voice only makes its soft rumble more dangerous.

"No." I look down, chagrined. "I didn't mean to say that, but it feels good to have it out. I came to ask if you can get me an interview with Robespierre."

His brows arch nearly to his hairline. "Why?"

"I'm going to confess that my uncle hired me to spy on the queen. It should prove his loyalty to the revolution."

Léon abruptly paces to the window, then back to my side, his movements tense. "It's dangerous, Giselle."

It's the first time he has said my name, and hearing it makes a spark leap through me. "Every day is dangerous and unpredictable," I say, and it comes out more harshly than I intended. "I went into Tuileries and saw the gory aftermath. It was burned into my eyes for days after. I know of the danger."

"It will bring your name to the attention of some of the most powerful men in Paris. Fervent revolutionaries prone to suspicion and drastic actions."

"Even so, it must be done."

He is quiet for so long that I think he'll refuse. I shift, preparing to leave, to think of another plan.

"All right," says Léon at last. "I'll come with you."

"That's not necessary." My mouth forms the words stiffly. "I know you don't want to be near me, that you won't forgive me. You've made it clear enough."

"No, Giselle." The dark glitter of his eyes matches his forceful tone. "I'm not offering because manners dictate it. I'm insisting because you have a better chance of convincing them if I'm there to vouch for your story. I've been too busy of late to go to Café du Foy, but I've had enough philosophical discussions with Robespierre and Marat and Desmoulins that they have at least a small measure of trust in me. You need me there."

"I—Thank you." My independent pride deflated, I lower my voice. "When will be convenient for you to visit Robespierre?"

"Tomorrow. I'll get the afternoon off at the shop downstairs.

We need to hurry. The jails are crowded—they'll start using the guillotine soon, just to make room."

The vicious, practical truth in his words makes me shiver. "I'll meet you here after lunch, then?"

Léon nods. "Wear a dress with a slightly lower collar, and the necklace. Let them see you wearing part of the Bastille."

"I will." I linger in the doorway, feeling awkward. "Well . . . good night. Enjoy your reading." I gesture toward *Le Morte d'Arthur*.

He shrugs. "I've read it many times, but it's comforting. One can't read Rousseau and Voltaire all the time."

"Of course not." A tiny smile springs to my lips. This is the most natural way he's spoken to me during our meeting, and it makes me happy to end it this way.

Chapter Twenty-two

Like me, Léon has dressed carefully for our meeting with Robespierre, cultivating a pro-revolutionary appearance. He wears a tight-fitting blue coat with red trim, and a crisp white shirt underneath. Instead of the white pants of his national guard's uniform, he has chosen black, and added a further revolutionary touch with a small tricolor ribbon pinned to his hat.

"You look well," I tell him. It's an understatement; I can hardly prevent myself from staring at the way the coat highlights the broadness of his shoulders and the narrowness of his hips.

He lifts his shoulder in a nonchalant gesture, but the corner of his mouth curls in a brief self-conscious smile. "It's an important appointment." Pursing his lips, he studies my appearance, and when he reaches a hand toward my face, my heart flutters in wild excitement. He only tugs a loose curl forward, though, letting it fall along the curve of my cheek. "There. It might help if you look delicate and soft, like you were entirely led into spying by your uncle, whose anti-royalists interests are so great that he recruited you to help him. Your dress is nice," he adds, almost as an afterthought. "Very revolutionary."

The small compliment is more than I ought to expect, so I squash the prickle of disappointment that he wasn't admiring me, only analyzing the strategy of my outfit. I did choose my dress with care, displaying tricolor against the formal cut of my bodice and skirt.

Upon reaching Robespierre's abode, Léon and I are admitted at once but directed to the library with instructions that Robespierre won't be available for about half an hour. Léon browses the books, but I'm too restless, and instead stride back and forth across the room, glancing at the papers on the desk with cursory interest, fighting the leftover spy's urge to memorize them. There's nothing interesting, though, only notes on the last constitution. Robespierre is too clever to leave secret plans lying about.

"Any other works you'd like to borrow?" I ask Léon, tracing my finger along the spine of a Latin book.

"No. There are things I'm curious to read, but I won't trouble him to lend them to me."

Wondering if this means Léon isn't as friendly with Robespierre as he once was, I glance up at his face, but I can't tell what he's thinking. He looks surprisingly serene, although he drums his fingers restlessly along the bookshelf.

"Your collar is a bit crooked," I tell him, noticing. "May I?" I reach toward a wrinkle in the fold of his white shirt.

"Please." He clears a sudden hoarseness free of his throat.

When I brush against his neck, expertly tugging the collar straight, he twitches. The movement is difficult to describe: stronger than a tremble, not vehement enough for a flinch. I try not to touch his skin, but the stiffness of the coat means that it takes me a moment to properly fix the collar, and by the time I finish, Léon has gone still again, like a stone settling at the bottom of a pond.

"Sorry." I tilt my face up toward his, inspecting my handiwork. "It looks better now, though."

He licks his lips, eyelashes flickering as he looks away, and then back again, his gaze sliding slowly across my skin. Heat trails along my collarbones, coiling around my throat behind the necklace. I can't help leaning closer to him, my head swirling with desire even though I should be frightened of the upcoming interview with Robespierre.

Léon rocks back on his heels. "We shouldn't stand so close together. It isn't proper."

"Since when have you cared for proper?" I ask, rather waspishly. "You got me drunk and kissed me on the first night we met."

A shadow curtains his face as he half-turns his head, scowling. "It was my wine—you didn't have to drink it. And you kissed me first."

"You wanted me to. And I wanted to."

"I don't want to talk about old, tarnished memories." His sharp words slice into me. "Things are different now. I didn't have to help you today, you know. Don't torment me in return; it's cruel."

The unexpected admission makes me blink in surprise. "I wasn't aware I had the power to torment you."

He begins pacing along the length of the room, moving with fierce, contained energy. "If you didn't, your betrayal of our trust wouldn't have hurt so badly. If I felt nothing, I'd be able to forget you. I'd never again remember laughing with you, and I'd never dream of bitter retaliation, of making you feel as wretched as I did."

"You want to forget me?" More than anything else he's said to me since Varennes, this feels like a knife twisted into my heart. "I can't help you with that, since I never succeeded in forgetting you.

I don't want to. But if it's retaliation you want, you have the means. You have the power and the opportunity."

"What do you mean?" He turns to face me, eyes narrowing.

My voice drops to a hiss. Even in a haze of fury, I'm conditioned to never speak openly about Varennes. "You know my greatest secret. You know what I did. You could have me bowing under the guillotine for it if you decided to tell your high-ranking friends."

His lips part, eyes widening in horror. "You believe I could do that? You think I crave such a terrible revenge—that I'm a monster?" He crosses the room to stand in front of me, moving so quickly that I've hardly adjusted to his new closeness when he reaches out his hands and places them on either side of my head, fingers tangling in my hair. My breathing falters, my pulse rocketing like fireworks.

"No," I whisper. My cheekbones grind against his palms. "I don't believe it. But I think, maybe, I would let you."

"Jesus Christ, Giselle." Léon's grip tightens, fingertips meeting behind my neck, and he draws me closer to his chest, tilting my head back. For one endless, ephemeral moment, my heart beats with frantic excitement and I revel in the warmth of his body pressing against mine. Then his lips cover mine in a hard, hungry kiss, hot as a brand and as dizzying as too much wine. My hands slide around his hips, linking behind his back and pulling him closer to me. I want to hold him forever. From the possessive way he slants his mouth over mine, deepening the kiss and gathering me more firmly into his arms, I think he wants the same thing, but I'm terrified to believe it in case I'm wrong. Then he makes a low growl in the back of his throat and trails softer kisses down my neck, across my exposed collarbone, and I stop thinking at all.

The rhythmic thud of hard-soled shoes on the wooden hall floor outside the library jolts us back to our senses. Léon straightens, loosening his grip on me. The footsteps move past the closed door, fading from earshot. Not Robespierre, not yet. Léon kisses me once more, gentler this time, and then takes a small step back. His eyes blaze with passion and his voice sounds smoky. "This isn't over."

I meet his scorching gaze. My lips feel swollen and my skin tingles. "No, it's not."

Aware that Robespierre could enter at any time, we seat ourselves in chairs on opposite sides of the fireplace, carefully avoiding eye contact, waiting in heavy silence. At least ten minutes pass before Robespierre swings the door open, and by then we've regained a semblance of composure.

"*Citoyen* Gauvain, how nice to see you," he says jovially. "It's been too long." He turns to me. "And you—*Citoyenne* Aubry, isn't it? It is an honor."

He and Léon exchange small news and pleasantries, and at last Robespierre leans forward in his seat. "What brings you here today, Léon? You wouldn't bring such a lovely companion to borrow a book." His politeness doesn't quite mask the curious glance sidling to me.

"Giselle has valuable information for you," says Léon. He speaks with a smooth balance of confidentiality and enticement, but I know him well enough to see the strained look around his forehead. "It's about a prisoner."

Robespierre turns to me, arching one brow in curiosity.

"My uncle," I say. "Pierre-Augustin Caron de Beaumarchais."

"Ah yes. The playwright." Robespierre's wide mouth droops in a frown. "His plays were celebrated at court, I believe."

"And throughout Paris. His plays pleased many people, although it is true that even the queen enjoyed his best one. He knew well enough how to interest the limp minds of the nobles."

I meet Robespierre's gaze squarely. His eyes glint like a cat's. "He spied on them for years."

He straightens, fingers splaying across his thigh, as if he could snatch the truth out of the air. "Indeed? This is a very interesting statement, mademoiselle. In what capacity?"

"He got his start spying for the old king, and it was there he started to despise the excesses of the court. When the revolution began, he returned to spy work, this time against the royal family. He helped me obtain a position in the queen's household as one of her wardrobe women and recruited me to spy on her. I reported back to him for two years."

Robespierre squeezes his fingers together, head tilting with attentiveness. "You must have witnessed many remarkable moments. Were you at Tuileries when the family was taken away? Is it true that the queen feared the Assembly would murder them all?"

"I wasn't present that day." I feign regret for missing out on such a notable event, but I remember the blood-splashed walls and think anyone would have been mad to want to be there. "I was there when Versailles was stormed and when a riot came through Tuileries in June. The queen was full of fear on both occasions. She trusted no one and wrote often to her family in Austria." I dislike sharing information with Robespierre, but I know I must give him some things in order to make him believe my story.

Robespierre scowls at the mention of Austria. "That stagnant nation knows nothing of the glory of France."

"Of course not. France moves toward enlightenment in a way that no country could hope to rival." Knowing I must bring the conversation back around to my uncle, I make up a small lie. "My uncle always felt such pride for France's progress." In fact, I am not sure what he thought of the matter, but I do know that he would swear it true in order to free himself from prison. "I suppose that is why he wanted me to watch the queen specifically. He feared her foreign influence."

"As all the wisest did." He leans back, watching me carefully. "If your uncle has been working against the monarchy for so long, why was he suspected of anti-revolutionary activity?"

"Someone must have made a mistake," says Léon.

Robespierre's gaze flicks to him, but he doesn't look satisfied by the simple answer.

"You were suspicious of him on the basis of his plays," I remind him. "Doubtless, others felt the same. He does have connections, but the reason for them—his espionage—remained a secret of necessity."

"Of course." Robespierre interrogates me further about the nature of my spying, asking intelligent, detailed questions that aren't always easy to answer. Although I hate to do it, I have to give him more anecdotes than I'd like. Still, my information is all so outdated now that it can harm no one. I'm careful not to say anything about Madame Campan, lest she become implicated in current events. I do mention Geneviève, with some reluctance. I don't think she'd mind talking with Robespierre, whom she admires, about the queen's household, but I still dislike dragging her into this. "One of the other wardrobe women also spied for my uncle. She can corroborate many of these facts, as well as his dedication to the revolution." I give him her name and watch the tense lines around his mouth relax. When he bends his head, he looks more trusting. At last Robespierre folds his hands together and reclines in his chair. "It does sound as though an error was made. I shall speak to your uncle myself. No doubt he'll be back at home again soon."

"Thank you, monsieur." Relief that the interview is finally over infuses my tone with an extra note of gratefulness.

He inclines his head. "The truth shall always prevail."

Fearing he'll want to visit longer, I try to catch Léon's eye, but he stands at once and shakes Robespierre's hand. "It was good to see you, my friend, and I'm sorry to rush away. I must return to the shop." I know it's a lie. He told me Monsieur Renard gave him the whole afternoon off.

"I also have work to do. I'm writing a speech to convince the Assembly to create a People's Tribunal." Robespierre turns to me. "If your watchful eyes and keen ears happen across any useful information, I trust you know where to find me." His courteous smile turns sharp. "Your uncle isn't the only one who knows the value of a good spy."

"Of course. It's the least I could do to repay you for your attention to this matter," I say, but my stomach twists into a knot. I've no desire to resume spying, especially not for Robespierre. His watchfulness and ruthless questions make me nervous.

Robespierre escorts us to the door. "One last thing, *Citoyenne* Aubry. If you see Madame Campan again, I'd be interested to hear of it. She's close to the queen, isn't she?"

Momentarily speechless, I try to hide it by ducking my head in assent. "Anything to help, *Citoyen*." My lips feel dry. I tell myself that he's watching Madame Campan, whose connection to the queen is well-known, but the idea that he knows she has visited me makes a knot twist between my shoulder blades. "Thank you again."

Robespierre sees us off with a cheerful smile, although he looks even more smug than usual to me. As soon as we step out the door into the clean air, I take a deep breath, feeling my heart race with belated nerves.

Léon links his forearm with mine, forcing me to either tug away or lay my fingers along his wrist and walk with him as a proper escort. I choose the latter, but it's a bittersweet reminder of old times.

Léon and I decipher every sentence of the interview. It helps me calm down, and I feel confident that my uncle's release comes shortly. When we've thoroughly discussed every aspect, Léon's arm shifts under my hand, sliding free of my grip, his fingertips grazing the underside of my wrist. Twining his fingers with mine, he guides us into a quiet nook around the corner from a bookseller's shop.

"Must we continue our earlier discussion now?" I'm aware it's a mild way to describe our fiery argument, the passionate embrace. My body quivers with excitement at his nearness and the way he grips my hand, but I'm also worried my longing for him makes me misinterpret things, that perhaps he only wants us to part on better terms than previously, not to reconcile. I press the wall, giving him space to talk.

"Yes, we must. We agreed it wasn't over." Léon leans very close to me. The silken warmth of his breath skims across my neck.

"What are you doing?" I whisper. His lips are mere inches away from mine.

"I'm going to kiss you. Unless you don't want me to?"

"I thought we were going to argue more."

"I think we've had enough of that," he murmurs. "It's behind us now." His mouth brushes against mine, feather light, with the last sentence, and his hand strokes my cheek gently, enticingly.

I lean into him, fusing our lips in a kiss as tender as the touches leading up to it. I feel like I melt into his arms, fitting there exactly right, nestled against his chest. His fingers move from my cheek, sliding behind my ear, and tangle tightly in my hair as the kiss changes into something fiercer. I let go of his hand and reach for his shoulders, sighing with delight when he wraps his arm tightly around my waist.

"We can't stay here," I say breathlessly. "It isn't proper." The repetition of his phrasing from our tension at Robespierre's house makes me giggle with dazed amusement.

"You're right: I don't care about proper," he says roughly, but he chuckles, too, and releases me slowly. "Can we go somewhere?"

"Yes, and quickly."

He leads us to the watchmaker's shop, rather to my disappointment. "I thought we were going somewhere to be alone."

"We are." Unlocking the door and pushing it open, Léon lifts me off my feet and swings me across the threshold. My skirt billows with the movement. "Monsieur Renard closed the shop for the day. Since I completed my apprenticeship, he takes his family to visit his mother across the Seine one afternoon a week. They won't be back until bedtime. They always stay for supper."

I slide my arms around his neck. "I must say, this is all very convenient. Did you intend to seduce me?"

"Until today I didn't dare hope we'd be so joyfully reconciled. But love always finds a way," he whispers. "Didn't you tell me that once?"

"I don't know. It sounds terribly sentimental."

"You certainly must have said it, then." Teasing me, he nuzzles my neck and pushes me toward the stairs. "I wish I could carry you up, but I'm afraid we'd land in a heap at the bottom."

I go first, deliciously aware of his eyes watching my hips sway. He pushes the bedroom door shut with a loud thump and pulls me willingly back into his arms, his mouth swooping over mine. Being utterly alone washes away the joking of downstairs, rekindling the heat between us, building it higher than before, outmatching the fierce tension of our embrace in Robespierre's library, eclipsing the excited joy of our reconciliation by the bookshop. Within moments, Léon has unhooked the top of my bodice and is tracing hot kisses along my breasts, his tongue dipping into the valley between them. Blindly, I wrestle with the buttons on his pants and manage to open the front of them, exploring the shape of him with eager fingers. His breath explodes against the side of my neck as he gasps with enjoyment, and then it's my turn to do the same when he rucks my skirt aside and trails his fingertips up the inside of my thigh.

"Don't wait," I murmur into his ear. Lightning flickers over my skin. I feel like I'm burning with desperate desire. It isn't anything like the first time, when I was nervous and uncertain. I want him badly.

"Oh God, Giselle. You'll seize all the control I have left." Instead of bearing me down to the narrow bed, as I expect, he slides his hand past my hips and lifts me onto the edge of the bedside dresser. He kisses me passionately while I rearrange my skirt, raising it higher. His fingers stroke against me until I gasp and squirm. He nestles his hips between my thighs, and I clutch at his shoulders as he sinks deep into me, staring into my eyes so I can see the rush of pleasure suffusing his features. Léon tries to go slow, reaching to stroke my breasts again, but I kiss him, arching my body against his, meeting each thrust. Our bodies grind forcefully together, and it makes me feel delirious. The sudden swell of delight leaves me gasping and whimpering against his mouth, while his motions grow rougher, jerky. I coax his tongue into my mouth, lightly sucking on it, and this sends him over the edge with a hoarse groan, his fingertips digging into my hips.

We smile at each other, breathing hard and pressing butterfly-soft kisses to each other's cheeks and foreheads. Léon lifts me down, and I sag against him, weak in the legs.

"Take off your dress, my love," he says.

My brow arches in surprise. "Already?"

"I wouldn't say that. I've been waiting over a year to see your bare skin again. I meant to look at you for a while first, get to know your body again, but instead we both succumbed completely to lust." He grins.

"Mm. We did." It feels very good when I stretch my arms over my head.

A wicked glint lights up his eyes. "But we still have a whole afternoon of no interruptions, and I plan on kissing every inch of you."

❋

Later, when I sleepily survey the room, I realize we broke the candlestick that stood on the dresser, knocking it to the wood-planked floor.

"Doesn't matter," says Léon. "It was always smoky." His voice softens. "It was good of you to risk so much to have your uncle released."

"I'm not such an angel. I did it for Eugénie, and also because my uncle knew of my role in Varennes. I feared he'd share, using it to procure his own release."

He stares at me, aghast. "Would he do that??"

I shake my head, pressing my lips together. "I don't know. But I couldn't risk it."

Pulling me close to him, he tucks my head under his chin, folding me in his arms. "I'm glad you thought of it, to protect yourself." He runs his hand along the outside of my arm in a long, smooth stroke. "The events of the past year have changed us, haven't they? We dealt with dangerous secrets, betrayal, riots, violence. . . . Are we scarred?"

I reach for his hand, squeezing it tight. "No. We are stronger."

He presses a kiss against my hair. "Good. I don't want to be apart from you again."

"You won't be, as long as I have anything to say about it."

He rolls me onto my back again, sweeping my hair across the pillow, gently twirling the ends around his fingertips. "I love you, Giselle." He brushes tiny feathery kisses across my cheeks. "I never stopped, not that whole year we were apart. I felt so hurt and betrayed, but I kept loving you, even when I thought it would be better for my sanity if I stopped. I could hardly understand my feelings, but now everything's right again."

"I loved you too, but I felt so ashamed for betraying you that I often avoided you. I worried I'd never be able to face you again, yet I longed for you every day. I've loved you for three years, and I'll never stop."

His fierce kiss burns like a promise. "And now we'll look to our happy future," he murmurs. "Varennes belongs in the past now."

Chapter Twenty-three

Robespierre keeps his word. My uncle is released on August thirtieth. Eugénie sends me a note to tell me, which I don't see until the next day. The day of his release is busy for another reason, for Léon and I marry at last. Neither of us wants to wait, in spite of the surprise our family and friends cannot quite conceal in regards to our sudden reunion. Our wedding is a small, intimate affair, with only my parents, Monsieur Renard and his wife and two young sons, and Geneviève and Étienne in attendance.

Maman roasts a chicken, and Papa fetches a couple of particularly fine bottles of wine from the cellar.

"I was saving these for a special occasion." He hands a glass to Léon, grinning at me. "This certainly qualifies."

Geneviève has somehow procured a dozen or so sugared rose petals, and helps Maman decorate the small cake with them, made after our cook was given permission to splurge on eggs and flour.

"Where did you get candied roses?" I ask her curiously.

"I made them." She laughs at my surprise. "Come now, I'm not entirely talentless in the kitchen. I rather like cooking. I started to do it myself after I left my parents' home. The hardest part was finding enough sugar."

Later, after we have eaten, she takes me aside, grinning. "I always cherished the hope that you and Léon would reconcile. I'm so glad it happened."

"What about you? Will you marry Étienne at last? You've been engaged for years."

She purses her lips, considering. "I always thought I wasn't ready, that I was too busy with the revolution, but it isn't a real excuse, is it? Especially as Étienne is an even more fervent revolutionary than me. It would be rather nice to live together. Where are you and Léon going to live?"

"Here, for a short while."

"It's a large house. You should be comfortable enough, as long as Léon and your parents are companionable?"

"Yes, so far." In fact, both of them are so pleased with Léon for moving past my decision to aid the royal family's flight to Varennes that he could probably consume the entire wedding cake on his own, and they'd find a reason to excuse him for it. "Still, I hope we find our own home soon." Now that Léon and I have fully resumed our relationship, I don't want to waste a single moment of time together.

❧

Three days after my marriage to Léon, the revolution, which has been relatively quiet since the captivity of the king and queen, spikes violently. Fearing that foreign Austrian and Prussian armies will invade France, causing the royalist prisoners to revolt against the population, Marat calls for the prisoners to be executed preemptively. It sounds like a drastic solution, given that Paris is free of invading armies, but it happens nonetheless. I've never met

Marat, but I know that Léon has, and I have difficulty imagining what sort of man could create a rationale for the prompt execution of over a thousand prisoners.

"I suppose he would say the end justifies the means." Léon sighs heavily. "But Paris has become so volatile that I often wonder if anyone has a clear vision of what the end should be." Just as I have given up spying, Léon has also withdrawn from the revolution, and never goes to Café du Foy for political discussions anymore. Instead he reads poetry and works of philosophy, rather than of political treatises, and devotes his energies to watchmaking and spending time with me.

One of the most tragic casualties of the spiking revolution comes in the horrific death of the Princesse de Lamballe, dear friend to Marie Antoinette. She'd been sent to La Force Prison shortly after the storming of Tuileries, and in the beginning of September a tribunal demanded that she swear to support liberty and equality, and of hatred for the queen and king. Allegedly, she agreed to liberty but not to betray her friends, and was condemned to death. Denied even the humane speed of the guillotine, she was thrown into the hands of a mob and torn apart. I feel sick thinking of it, imagining the invasive hands, and maybe other body parts, the jeering voices, the pain and humiliation that must have filled the last moments of her despicable death. Later they paraded her head on a pike. I heard they tried to deliver it to the queen but were not allowed to reach the Temple. At least the queen was spared this additional terror, but how she must weep for her friend.

I didn't know the princess well, and never spoke to her, but I saw her often at Versailles with Marie Antoinette. Most of the time, she comported herself with all the discreet manners and elegance expected of her noble blood, but she appeared to have genuine affection for the queen. When they spoke together, she listened intently, eyes glinting with sincere interest. Once, some joke that I couldn't hear set them off into peals of laughter. They giggled together until their cheeks glowed pink, and they breathlessly fell back against the velvet sofa. Even with the gilded wall decorations and their elaborate powdered hairstyles and silken gowns, they looked just like two regular woman enjoying a moment of friend-ship.

Although I don't verbalize my sorrow for the princesse, Léon notices my somber mood and understands the cause.

"Perhaps it would distract your mind to read something." He draws soothing circles on my back with his hand. "No? Could you fall asleep? Rest might ease your mind."

"I don't think I could sleep."

"Even if I tired you out first?" His crooked, suggestive smile makes my skin grow warm.

"Maybe then," I relent. "But it's the middle of the day." In our own home, it might not matter. I can hardly wait for when we find a house of our own to live in. We have enough savings, especially if I sell the brooch the queen gave me, but it hasn't been easy to find a suitable place.

"What about sewing?" he suggests. "I could walk with you to pick out some new fabric, and you could design a new dress. Some-thing that will be all the fashion next year."

"Your confidence is sky-high, my love. But maybe the fresh air will help."

As we walk, Léon sighs when he sees a trio of national guards march past us on the other side of the street. "I am thankful that I wasn't on duty that day," he says, referring to the violent inva-sion of Tuileries. "I wish I could leave the national guard."

"Papa does too, although he's fortunate enough to be given mostly clerical duties." Since October of the previous year, all active citizens and male youths over eighteen years of age have been obliged to volunteer.

"I was a fool to join before it was required," says Léon. "I only did so because I was angry." Tactfully, he does not explain that his ire was with me for aiding the royalists, but we both know it. "Being in the Guard never was what I expected."

In the store, I run my fingers over rolls of fabric, scanning the colors. I turn away from the fathomless blues and heated reds. Even snowy white holds little appeal right now, for I feel I've seen enough tricolor to ensure it will never be a novel color combination again.

"Which colors have you sold a lot of lately?" I ask the woman working in the shop. "Which pattern is popular these days?"

"Red, white, and blue, of course." She stares at me as if it was a foolish question.

I suppose it was. "What other patterns have you sold lately? May I see the lists?"

To my surprise, she agrees, passing me a sheaf of paper.

"It's because of the way you asked," Léon whispers in my ear. "Without a shade of doubt that she'd refuse, and so she didn't."

She's not very clever, then, but I refrain from replying, afraid she'll hear me. Instead I scan the list, noticing a large purchase for brown and white sprigged cotton, and white dimity, as well as lace, of the sort that would be used for caps. The order captures my attention because the procurer was Madame Éloffe, who was always hired to remake the queen's wardrobe. I feel certain that these must have been ordered to provide her with dresses.

I choose something similar, but with pink sprigs instead of brown. As we exit the shop, I notice a man striding toward us down the street, and his face looks familiar.

He seems to recognize me too, slowing his steps, although his expression remains wary, and he doesn't speak.

I stop and call to him, suddenly remembering where I know him from. "You were in the kitchens at Tuileries, weren't you?"

"Were you a servant too? You look familiar," he says

"Yes, I worked with Madame Campan."

He nods. "I remember her. How did you like her?"

"She's a very kind lady," I say honestly.

He jerks his head in a nod again, looking thoughtful. "She isn't at the Tower—out of a job now, just like you, I reckon."

"Aren't you?"

He lowers his voice, beckoning farther away from the bustle of the street. "I'm in the kitchen of the Tower now."

I can't tell if he is loyal to the queen or not. "And do you like it?"

He shrugs. "The food is served liberally enough, but there isn't much else to recommend it. Guards everywhere, and you wouldn't believe the way they treat the family."

His words are innocuous enough that I could interpret them gleefully, that the royals are treated badly or sorrowfully. It's the way he says *family*, filling the word with importance, that finally tells me that he's loyal to them.

"Are they all right?" I ask, my voice quieter. Léon squeezes my wrist in warning, but I pat his hand reassuringly.

"As can be expected," says the man. I remember him better now—his surname is Turgy. "There's a library there, surprisingly enough. They say it has fifteen hundred books, leftover in a turret room that was the archive for the Knights of Malta, years ago. The king reads one a day, and seems as content as he ever was. The guards are the worst part. One of them likes to blow smoke in the queen's face, carrying his pipe with him at all times. He loves making the family pass through a low wicker gate, because they must bow their heads before him to do so."

"How unpleasant." It's a vulgar, cheap revenge, but at least they aren't actually being harmed.

"If you have any news, I could pass it on," he says, so quietly, I almost don't hear him. "I'm allowed out three times a week to get supplies. Sometimes I take back information, or messages, too."

"How are you allowed out without an escort?" asks Léon suspiciously.

"I managed to make everyone believe I'm at the Tower on the order of the Commune," says Turgy. He looks back to me.

"No messages," I say. He seems legitimate, but I have nothing to say to Marie Antoinette. Even if I wished to endanger myself again, I'm powerless to help her.

When Léon and I return home, I put aside my sewing long enough to send a note to Madame Campan.

"Is that wise?" asks Léon, fidgeting with the sleeve of his shirt.

I put my arms around him. "Madame Campan's desperate for news of the queen's well-being. I kept my wording very innocuous, just in case anyone sees the letter. Now it's her choice to contact Turgy or not. My conscience will be clear, and I'll be free of obligations." I don't dare visit Madame Campan, although I wish I could. If Robespierre's still watching her, it would only draw unwanted attention to me, and she'd never renounce her loyalty to the queen, no matter how hard I tried to protect her. A short letter will have to suffice.

Léon brushes his lips sweetly across mine. "I'm glad to hear it. It hurts me to see you pulled in two different directions."

"I didn't enjoy it either. I won't repeat the situation."

❧

In the new year, the Convention holds a trial for King Louis, officially still known as *Citoyen* Louis Capet. Referring to him otherwise would be dangerous in the wrong company, although it does happen. I hear whispers about the king, or the queen, sometimes in the marketplace.

"The trial of *Citoyen* Capet is the embodiment of the opposition between the royalists and the revolutionaries," says Étienne, topping up his wineglass and passing the bottle around the table. He and Geneviève have invited Léon and me to dine at his house, which she moved into shortly after they married at Christmas.

"I don't think the trial is in his favor," says Geneviève thoughtfully.

"The iron chest incident certainly didn't help him," I say. In November a locksmith came forward with information about a secret iron chest he'd built. Inside, Louis stored clandestine documents and correspondence with foreign nations, colluding with them to end the revolution. Other high-ranking men had been implicated as well, including Mirabeau, who died a celebrated revolutionary. Posthumously, his reputation has been destroyed by the secret correspondence.

"I read an interesting argument recently," says Léon. "It said that if we sacrifice one person, such as *Citoyen* Capet, for the happiness of many, it sets a precedent that could lead to the acceptance of violence as a means to happiness."

Étienne shrugs. "Capet hasn't been executed yet, but there's plenty of violence because of him already. Maybe it would stop if he were gone."

"But if it doesn't?" Léon's eyes glitter with interest. He enjoys philosophical discussion more than Étienne does, I think. "Where would it end, hypothetically?"

"Probably with his wife," says Étienne. "She has caused rioting and starvation as well."

"And their children?" I ask in a low voice.

Silence falls around the table until Geneviève clears her throat. "They're young enough to be raised as true citizens contributing to society."

When the Convention votes on the matter, a slight majority wins in favor of Louis's immediate execution. Many members of the Convention allegedly voted for his death, but with conditions and reservations. In order to come to a more forceful decision, the Convention votes again the next day, on a motion to grant Louis a reprieve from execution. Once again, the majority overrules for his death.

"This newspaper has the same account as the last." Léon tosses it aside in disgust.

"I doubt there are any that could have enough details to satisfy your inquiring mind." I ruffle his hair as I pass through to the kitchen.

"Étienne will be clamoring to witness the execution. But I'm not sure if we should go."

"I have no desire to witness it."

"It would make us look more revolutionary," says Léon slowly. "Still, it'll be crowded enough that anyone could be missed in the crowd."

We've both fallen into the protective habit of pretending to be more fervent revolutionaries than we truly are. The revolution has marked both of us. We've both faced the crushing terror of riots, and I walked through the carnage of Tuileries. Léon killed a man while on duty with the national guard. The revolution also tore us apart once. We've already paid a price for our involvement, and it could have been higher. We're afraid to risk more.

For the execution of the disgraced and deposed king of France, the guillotine moves from its months' long fixture at the place du Carrousel to the place de la Révolution. On the twenty-first of

January, *Citoyen* Louis Capet's head rolls into a basket in front of a large crowd.

Léon and I stay home during the event, in the small apartment we rented for a few months, deciding not to find somewhere more permanent until after we visit Toulouse so I can meet his family. Still, we hear all about it from shop owners, neighbors, newspaper columns, and Geneviève and Étienne, who attended.

"He was surprisingly brave," says Étienne. "He had an air of dignity and resignation." He sounds more admiring of Louis now than when the king was alive.

"He was never a coward," says Geneviève. "Remember how he dealt with the mob during the first invasion of Tuileries, drinking a toast with them? I think he was too accustomed to impassivity to ever feel a strong emotion."

Étienne snorts in amusement at her observation. "Well, it didn't last long. He made a speech for his innocence, and I think he'd have said more, but the drums started up while his mouth was still open."

A flare of indignation leads me to speak without considering the prudence of it. "That's dreadful. They killed him without letting him finish speaking? He'll never speak again, and even so, they could not grant him another moment to express his last thoughts?"

Étienne narrows his eyes at me. "*We*—the people of France—executed him for crimes against the people. It's perfectly appropriate that *we* did not allow him more time to spread his poisonous beliefs among the crowd. Even after everything, there are those who believe he was somehow superior, that he deserved to have everything while so many people have almost nothing." His glare seems to imply that I'm one of them.

"I wasn't aware you were a member of the court who decided his sentence," I snap, angry at the way he speaks to me as if I'm an outsider, treating me so rudely—in my own house, no less. "And I speak not as a royalist, but as a person who believes life is important enough that even those who deserve death should be allowed dignity in their final moments. You may call me a humanist."

Léon leans forward. His lips part slightly, showing his teeth, as he stares at Étienne. In spite of Léon's lapsing revolutionary ideals, he and Étienne have managed to remain friends thus far. Now I'm not sure how long it can last.

Geneviève smacks her palms on the table. The wine ripples in the glasses. "Giselle is softer-hearted than you, Étienne. I think it makes her very admirable, especially in these violent times." As Étienne subsides, looking abashed, she turns to me and wrinkles her nose. "It's just as well you weren't present, Giselle. I could hardly believe how many people ran up to dip their handkerchiefs in the blood after. A gruesome memento, but if we had known such things would be popular, we could've made extra money. Perhaps people would have wanted to collect handkerchiefs that the royal family had blown their noses into, or for bits of hair cleaned out of a brush." She tilts her head in half-forced amusement, mouth quirking in mild scorn at the idea of collecting such items.

"A wasted opportunity for us," I say, joking back with her even though my heart isn't in it.

⚜

I find myself easily distracted and restless at night over the next few months. I throw myself into my sewing during the day, determined to create a repertoire of items to demonstrate my skills and start a new job in a dress shop. After working so hard, I should be ready for sleep, especially after Léon and I go to our shared bed at an early hour, still excited by the novelty of it. During the day, I find myself thinking of Marie Antoinette at unexpected moments, swept with sympathy for her now that she's a widow and a prisoner with a hopeless future. Sometimes a rose-colored ribbon will remind me of her, or a sleekly ironed fichu will remind me of Madame Campan, and I wonder if she managed to find some peace.

One night, when Léon and I curl our bodies together under the heavy blankets, replete with loving and nestled away from the rainy June night, he clears his throat in the soft way that I've come to recognize as a herald that he has something important to say, and he isn't sure how I'll respond to it.

"I've been thinking about Toulouse," he says, stroking my hair away from my forehead.

I roll around to face him, nuzzling his neck. His skin tastes a little salty and feels cool against my lips. "About our visit there? I'm excited to meet your family, and to see your dog, Octavia."

"I have a different idea. Giselle, what if we stayed there for a while?"

"You want to live in Toulouse instead of Paris?"

"I think part of me has always assumed I'd return there someday. But it's not my main reason for suggesting it. I just think Paris isn't good for us any longer." He bends his face to peer into mine earnestly. His nose brushes against mine. "So much has happened to us here. Dangerous things. Dark things. I know it was hard for you when Louis was executed. . . . They say that Marie Antoinette will be next. How much harder will it be for you if that happens?"

"There won't be anything I can do to prevent it, so I suppose I'll manage." The hesitancy in my tone doesn't quite fit with the practical words.

Hearing it, Léon plays with my hair again, twirling the ends gently between his fingers. "In Paris you'll have to hear all about it, see mementos . . . perhaps even see it. It won't be easy, but it may be easier if we're farther away." His lips skim across my cheek.

"You've been torn between two loyalties long enough, and I don't want to see it hurt you again."

I tilt my head up, seeking his mouth with my own, touched by his thoughtfulness. It never occurred to me we might leave Paris for good, or at least years, and I find that the idea holds more appeal than I would have expected. We might have more luck with his watchmaking business, and my dressmaking trade, in a less turbulent city. All of France is affected by the revolution, but we live in the bloodiest heart of it. After all that has happened, sometimes I peek over my shoulder as I walk, fearing people will point fingers at me, shouting that I'm the queen's lady. . . .

"Do you mind? You were so proud to come to Paris on your own, to build your fortune here. It's not only because of my mistakes that you want to leave?"

"No." He squeezes my hand for emphasis. "I don't mind. It will be easier for me to leave Paris than you; I have no family here. But if you're willing, I think we can be very happy." His hand slides down past the slope of my breast, stroking my stomach. "We'll build our life in Toulouse, maybe start the family we've dreamed about. As long as we are together, I think we can do anything."

"Just the two of us," I murmur. "Making the life we want for ourselves." I picture it in my mind, Léon and I setting up business together, raising children who have his eyes and my hair. Imagining it makes me happy. I no longer have grand dreams of designing dresses for nobility, or being embroiled in court politics. I only want a peaceful life with my husband.

Chapter Twenty-four

JUNE TO OCTOBER 1793

Léon writes to his parents to let them know of our plan, and to enlist their assistance in helping us find a place to live. We intend to travel to Toulouse in January, after spending Christmas in Paris with my family. I'll miss them dreadfully, but I still look forward to the future.

"It's warmer there," Léon tells me. "In the summer, we can walk in lavender fields. I loved to do that. I missed it very much during my first year here."

"It sounds lovely," I say, imagining the sight of rows of purple flowers under a bright summer sky, and how heady the scent of the lavender must be, perfuming the air for miles around.

I spend more time with my parents, taking advantage of the time remaining in Paris. At first Maman resisted our decision, but Papa reminded her the world is larger than Paris. The distance is a sorrow for me, too, but I know leaving Paris is the right choice.

The revolution doesn't rest in the summer, during which time many new laws are passed. Due to the scarcity of resources, hoarding is declared a crime. Léon and I have little enough to fear from this law, but I wonder if my uncle may be hiding some of his resources, particularly his wine cellar. As well, a new national standard of measurement called the metric is introduced, and supposed to have greater accuracy. In July, Marat is killed in the bath by a woman called Charlotte Corday. For weeks afterward, one can hardly leave the house without hearing lurid details of the murder. Having a poor opinion of Marat, I can't say I mourn him. This isn't an opinion I speak outside of the house, though, for his death renders him a kind of revolutionary martyr, and he's better liked in death than he ever was in life.

In October the current government introduces a new calendar, which has ten days in a week, and each day of the year has a unique pastoral name. While the names are poetic, they're also extremely confusing. October is now called Vendémiaire, a month that spans from old mid-September to mid-October. On what would have been the fifteenth day of October, but is now called Amaryllis, I go to the market, an unassuming task for a grandly named day. I expect to return only with vegetables. It's a good thing Léon and I both like soup, because I seem to be making a lot of it lately.

When I return from the market, Léon stands by the window of our small sitting room, staring listlessly outside. Two glasses stand on the table, both mostly full of wine. I put down my basket of carrots and go to his side, laying my hand on his arm. The tension in his body flows through to mine.

"What's wrong, my love?"

He turns slowly to face me. "Robespierre called on me. He just departed."

The reluctant cadence of Léon's voice and the pinch of dread around the corners of his mouth and eyes tells me it wasn't a welcome visit. Dread frosts across my skin and kicks my voice into a higher, tight note.

"What did he want?"

Léon slides his hands along my arms, settling them on my waist, holding me close. His fingers grasp protectively at my body. "He wanted to warn me that you'll be facing investigation. He says they're questioning everyone who may have been close to the queen. The Widow Capet," he amends, clearly quoting Robespierre's way of referring to her.

"What?" I stare wide-eyed into his anxious face, trying to quell the swirl of panic rising in my throat. "I'm not close to her. I was a servant—I haven't worked for her in a year!"

"I know. I told him. I insisted you had no pertinent information you hadn't already shared. He told me he was investigating your uncle, too, but that he proved his dedication to the revolution—for now. Apparently, Pierre has committed to provide sixty thousand rifles to the revolutionary armies. He's probably going to Holland soon to arrange the purchase."

This information registers in my mind, but dimly. My uncle has experience with munitions; he supplied them to the American Revolution a few years ago. He can take care of himself. "I don't have any information for Robespierre—he can ask me himself. Why didn't he?"

Léon cups my cheek in his hand, and his voice drops to such a gentle note that I know how deep his worry really goes. "He came to me first because you're my wife. It's proper that he didn't approach you directly, and better this way. At the very least, I'm thankful he warned me. He said he felt duty bound by our friendship." His mouth twists on the last word. Léon doesn't consider them friends at all anymore, and hasn't for some time.

"I still don't know anything of use to him, not anymore."

Léon presses his finger against my lips, stroking the shape of them once I stop protesting. "I know, *mon ange*. But if he asks too much—if he searches too far—there are things he could discover."

"Why is he looking now?" I whisper. "The queen has already been sentenced to death. Her execution is tomorrow. He has won—he needs nothing else to condemn her. She's past saving." My voice cracks.

"He says he's determined to promote the revolution, even if it means seeking out every royalist in Paris."

"What else can I do? I've been wearing tricolor for ages, far longer than many." Three weeks ago a decree had passed that all women must wear a tricolor ribbon in public. It hadn't made a difference to me; I already did so.

"There is one thing." Léon's face creases with sorrow. "I'm sorry, Giselle. I told him we would be present at her execution tomorrow. I had to—he pressed me."

His words make me flinch. He releases his gentle hold on me, letting me stagger back. "I can't watch her die. I can't save her, but she doesn't deserve this fate. I can't be part of it." Her trial had ended only earlier today, but already news of the guilty verdict swarmed through Paris. People fairly shouted about it in the streets. I'd known about it before I even went to the market. "I can't," I repeat.

"You must." A kind of wild steeliness enters Léon's tone, and his hands reach for me again. "You must, because I can't watch you die. And if we can't turn Robespierre's attention away from us, I fear that may happen. Paris is going mad for the guillotine, Giselle. And make no mistake, his attention is on us. Do you think it's a coincidence he called when you weren't home?"

I feel cold inside. My fingers tremble against Léon's. "He has spies watching me?" I shouldn't be surprised, but I hear it echoing in my voice. I'd suspected what kind of man Robespierre was from the first moment I saw him at Café du Foy, when he memorized my face. I'd brought myself into his notice when I described my closeness to the queen. And he must have wondered why Léon became estranged so suddenly. . . .

I know he's right about the execution tomorrow. I sink onto the worn sofa, dragging him down beside me. "I must witness her death and appear as a fervent revolutionary." My voice sounds dull, heavy with dread as I recite my duties. "I must not let my true feelings show."

"Yes," says Léon simply. "I'm sorry. But I will be with you. I'll support you however I can. If we can make him believe you feel no pity for her, that you truly support the revolution, he will turn his attention elsewhere."

"I hope you're right." I press my fingers to my forehead. My skin burns with dread. "I thought the horrible rumors I heard in the market this morning were the worst news I could receive today. I should have known better." Each drop of blood dripping from the guillotine brings more horror to the city.

He wraps his arm around my shoulders, pulling me comfortingly close. "What did you hear?"

"Stories of Marie Antoinette's trial. They interrogated her children." They must have been so afraid, surrounded by unfriendly strangers.

"I know." The softness of his voice tells me that he's also heard the terrible things said of her, with her own son's word as evidence. Robespierre probably told him, and in my current bitter mind-set, it is easy to imagine that he enjoyed sharing such crude information.

"Everybody knows now that poor little Louis said his mother molested him." Even saying the words makes me feel sick inside, and Marie Antoinette must feel even worse, knowing that some people must believe these vile, trumped-up charges against her. I try to quell the curious kind of emotional nausea rising in my throat. Marie Antoinette has her faults, but she was always the best mother she could be, and I know the chance of an inappropriate relationship with her son was nonexistent. Aside from the fact that her personality didn't seem capable of such atrocity, the servants would have known about it. In Versailles and even Tuileries, crawling with attendants, such a thing could never have been kept a secret. Thank God, Madame Campan has fled to the country and isn't in Paris to hear these disgusting tales. I hope they don't reach her for a long time.

"It isn't true," I say to Léon, even though I know he doesn't believe it. I stare at the floor, since he doesn't deserve my vehemence.

"Robespierre all but admitted that the boy agreed with any question posed to him. He's frightened enough to go along with anything." The sharp edge of condemnation in Léon's voice matches the spasm of pain I feel when thinking of the little prince's spirit being broken.

"And Madame Royale? What did she say?" It's a dangerous way to refer to Marie Antoinette's daughter, but we're safe from judging ears in our own house.

"Upon seeing the brother she's been parted from for months, she rushed to embrace him. They wouldn't allow this until she answered their questions satisfactorily." Léon paused, and his dark eyes glittered with approval. "She did not. Over and over, she refused to repudiate her mother."

I feel a surge of pride for the headstrong princess. "But it was not enough to save the queen."

Léon shakes his head slowly. "How could it, when the decision was made before the trial? They never intended to acquit her."

Indignation blazes through me, burning my cheeks. "And incest was the only way they could think of to ensure her execution?

It's shameful, and it shows just how much they fear her, even now."

"Yes," says Léon. He watches me with stark sympathy. I know he loathes this situation nearly as much as I do. He folds my hands gently between both of his. "Giselle, I see the fire in you—I know how strongly you feel. If you can channel your resentment tomorrow, pretend it is instead fervency for the revolution. Convince Robespierre to turn his dangerous attention elsewhere."

I know he's right, and I will do it, but the idea of Robespierre chasing after another, someone who might even be more innocent than I am makes me sad. "Thank God, we have plans to leave Paris for Toulouse."

⚜

For Marie Antoinette's execution, I dress as revolutionary as possible. Robespierre will be watching me, and if not him personally, he'll have spies in the crowd to do it. Both are a possibility. I wear my white dress embroidered with tricolor, and pin a tricolor cockade to one shoulder of my red fichu, and one to my hat, also displaying my Bastille necklace. I can't help remembering the times when I helped Marie Antoinette coordinate her outfits to appear revolutionary. She would loathe my outfit today. All the tricolor ribbons make me feel like a horse decked out for a parade. To complete the parade feeling, I also carry a red-white-and-blue handkerchief, waving it like a revolutionary flag.

"Are you ready?" asks Léon. He has dark shadows under his eyes.

"I have to be," I say simply, and take his arm so we may walk together to the place de la Révolution.

Before the queen is brought for her execution, the crowd gathers. I can't bear to look at the guillotine, stained and looming before us, so I furtively scan for Robespierre's possible spy, without much luck. I feel as though I'm on a stage, and when I think that this is how Marie Antoinette must have felt for much of her life, hysteria threatens to summon wild laughter. My breath shakes.

The ugly roar of jeers and screamed insults tears through the air long before the cart carrying Marie Antoinette comes into sight. For a moment I worry the sound will smash through my composure, but I breathe slowly and guard my expression. I lift the little tricolor flag I brought and wave it, a testament to my supposed revolutionary fervor.

I'd been told that the late king had been transported to the guillotine in a closed carriage. Marie Antoinette is afforded no such dignity or protection. The rough-planked cart is hardly better than what a cabbage farmer might use, and even the clergyman sitting beside her looks uncomfortable. He wears the recognizable attire of a constitutional priest who has taken a civic oath, the only order now allowed to attend to prisoners and enemies of the state. Marie Antoinette sits straight-backed and proud, but as the cart swings past me, I see that her eyes look huge and wild. I recoil back against Léon, who clutches at my arm and randomly shoves at the person nearest as if they had pushed me. His wariness for potential spies watching me reminds me that I must put on a show to rival the most talented actress. I wave my little flag again as Léon shouts for liberty.

Fortunately, Marie Antoinette stares straight ahead the entire time and doesn't see me. I'd be heartbroken if she knew I was part of this abominable crowd. In her white dress, clean though plain, she still looks regal. The stark, pure whiteness of her gown stands out in the crowd, more so because she wears no other color. No black widow's ribbons, no jewelry. Her hair looks pale now too, where it curls out from under the plain white bonnet. Even on her way to her death, she projects a bold image. The horrors of her imprisonment and the execution of her husband have aged her, made her thin and gray, but they haven't destroyed her innate elegant poise.

She climbs down from the cart nimbly enough, and thankfully the guards keep the crowd back so she has space to disembark and climb the steps to the guillotine without being swarmed. She stumbles slightly halfway up the stairs, and her scuffed purple shoe falls down to the ground. It reminds me of *Cendrillon* losing her glass slipper, and how Marie Antoinette liked to tell the story to her daughter. Watching her avidly, I see her pause for a heartbeat, and then she hurries the rest of the way up the stairs, clearly deciding that she can meet her fate with one bare foot. I wish I couldn't see her as well as I do—Léon had suggested that we push our way to the side of the crowd, almost behind the guillotine, so that we will be near enough to please Robespierre but also have little risk of being spotted by the queen herself.

At the top of the steps, she seems dismayed by the swell of the shouting crowd before her at such a near distance. The executioner moves closer. With her gaze focused on the vicious crowd, she accidentally steps on his foot with her bare one.

"I'm sorry; I did not mean to," she says. I can mostly make out the words by watching her lips—knowing her as I do, and the practice I had watching faces during my time as a spy, it's easy to read the brief, polite apology. I wave my flag harder, lifting it to face level, struggling not to show my wonder and sorrow that she can retain her manners even now.

The executioner shrugs it off and helps her to stand behind the guillotine. His motions brisk, but not rough, he removes her white cap and lifts a handful of her gray-streaked hair and slices it away, leaving her neck bare for the guillotine's blade. Marie Antoinette is not given the opportunity to make a final speech. Her last thoughts shall be hers alone. The executioner reaches to help her kneel.

I feel a burst of empathy for her, that she must face this death alone, with a crowd of enemies in front of her. Before I've really thought, I bash my way through the crowd, moving closer to the front of the guillotine where she might see me. A few people punch at my shoulders for getting in their way, but I hardly notice. Léon clutches at my arm, following close behind me.

At first I don't think she'll see me, but as I wave my flag furiously, her eyes flick toward me. Our gazes lock, and I feel connected to her. I wave my flag harder and feign dropping it. While righting myself, it allows me to bend slightly, to show I would still bow to her if I could. It's the best I can do; I can't speak any words that she'd hear above the catcalls of the crowd. There's no other way for me to convey my feeling that she's a woman who does not deserve her fate, or all the blame heaped upon her personally, no matter what errors she's made.

I think she understands. She watches me a heartbeat longer, then lifts her chin high. Her gaze sweeps skyward for the last time before she lets the executioner help her to kneel. With her neck outstretched on the base of the guillotine, she can see nothing but the scaffold. The sight of Marie Antoinette in such a vulnerable position hushes the crowd. Even though it's not completely silent, the sudden shift to quiet feels eerie. The blade of the guillotine flashes in the noonday sun during its rapid descent and collides with Marie Antoinette's slender neck with a soft, wet sound. The following thunk as the blade rests at the bottom of the scaffold again seems loud in the tense silence.

The quiet grows in an endless second, and then the crowd shrieks again, with approval and patriotism and excited horror. My flag flutters crazily in front of me, my fingers knotted so tightly around the cloth that it cuts off the circulation of my blood. I shout about France and freedom, and my voice cracks with hoarseness. I hardly know what I say because I don't care anymore about the revolution. My mind swirls between the shock of the queen's death, and the reminder not to show any sorrow, so I channel it into pretended revolutionary fervor instead.

A group of Girondins are to be executed next, and the Duc d'Orleans as well. We have to stay for it all, but Léon draws us to the side again, away from the worst crush of the crowd. One of the Girondins somehow commits suicide while waiting for his turn to approach the guillotine, but they still lay his lifeless body on the scaffold and slice his head off.

The Duc d'Orleans is granted the chance to say a few words, and he spits about regretting that he must shamefully die under the same blade that killed the deposed King Louis. I feel numb, watching him die, still mired in the aftermath of watching Marie Antoinette's life be chopped away. I dimly remember when Geneviève and I mocked the *duc*'s attempt to appear Third Estate by wearing bourgeois clothing. It feels like a long time ago.

Robespierre finds us when the crowd at last begins to dissipate and sawdust has been scattered around to soak up the blood. The fact that he spotted us in the mad bustle of the place de la Révolution tells me that he must indeed have someone watching us. The knowledge forms a knot underneath my ribs and makes it hard to breathe.

I greet him respectfully and make sure to hold my tricolor flag high.

"Madame Gauvain, how nice to see you again," he says. "I didn't know if you would attend today. I know these events can be rather intense for women, who tend to be of more delicate sensibility. And you knew the Widow Capet, didn't you? I'd nearly forgotten."

I stare back into his lying catlike eyes, narrow and cold. "I would not have missed it. Today I witnessed history in the making. France is fortunate to experience such liberation." Somehow I keep my voice free of bitterness and manage to sound slightly awed. I refrain from remarking upon his reference to my past at Versailles.

"Of course. Washed free of the heavy inadequacies of the past, France will be a leader in politics. We will create an egalitarian society never before been seen, even in classical times." He clears his throat. "You missed the execution of Louis Capet, though, I believe? Another momentous day—a pity you were absent."

"I wanted to be there, monsieur. Unfortunately, I was ill." He looks skeptical, so I lay my hand across my belly, making sure to drape the tricolor cloth across my dress. "I thought I might have been with child, but unfortunately it wasn't so. Perhaps now that Paris is cleansed, I may conceive a child who will be born into better times." For a moment, I fear that my zealousness was overdone, but after regarding me for a moment, his face relaxes.

"Permit me to wish you all the best, then." He speaks for another moment with Léon, behaving more naturally. When he turns to depart, tension unrolls down my spine and the air stops choking my lungs. Then he turns, calling over his shoulder.

"Perhaps I might call on you soon. I hope you may be able to share some of your knowledge of the old court, Madame Gauvain."

"I'm glad to help," I say, and it's a good thing that he departs and I'm not required to speak further, because my throat constricts with fresh nervousness.

"Let's go home." Léon's fingers clench mine. Almost, I think his grip will bruise me, but I still don't want to let go, clinging back to him.

We travel home in silence. Once we cross the threshold to our house, peacefully quiet and draped in afternoon sunbeams, I sag against him, feeling the sudden urge to cry.

Léon lifts my face so he can look into my eyes. "We must leave tonight, *mon ange*." He sounds unbearably gentle. "Can you be ready? I know it's sooner than expected, but it's not safe here anymore. We cannot delay."

I think back to the cunning way that Robespierre tilted his head as he bade us farewell, the glint of excitement in his eyes. He reminds me of a hunter, one fixated on the chase, and it makes me shiver. "Yes." I clear my ragged throat and meet Léon's beloved, worried gaze. "Yes, I can be ready. Even though right now all I wish for is to curl up and cry."

He slides his fingers through my hair and kisses me softly on the mouth. "You were so brave today, my love. You're always so strong. . . . I promise, once we are safely in a carriage and outside of Paris, you may cry all you like. I'll stroke your hair away from your face and hand you fresh handkerchiefs." He tries for a smile, but it comes out crooked.

My voice drops to a whisper. "I'm so afraid."

"Me too."

Hastily, we gather our belongings. We can't take any of our furniture, of course, but we are so newly married that we haven't accumulated very much. Although I worry there isn't enough time, I can't leave Paris without seeing my parents again, and Léon takes us straight there before I even have to ask.

"I knew you would leave for Toulouse sooner than later," says

Maman. "But I imagined it wouldn't be so hard to say good-bye for some reason." She smiles sadly, reaching to hug me.

"I'll see you again," I promise. It wasn't something I could necessarily say if I remained in Paris. "And if it becomes worse here, if you think that you'll be targeted, you must come to us in Toulouse."

"I've thought of it already," says Papa. "We may end up joining you there. I find I don't like Paris when the streets turn scarlet with blood."

Maman insists on feeding us, so we have supper together, and then Papa helps Léon arrange for a carriage leaving the city.

"He's a trustworthy driver," says Papa. "You'll have to change horses and drivers outside of the city, but once you're away from Paris, it will be easier. Robespierre's reach doesn't extend that far, I don't think."

I peer out the window as the carriage rolls out of Paris. The cool fall air bites at my skin, but it makes me feel alive, too. Night has fallen, and I try to guess which way is south from the sprawl of stars, but I can't tell. In the dark, the landscape outside of the city looks vast and endless, and the view feels like a harbinger of freedom. Goose bumps tickle along my arms and down my back, and for the first time in over a year, I feel somehow secure, safe in my own skin instead of behind an armor of secrets.

Author's Note

The French Revolution is a complex part of history, with richly detailed records left to us today. Sometimes in my research, I found myself almost overwhelmed by the incredible amount of information available. While I tried to include as much as possible, some details had to be glossed over or slightly altered in light of plot or characterization.

One of these changes is that I have portrayed a simplified version of Marie Antoinette's household, which was very large and included a complicated hierarchy. I have limited the arc of the story to a few key members of it. While it is implied that Giselle and Geneviève are not the only tirewomen, they frequently appear to be working alone; in reality they would have been part of a larger group of household women and ladies-in-waiting.

Both Giselle and Geneviève are fictional, although one of the queen's tirewomen really did suspect the plan to flee to Varennes and was dismissed a day before the escape occurred. In Madame Campan's memoirs, she is only named as R——. I gave this bit of history to Geneviève.

As Giselle is fictional, so too are her parents. Her uncle Pierre-Augustin Caron de Beaumarchais, however, is a real figure, as is his daughter, Eugénie. De Beaumarchais had several sisters whose lives are not well documented, so I forged the family link by making Giselle's mother one of them. As soon as I read of de Beaumarchais's connection with the Secret du Roi, I knew I wanted my main character to be part of his family.

Léon is also a fictional character, but his trade as a watchmaker is a real one, and his initial support for the revolution is also fitting for a person of the time period. Léon probably joined the national guard earlier than someone of his ideology would have. In October of 1791 active citizens were obliged to join the national guard for maintenance of law and order. In the summer of 1792, the fundamental character of the guard changed, becoming more pro-revolutionary. Given this shift, it's possible that someone like Léon would not have joined until obligated. However, I wanted Léon to be a member of the national guard for the Massacre of the Champ de Mars in July of 1791, and since its commander, the Marquis de Lafayette, had a strong reputation for his involvement in the American Revolution, it seemed plausible that Léon would be drawn to his leadership.

I also took a liberty with Madame Campan's movements. In late May of 1790 she was sent to the Auvergne, in the south of France, to undertake tasks for the queen. She did not return to Paris until August of 1791, and was thus not present for the June flight to Varennes, and did not hear a full account of the ill-fated journey from Marie Antoinette until August. I have omitted this and kept Madame Campan in the loop, since she is a central character with a deep emotional connection to the queen.

Perhaps anticipating a wild portrayal of Marie Antoinette drinking champagne and dancing all night, some readers might be surprised by my more understated depiction of her. I was too, for when I entered my research, I fully expected to encounter the flighty queen. However, much of her reputation as a party girl stems from her time as dauphine, before she became a mother. By the time the revolution began, Marie Antoinette was thirty-four, and while she lacked the political and economic skills to aid the revolution or the societal issues that provoked it, she was always a caring person and appears to have been sincerely troubled by the outbreak of the revolution. From my research, I believe it had a somber effect on her behavior.

During the revolution, the government changed many times, going through several different names. Any errors in the naming conventions, or indeed any other factual errors, are entirely my own.

About the Author

CHIPPERFIELD PHOTOGRAPHY

Meghan Masterson graduated from the University of Calgary and has worked several unrelated jobs while writing on the side. As a child, she gave her parents a flowery story about horses every year for Christmas. Meghan loves reading at all hours, cooking, and going for walks with her dog. She and her husband live in Calgary. *The Wardrobe Mistress* is her first novel. Visit www.meghanmastersonauthor.com for more information.